D . G .

...DOOMED

to repeat it

THE DESIGNIMAGE GROUP, INC.

This Edition Copyright ©2001 D. G. K. Goldberg

Inquiries may be directed to:
The Design Image Group, Inc.
P.O. Box 2325
Darien, Illinois 60561

ISBN: 1-891946-12-9

First Edition

DESIGN IMAGE

THE DESIGNIMAGE GROUP, INC.

Visit us on the web at
www.designimagegroup.com

Printed in the U.S.A.

10 9 8 7 6 5 4 3 2 1

*I have a lot of people to thank
for helping this book exist.*

*I'd like to thank my spousal unit Ronnie Shull who benignly
ignored lunacy and demonic possession during the writing of
Doomed to Repeat It. And who tolerates me no matter who I
happen to be at any particular point in time. (Ronnie has even
forgiven me for using his hair as the model for Ian's hair.)*

*And...
Jacob Goldberg-Hilbert, who introduced me to the amazing dog
Sarah and his corner of the universe. Robin (she really is a
rocket scientist) Alldredge aka Birdy, who went above and
beyond the call of friendship in encouraging me, catching
inconsistencies in the manuscript, and making me finish the
damn thing. Kelly Lockhart, whose thoughts about entropy
defined my approach to this story and whose kindness to the
drunk and deranged has been a blessing. Julie Ann Parks,
author of Storytellers, who gave up some of her own precious
writing time when I hit neurotic overdrive, and who was
willing to engage in crazed discussions on "what would it be like
to have sex with a ghost". Fred Grimm, who listens to me
whine, feeds me, puts up with me when no one else will, and
gets me out of the house. Linda Avey Bullock for teaching me
anything I know about the craft of writing and keeping me
going when I am ready to give up. Michele McDonald, the
incomparable Air Goddess, who puts up with my hysteria.
I would not have written this one without you guys.*

And...
Judy Johnson for her willingness to assume the role of big sister,
comforter, and voice of reality. Brian A. Hopkins for selling his
first novel so I could sell mine. Charles Anders for being the
daughter I've always wanted, and the shopping partner of my
dreams. My sister Donna Jones, who feeds me, humors me, and
hasn't pushed me in front of a truck (yet). My cousin
Elaine Dinerman, who always suspected I was a writer and my
cousin Gail Safrit, who doesn't give a rat's ass what people
do as long as they're happy. My world would be
fairly hopeless without all of you.

And...
Tera, James, Bill, Wendell, and the rest of the Stellarcon crew —
I hope that you'll never regret making me the
property of Stellarcon.

And...
O.P. Goldberg, for loving me unconditionally. Were he alive,
he'd say, "Why do you write about such horrible things?"

And...
Johnnie Goldberg for making me think love is conditional.
Someone had to make me get off my ass.

It wasn't God who made honky tonk angels.

ONE

Layla slumped across the scarred picnic table in front of Down Under and glanced blurry eyed at the shot of tequila in front of her. A girl wearing a belly dancer's coin belt over a black tank dress squeezed past her, clutching a beer. The jangle and glint annoyed her. Layla shook her head; unbrushed black hair fell into her face. She took a pull off her bottle of Miller Light before tossing back the shot of Cuervo Gold. It burned going down. She almost gagged. Catching control, she swallowed hard and sipped her lukewarm beer. The burn in her belly was satisfying, comforting, it reminded her of why she'd laid out of work today.

Work: answering the phone at Amanda Windale Maternity Home, where the clinical director routinely blasted her for not immediately putting through whatever man she was stalking. Keep up with the program? Layla couldn't even figure it out. Saundra wore five hundred dollar blazers and had boyfriends who left her for Waffle House waitresses. Linda, the office manager, kept bringing cakes for the staff and idiotically saying, "Try this, it's so yum" while advocating further cut backs in the food for the residents.

Everyone else who worked at Windale Home had some weird agenda from their own closet – a baby born in '75 or a daughter who did crack. Layla had simply stumbled into what seemed an easy job.

She picked at the label on the sweating beer bottle with the edge of her thumbnail. Her nails were a bland shade of mauve. Her hair was naturally black. Layla reached into the pocket of her Levis for matches. She squirmed a bit while she extracted the matchbook. Her jeans were tight. She lit a Marlboro and looked up. The sun was strobe bright and piercing. On the sidewalk in front of Down Under, DJ argued with his rent boy. Between the tables, Tracy, the ring in her belly button bouncing, paraded around, shaking her boobs to hustle a beer. Tracy stopped moving for a second to talk to Mazie. Mazie always got on Layla's last nerve, noisy bitch. Two guys in expensive Goth drag lounged on the old sofa, stuffing spewing from its seams. They smoked clove cigarettes.

Through the haze of memory and alcohol, Layla heard Matt complaining about Bob: "One freaking Marshall amp and he thinks he needs help carrying it, what a wuss. Bob is so damn nelly. I am so over him."

Mazie's shrill giggle followed Matt's words into the din. Layla lit a match and watched it burn out. Mazie grabbed Layla's arm like they were friends sharing a joke.

Layla jerked her arm away and lit another match. A strawberry blond guy in a patchwork shirt walked out of the Center Of The Earth Gallery and turned toward the crowd drifting into Down Under. "There's one for you, Matt," she said. "Go talk to him."

Layla looked out for Matt. Got to get Matt laid, definitely need to get Matt laid. And, need another shot of Jose. Does that rhyme? Oh yeah, she was going down. Three in the afternoon, sitting outside Down Under with the artsy-farties, the losers, the wannabes, the gonna-bes, the used-to-bes, the Goths, Punks, rockers and drunks, Layla felt the glorious apathy of alcohol numbing her brain. "It starts in the gums, you know?" She grinned at Matt.

"What does? What are you talking about?" He leaned back to escape the blue stream of cigarette smoke and bumped into a cheesy metal table. Layla giggled at the sound.

"Oh, dissonance. Entropy and dissonance. They go together somehow." Layla peeled another bit of paper off the beer bottle. "Entropy," she said. She tapped the bottle against the heel of her purple cowgirl boot, "Dissonance," she added.

"I'm sure you think you've made your point, but I'm clueless. What about gum?" Matt seemed to be weaving. Layla squinted so that he'd hold still.

"Oh, not gum. Gums. My mouth gets drunk first. I can

feel my gums go numb. I need a dentist that uses tequila instead of Novocain." Maybe she should ask Dr. Trusdale about tequila, he was okay for a dentist. When Luke had hit her jaw and she'd needed a molar pulled, Dr. Trusdale had said, "Just open wide and pretend I'm an expensive blind date." Layla giggled drunkenly at the thought. He was okay for a dentist; maybe she had a mild case of the hots for him. No. No more cases of the hots. Not since Luke. She zapped from giggly to weepy faster than the speed of life.

"You okay?" Matt said. He had beagle eyes. The same eyes ever since he was a skinny eight year old. He leaned toward her. The sun caught the strands of red in his dark brown hair. He gnawed his lower lip.

"Need more tequila," Layla mumbled. She patted his cheek, no razor stubble, just soft skin. "Did you wax?"

"Yeah," Matt answered. He blushed. "I have no secrets from you, never have." He dipped his chin. She couldn't see his face.

"We have no secrets from each other. Never have. Never had? Not since the first. Do you remember when Mrs. Lewis busted me for smoking and you said it was you? She was a real piece of work. How'd she stay licensed as a foster mother? Crazy as a bed bug she was." Layla swallowed more beer.

No secrets: Layla's mother had died spectacularly in a murder that dominated the front pages of the Charlotte Observer when Layla was fourteen. Her mom, Ressa MacDonald, had been an ex-hippie, debutante turned tough businesswoman, who turned her father's flagging antique business into the place where Myers Park matrons spent their trust funds. On the side, she'd done most of her clientele's husbands while Layla was cosseted by a series of pillow-breasted African American housekeepers with names like *Queen Esther* and *Glaciations*. Her father, who Layla always thought of as *Daddy Useless*, hadn't seemed to know or care as long as he could drink Johnny Walker Black and play poker three nights a week.

Daddy Useless had her mamma's blood splattered across the front of his tux when he woke Layla to tell her that her mother was gone. Gone? Layla's eyes filled with tears. Not gone, dead. Freaking dead. May Louise Thompson had blown her away, one shot in the cleavage, in the middle of a reception for the Southeastern Museum Guild at Ferndale Country Club.

Fourteen years ago today, Layla thought, fourteen. What kind of a number is that? Layla had been in the same algebra class as May's son.

"You okay?" Matt asked again.

"Just remembering," she answered. Remembering the two years of smoking dope and reading all night long after Daddy Useless dumped her on Grandma MacDonald so that he could deteriorate into a convenience store clerk. Recalling the times that she thought she heard Mama in the achromatic dawn after scurrying out the window to walk around the sleeping streets. Then, some concerned neighbor or teacher called child welfare and she was beamed into foster care. She'd stomped across the hardwood floor of Mrs. Lewis's living room making the statues of Jesus on the mantel shimmy while she tried to figure out how to get thrown out fast. Then Matt spoke to her for the first time, "You're the murder girl. My parents are deaded too. Will you be my sister?" He was eight, all long legs and big eyes, the other kids called him sissy boy.

"I remember meeting you for the first time. You were so cute."

"I still am. What I remember most is when all the jocks who called me fag and pounded on me were drooling over you in that sequined number you wore in your guise as 'mysterious older woman prom date.'" Matt's voice was soft.

"Yeah, I wash up real nice," Layla said. She winked at him, and then rubbed her eye with the back of her hand, smearing mascara all over her cheekbone.

"Well, dear, let me tell you, the panda bear look isn't you. Wipe that mess off your face." Matt relaxed visibly.

Layla rummaged through her backpack for a compact. She squinted into the mirror. Flecks of mascara and streaks of eyeliner covered the left side of her face. She was pale above the black 'Honky Tonk Angel' t-shirt. She snapped the compact shut. "You'll have to do it for me," she said.

Matt turned to straddle the bench. He poured a bit of his Pepsi onto the edge of Layla's shirt and dabbed at her face. "Well, that's the best I can do, precious," he said. "It may be best that you've taken a vow of celibacy. You're not looking tres chic."

"I'll take it up with my fashion consultant," she said.

Matt rolled his eyes. "Girlfriend, that look is not my fault. I disavow any and all responsibility for the cow girl theme." He leaned his head on his hand. "It's them, isn't it? Your parents. The cow girl theme is the rebellion du jour."

Layla shrugged. "Jasons plural at six o'clock." Jason and Jason, two dissimilar, ubiquitously named habitués of Down Under were the center of a loose group that more or less included Matt and Layla. Matt turned to spot both Jasons walking down Davidson Street. The taller of the two Jasons was sporting a lime green cape. He was famous this week for not missing a beat drumming Freebird when his stool broke; he had great balance. "That color could make me hurl," Matt said. "Who dresses straight men?"

Over the bar sounds, Layla heard Mazie squeal a greeting at the Jasons.

Layla lit another cigarette. The diversion relieved her. She wanted to talk about her mother and didn't want to talk about her mother. She had some secrets from Matt, predominate among them was the sense that her mother was occasionally around, and the sense that some one else was following her. Stalking her. She watched the smoke rise and curl in the humid Carolina afternoon. Smoke like ghosts, wispy, something else. It wasn't exactly that she lived in a haunted house.

Layla lived in a huge house in the center of Myers Park, an exclusive area of inherited money and madness, where incest and mildew are commonplace. Discreet psychosis and arrogant kudzu choke out change. Most families contain the requisite alcoholic university professor or fragile beauty vaguely connected to the mysterious unspeakable death of someone. Some older families have a never-mentioned relative in prison, three kids in rehab, and a man who shot his brother in a hunting accident. Yet, they are the "right sort" of people.

She'd inherited the house from Grandma MacDonald. Daddy Useless had tried to sell it, but Grandma had left a will as well constructed as the three-story brick house. In Myers Park, carpeted lawns maintained by expensive lawn services stretched out an acre or more before bumping into broad sidewalks beneath a canopy of tall, leafy trees. Layla rented two bedrooms out, one of them to Matt. She had to; she couldn't have afforded to maintain the house otherwise.

If anyone else had wanted to take in boarders, there would have been hell to pay. The SUV-driving soccer moms would have gone on a rampage, roaming the streets with petitions, whining before the zoning commission and involving the attorneys they'd married. But, Layla was one of their own. She might drive a crunched Toyota in its second decade and dress like a refugee from a country western bar, but she was theirs, she was Southern, they knew her people. Even though those people were an adulterous corpse and a useless alcoholic, they were from good families.

The right sort of people.

Just outside Layla's window was a silvery birch, the color reminded Layla of one of her mom's evening gowns. If she sometimes spoke to the tree, narrowing her eyes in the twilight so it seemed to shimmer and move–well, it wasn't that she thought that her mother had taken up residence in the tree. The house wasn't haunted. The tree wasn't haunted. Layla was haunted. She thought. Maybe. She needed more tequila. She knew that she needed more tequila.

"Our girl Layla's fading in and out," commented the shortest Jason. He had a long braid down his back. "Did Bob manage to struggle in with the massive behemoth amp?"

The taller Jason played with his drumsticks, tap–tap–roll on the edge of the table. He shook his short dark hair in sync with his motion. "What are you doing, Layla?"

"Renewing my longstanding friendship with Jose Cuervo," she answered. "I think Bob's been set up, probably having a hissy fit wondering where you guys were. Matt, please, I really need more tequila. By the way, that lime green sucks more than just a little bit."

Matt put another shot of tequila and a Miller Light in front of Layla. She shook her head, squinted and focused on the drinks. Matt took a swallow of Pepsi.

"It's early man, what's the soda about?" asked short Jason.

"Oh, I'm designated sober tonight," Matt answered. "You know, driving Miss Crazy." He averted his face and reached over to Layla. He squeezed her hand. She didn't respond. He made a mock courtly gesture and kissed her hand. She smiled briefly but there was a vacant look on her face, she didn't really notice Matt.

Deep inside, somewhere very near her heart, Layla felt a tug, a pull, a tiny glimmer of something dark and bright. Tequila, liquid schizophrenia, definitely different from other drunks, more like mescaline than alcohol, really.

She slammed down the shot of Cuervo and unfolded herself from the bench. Her legs were wobbly, drunk legs, rubber legs. Layla grinned like a stoner. Getting to the ladies room was going to be an adventure. She cautiously stepped down the concrete stairs. One, two, three, four, five. Good, very good. This walking thing was okay, she remembered how to do it.

She held up her arm as she passed from the patio into the building. She displayed the orange plastic 'cover charge paid' bracelet encircling her bony wrist. The guy at the door – new guy, she didn't recognize him and he didn't acknowledge her – scrutinized it. His shaved head and multiple piercings put her off. Layla got the giggles over people whose efforts at individualism fit neatly into the times. *Yeah, I bet he has a pierced nipple and a dragon tattoo, she thought. It's a good thing I'm not into sex, there aren't many men around worth shaving my legs for...Lord, I'm drunk.*

She stumbled on the doorstep and reached out to grab an old stove that leaned against the wall. Layla wasn't certain whether it was DJ's love of kitsch or laziness that resulted in Down Under being a hodge podge of mismatched kitchen tables, derelict appliances and yard sale rejects. She clutched the cold porcelain surface of the stove to steady her weaving. Okay cowgirl, got the blues? But, you still need to make it to the ladies.

Bob was prancing around the small stage in the front of the room making macho stallion noises as he stacked his amps. Layla kept her hand on the wall and tried to slide by the sound booth undetected. Scott was running sound, playing oldies until the band took over around nine. She couldn't slither past. He spotted her. He put on "Tiny Dancer" by Elton John. She freaking hated that song.

Layla stumbled and reached out for the wall. She got Fred instead of the wall. "Hi...you're not a wall," she slurred.

"And if *you* drank less you could make all kinds of great discoveries," Fred answered. "Even more profound than distinguishing between a massive man in an Hawaiian shirt and a wall."

He'd lecture her about smoking next.

Friends can be a real pain in the butt.

Layla escalated the stomp quotient of her boots. She really hated being a small woman. She thought that if she were a big old healthy looking cowgirl, an Amazon type, that maybe people would take her seriously, maybe they wouldn't be so quick to tell her what to do.

She stepped on Styrofoam cups advertising a NASCAR race. One of DJ's brilliant economies involved buying leftover odd lots of cups and plates from every event that hit Charlotte. Pina Coladas in concert cups and wine in plastic emblazoned with the Charlotte Hornet's logo were part of the Down Under ambiance. Layla staggered past posters of Jim Morrison, Nine Inch Nails, and Rick Flare to join the line to the ladies.

The lyrics to "Tiny Dancer" bothered her; she hated it when men thought there was something childlike about her because she was small. Layla had spent a large part of her life feeling 'less than'. She had never even discussed it with Matt, this feeling of 'less than'. She wasn't a kid, damn it. She didn't have sex anymore, she didn't think she even wanted to, except sometimes when she was drunk. Layla held herself upright by placing her palm square against the empty paper towel dispenser. *DJ must not have found any towels on sale. I hope there's toilet paper.*

Layla struggled through a miasma of hairspray, Charlie, and bathroom disinfectant. She ignored sink-side comparisons of penis sizes and incomes. Washing her hands, she started humming an oldie. Maybe it was time to think about Mamma, that was what this drunk was all about, wasn't it? Losing Mama before her junior-senior that wasn't, the debut she never made, the white wedding she wouldn't have. Yeah, throwing a drunk over losing Mama. The song that ran through her sodden mind was *One Toke Over The Line*. Pretty harmony. She banged her shin on something and fell out of the ladies into the dark smoked filled club.

Weird song for her to think of, Layla wasn't much of a stoner.

She stumbled into Fred again. He straightened her up and turned her back toward Matt.

Layla. Why had her cursed parents bestowed that name on her? She perceived it as a handicap. A Layla ought to be impossibly beautiful or at least blonde, she ought to bring men to their knees or at least make them look twice. Layla was Patti Harrison with the charms to ensnare Clapton. What was *she?* Layla? A skinny cowgirl with a dead mother. A skinny celibate cowgirl. Layla suspected that men only came on to her when it was close to closing time. She had never even told Matt that.

She shuffled back to her place on the picnic bench. Tracy was talking non-stop about wanting to have her hair done light pink with streaks of dark blue. The Jasons had disappeared to play drums and bass. Two more shots of tequila sat in front of her, she thought she should think about her mother, who was, after all, the reason for this particular drunk. But she couldn't, she just couldn't.

In one of those moments of clarity that haunt drunks, Layla looked at her pale hand on the table, next to the glasses of Cuervo Gold. It was an aristocratic hand, slender and pale, soft and flawless. Her hand reminded her of the ballet lessons, the piano lessons, the beautiful world of structure and artistry before her Mama died.

"I'm ready to go," she said. Matt didn't move, had he heard her? Tracy was monotoning about some party in Raleigh where she'd pulled all the fire alarms in the hotel. "I need to go, Matt."

"Driving Miss Crazy," Matt said to the man he'd been talking with, not a rent boy, but a muscular accountant for First Union, deep in the closet.

"Oh, yeah," said the accountant, passing Matt a business card, home number scrawled over the office telephone. "I see."

He didn't.

Matt took care of Layla. Layla took care of Matt. No one else saw what they saw.

"I didn't really think about her," Layla slurred, leaning into Matt's embrace as they walked to his car.

"Sssh, you don't have to," he said. He had his keys in hand.

"I do," she said. "I do need to think about her, today if no other time. This is the day I need to think about her and I didn't. I got wasted instead." Layla whined. She was near tears. She wore a holographic bracelet. For a moment, she was distracted, staring drunkenly at the hologram, forgetting Matt, forgetting Mama.

"You needed to get drunk," Matt said. "And tomorrow you'll need a facial, trust me."

Matt shoved her into his Saturn. "Yes, they want to be my car company as long as I make payments," he said. The night was grainy, artificial somehow. Charlotte lit like a grade B horror flick, the First Union Tower Christmas treed against an ebony sky.

Matt sped down 7th street.

"I want to stop for another drink," Layla said. "No, I don't.

I just want to go home"

"Home it is, then," Matt said.   He cut over toward Presbyterian Hospital, took Kenilworth past CMC, and headed down East Boulevard. The streets were deserted.

As he turned onto Queen's Road West, Layla began hyperventilating. "I swear I won't get into any trouble, please just let me walk from here. I need to clear my head."

Matt slowed just past the intersection where East meets Queen's Road West. "I just need to walk a few minutes." She hopped from the car at the light.

Layla stood and watched Matt's headlights. He circled and then went down toward Princeton. She exhaled. He obviously decided that it was easier to go home and wait for her than to troll the streets behind her.

Layla bounced as she moved though the dark.   She liked being in the film noir light of 3 AM. She loved the sound of her boots tapping along the sidewalk. The cooler night air gave her the illusion of partial sobriety. She adored the stark lines and odd contrasts of shrubs and houses in the dim black and white night. It was all wonderful–a macabre fairy tale, a dark wonderland.

Right up to the moment five fingers imprinted themselves in her arm, squeezing and chaining the soft flesh.

"Oh, shit," she muttered. "Oh, shit." This is Myers Park; land of old money, why is some one grabbing me here? This is a safe neighborhood, right? Layla jerked her arm forcefully and swung her backpack around in front of her.   She took off running.

"Bitch, you think you too good."

Layla caught a quick glimpse of him; hat pulled low, red shirt, running shoes.

She ran through yards across the sprinkler systems, beneath the fake Tudor windows, scrambling over low decorative walls. She ran through the hyacinth bushes and azaleas. She heard him gaining on her. He crashed through the hedges just seconds behind her. She couldn't lose him in her neighbor's yard. Her chest ached, her own panting sounded incredibly loud to her, it filled the night.

Her boot heels hammered the ground.

The thump of his running shoes maintained a steady pace.

"I just be willing to do you a favor," he said. His breathing did not sound labored. He moved right behind her; she felt the tug of his fingers on her t-shirt

Layla twisted and ran. Her quick motion pulled the fabric from his grasp. Still, he was just behind her, she could almost feel his breath on her neck. Her side hurt. Yeah, doing me a favor. Even a rapist comments on my lack of allure. She didn't have the energy for a manic giggle. She ran and wanted a cigarette.

Cutting through a hedge of sultry gardenias, she hit her back yard. Layla ran up the back stairs two at a time. She didn't look back. She heard a thud. Had he tripped? She'd thought he was keeping up with her until the stairs. She didn't look back. Layla only heard the pounding of her own heart, the sound of her own footsteps on the stairs.

Despite the thick August heat, she was chilled. The air felt heavy on her skin. On the top step, she paused, gulped air. She jammed her key in the lock.

She heard a voice say, *"I tae care of me own."*

Going mad. Voices. Layla shook her head. *"I do lass, I tae care of me own."*

Layla unlocked the door. She went in without turning on the light. She put on the chain lock. Cold sweat plastered her hair to her neck. Her chest ached. Layla held onto the wall as she walked to her bedroom. She couldn't quite catch her breath. She slid her backpack off her arm in the hallway and stumbled over it as she entered her room.

Still dressed, boots on, she passed out on the bed.

"I tae care o' me own," was the last thing she heard.

TWO

The sound of Roberta Flack mingled with Matt's off key caterwauling. The clang of pots and pans and a vicious sliver of sunlight shattered the remnants of Layla's sleep. Her mouth tasted like she'd eaten an ashtray. She opened her eyes and scanned the characteristic wreckage of her bedroom; books covering the foot of the bed, empty Miller Light cans standing sentinel on the dressing table and clothes heaped by the door. The ruffled curtains over the wide windows betrayed her by allowing the killer morning sun into the room.

She knew that Matt would be flittering and fussing around the kitchen, Tinkerbell in khakis, fixing pancakes with chocolate chips or omelets with elaborate ingredients. Why did he always want her to eat when her body ached from alcohol and her stomach rolled? Food struck her as an obscene proposition.

Her body hurt in places she didn't think she had. *I can't drink*, she thought. *Not like that*. Layla surveyed her body still clad in yesterday's jeans and t-shirt with disgust. *Thank God, it's my day off.*

Moving with caution, as if a sudden or random movement would break her bones, Layla rolled first to her side and then struggled upright. She wasn't even steady enough for a cigarette. She sat, legs dangling off the bed, head throbbing, eyes swollen for a second. In the dim recesses of her brain, she knew that coffee, food, and a shower would restore her. Yet moving seemed so incredibly difficult.

She stopped for a moment. The chirping of birds, the clang of trashcan lids, the slam of car doors filled the air. *Life goes on*, she thought. Through the years since her mother died, she had that thought over and over. *Life goes on, don't think about it, don't think about anything.* Gingerly, she stood. Layla was so hung over that she wobbled slightly. The faded floral rug felt soft beneath her feet.

She blinked a few times. Layla ducked her head to avoid the mirror and staggered to the bathroom. Roberta's voice filled the house. Cold water on her face, like the slap of rejection from a long time lover, she brushed her teeth and ran her fingers through her hair. She shuffled to the kitchen; picking up her feet would have done her in.

Matt placed two Tylenol and a glass of orange juice in front of her. "Drink up, precious. I know you know how."

"You're infernally perky this morning," Layla said. She sat at a scarred table that had been in her family who-knew-how-long. Its broad wooden top was scantily covered with woven placemats. She blinked at a cluster of orange dahlias in a blue jug.

Matt ran around the kitchen like a hamster on a wheel. He slid pancakes off his frying pan onto a metal tray heated with a candle. He sliced strawberries paper-thin while he sang along with Roberta. He darn near pirouetted between the refrigerator and the tiled counters. He flipped an omelet expertly while he sang.

"You're disgusting," Layla said.

"*I'm* Martha Stewart in drag. *You're* disgusting. You try hard to be, and a damn fine job you do of it." Matt sat down opposite her after fussing with two stoneware coffee mugs. "So, have we thrown our annual drunk?"

Layla wrapped stiff fingers around the steaming mug of coffee. The warmth of the cup seeped through her flesh. It was comforting. She stared into the black liquid.

"Finding our future in coffee grounds, are we? I thought that was strictly a tea drinking thing." Matt piled food on a plate and placed it on the woven placemat in front of Layla.

"I've killed for less," she said. Roberta was silent.

Matt walked toward the counter where the CD player squatted.

"I really am in the mood for Merle Haggard," Layla said.

"Puh-lease," said Matt rolling her eyes. "Must we bring this redneck charade into our home? It's bad enough that you're an ersatz unlaid barslut in public. Must the hideous strains of country music invade my living space?" He put in a jazz CD, something Layla didn't recognize.

Layla stared at a bright yellow omelet, festooned with orange swirls of cheese on the blue plate in front of her. She wrinkled her face in disgust when she spotted the pancakes and strawberries beside it. She was certain Matt had cooked and color coordinated simultaneously. She wasn't quite certain what had happened last night. She wasn't a very good drunk. "I'm really kind of hazy on last night," she said.

"Oh, it was wonderful, precious. You took your clothes off and danced naked on the tables outside of Down Under. Then you decided to become a Jehovah's Witness, you called some 800 number and arranged it. They'll be by for you at noon." Matt deftly cut a bit of his omelet with the edge of his fork. Cheese oozed onto his plate.

Layla looked at the food in revulsion. She felt queasy, headachy, and near dead.

"It's fortunate you don't drink liquor often, precious." Matt ate a bite of omelet and then dived into his pancakes and strawberries.

"You seem relentlessly cheerful," Layla said. "I could kill you. Easily."

"Protein first, precious, then homicide. It's a rule." Matt ate, fueling himself efficiently.

Layla sat across the table and stared at him. The room had changed little since her grandma's time. Glazed planters full of herbs lined the windowsills, tended by Matt. Layla's gran had grown herbs in the same place. The pots and pans hanging above the stove, the sideboard laden with whisks, garlic presses, and other unfathomable kitchen gadgets Matt used expertly had belonged to Layla's Gran. Matt had bought the blue dishes at Pier 1, but on fancy occasions he preferred Gran's bone china.

"Well, are we eating our breakfast or committing it to memory? Come on, precious, the only thing worse than cold eggs is a bad perm."

Layla sipped her coffee and glared.

Matt cut a small bite of pancake and stabbed a bit of strawberry with his fork. Waving it in front of her face he said, "Eat a bite for baby brother."

Layla opened her mouth to protest and he shoved the food through her lips. The pancake was surprisingly comforting.

Layla sighed, picked up her fork and ate half a pancake in silence.

"There's my good girl," Matt said. "And a shame it is, she'd have so much more fun if she was bad." He refilled their coffee cups. "Now, Holly–there's a bad girl. Voyeur's dream. Did you see that sweet young thing she dragged home from Myrtle Beach last week? Honestly, if he ever decided to switch hit, I could make me a very happy boy."

"No, I didn't meet him." Layla was feeling as if she might live, but still the sexual adventures of the third member of their little household didn't really interest her.

"More pity that," Matt said. "Definite eye candy. And, by the time she's through flying the Charlotte–Orlando route this month she'll have lost track of him."

"Holly is in many ways the perfect room mate. She's never here," Layla said.

"Oh, we are a bit snippy this fine morning," Matt said.

"Oh, honey. I didn't mean you. I mean, we're like family, we're kind of set in our ways. I just think we'd both have a lot of adjusting to do if Holly was here all the time." Layla lit a cigarette and coughed. Holly had come to them through a connection with a hairdresser Matt dated briefly. She flew out of Charlotte and Chicago, splitting her time between the two places.

"Set in our ways? Oh please, that sounds like they're about to drag us off in tandem, you to the aging recycled virgins rest home and me to the happy hostel for fossilized fairies. Save me, I'm still years away from dirty thirty." Matt finished his breakfast and started clearing the table. He left Layla's pancakes in front of her.

"Did you hear anything last night?" Layla asked.

"Let's see. Last night. Well, I heard you nattering on about entropy and dissonance, a boring mix of clichéd conversation, the bad Jasons band in its current desultory incarnation, the clang of beer cans, and some traffic noise. May have left something out." Matt filled the sink with hot sudsy water and sniffed the lemon scented dish soap appreciatively. He rinsed the plates and put them in the hot water methodically.

"No, I mean...when I came in," Layla said. She played with a bit of cellophane from her cigarettes, swirling it around the tabletop with her index finger.

"Well, you're here now. So, we've established that you did in fact get home." Matt swept the spotless linoleum and hung the broom and dustpan back up on the inside rack concealed behind the panty door.

"No, something happened. Or, I think it did. I think I remember someone chasing me on the street. I ran. He should have caught me, but he didn't. Something else happened." Layla lit a cigarette, ignoring the one that already burned in the ashtray. "It's weird, I was so drunk. Maybe I got a dream confused with stuff."

"Dreams are confusing stuff.   Everything is confusing, precious. It's because you try to figure it out. If you just wouldn't think so much, it would all fall together." Matt poured more coffee and perched on the edge of the kitchen counter.

"Been watching Oprah again? I'm not into visualizing or going with the flow." Layla spun the ashtray around. She rubbed her finger along the fringe of the placemat and jiggled her left leg, shaking the kitchen table. "Sorry, I'm a bit out of sorts."

"Well, you earned it."

"It's just that I remember being in danger last night. A man on the street chased me. Then, something made him go away. And then I thought I heard someone else speaking to me, he had an accent. Scottish, I think. But there was no one there. I mean, there was someone chasing me. But after he went away, the voice I heard – the accented one – no one was there then." Layla stared at the corner of the refrigerator. She didn't actually see the refrigerator; she was thinking this same room, long ago, before Mom died. "I don't know. Now I'm imagining strange men."

"Precious, we all imagine strange men. I know I do." Matt shrugged. "You're hung over, tired, all of that. And it wouldn't hurt to do a tad more than imagine a strange man."

"A new man doesn't solve every problem on the planet," Layla said.

"And you would know this how?"

"It's just that after Luke..." Layla's voice trailed off. She picked at a chip in her nail polish with her thumbnail scattering flakes of mauve across the table.

"After Luke." Matt sounded exasperated. "After Luke." He jumped to his feet, stomped across the room, and cleaned the nail polish off the table. "If you ask me, *precisely* what you need *after Luke* is a man. Luke wasn't a man. He was a warped experiment in intermittent reinforcement. Now he loves you, now he doesn't. This morning he has the hots for you, this afternoon he's not interested. He doesn't want you, but he doesn't want anyone else to have you. He wasn't consistent from one moment to the next."

"Like you would know anything about consistency?" Layla said. Tears brimmed in her eyes.

"I'm incredibly consistent, sweetie. I want sex. All the time, if I ever find a man that feels the same way, I'll be his love slave for life," Matt flung back his head dramatically and camped a sex goddess pose.

"Until Labor Day, you'll be his love slave," Layla said with a faint smile.

"Life, Labor Day, they both begin with 'L', I get confused." Matt sat down opposite her and held her hand. "But, it's different for you. You need a guy that's steady. One that won't flake off, or lose his temper six times a week, or get crazy with you."

"Getting crazy might be a good thing," Layla smiled like a naughty child. She stubbed out her cigarette and ran her hands through her hair. "Getting violent is not a good thing." Her voice was flat, her smile evaporated.

"I didn't want to mention it," Matt said. He bit his lower lip and squeezed her hand. "Seriously precious, consider Luke an anomaly, a throw-back to the Neanderthals, just a weird bad thing. Most men aren't violent."

"Most people don't have their mothers blown away." Layla said, then burst into tears. Horrible keening animal noises erupted from her throat, sobs that seemed volcanic, as if they ought to crack her ribcage. She moaned and wailed, lost in a sea of grief, tossed helplessly on the storm currents of loss.

Matt knelt beside her, wrapping his arms around her shuddering body, cradling her as if she were a child. He stroked her hair and made vague soothing noises. He rocked Layla. She leaned against him, weeping copiously and allowing her grief to devour the moment.

"Luke wasn't violent," Layla said. "Not violent, not really. It was something else." She snuggled into Matt's chest, resting her head on his shoulder. Absently she watched a few crumbs on the table, wondering when he would see them, when he would compulsively mop them up. His shirt smelled of detergent. He smelled of deodorant, soap, and shampoo.

"Shh, precious." Matt reached over her and grabbed a Kleenex. "Blow your nose."

"No," she said, an undertone of petulant childishness permeating her voice. "Besides, I can't blow my nose. I never learned how properly." Layla grabbed the Kleenex and mopped her face. "All better now."

Matt stroked her matted hair. "A facial and a hot oil treatment, the bare minimum."

Layla giggled. "Mother hen."

After a moment, Matt got up. He evidently spotted the crumbs on the table and attacked them with a sponge. His face was contorted. He appeared about to speak. He coughed and frowned. He rubbed the table viciously. Suddenly, he stiffened. He threw the sponge in the sink, like a major league pitcher hurling the ball to first to pick off a cocky batter. "All right," he said, fire in his voice, "What do you mean by 'not violent'?"

Layla paled. "Oh, I think he did love me. Really. I think that the way I am just made him crazy." She hung her head down. The knees of her jeans were faded, why did the knees always fade first? Using her thumbnail, she tore at a hangnail until it lengthened and then bit it. Her index finger began bleeding. She pressed the Kleenex against the wound.

"Precious, that wasn't love. That was rape."

His words hung in the air like dust motes.

Rape.

She never thought about that word in connection with her, with Luke. Rape was something strangers did to you. Sudden, unexpected. It couldn't be the slow, gradual hounding, the sudden lunges, the tearful protestations that "I'll never hurt you," that Layla associated with the awful night Luke had lost control.

Abruptly, Layla stood. She paced around the kitchen. She paused in front of the window, staring out at the green canopy of trees that shaded the back yard, remembering the precise location of the clothesline. The morning sun pierced the shade. Layla squinted, and stared intently at the multiple textures of moss, grass, and leaf. "It's like a monochromatic quilt, isn't it? The yard."

From behind her, she heard Matt. "You don't want to talk about Luke."

She strained her ears. Would Matt start cleaning or baking or organizing the CDs she'd scattered across the counter? Would he please do *anything* other than remain motionless while speaking to her in that soothing concerned voice? She reached into her pocket for a cigarette. She'd left them on the table. Layla didn't want to turn around and face him. As long as she looked out the window recalling the clothesline, she felt safely detached.

Her body felt heavy. Her legs inside loose denim felt weighted with lead. Something seemed to reach into her chest and squeeze her heart. Layla expelled her breath in short desperate bursts. She stood in the kitchen drowning. For an instant she saw her own thoughts like a maze, a series of interlocking corridors walled by locked doors. Somewhere, at the end of a twisted unlit hallway was an entity akin to the voice of reason. She knew that Matt wanted to help, wanted her to purge the dreadful guilt that had wrapped viselike around her soul since the night Luke assaulted her and left her shaking and crying, unable to explain the depth of her pain. Matt wanted her to cry and wail and externalize the blame. Matt wanted her to get angry.

Layla tilted her head to the side, watching a yellow finch perched on the bird feeder outside the gingham curtained kitchen window. She wasn't angry. She knew she ought to – needed to – talk to Matt, but her throat felt tight, constricted, as if someone was slowly squeezing the life out of her. The bird took wing and vanished into the leaves of an oak tree.

"Layla, you can't hold it in forever. It's eating you like cancer."

"I'd let it out if I knew what it was." Layla shrugged. The statement and movement were affectation, suited to the country cowgirl personae she'd adopted. She felt dirty, cheap, and dishonest. Matt was her dearest, her closest friend. She felt like she was lying to him, striking a pose. She exhaled, her breath, a gust. Her hands were shaking.

Layla paced back and forth for a few seconds. She ran her hand through her unkempt hair, and then grabbed one of the straight-backed kitchen chairs, spun it around and straddled it.

Then, as if she'd suddenly remembered an important errand, she jerked herself erect. "Matt, it's more complicated than you think, what happened. I feel responsible. When I broke off with

Luke, I guess I was kind of ambiguous. I mean, I was flattered that all of a sudden I seemed so important to him. Me, little Layla, the dumb cow that waited in the corner of the bar until he got tired and was ready to go somewhere to crash. I always felt like a last choice, like he saw me when whoever he really wanted was busy. Then, when I decided not to do it anymore, he acted like he loved me."

"Love," said Matt. He snorted. "I might be inclined to put on Tina Turner at this point. Oh, precious, that was outraged ego, not love."

"It felt like love. So, when he wanted to talk about it, of course I was willing. I mean, I'd been dying for him to actually talk to me for months." She jiggled her left leg. The table shook. "Okay. So, then we started kissing. Then, when it went beyond that, I was confused. I kept thinking, this isn't what I want, but he wants me. I'd have given anything for him to want me as much I wanted him."

She leaned over to the table and got a cigarette. She squinted as the blue smoke shrouded her face. "So, when he started getting forceful, he kept telling me, 'You're making me do this, you know you want me'. He kept saying, 'You always want me, bitch'. I didn't want him. Not then, not like that. But, I felt like I'd caused it. From all the times I had wanted him. I know I didn't. I know it. But, I felt responsible. Crazy."

"Precious, you did nothing wrong."

Layla shrugged. "I *know* that. But, on some level I don't really believe it." She watched the smoke drift up to the ceiling.

"You have to believe me, Luke was fucked. Men aren't like that." Matt sighed. "You really need a facial precious, and a hot oil treatment for your hair."

"I'm not ready to go back on the market, dear one." Layla smiled weakly.

"Oh, we aren't talking marketability, precious. We are talking about not offending the delicate aesthetic sensibilities of your room mate." Matt leaned back. "Come on, into the shower and I'll give you a nice moisturizing facial afterwards."

Tears leaked out of Layla's eyes. 'I don't care what I look like."

"Of course you don't. That's why you need me." Matt stood. He took the cigarette from her and stubbed it out.

The phone rang. The pair stopped, remaining motionless

while the recorded message clicked on. *'This is Matt, Layla, and Holly's refrigerator. The answer machine is on vacation in Barbados. If you'd like to leave a message please scribble it down and use a magnet to attach it to my door.'*

They looked at each other, wide-eyed and shallow breathed. "It's okay, precious," Matt said. "They can't see us not answering."

Layla giggled. The shorter Jason's voice started, reciting a list of places and times to meet up and do nothing in a hurry. As soon as he said, 'Café Dada at three', the tape ran out.

Layla laughed. "Do they ever do anything other than hang out?"

"I don't think so. Now give us a smile and run take your shower. That's a good girl."

Layla smiled bravely and walked toward her room. She heard the sound of Tina Turner singing, "What's Love got to do with it?" She peeled off her dirty clothes. It took a few seconds of rummaging through the pile of clothes on the floor to find her terry cloth bathrobe.

Her bedroom was at the top of the stairs, with a huge bathroom right next to it. Holly had a smaller room next door to Layla's, with a newly installed adjoining bath. The modern bath didn't tempt Layla. She loved the big claw footed tub and spacious linen closet in her own. She kept the bath scrupulously clean in stark contrast to the clutter that covered her bedroom.

Matt's room was a half landing down. It had been Layla's room when she was a teen. Layla often wondered if Matt heard her pace the floors during her sleepless nights.

Over the sound of Tina's voice, woven like a gilt thread into the fabric of the day, Layla heard a soft brogue, "Lass, didna fash yerself. He wasna worth it. Everythin' will be set right."

She stopped dead still in the hallway.

"Matt, Matt?" She yelled, straining her throat. She coughed a nervous cigarette cough. "Matt?" Her heart beat so rapidly she thought her chest would burst. She struggled to breathe through the fog of fear that enveloped her. Layla shook all over, even her voice shook as she screamed, "Matt!"

He slid through the hallway and caught the end of the banister.

"Matt did you hear anything?" She looked down at him,

studying his face.

"Only you and Tina," he answered.

THREE

Moisturized, manicured, pedicured, styled and facialed to Matt's satisfaction, Layla sprawled on the chintz covered chaise lounge in her Gran's sitting room. Her clean jeans and freshly laundered t-shirt cuddled her body. The room nearly wrapped itself around her in a hug. The violet sprigged wall paper, the white Priscilla curtains, the delicate lines of the Queen Anne furniture all reminded Layla of a period she thought of as 'the before time,' back when Gran was energetic, vital, and full of laughter, when her mom was alive and she'd spent evenings with Gran in the big house. She'd perched on the window seat in this very room and watched Mom and Dad drive off in the big black Cadillac, Mom's hair upswept, the snowy column of her slender neck ringed by a strand of glowing pearls.

She felt safe in her room. The piles of clothes, scattered papers, and countless books that sat on every surface served as a barricade against the world. She felt sane among her familiar cushions; able to stop wondering what was wrong with her, why she suddenly seemed to he hearing voices, why she'd driven Luke to such extreme behavior.

Layla flicked her ashes into a bone china dish.

"Peasant," Matt said.

"Please, don't start in with me about smoking." Layla sipped coffee.

"Precious, cigarettes are way down the list." Matt tipped up her chin and examined her face. "Your eyebrows are great. I'm a freaking genius you know."

"Absolutely," Layla agreed. She set the coffee cup down on an end table, put out her cigarette and leaned back into the cushions.

"So, have you recovered sufficiently from last night's debauchery to participate in the essential Saturday night rituals?" Matt paced, thumbs hitched in his belt, maneuvering around the room, keeping sight of himself in the mirror over the small fireplace.

"You know, I think I am still in do-it-yourself detox. I think I'd really like to stay home tonight. Somehow migrating from bar to bar doesn't do it for me. But don't let me slow you down, pardner. I know there are drinks to drink, men to be had and Jasons to ridicule."

Matt looked at her as if he was assessing the truth of what she was saying.

"Besides, I want to read. I have that new book about Flora MacDonald I want to look at."

"Well, I certainly wouldn't want to keep you from the dead." Matt ruffled her hair. "You probably do need a night off. That table dance at Down Under was a bit much."

Layla pantomimed tossing a pillow at him. "Don't worry about me. I'll rest and wallow around here. I sort of need down time."

"Well, all right then," Matt said.

Layla cradled her coffee cup and smiled. She listened to his footsteps going down the stairs. She heard him shut the door and then heard his car start. Reassured Matt didn't feel the need to baby-sit her, she put down her cup and eagerly opened her book.

Twisting a strand of hair around her finger, Layla curled on her side and began to track the fictionalized adventures of Flora MacDonald. An hour into the book, Layla was disgusted. It seemed too neat, too much of one event fitting into the next. Sheesh, Flora had only known Bonnie Prince Charlie a week, and the author was transforming this adventure into a star-crossed romance. Disgusted, Layla dropped the book on the hardwood floor. She felt foolish. She'd always thought Flora MacDonald had to be a mythic heroine. Stuff was named after her: schools, highland games, and such. When she thought about it, it seemed that Flora was simply a single girl hanging about when the Bonnie Prince needed a traveling companion. Layla wanted Flora to be wonderful.

They shared the same last name.

In 1746, when Bonnie Prince Charlie's efforts to gain the Scottish throne failed, he was forced into hiding so he could escape to France. Flora had been 24. The book said she was beautiful. But it would, wouldn't it? After all, who writes a romance about a normal looking woman? Flora's foster father and fiancée had been on the other side politically; her fiancée actually served in the English King George the II's army.

The guys that supported Prince Charlie told Flora that her foster father was in favor of the rescue plan. With the Bonnie Prince in drag, Flora helped conceal him until he was able to get safely to the ship that took him to France.

The author had been liberal with her use of long smoldering glances between the two and glossed over the fact that Charles was wearing skirts. Following the escape, Flora spent some time in the Tower of London. Upon her release she married her redcoat fiancée. They immigrated to North Carolina. The couple shared a knack for betting on wrong horses. He was a redcoat during the Revolutionary War. Ultimately, Flora returned to Scotland. When Layla read that a sheet upon which Bonnie Prince Charlie had slept was used as Flora's shroud, she made gagging noises.

Flora probably loved her husband, if she loved anyone. The Bonnie Prince sounded a bit like a Bonnie Jerk. Shoot. It was probably the North Carolina connection that had hooked her, or that Flora was Scottish. Layla had always had a weird desire to see Scotland, maybe because her name was MacDonald, or maybe because like everyone else she knew, she was going to travel 'sometime'.

Leaving the book on the floor, Layla toddled off to the kitchen. Surely, one of her food conscious roommates had left her a scrap of something. Matt was always good for leftovers, and Holly brought in multiple bottles of salad dressing and salad greens that turned to slime before her next layover in Charlotte. Holly was a good roommate, Layla thought. Despite her omnivorous sexual appetite, Holly was so sweet, she was near old fashioned.

Holly acted big sisterish toward Layla, despite the fact that Layla had two hard years on her. Holly was a caretaker. She was the roommate that checked to see that the Freon was in the air conditioning unit and milk was in the refrigerator, even if she wasn't coming home for two weeks. I wonder where she is tonight, Layla thought; I can't remember where she sticks her schedule. Did she bid on Chicago or Paris after Orlando? Oddly lonely, Layla wished she could call Holly, just to say something inane like "what's up?"

Sometimes Layla could talk to Holly about things she couldn't talk to Matt about. It wasn't that girl-talk thing – it was that Holly didn't know her quite so well.

Layla shook her head. *Of course, I feel bad.* Yesterday was the anniversary of Mom's death. It seemed extra significant because I was exactly twice the age I was when she died. For fourteen years, I had a mother, and now I've lived just as long without her. I'd been drunk as a human can get, and I imagined both an assailant and a rescuer. Something murky and Jungian in that last bit of tequila no doubt.

Everything in the refrigerator seemed grotesquely unappealing. Matt had bought some designer cheese. *I bet it tastes like a Serbian soldier's socks.* Holly's collection of diet salad dressings rimmed the door like a guard unit. The freezer cradled six Lean Cuisines and an interloping box of Dove bars. Layla spied half a corned beef sandwich from Leo's. *I bought that when?* Wednesday. Yeah. Wednesday. She knew the edges would be hard and curled, the rye bread soggy, saturated with the memory of dark mustard. *I should toss it,* she thought, and instead shut the door.

Layla grabbed a handful of vanilla wafers from the box perched on top of the refrigerator. She assumed they were hers, she couldn't fathom what Matt or Holly would do with such a caloric, pedestrian treat.

Crunching the stale vanilla wafers, she sat on a kitchen chair. She bit angrily, the sweet synthetic taste disappointing her–the cookies were vapid, shallow, overly artificial. Layla chewed furiously and considered the problem of Flora MacDonald.

Flora hadn't been who Layla wanted her to be–oh, the author had tried all right, concocting a romance, attributing bravery to a Highland lass with a capital "c" cause, but between the lines Layla read what she thought was the truth: Flora was immortalized because she happened to be at the right place at the right time. Flora seemed to have had no burning ambition or fervent desire to change the world. She'd been a presumably pretty girl caught in the current of history.

Damn. Layla crunched on the cookies, leaving a trail of crumbs on the floor. Layla wanted a heroine. Joan of Arc was a nutcase, Mary Queen of Scots a wretched codependent who married poorly, Elizabeth the first seemed to be without a heart, a nasty piece of work who punished her lovers for her mother's death. Layla winced at the thought of little Elizabeth coping with step moms after her mom was beheaded. At least Daddy Useless never remarried. Maybe I should call him, we could go out for a few drinks.

Okay. Layla brushed her hands off on her legs. This has gone on long enough. I can be mad at Flora MacDonald for having been no more than a pretty young girl some other time. I need to deal with dinner. Still standing in the center of the kitchen, Layla considered the options; they came down to stay in and scrounge or go out. The Lean Cuisines suddenly looked appealing. Certain that they were Holly's, she scrawled a note on a sticky and patted in onto the refrigerator door. She'd replace the honey-glazed chicken before Holly returned.

Darn. Microwave meals got complicated. Layla read the instructions and jabbed a hole in the film over the meal. She shoved it into the microwave and lit a cigarette. Outside she heard a few birds, no cars. The house was set quite a distance from the road across a carpet of neatly trimmed grass contained in a careful border of azaleas, gardenias and ferns.

She sat. It felt good to be alone. Layla reflected on how long it had been since she'd had an empty expanse of hours laden with solitude. She uncoiled, moving slowly from the chair to the counter. She popped in a CD, soon the voice of Merle Haggard harmonized with her sad tranquility. Luke hadn't been bad, not really. They just couldn't communicate. Maybe in part it had been her fault; she'd been clinging, demanding. He had told her he needed 'walking around room.'

Layla hummed along with the music. She didn't feel sad, more bittersweet. Matt was wrong. Luke hadn't been violent, he hadn't raped her, it was what she had done. She made him crazy. It was weird, though. He seemed to take her for granted until she broke off with him, and then he went crazy as a country song.

Layla had decided the relationship was going nowhere at ninety miles an hour with the brakes off. Seeing thirty a few miles down the road, she'd ended it. Once she had, Luke had gone crazy. Holly said men were like that, ignore you until you leave, and then they lose their shit.

Layla didn't know what men were like at all.

The microwave dinged. Merle sang. Layla grabbed a soda – Matt's? Holly's? – from the fridge and danced over to the table.

She had a forkful of peas and carrots halfway to her mouth when the telephone rang. The answering machine babbled the familiar message. She heard Luke's voice, "Baby, Baby. Come on, we have to talk. Layla, I know you're there. Pick up the phone, Baby. Please." Luke paused. Layla sat rigidly, her spine stiffened, the peas rolled off her fork onto the table, a few scattered onto the floor. The sad sweet mood of loss vanished, replaced by a heart hamstering fear.

"Bitch."

Layla drew back from Luke's voice, recoiling from the slap of the stark curse. She dropped her fork. She trembled. That was it, the "Oh Baby I love you if you'll answer, and I hate you if you aren't at my beck and call." Her arms wrapped around her rib cage, she could hear her heart thundering against her eardrums. She feared that something inside her would burst.

The night jeered at her. Tree branches transformed into skeletal fingers and clawed at the screens. The floor creaked, as if a murderer came by stealth and cunning across the broad pine planks. Odd whinging noises, the house whines, the noises of a coffin settling in the receptive, hungry earth.

Layla felt something rise in her throat. Outside she heard the crunch of gravel. Or did she? Did the steps groan beneath hostile weight? Was someone walking through the yard, coming closer to the door, or was it wind? Her ears hypersensitive, she heard an airplane fly overhead, the roar of its engine sounded disturbingly close. Layla had never noticed an airplane overhead before.

Ring.

Message.

Dial tone.

Did Matt lock the front door on his way out? Matt never remembered to lock the door.

Layla exhaled in tiny puffs, trying to catch her breath. Her heart roared in her ears. Her hands were icy. She thought about a cigarette but had a sense that the flick of her lighter would reveal her whereabouts. She was foxholed, paralyzed like a bug in amber, melded into the night.

Ring. Message. Dial tone.

Damn him.

Damn him.

And, damn me. Damn me for wanting a romantic fantasy. Hadn't she learned anything from her parents' tragedy? The ticking of the kitchen clock bit into her molars. Jaw clenched and sweaty, Layla rose carefully. The house seemed to be rejecting her; the same house that had held her tenderly seemed to want to expel her into the night. She felt vulnerable, exposed, unsafe in the brightly lit kitchen.

Like a manic lemming, she rushed to her room and grabbed her backpack. Several beer cans tumbled onto the rug when she scrambled through the wreckage on her nightstand for her car keys. Hyperventilating, she rushed out of the room, leaving crumpled cigarette packs and tumbling paperbacks in her wake.

In the hallway she bounced from left to right, her thoughts racing, her mind jumbled. Okay then, lock the front door, go out the back. Decision made, she ran to the front door like a four-year-old running to the toilet down an unlit hallway, eyes near shut to keep out the dark. She broke a fingernail fastening the chain lock. Sucking on her finger, she pivoted and ran toward the back of the house. Layla's shoulder brushed a picture on the wall. It scraped against the wallpaper. She held her breath.

Not bothering with the lights, she set the lock on the back door and jogged down the stairs. In her peripheral vision she thought she saw Luke. Luke standing near the corner of the house, hands in his pockets, a threatening grin on his face. She flashed back to a bar tending job years ago when the thick fingered manager had grabbed her breasts and smeared her face with his thick liver lips, 'You know you want it, girlie.'

The manager had the same smile.

Was Luke there or was she spooked?

She ran to her car and fell into the driver's side like a little leaguer sliding home. Lights off, she cranked the engine and reversed. She flicked the lights on as she backed down the drive. Luke wasn't anywhere to be seen. Had he been, or was she just frightened into insanity? She was spooked, no doubt about that, voices, ex-boyfriends, what was happening to her?

She turned on the radio. Jabbing the buttons repeatedly until the soothing strains of a familiar country song filled her car, she drove down Queens. How could Luke have called her if he was in her yard? Cell phone, stupid, she answered. Damn.

Layla loved driving down Queens, the green tunnel of trees making the street dark during the day, blocking out the stars at night, muffling the city sounds. The street seemed enchanted to her, safe, fairy-ish. Fairy-ish she thought, is that a word? Knowing what Matt would say, she smiled "It is now."

She turned onto Chilton and drove down to Sharon Road. Taking a right, she crossed Briar Creek. It pissed her off that whatever brilliant things the engineers had done to stop Briar Creek from flooding had slowed it to a trickle. The bridge wasn't really a bridge anymore, just another bit of road with flimsy railings.

When Layla was a little girl, Briar Creek had been a virago, a creature more river than not, who periodically overflowed her sloping banks and washed away children foolish enough to disregard maternal warnings. Layla recalled being tiny and thinking that the muddy water frothing past was a stream of chocolate milk. She'd tasted it once. It was nasty. I'm a slow learner she thought, I keep dreaming, even when reality is nothing but mud.

When she was around ten, she'd gone sort-of fishing in Briar Creek. She and a bunch of kids. They kept trying to catch crayfish. None of them really knew exactly what a crayfish was, or what they'd do with it. They weren't even sure there were crayfish in the creek. Only someone said that they knew someone who caught crayfish there once. It was a pleasant way to spend a summer afternoon.

Probably weren't any damn crayfish, Layla thought. I haven't learned much. I still spend all my time looking for things that aren't there.

She cut down Wendover and followed the road until it became Eastway. The manicured lawns and Mercedes were behind her; she drove past Food Lion and Wal-Mart to the light on Central. Turning right, she was in the center of chaos-light, a Latin grocery shared a parking lot with a Vietnamese grocery. Video stores with oriental lettering in their windows rubbed bellies with Laundromats wearing Spanish and English signs. She pulled into the parking lot of the Landmark Diner, thankful for a space in the brightly lit area in front of the windows. After she turned the key in the ignition and cut off the lights, Layla exhaled. She sat in the car, forehead pressed to steering wheel, spine limp. After taking a deep breath, she grabbed her backpack from the floorboard and got out. The amber lights of the restaurant seemed warm, welcoming. Forgetting her uneaten dinner, Layla started thinking of the desserts enshrined in a glass case by The Landmark's front entrance, huge mounds of whipped cream, cheese cake swirled with chocolate, frothy meringue gracing tart lime dancing across a graham cracker rink, and the papyrus thin layers of baklava. Salivating, she took the stairs two at a time without even pausing to pick up a "Creative Loafing" to scan with her food.

She pushed on the glass door and was blasted by the air conditioning. While she waited by the register, she glanced at the dessert case—food porn, erotic confectionary, an apple pie spiced with cinnamon sprawled indolently between salad plate sized oatmeal cookies and sand-toned turnovers. A mountainous black forest cake quivered beside a wedding dress coconut cake crowned with pineapple. Strawberry shortcake stood in solitary splendor near the front of the second shelf. Blueberry coiffed cheesecake towered above it.

As the hostess approached, Layla spotted the two Jasons and Mazie in a back corner booth.

"Smoking or non?"

"I see some friends of mine here already," Layla said. "I'll just go join them." She brushed past the other booths to the corner where the Jasons sat. The taller Jason was drumming on the table, his head bouncing to music no one else heard. The shorter Jason had his skinny arm stretched around the fleshy shoulders of the busty young woman wearing dark rimmed glasses. Mazie sucked smoke from a clove cigarette.

Shit. Mazie. First, she was at Down Under with her loud giggle and now it seemed she'd latched on to Jason.

"Those things are bad for you," said Layla, taking a Marlboro out and lighting it. The taller Jason moved over a few inches without interrupting his drumming.

"Mazie, Layla. Layla, Mazie," said short Jason.

"We've already collided," said Layla, exhaling a stream of tobacco smoke.

"Hey, *those* things are worse for you," squawked Mazie. She poked out her lower lip and stared at Layla with little piggy eyes. Her breasts bobbed up and down in her embroidered cotton smock.

Tall Jason looked at Layla and rolled his eyes.

"I was making a joke," Layla said. She shrugged and gave Mazie a conciliatory smile, almost rolling over on her back to expose her tummy.

"Well, it wasn't very funny," Mazie said. She sniffed. Her nose was red.

Tall Jason drummed louder. Short Jason's skin was tinged an embarrassed pink.

A waitress appeared and put iced tea in front of the Jasons and Mazie. "Hi, hon. I didn't see you slip in. What can I get you?"

"Coffee please," Layla answered. "And a piece of blueberry cheese cake."

"Okay, I'll get ya'll's order out in a minute," she said. As she walked to the kitchen, her ponytail bobbed up and down.

"Do you know how many grams of fat are in cheesecake?" Mazie asked.

"No, do you?" Layla blinked innocently and thought about strangling Mazie. She could just hear Matt's take on this deal – "The things men will do to get laid. Honestly, precious, gay or straight we'll fuck mud."

"I don't believe in grams of fat," said the tall Jason.

"How can you not believe in them? They're a fact." Mazie looked at him as if he'd set himself on fire or sprouted a second head.

"I just don't. I don't have to believe in anything. It's all choice. You choose what to believe." Jason tapped out a complex rhythm with his spoon and fingers; he hit the iced tea glass and the sugar jar in sequence. His friend, the short Jason, looked like he had a severe headache. Blotches of red patched his pale skin.

"You have to believe in things if they *are*." Mazie said. Her voice was slightly nasal.

"But, how can you be certain what is?" Layla continued,

"Besides, why do I *have* to believe anything?" She was halfway curious and halfway baiting the girl. She leaned back as the waitress slid coffee in front of her. "Thanks."

"Well, things are." Mazie affirmed. Her face was contorted. She looked over at short Jason; he was staring out the window to the parking lot.

Tall Jason drummed.

Suddenly, Mazie gathered her purse and wiggled out of the booth. "I think I'd better go." Flinging back her dark curly hair, breasts dancing and chin tilted upwards, she stomped out of the diner.

"Shit, I'll never get laid," said short Jason.

Layla giggled.

The waitress returned with three hamburgers and a slice of cheesecake. She placed them on the table. Tall Jason claimed Mazie's hamburger.

"Yeah," said short Jason. "You got something out of it. You'll eat her hamburger."

"I take what I can get," answered tall Jason.

A group of well-dressed African American women took the large front booth. A few of them wore corsages. Three Goth girls in the front booth shared a salad while casting furtive glances at the dessert display. A couple in their sixties in the booth ahead of Layla's reminisced about everything they'd eaten on prior trips to this particular diner, the woman fretted, had she ordered the right thing? The French toast she'd had two trips ago had been really scrumptious. Did she even like western omelets?

Layla licked the fork, savoring every bit of the rich cheesecake.

"Watch the tongue action," tall Jason said. "You're turning him on."

"Yeah, like *you've* been laid this year," short Jason said.

Tall Jason shrugged and Layla laughed. The tightness in her chest, the rigid cord between her shoulder blades, the smothering fear, all of those dark horsemen had gone. She was sitting in a fluorescent-lit diner with two predictable friends and her fears dissipated, lost in the clank of glassware and the muffled sound of shouting in the kitchen.

"I'm glad you guys were here tonight," Layla said. She went through her backpack for her wallet.

"We're always somewhere," tall Jason said.

"Asshole," said short Jason. "Him, not you," he added, pointing at his roommate

"No really," Layla said. "I'm glad you were." She pulled out a ten and handed it to them. "For my share."

"Well, thanks for coming out," said the tall Jason with a mock bow. 'You'll find us next weekend at Down Under and through the week right here at the Landmark."

Impulsively, Layla hugged them both. "Bye."

Driving home, Layla switched to a soft rock station and sang along with something upbeat and forgettable. She parked close to the back stairs. The lights were like she left them. Matt's car was still gone. Nothing disturbed the yard.

Layla carefully locked the back door behind herself. Cleaned up the remnants of the microwave dinner, even sweeping the orphaned peas off the floor. She shut off all the lights, clicked the power switch on the CD player, and ambled off toward bed.

With a guilty twinge at the effort Matt invested in her appearance, she detoured to the bathroom and did the floss-brush-wash-moisturize routine. Body chores done, she continued onto bed. Layla toed off her shoes, dropped her jeans to the floor.

Tugging her t-shirt over head, she heard a faint voice. "She wasna as bonnie as ye."

Layla gulped, she pulled the shirt back down. No one was there. She waited for the voice to speak again. All she heard were night bugs, raspy and fading. "All right, who are you?" *I must be crazy. I'm talking to the fucking voices.*

Only the strangle tree fingers answered.

"I"ll try again." she said, "Who is *she*?"

A rich baritone laugh filled her darkened bedroom. "Weel nae. I'd thought ye' knew tha'...she was Flora MacDonald. She had a nice bosom, tis true. But, she were a bit horse faced. She wasna as bonny as ye."

Layla was alone. She was sober.

"Maybe I'm going barking mad," she said. It was a brave statement, a whistling in the dark statement. No answer.

Layla took two Tylenol and got into bed to wait for sleep.

Sleep was a long way off.

FOUR

Monday, Monday, by the Mamas and the Papas blasted the remnants of sleep out of Layla's brain. She squinted at the digital alarm. After smacking it several times she concluded that once again it was Matt in the kitchen, not her clock radio, that had shattered her slumber.

"Damn right you can't trust that day." Layla threw on her robe. "What was I thinking when I turned that boy onto oldies stations?" She slumped toward the kitchen nattering, "Coffee, must have coffee."

Matt handed her a cup of coffee.

Layla shut off the CD in mid-chorus. "I really don't need a musical medley on suck day. Work is going to be rotten enough without Top 40 haunting me." She opened the refrigerator, looked over the contents and shut the door again.

"New concept. How about a job you'd like?" Matt grabbed toast and slammed it onto a plate. He put more bread in the toaster and pushed the lever. "Think about it, instead of forty hours of hellish torment you could actually – hold onto your hats, folks – be *not* miserable."

Layla swallowed her coffee. "I don't want any toast." She turned and stepped toward the door.

Matt caught the belt of her bathrobe. "But I, on the other hand, want you to eat. And as you are resigned to a life of deprivation and suffering – whereas, I am committed to hedonistic gratification – it's only fitting that you eat the toast to please me."

Layla shrugged.

Matt smeared his own toast with butter and honey. He

refilled her cup and his own. "Don't worry dear, you can fret and fume all day in your little cubicle. While I spend my eight hours with bright, funny people who deal with their neurosis during happy hour." The second serving of toast popped up. Matt stuck it on a plate. Shoving it to Layla, he added, "Consider it penance for abandoning me on Saturday and spending all day Sunday sprawled in bed reading. Now, if you were reading because you were in school, like maybe to train for a job that you actually liked, you wouldn't have to atone."

Layla chewed dry toast.

"News flash. Some of us like our jobs. To get those jobs we actually finish college instead of taking a series of random courses and recurrently dropping out."

Layla glared at Matt. "First thing Monday morning is a bit early for this routine. I know it's one of those for-my-own-good lectures, but *please*." Matt pushed the honey down the kitchen counter to Layla. She spread a bit of it on the second piece of toast. "So, you didn't get laid this weekend? Is that the reason for this charming intervention? Slutboy seems a tad out of sorts."

Matt laughed. "You got me. But, you remember that hunky guy from Friday night?"

She shook her head.

"Silly me. You don't even remember getting naked and table dancing. Anyway, I talked to him right before we left. I called him yesterday. I'm meeting him for dinner tonight at Planet Grill." Matt rinsed his cup and dish. "You won't mind another evening alone?"

Layla blushed. She really didn't like being so vulnerable that her friends felt she needed constant care taking. " 'Course not. Besides, I have lots of pointless non-degree generating books to read and if I want company there will be forty five messages from a Jason telling me which bar, café or restaurant they'll be occupying. I could even go listen to Fred tell me to quit smoking and drinking and start eating."

Matt bent down and gave Layla a dry peck on the cheek. "Have a nice day, June. Make sure the Beaver does his homework."

Layla left her plate on the counter, poured another cup of coffee, and leaving it to cool, went off toward a quick shower. With her damp hair pulled back into a ponytail, she put on a pair of black pants, her boots and a white blouse. Back in the kitchen she looked out the window, drank her coffee and smoked a cigarette. The day was clear with a slight breeze ruffling the leaves. Deciding to walk to work, she shoved cigarettes and a book into her backpack, picked up her keys and doubled checked that she'd shut off the coffee pot.

With her backpack on one shoulder, she walked toward Freedom Park and down Lombardy, to cut through the back way to Windale. The tennis courts in the park were already active; two women in whites were running each other around the court. A young mother with a strollered baby moved down the sidewalk. Layla felt a familiar ache in her chest. Her job broke her heart; maternity home pregnancy was nothing like the middle class having-a-baby thing. The young woman flashed her a smile as they passed on the sidewalk. Her neat cotton dress, chubby baby's expensive stroller, and the young woman's beautiful teeth defined her as middle class. The girls at the home usually came from households where the family car cost less than that stroller.

Layla paused by the home's back gate and lit a cigarette. Staff weren't allowed to smoke, not even in the parking lot of the facility. It drove her nuts. She looked over the fence and saw something shimmering near the front gate. She recalled family trips down to Myrtle Beach when she was a child. Daddy Useless had explained that the black pools of water she saw on the highway were only mirages. She'd been disappointed, before that she thought a mirage had to be a full-blown oasis from a fantasy world like the setting for *One Thousand and One Nights*. She'd always been a reader, even as a small child.

Stepping on her cigarette butt, she unlocked the gate and walked downhill to the red brick building. It looked more like a college dorm than an institution. Maybe she should resume college instead of staying in this stupid job. Yeah, Matt got to me, she thought. But, maybe I can't really do it; even as a kid I neglected my homework to read whatever book struck my fancy at the moment.

Layla entered the building through the kitchen, collecting a cup of coffee. The hallways were deserted. She unlocked her booth and switched the phone system back to the front desk from the overnight voice mail. Since no one was around, she took out her book, a history of Scotland, and started reading. Layla chewed on a pencil while she read about Bonnie Prince Charlie meeting with his council in the wood paneled drawing room of Exeter House. Days before Culloden, with three English armies assembling, the darn Prince was discussing what to wear for his entry into London. So much for optimism, Layla thought.

The phone rang, an internal call. "Has anyone called me?" Saundra's voice was harsh.

"No, not since I've come on," Layla answered. She stuck a scrap of paper into her book to mark the place.

"Well, I'm expecting several calls," Saundra said. Her tone implied that it was somehow Layla's fault that she hadn't received them.

"Yes, ma'am." Layla spoke to dead air. Saundra had hung up.

Layla shuffled through the notes that Annie had left for her – insulting really, all the underlined do-not-forgets and be-certain-to's. Oh damn, her schedule request for the next few weeks had been denied, hello second shift. Layla gritted her teeth, then quickly forced her jaw to relax. Dr. Trusdale had said something to her about grinding her teeth and how it would ruin the enamel. She hated second shift. It gave her no time with Matt.

"Happy Monday," Annie said as she came through the double doors, weighed down with a cake carrier, an umbrella, and a huge satchel. "Have you seen the sky lately? It looks like there's going be a downpour."

"It was clear when I came in," Layla answered, getting up to open the door of the booth.

Annie set the cake down on the counter next to the staff mail slots. "This is delish. I got the recipe from *Family Circle*. It's a strawberry cake, better than sex, you'll love it." She retrieved her mail from her box. "Did you see the schedule? Katie needed to work a few day shifts. Her husband, you know how men are. He wants her home more in the evenings. God, men are such babies, can't feed themselves, can't function."

"I have a problem with this," Layla began.

"Excuse me," Annie said, nastiness creeping into her voice.

"I'm full-time, she's part-time. I was hired for day shift six months before she came on board and you're changing my hours to suit her needs." Layla did rapid head calculations trying to figure out how much unemployment she'd draw if Annie booted her out the door.

"I supervise support staff. The policy about hours has been changed. I draw up the schedule every two weeks. You don't own day shift." Annie made an elaborate show of going through the supply drawer and rattling pens and paperclips as she spoke. "You need to learn how to accept authority."

Annie shut the door emphatically and trundled off to her office, her footsteps heavy on the carpeted floor. "Saundra, I left a super cake up at the front desk. Go get some."

"Thanks, I need to check for messages anyway. I have no idea what Layla does with my messages."

Layla put her head in her hands. The bitch didn't even bother to whisper. I can hear her all over the building and so can everyone else – like right, it's *my* fault that whatever guy she has the hots for hasn't called.

Saundra jerked on the door to the booth. "I forgot my key, let me in."

Layla got up and opened the door.

Saundra cut a slice of the cake; the sickly sweet odor filled the receptionist's booth. "Are you sure no one has called me?"

"Nope. No calls." Layla shoved her hands in her pockets. She really wanted to say, 'Oh yes, they've called. I just eat all your phone messages.' Suck day is right. Have to get another job.

The phone rang. Layla answered with her standard how-may-I-direct-your-call-routine. Saundra looked at her expectantly. Luke's voice. "Layla, I'm sorry about everything. Can I see you tonight?"

"I can't talk right now," Layla said. Saundra's eyes narrowed.

"Well then, what time can I come by?"

"You can't. Oh, I don't know. I really can't talk now,"

Layla twisted the chord to her headset. She actually felt Saundra's scrutiny.

Saundra cleared her throat loudly.

Drama queen, bitch, Layla thought.

"Don't tie up the agency line with personal calls." Saundra's voice was loud.

Luke obviously heard Saundra on the other end. "Oh, I get it. I'll call you back this afternoon, babe."

"I see what the problem is. As long as you tie up the line

with your calls, no one can get through." Saundra's face had a near feral expression beneath her make-up. She pivoted on her high heels and strode off in the direction of Annie's office.

Layla heard Saundra say, "I have to talk to you about that girl."

Then Annie responded, "Yeah, she's got an attitude problem," before the door shut.

Layla took several calls in rapid succession, sorted the mail, and covertly scanned the want ads in the *Charlotte Observer*. She was considering an exciting career in fast food when she heard a tentative tap on the front desk.

"Ma'am, excuse me. Ma'am?"

Layla looked up and saw one of the younger residents of the maternity home, a waifish little teen from eastern North Carolina. The tattoo on her upper arm and pierced tongue conflicted with her angelic blue eyes and the wispy pale bangs that fluttered into her freckled face. "Yes, Brandy. What do you need?"

Brandy licked her lips as if she was nervous. Her eyes darted around the reception area. She leaned into the booth and lowered her voice. "You been working here long?"

Too long, Layla thought. "A while. What can I do for you?" The girl seemed tense, Layla wondered if she was in labor or something. Even though she was friendly with the residents, they usually took their concerns to the nurses or the social work staff.

"Well, you know that picture of the girl this place is named for? Well, did that girl die in this building?" Brandy's voice was barely audible.

"No," Layla answered.

Brandy looked skeptical. She twisted a strand of pale hair around her index finger. "You sure?"

"Yeah, this isn't even the first place in Charlotte named Amanda Windale Home. The home has only been in this building about ten years." Layla tried to think of an easy way to explain it to Brandy. "You see there are Windale homes in lots of cities. The girl we're named for, well, her Dad started the first one. She passed away somewhere else. She wasn't ever in Charlotte."

"Well, did anyone here die while she was having a baby or something?" Brandy moved in closer. Her face was pale beneath the freckles.

"No, that didn't happen. People hardly ever die in

childbirth. Are you nervous about something? Do you need me to call the nurse?" Layla wondered if Brandy was having pains. "Are you hurting anywhere?"

"No. It's not me. It's the building. I think it's haunted and I thought that you might know who it is that's haunting it." Brandy spoke in a matter of fact tone, as if haunted buildings were a given. "I just kind of reckoned you'd know. You just kind of feel like someone who sees spirits." Brandy smiled slightly. "You can see haunts, can't you? I might be haunting this building soon if I don't get to math class. If I lose any more privileges for cutting school, I might die for real." She gave Layla a childish wave and walked away.

Layla checked the schedule. Another hour until someone would relieve her for lunch. Between Saundra and Annie's nastiness and Brandy's strange comments, she was about to die for a cigarette. Maybe Matt had a point, maybe she needed to do something different about the job thing, this gig was getting old, all the stress of a real job and none of the power.

By the time suck day moved into the home stretch, Layla vowed she'd at least get a job where she could take more smoke breaks. Saundra had stomped around in a vile mood because she hadn't received any personal calls. The phone rang constantly. Brandy had come by several times with her soft drawl and recursive Madonna smile. The spooky kid kept questioning Layla about ghosts, was Layla "for real sure" that she didn't know anything about some ghost hanging out in the building?

The clock moved toward five at glacier speed. Layla had her backpack organized, ready to spring when quitting time paroled her. Quarter of five, the phone rang. "Layla, it's Luke. I'm sorry. Really. About everything. I swear. Can I see you? Please."

He sounded sincere. Layla wavered. It had been a shit day after a shit weekend. Matt wouldn't be home. Layla wondered if, maybe, she was avoiding Luke because of what Matt might say. "I'm thinking," Layla said. She rifled through her mind, but seemed fresh out of clever things to say.

"Look, I know things went bad wrong. But, I swear, I just want to talk to you."

Layla glanced through the front doors. The sky was dark. Rain splattered against the parking lot. "Okay," she said. "Why don't you pick me up at five?" At least she'd avoid getting soaked walking home.

Huddled under the entranceway, Layla squinted into the storm looking for Luke's car. She was desperate for a cigarette. The rain was hammering the ground so hard that drops seemed to bounce off the parking lot. The air was thick and moist.

Luke pulled up and reached across the seat to push open the passenger side door. Layla slipped in quickly. "Hi," she said. She lit a cigarette and took a deep drag. "Don't start in with me about smoking. I swear I was three seconds away from total psychosis before I lit this. All that stands between me and chaos is nicotine."

"It's alright." Luke had a slow southern drawl that a lot of women found sexy. "You go right ahead. Rough day?" Water splashed alongside the car, lightening split the sky. As he drove out of the parking lot, they were immediately stuck in five o'clock traffic. Sheets of rain covered the windshield. "Where to, pretty lady?"

Layla leaned back and smoked. "I don't know that we're going anywhere until they build a few more roads. We may be sitting here for decades."

Luke pulled open the ashtray. "Well, it would give us time to talk."

Layla looked at him. Even when she was angry with him she found him attractive. What was wrong with her? Two days ago she'd have sworn she wouldn't waste spit on him if he caught fire. "Just let me decompress from work before I'm expected to have any kind of serious talk."

"Look, I need to make this easy. It was all my fault. I kind of went nuts when you broke off with me. I sort of figured you'd always be there. I guess I took you for granted."

Layla lit another cigarette off the butt of her first one. A muscle in her jaw jumped. She looked at the wall of water sloshing down the window.

"Let me try again," Luke said. "I just want to start over. Be friends. Or whatever. I know you don't trust me. I just want a chance to rebuild trust. Please."

Layla couldn't risk looking into his eyes. Sucker bait. Telling her she could call the shots. She turned her face to the window.

"You got me where you want me, lady. Wherever that is." Luke reached across the car seat and traced her jaw with the tip of his finger. Layla shivered. She blinked tears. Matt would be so pissed.

"Look," Luke continued. "I can understand it if you don't feel comfortable alone with me. You want to go get dinner or something and then I'll drop you off?"

"Sure. If this traffic ever moves." Layla exhaled. *Sure, a restaurant, they wouldn't be alone. Friends, they could be friends.* She stole a glimpse of him, his hair fell across his forehead and he shook it back. Luke leaned forward and wiped some fog off the inside of the window. Layla felt first-date stupid. She leaned into the car door, unable to think of anything to say.

"Anywhere in particular you want to go?" Luke finally pulled onto Kings Drive where traffic was moving.

Layla panicked for a second. "Well, not Planet Grill. I'm in no mood for stir fry. Not Down Under, I only like it when I can sit outside. Anywhere else is fine."

Luke headed in the general direction of the Landmark. Layla wished he'd talk. The quiet in the car unnerved her. The windshield wipers, the traffic sounds and the silence between them seemed ominous. She giggled nervously. "This is like one of those really cheesy horror movies. You know, the young couple was only going out to dinner and then something went horribly wrong." She giggled again.

Luke picked up on it. "Or maybe, it was a rainy evening when they set out, but little did they know what awaited them." He laughed.

"Or maybe, the storm was just the beginning." She put out her cigarette.

"How about, they could so easily have chosen a different road." Luke flicked on the radio. The traffic report came on. Layla was edgy around him, tense, fearing she'd do or say the wrong thing.

"This rain may mandate the building of an ark," Layla commented when Luke stopped in front of the Landmark.

"I don't have an umbrella," he said. "Sorry. We'll have to run for it."

The restaurant was half empty. They dripped to a booth in the smoking section where Layla lit up again. He used to insist on nonsmoking when they went out.

The ritual of ordering drinks and reading the familiar menu

soothed Layla. The rain kept the crowd away. Most of her friends were late nighters anyway. It felt odd to be in the diner before ten PM.

Luke put down his burger after a few bites and stared at Layla. She stabbed a piece of lettuce with her fork. "I'm not good with words," he said. "I just wanted to tell you that I really appreciate being with you. I like talking to you." He reached across the table and put his hand over hers for an instant. It was awkward. She was still assaulting salad. He smiled sheepishly and pulled back his hand. "I just like being with you."

Layla wanted to keep him guessing. Lord knows, between Matt and Holly, she had heard enough man-handling advice to fill twelve issues of Cosmo. Luke was acting like she'd daydreamed he'd act. "I like being with you when you're nice," she said. "How long is it going to last?"

"A long time," he said.

Layla looked down at her salad. Damn. He must have been studying romance novels. She lit a cigarette and pushed her food aside. "We'll see."

"Okay then," he answered with a smile.

Damn, he's well rehearsed.

The rain let up and the restaurant began to fill. A familiar looking couple in Harley t-shirts occupied the next booth. Two Goth guys that hung out at Down Under waited by the door. "Can we leave now? I had a rotten day at work."

"Sure," he said, reaching for the check.

He drove her home with the radio on a country station. It was still drizzling. Occasional orphaned lightening cracked the swollen sky. When Luke parked in the drive, Layla felt his anticipation like a palpable presence. No, she thought, let's see how real the reformation is. "I'm really burned crispy," she said. "Thanks for dinner."

"No," he said grabbing her hand. "Thank *you*." He kissed her hand, then quickly released it.

She picked up her backpack and left the car.

FIVE

Matt was conspicuous in his absence. She flicked on the light. Nothing happened. Damn, another power outage. Layla felt along the wall to the refrigerator. Standing on tiptoe, she patted the top until her fingers brushed the box of candles. She lit a fat white candle, dropped her backpack on the floor, and got a can of soda from the dark refrigerator.

Holding the candle aloft, she went to her room. Layla set the candle on top of an old beer can and lit a cigarette. She doubted that Matt would make it home tonight. The rain pattered against the roof and windows. She peeled off her clothes and padded to the bathroom for the cleanser and moisturizer routine. Matt's got me trained.

When she returned to her room, she saw him.

Layla gasped.

Standing in front of the window, hands clasped behind his back. She saw the figure of a tall man, red-blonde hair spilling down his back, illuminated in the tentative flicker of candlelight.

Her mouth went dry. She began trembling, then segued into shaking all over. She thought she should turn and run but her legs were leaden. Her fingers stretched spastic. Holding her breath, she bent slowly and picked up a t-shirt from the floor, every creak, every infinitesimal sound reverberating in her bones. She pulled the t-shirt over her head and down her thighs. She thought she could hear the cloth move across her skin.

A scream was stuck in her throat, choking her, forcing her to fight for air.

He was tall. He seemed a foot taller than her, his shoulders broad, his bones large. He seemed too slim for his frame, yet not skinny, more as if muscle and sinew were refined to the essential, no extraneous flesh or bulk.   He lifted his head and the candlelight caught copper across his hair.

Lightening slit the sky and the man seemed transparent. She could see the arthritic branches bent in the wind through his body.

She had no words. Only terror, raw and ruthless, paralyzing in its enormity.

She couldn't swallow. Layla's tongue felt thick, her throat closed. Every bit of her skin surface tingled and twitched, alive with the fear hammering her heart. Her skin seemed a separate entity radiating fear, each bit of it sensitive. The softness of the t-shirt, the smooth wood underneath the soles of her feet, every sensation sharp, etched into the moment.

What was he doing here? This stranger who in silence slipped into her home? Matt wouldn't return until tomorrow at the earliest. Would he kill her? She stared at his hands, slim fingers, large knuckles, the hands of a surgeon.

Or a strangler.

She flashed back a few hours to the spooky kid from down east, "You look like someone who sees ghosts." Why am I thinking about that? Why don't I run? I should run.

She could see through him.

Layla shifted her weight. The floor creaked. She held her breath.

He turned around without a sound. He flowed, moved like a dancer despite his height. He stood, legs slightly apart, hands clasped behind his back. He looked down at her, caught her gaze and held it like a firefly in his hand. She stared into his eyes and could not tell what color they were.

What color *exactly* were his eyes?

The candlelight seemed brighter. *Why couldn't she tell what color his eyes were?* She didn't understand her confusion. Trick of the light. Trick of the night. Fear, a metallic taste in her mouth.

Layla shook all over. He looked at her. He remained motionless, stood like a moonlit statue. Her nipples puckered and hardened. She longed to fold her arms across her chest to cover them. Crazy bitch, he's going to kill me and I'm turned on. He never moved, but she felt his gaze like a stroke of his hand. A smile flirted with his mouth, a vague amused smile. She was certain that he knew the effect he was having on her.

Layla pressed her legs together. She could still do that despite being mesmerized, unable to run, paralyzed, unable to move. She licked her lips involuntarily. His smile broadened. She blushed and lowered her eyes. She was wet. Her legs unsteady, a gnawing longing filling her entire body. Layla willed herself to stop quivering; it was pointless.

The intruder wore a kilt with a piece of plaid wool tossed across his shoulder. It wasn't a kilt like the ones Layla had seen in movies. It was thick and heavy, gathered rather than pleated, and the cloth over his shoulder seemed part of the garment, more like something Roman than her image of a Highlander.

His legs were smooth muscled, neither slender nor bulky. She could not stop herself, she looked at his legs and felt the sensation of their muscled length between her thighs, she could feel the hair on his legs rub against her skin. *What was wrong with her?* He was doubtless going to kill her and she was dissolving into erotic fantasy.

Is this how it was for my mother, she wondered? Did she feel this compulsion, this wicked pull? Is that why she did half the men in town? Am I doomed? Layla looked around the room, the messy dressing table, piles of books and clothes on the floor, over-flowing ashtrays, all familiar. And, the stranger, the stranger with his smooth features, and altering eyes who stood motionless, charging the air between them.

She knew how he would kiss.

Layla knew that he'd swirl his tongue around her mouth while kneading her butt, his skilled hands would slip round her ribcage to tease her breasts, then he'd lift her onto the bed and move inside her with practiced ease. Weak in the knees, she thought. I've never believed a man could make a woman go weak in the knees. Always thought that was idiot hyperbole, stupid romance novel crud, and now I'm going weak in the knees, wobble legged and wet.

Layla focused on the rhythm of the rain.

"Good evening," he said, his voice a drug, his voice like honeyed wine pouring into her, soothing her distress and intensifying her longing.

Layla couldn't think of what it was she should do or say. She felt awkward, her hands seemed extraneous, her legs superfluous, every word, every thought that came to mind struck her as stupid, embarrassing.

He nodded. A slight incline of the head causing his hair to fall forward and shadow the planes and angles of his face. It wasn't a bow; it was an acknowledgement of her presence.

"Good evening," Layla answered, her voice a squeak. She felt her cheeks hot with the shame of her thin reedy voice. She dug her fingernails into her palms. "Do you mind if I smoke?" Inane, she thought, he's going to kill me and instead of running out of the house screaming bloody murder at the top of my lungs, I'm asking if he minds if I smoke.

I really am fucking crazy.

The intruder tilted his head to the side, a quizzical expression covering his face. "Weel, lass, ye can do what ye will, I reckon," he said. He took a few steps in Layla's direction. She watched the play of muscle beneath skin and wondered at his transparency.

She could see through him.

The back yard beyond the window was clearly visible through his chest. Yet, she longed to fling herself into his arms, to wind her own arms around his neck and press herself against his body, then to lick the length of him.

Do what ye will.

"Are you Wiccan?" she asked. Layla thought of the random bits of Wiccan thought she'd heard from one of the Jason's rapidly cycling girl friends. The stranger seemed partially Wiccan, do whatever she liked? She'd like to start licking the sweet spot between his neck and collarbone and trace his ribcage with her tongue, then kneel before him and...oh no, she'd do nothing of the sort. She couldn't, she wouldn't.

Would she?

He continued his unbroken gaze. "Whatever ye like, lass." Layla fumbled through the packages and books on her nightstand and found cigarettes. She lit one by rote, by habit. What else was she to do? "Are you going to kill me?" She inhaled, backed up to the edge of the bed, and waited.

"God's wounds," the intruder said. "What do ye tae me for?" He seemed pissed off. Layla sucked smoke. Her legs collapsed beneath her and she perched on the side of the bed. He was so damn hot. It was all she could do to keep from wiggling around.

He walked the length of the room, turned sharply and then took long strides back across.

No sound punctuated his steps.

Layla cringed into her pillows. The stranger paced. Layla smoked. After a few minutes she put the cigarette out in an abandoned soda can. The candlelight flickered across his cheekbones. Layla wished he was less perfect, less the image that haunted her dreams, less the fantasy man that sent her fingers into her panties and her brain into null thought. He was who he was.

She wanted him.

He stopped moving and stood before her. Layla opened her mouth to say something – what? She didn't know. A small noise, the mewling of a kitten, a moan, escaped her lips. The stranger reached toward her. Would he strangle her? Would his hand reach around her throat and crush her larynx, snap the small bones in her neck?

His fingers brushed her lips. She felt and did not feel his touch. Icy hot burned her mouth, his touch was there and was not there, his fingers insubstantial, candlelight whispered through his body.

Layla heard her own heart beat.

"You're in danger, lass." His look was not tender but implied no threat. He examined her closely, his eyes drifting across her face and down her body.

Layla pressed her bare legs together. She clasped her hands together in her lap. He's wearing a kilt, she thought, what kind of sociopathic murderer wears a kilt? *Killed by the Kilt*, what a great name for a cheesy true crime book. She shook her head. Can't even take homicide seriously when I'm the victim.

He studied her face. "The danger's no from me. I'll not harm ye. The danger is all around ye. I can feel it."

Her stomach tightened. She took short, shallow breaths. Her hands were sticky with sweat. Layla looked around the room, piles of newspaper, empty shopping bags, crumpled cigarette packs, the flitting candlelight cast shadows on the walls and pinpointed the disorder and debris. It's a shame I won't be around to see them try to analyze the crime scene. Wonder what they'll make of the candy wrappers under the bed?

"Stop it now." He sounded exasperated, like a parent dealing with a bratty child. "I'm here to protect ye." He sat next to her on the bed; again she was oblivious to how he had moved. The bed did not sink beneath his weight or move at all. His arm slipped around her shoulders.

Layla shook like a small animal in a trap. She blushed. She could not stop shaking: The harder she tried to control her rebellious body, the more she shook.

He laughed. He sounded very pleased with himself.

Unnerved, Layla looked up at him. He turned to her, and she licked her lips. She couldn't stop herself. She raised her chin and prepared for a kiss. Damn him. A woman would have to be dead six days and buried to miss how seductive he was.

He shook his head from side to side, still laughing. "You shake whenever I look at you."

Alarms went off in Layla's brain; his accent had changed. No, not his accent, the *way* he spoke. What did that mean? "You're talking differently from how you were before."

He tossed his head, shifting the long red blond hair, rearranging the shadows across his face. "I've watched you for a while. I've learned the speech patterns of your time. It will be easier for you to understand me if I speak in a style that you're familiar with."

Their faces were inches apart. Layla did not feel his breath. His skin was darker than the red gold hair would suggest. A lot of time outdoors? 'Speech patterns of your time'? What was he? A one person LARP? That spooky kid at work intruded again, 'You seem like someone who sees spirits.'

She licked her lips again and inclined her face toward him. Idiot, he couldn't possibly be attracted to you. He was devastating. Mortified, she averted her eyes; through her eyelashes, she saw his lap. He was attracted to something, whatever he was. The stranger's arm seemed to be around her shoulders, it was weightless.

Near panic, Layla looked around her room, things familiar seemed different bathed in candlelight. A picture of her mother in a sterling silver frame perched on top of Layla's jewelry box. Her mother had been a petite woman but not at all childlike in appearance, with thick wavy hair cascading to her small shoulders. Every line of her body conveyed a feline seductiveness. Even in the posed portrait, she seemed to have just got out of bed. Despite the formal gown, the strands of pearls, the flawless make-up, Layla's mother looked well loved, her mouth kiss-swollen, her eyes wide.

Screwing around had killed her mother.

Layla sat next to the intruder, aching with lust, craving his touch, desperate for a kiss.

Thunder, Armageddon loud and echoing, startled her. She jumped, bouncing the bedclothes. Another clap, a roar, a crash through barriers, and the rain pistoned into the windows. Wind moaned, a funeral sound, a wailing, a sound like Layla's sobs when she dealt with her mother's death.

Then, a flash of lightning flooded the room. Bleached light outlined the furniture, the stranger, and the photograph in precise detail for a few seconds. The light died swiftly, devoured by darkness. Complete darkness, even the candle deserted her. Tentatively, she moved her hand in the intruder's direction.

Layla's hand fell onto the bed.

The lamp beside her bed came on suddenly, the answering machine started beeping and babbling. Layla sat on the bed alone. She could hear tall Jason's voice, "I guess you aren't there, if you were there you'd know that we're going to be at Down Under tonight and we wanted to know... Hell, I don't know what we wanted to know."

She checked her watch and reset her clock radio. It was only nine thirty. It felt later. Layla had a bad case of tight-headed three in the morning. She blinked recurrently. Her eyes felt too dry. She kicked at a heap of clothes on the floor by her bed. Then she stiffened, sat up straight, and flung herself face down into the pillows as if she was having a seizure. "I am very good at not thinking. Not thinking is what I do best. I not-think about my mother, I not-think about Luke. I not-think about my shitty life. Right now, I am really not-thinking about whatever happened here tonight. Nothing happened and I am not-thinking about it."

I'm completely fucking crazy.

I'm haunted.

Layla screamed until her throat felt raw. Then she pummeled the pillow until her hand hurt and her shoulders ached. "Okay, I'm not-thinking."

Layla punched the bed a few more times. The creak of the front door, followed by Matt's footsteps stopped her tirade. She ran her fingers through her hair and went to the kitchen. Matt was already pouring a glass of wine when Layla got there. "I thought I wouldn't see you till Wednesday. I was sure you'd get lucky." There, she thought, that seemed normal enough.

"Oh, please. That man was just too intense. I was ordering desert and he was plotting the joint adoption of a cat. Siamese versus long haired Persian on the first date is a bad sign." Matt gestured with the wine bottle. Layla nodded and he poured a second glass.

"I thought you were in the market for a love puppy." Layla sat down and gulped wine, feeling the muscles in her neck relax. She jiggled her leg.

"A love puppy perhaps, but when a butch type starts talking cats on the first date, I see myself on a virtual leash by the third. That man needs to slow down." Matt shook his head.

"So, are you going to see him again?" Layla ran her fingers up and down the stem of the wineglass.

Matt tossed his head from side to side. "I don't know. I might. I liked him until he developed a pronoun problem. You know, changing 'I' to 'we' within an hour. He made a quick leap from 'his' hobbies to what movies 'we' had to see. But still, I do like him. Maybe, I'm just scared." Matt poured himself more wine. "Ah, a light fruity blend similar to the light fruit that ducked into the Harris Teeter to buy it on the way home. That was some serious rain we had earlier."

"Yeah," Layla said. She had no clue how to explain the stranger that had appeared in her bedroom, and telling Matt she'd had dinner with Luke would be as pleasant as root canal work. She drummed her fingers on the table.

"So," Matt said, "What did you do about dinner?"

Layla winced. She should have known he'd pick up on her discomfort. "I had dinner with Luke."

"Oh, great. I'm living with a lemming. Dinner or dinner and a rape?" Matt's mouth thinned, he close to shouting. Layla drew back. She didn't think it had been rape. Not at all, not really. She'd lead him on that night. Shit, she thought, I was wearing new black lace panties from Victoria's Secret, that kind of rules out rape, doesn't it? I sort of planned to be seduced.

"Precious," he said, "I'm sorry I yelled. Believe me I'm not mad at you. It just scares me. Really. That boy is no good. He's so bad that he needs three more incarnations to even make it to pond scum. Trust me, I can see why you find him attractive, but you just don't get it. You aren't a person to him, you're a form of property."

"No, really. He was okay tonight. We went out to dinner and he dropped me off. He was perfectly well behaved." Layla reached for the wine bottle. "One more glass and then cut me off. The idea of working in hell with a hangover is not appealing."

"What you don't know about men would fill a library. Look precious, I have no doubt that Luke is quite capable of a sort of casual redneck charm right up to the point where he believes that he's got you hooked again. Then history will repeat itself. And while we're at it, dear one, please try to recall that he's a mean drunk. Mean drunks are not our friends. We like happy drunks, we can even stand a sad drunk, but we do not like mean drunks." Matt poured himself another glass. "I am a very happy drunk."

The phone rang. Matt reached out and put his hand on Layla's forearm, "Let's not be a Pavlov doggie, dear one. Let's see who has the audacity to interrupt us."

"Probably a Jason," said Layla over the machine's message.

An unfamiliar whiny voice said, "Layla, this is Mazie. Tracy or somebody had your number. I'm sorry we didn't hit it off. I had killer PMS the other night. I'm sorry. Please pick up if you're there, I'm sorry. Have you seen Jason in the past few days? I need to find him. Maybe we should get together sometime and go out, I'm sure we'd have a really great time. Well, sorry. I'll try back later."

"Well," said Matt, "We know who's sorry now. Who was that wretch?"

"Oh, Mazie. I think I may have insulted her."

"You met her, therefore you insulted her, precious. It's a fundamental part of your charm." Matt reached over and ruffled her hair. "You know that I only lecture you about Luke because he scares me."

"I know." Layla ran her fingertip across a deep scratch on the wooden table. She thought about telling Matt what else had happened this evening. Gnawing her lower lip, her shoulder muscles tensing, she decided against talking about it. Whatever it was. She shoved thoughts of the intruder into the dark recesses of her mind. "I'm real good at putting things out of my mind. It's easier to just forget about what happened when Luke got so crazy."

Matt put his hand over hers, giving it an affectionate squeeze. "You okay?"

"Yeah, I'm okay," Layla answered. "I'll be careful with Luke. I won't take any chances." She thought that maybe Luke and she both deserved a second chance. He had met her halfway, acted like she'd begged him to act long before the break-up. "It's not really cut and dried, Matt. Part of it is my fault."

Matt's chin jutted out exactly as it had when he was a little boy gearing up for a temper tantrum. His eyes widened as he locked his gaze with Layla's.

"Slow down partner," Layla said. "Don't get all politically correct on me. I know all about 'no-means-no' and 'if she says no, it's rape.' Let's talk down and dirty. I was all over him. I had my hand up and down his dick for a quarter of an hour, and then something threw my off switch. Luke had every reason to believe I wanted him. Hell, I *did* want him." Her words came out in a loud, flat-toned, staccato gush. She sucked air and then lit a cigarette. "I wanted him and then I snapped. I just...*didn't* want him. It felt like a dead end, like getting sucked back onto a merry-go-round that I didn't want to ride. I wanted him while I thought he could really want me. Then, it suddenly seemed like if we made love, I'd be property again, parked in the corner until he was ready to go home. It didn't feel like he was going to make love to me. It felt like he was reclaiming a lost object."

Matt looked at her. His voice was soft. "I understand that you feel some responsibility. But, he hit you. That changes everything." His lip trembled. "You may forgive him. I can't."

Tears drifted out of Layla's eyes. For the second time that week, she fell into her roommate's arms sobbing while he cuddled her like a child. Matt took the burning cigarette from her hand and put it out. Layla's sobs became silent tears and then ceased. "You know, you are right about one thing, Matt." A smile invaded her face.

"What's that, precious?"

"Water-proof mascara. If I'm going to keep doing this, I need water-proof mascara." She laughed.

Matt giggled. "You're okay?"

"I swear. But I need to get to sleep. I have another exciting day responding to the challenge of a ringing phone." She kissed Matt's cheek.

As she stood, she heard a voice as Scottish as Highland mist that said, "My name is Ian. Ian Macgregor."

Layla jerked. She turned to Matt. "Did you hear that?"

"All I heard was the house shake when you jerked for no reason, precious." He looked concerned. "You sure you're okay?"

"I promise I am. I'm going to sleep." Layla walked down the hall. *I will not-think; I will not-think ran like muzak through her mind.*

SIX

Layla accepted a glass of wine from tall Jason and maneuvered through the people to the counter dividing the living room. "Happy Friday, this week was a bitch," she said before the crowd swallowed him. She looked at the chopped veggies, dip, chips, and pastry wrapped salmon without appetite. Someone put Clapton on, liability of my stupid name, Layla thought; everywhere I go, I get theme music.

The Jasons had decorated their house in cast offs and crap. Very little legitimate furniture intruded into the mix of block and board shelving, beanbag chairs, and oversized pillows. An empty aquarium filled with books and video cassettes took up a large portion of one side of the room. Weird masks and music posters covered most of the wall space. Indian print bedspreads served as curtains. The front window overlooking 35th Street was cracked. The Jasons avoided mentioning it to their landlord; they shared a mutual distrust of landlords, police, and employers.

"You can count on the Jasons for food," said Tracy. She stuffed a small quiche into her mouth. "Nothing like good friends who are sous chefs." Tracy stepped on Layla's foot, fell through the crowd, elbowed her way through the kitchen and joined the people smoking dope in the back yard.

Tracy had sprayed bright blue into her hair and was wearing her usual belly-baring clothing. Most of the crowd wore the ubiquitous uniform of jeans and black t-shirts with a scattering of second hand chic. Layla knew everyone swarming the house, if not by name, by sight.

She moved around the edges of the horde, wondering how so many people had crammed into the tiny house. After skittering crab-style along the edge of the throng, she reached an unoccupied beanbag chair in the corner, and sank down gratefully to sip cheap wine and watch her friends. Dave was already ripped, being an asshole per usual, but a friendly one. The Jasons were handing out wine and opening the door every few minutes.

Short Jason peered around the corner at Layla. "Did Mazie call you? Do you think she's coming out tonight? What did she say?"

Layla scooped up an abandoned beer can to use as an ashtray. "Yeah, she called. I have no idea if she's coming out. I only got the message. I didn't actually talk to her. All she said was that she was sorry, I don't know what for."

Jason paused for a second. The crowd ebbed and flowed around him. He grabbed the end of his braid and thoughtfully examined it.

"Split ends?" Layla's male friends fussed over their hair far more than she did.

Short Jason didn't speak for a second. "No. I'm just wondering if she sounded like she liked me." He looked down at the floor. Sarah, the huge mongrel dog that lived with the Jasons, slurped his knees. Jason gave Layla a self-deprecatory shrug, an expression that seemed to suggest that he thought it an extremely remote possibility that a woman might find him attractive.

"Shoot, Jason. I don't know. I mean, I don't know how she'd sound if she liked you." Layla exhaled smoke. "I mean, she didn't scream, 'Jason's a prick, save me,' if that's any help."

Jason chewed on the end of his braid.

"Stop that, it's gross," said Layla. "She did say she needed to talk to you."

He flushed and let his hair fall out of his mouth. "Do you think maybe we ought to go up to Down Under?"

"No," shouted tall Jason. "I'm pissed off at DJ, I'm not going up to Down Under tonight." The crowd had gathered at the Jasons to party in lieu of their usual Friday invasion of Down Under. Jason had been bitching all week about the money that DJ owed him.

"Look, man. Every few weeks DJ flakes, he just doesn't pay people. He'll catch you up," short Jason said.

"Fuck that," hollered Dave. "It's been old already. That shit was old last year. Sooner or later we need to quit spending our beer money there if he doesn't pay sound men and musicians on time."

"Well, he never said he'd pay up this week," short Jason persisted. "Besides, you didn't even go by the next day to check with him. He may have had your money."

"Oh, you just want to see if Mazie's there," someone said.

"This is a man who only cares about one thing," Dave indicated short Jason with his extended hand, as though he were introducing a politician to a cheering crowd. "This man only cares about getting laid. Everything else is irrelevant."

The entire room broke up in laughter. Layla almost choked on her wine. Several guys started applauding.

"Watch it. I haven't fed you assholes, yet." Short Jason extended his hands in front of him and mimed swimming through the crowd to get into the small kitchenette where a huge pot of spaghetti sauce simmered on the stove. Wagging her tail hopefully, Sarah followed him.

"Check out Sarah," said Dave. "At least one woman is after your ass, Jason." He had one arm around a skinny redheaded woman with a rose tattooed on her upper arm, and his other arm around a short brunette in a thrift store lace dress. Twyla, the redhead, gave the brunette a nasty look.

"Cute," said Jason. "Real cute."

"Don't knock it, Dave," said tall Jason. "Our secret spaghetti sauce recipe is a real chick magnet."

"Yeah, and next week, ya'll are going to test out the 'have regular shower' theory out and see if that works with women." Dave gave both girls a hug.

Layla sank deeper into the soft chair and took a sip of wine. Annie and Saundra had been riding her butt all week. She wondered if they were plotting to make her quit. She'd seen it happen before. Those two and a few more members of their coven would ride someone until she bailed. Great policy, the agency got rid of folks without ever having to pay unemployment. It was probably time she started looking anyway. With next week's second shift schedule, she'd be cut off from most of her friends.

Stupid nowhere job. Layla liked some of the maternity

home's residents. She had been impressed by the difficult decisions the young women at the home faced. Adoption was out-of-fashion; these kids were under heavy peer pressure to keep their kids. Yet, some of them chose to place their babies with couples. Parenting looked rough to Layla. She couldn't imagine facing the world alone with an infant. She shook her head. Sad world.

She thought of Brandy, that strange spooky kid, only seventeen. Brandy's eyes seemed old. Brandy had stopped by the receptionist's booth several times during the past week. The girl seemed unwilling to accept that Layla didn't 'know' the ghost that Brandy kept feeling in the building.

Layla shook her head. I've got to get another job.

"State of emergency," Dave blared. "Empty wineglass in the corner. Take immediate corrective measures." Twyla giggled.

Tall Jason stepped over a couple on the floor and avoided tripping over his dog. Sarah, tail still wagging, wove around his legs. "Coming through," Jason announced. He leaned over a slightly stoned couple sprawled on the floor and deftly splashed wine into Layla's glass. "That's the vin de casa. Really cheap red."

"Thanks," said Layla. She felt the impact of the second glass after one sip. "Whew, I better slow down. Too much to drink on an empty stomach."

"Hey, Jason," tall Jason yelled. "Start boiling water for the pasta. We have hungry women out here."

"Hot damn, hungry women." Dave laughed. "They're the best kind." Shrieks of getting-high giggles combined with a few dirty looks from some of the females greeted his comment. Twyla clutched his arm with a territorial expression. The brunette wandered off toward the back yard. Twyla's face smoothed into a smile at the brunette's exit.

Short Jason slithered through the crowd until he bent before Layla, his long braid sweeping her knees. "Come on into the kitchen with me. I'll fix you a plate before the Mongol hordes are unleashed and we can go sit on the porch. I want to talk to you. Okay?"

"Sure." Layla and short Jason went back a few years. They'd worked in a string of restaurants and bars together before she'd switched to office work. She held out her hand. Jason pulled her to her feet, and she followed him to the kitchen.

"Cool, when did ya'll get that?" On the wall, opposite the refrigerator, was a large poster. A young woman's figure stood in a meadow, blue tinged mountains reaching into the sky behind her, their stark black rock a startling contrast to the tender sky. Hair, black as volcanic dust, spilled down her straight slender back. A tall man in a kilt, red blond hair framing his face, looked down at the petite woman in a flowing white dress. The man reminded Layla of something she wanted to forget. His expression was tender but something else lingered in his gaze, a proprietary shading, the woman was his, he owned her.

Layla shuddered. Then, she crept closer to the poster, "Hey, this isn't a print."

"Nope," said short Jason. "Jason is painting again."

"I really wish he'd take it seriously. He's good. Damn good." Layla stepped back to gain perspective on the artwork. It filled her with an ineffable sadness; something doomed and lost reached from the image and wound tendrils around her heart. For an instant, the woman in the painting looked like Layla's mother. Not her mother, really. A younger, innocent version of her mother. But, the mountainous setting, the stark rock rising into a lavender twilight beneath crystal blue – they were unfamiliar to her. "What does he say about this one?"

"Oh, you know him," his roommate answered. "He never says anything serious about anything, it'd spoil the show. These days he claims he visualizes the past lives of his friends whenever he's stoned. He says he's painting other people's incarnations. Typical bullshit."

Layla hugged short Jason affectionately. "He's a tough act to follow."

"Oh, I don't follow him. I just watch the show." Jason dished up two plates of pasta and drizzled sauce over them. "We better grab this now. I have a distinct impression that Captain Annoying, also known as tall Jason, is going to throw habanero peppers into the sauce."

"For crying out loud, why?" Layla covered her food with grated cheese.

"Just cause he's that kind of guy," answered Jason. "Come on, let's sit out on the front porch where the crowd isn't. I want to talk."

The sound of the party became a muffled mix of music,

phrases, and occasional laughter. Layla and Jason sat on the porch steps chewing in companionable silence. Next door a heavy set woman peered out the front door, a look of contempt plastered across her face, pink foam hair curlers bobbing. Jason smiled and waved. She stiffened and slammed her screen door. In the street, a group of gawky boys showed off with a basketball, their pants slung low, their occasional curses self-important and loud.

Layla set her plate on the step and lit a cigarette. "So, you really like Mazie?" She watched the kids dribble the ball.

"I don't know, I think I might want to find out if I do." He finished his plate and eyed Layla's, which was still half full.

"Go ahead, you're a growing boy." Layla leaned back against the porch railing. "So, tell me."

"Nothing to tell," Jason said. "I just would like to get to know her."

Layla took a drink of her wine. She didn't like Mazie; she found her intrusive, pushy. Why is it that nice guys like Jason fall for irritating twits? She didn't want to screw up her friendship with Jason over Mazie. "Tell me more about tall Jason getting stoned and painting other people's past lives."

"Nothing to tell...not really. I just asked him where he got the idea for that painting in the kitchen and he said when he gets stoned that he sees pictures. He thinks that he is picking up on energy from other people around him, about lives they lived before. I don't know if he even believes that, you know how he is. I swear when I'm not home I think he bullshits the sink."

"What if he's telling the truth?"

Jason snorted.

Layla gnawed on her lower lip. "Seriously, what if he is?"

A battered Ford Fairmont, more primer than its original blue, shuddered to a stop. Mazie spilled out in a long flowing burgundy dress and multiple strands of beads. Layla caught sight of her covertly straightening her skirts and smoothing her hair. "Looks like you'll get the chance to get to know Mazie. Here she comes," Layla said. Mazie wore shiny new boots; she teetered on their high heels.

Jason stood up and waved, "Hey, Mazie!" A grin lit his face.

Oh, yeah, he's gone, thought Layla. Must be the boobs. Mazie's unleashed breasts bobbed as she moved awkwardly up the walkway in her three inch heeled boots. Layla arranged her face in a smile. Mazie's weird phone message, the random apologies, had left Layla uncomfortable. Something about this lady ain't right, Layla thought.

Mazie half fell into Jason, giving him a boob-smashing hug. "Good to see you," she tossed at Layla.

Mindful of her friendship with Jason, Layla forced a smile, "Yeah, good to see you again. Let me see if I can get you a glass of wine. I'm running on empty myself." Layla stood and gathered the plates and her wineglass.

"Super," said Mazie. She huddled into Jason, her plump body contrasting with his bony frame. Layla found herself thinking about Jack Spratt and his wife. Stop it, she admonished herself, why do you have to be such a bitch? Don't you want your friends to be happy?

Annoyed at her own attitude, Layla filled two glasses of wine and fixed a plate of spaghetti for Mazie. She stuck a fork, knife, and napkin in her back pocket. Balancing the plate and glasses, she moved through the crowd sideways until she reached the front door. Layla bumped the screen door open with her hip and handed Mazie the plate. "Where's Jason?"

"Oh, he had to go tie Sara up in the back yard. With all of you guys coming and going, he was scared she'd freak and get out in the road or something." Mazie looked at the plate curiously.

"Hang on a sec," Layla said bending to set down the wine glasses. "Voila." Layla produced the silverware and then sank to her perch on the top step.

"Thanks." Mazie put the plate of food beside her and took one of the wine glasses. "Ugh," she wrinkled her nose after sipping the wine. "What's this?"

"Really, really cheap red. The other house specialty is really cheap white alternating with slightly flat generic soda." Layla smiled. She felt like a little kid sucking up to the class bully.

"I'm really glad it's just us for a while, Layla. I've really wanted to get to know you. I feel really bad about walking out like that the other night. I mean, I really like Jason." Mazie gnawed her lower lip, getting flecks of brownish lipstick on her front teeth. "I'm not going to get anywhere with him if his friends don't..." She twisted one of the many silver rings on her fingers around and round. "It seems like all of Jason's friends really value your opinion. Jason is always saying Layla says this or Layla likes that. That must make you feel special."

Layla felt queasy.

She detected a whine of resentment in Mazie's voice. "I don't know about that. We just go way back." Layla fixed her gaze on the white frame house directly across the road. She could see the flicker of the television screen through the thin curtains. Two heads were silhouetted. The front yard was littered with a Big Wheel and a wading pool, a family.

"Did Jason know you all the way back when your mom was killed?" Mazie's voice was strangely excited; it reminded Layla of the school counselors and teachers whose compassion was a thin veil over their morbid curiosity.

Layla's chest tightened. She wanted to fold inward, disappear. "Not that far back." Bitch. What is her deal? She lit a cigarette off the end of the one she'd been smoking. Her hands were sweaty. She wished Matt had come over with her instead of arranging to meet his new potential sweetie for dinner. She wished she'd stayed home or that Mazie hadn't showed up. "I don't talk about that."

Mazie made a squeaky little sound somewhere between a nervous giggle and a moan. "Sorry, I mean, I just wondered how long ya'll had hung out."

Yeah, right. Death groupie.

Layla swallowed the rest of her wine in one gulp. "We met about six years ago. Jason cooked at the Pewter Rose and I was on wait staff." Damn, I wish Jason would get back, or that someone else would come out. A few fireflies hung in the heat. Across the street, a dog barked, setting Sarah off. Soon a chorus of barking filled the evening.

Mazie picked up her plate and put it on her knees. "Looks good," she said.

"Yeah, that's the double Jason special recipe sauce. Neither one of them will tell anyone what's in it. Probably full of old socks or something." Layla stared straight ahead. She didn't want to look at Mazie.

"Shit!" Mazie flung the plate up in the air. "What is in this stuff, you trying to kill me?"

Oh God, the habaneros, Layla thought–just as the spaghetti covered her.

"Jason!" Layla shrieked, spaghetti spilling down her blouse, strands of pasta hanging in her hair, and a blob of tomato sauce staining the front of her jeans. "Jason, damn you."

"Why are you yelling at Jason? You gave me the shit. What did you put in it?" Mazie's caterwauling summoned half the party to the front of the house.

Over the waves of laughter, Layla could hear tall Jason's distinctive cackle. "Jason, I'm gonna get your ass."

"I got the deal," said Dave. "A chick gets covered in sauce and she takes off her clothes. Your master plan to get laid." Twyla leaned forward and whispered something into his ear. He responded with a quick squeeze of her ass.

Short Jason's skin was a mottled, botchy mess of sickly white and bright pink. "It's not Layla's fault. It's my goofy roommate. He put hot peppers in the sauce."

Tall Jason, still laughing, offered Layla a grubby dishtowel. "I've got to get home and take a shower. Can anyone give me a ride? I had Matt drop me off, I told him I'd catch a ride home." Layla started giggling at her dilemma. She looked like an extra from a slasher film.

Glancing at short Jason, Mazie spoke in honeyed tones. "Gosh, Layla. I'm sorry. Let me give you a ride home."

Layla made eye contact with Twyla. Twyla cocked her head toward the brunette threat, and shook her head 'no' while she clung to Dave's arm.

Unable to come up with a legitimate protest, Layla said, "Sure. Jason grab me a towel so I won't get this crap all over Mazie's car." Jason disappeared and quickly returned with a faded towel and a plastic garbage bag.

Layla spread the garbage bag on the passenger side of Mazie's Ford and hopped into the car.

"We'll be back," Mazie yelled and cranked the engine. She drove like an old lady, stomping the brakes and speeding up for no apparent reason.

"It's over on Queens, near Freedom Park," Layla said, hoping she could get through a brief spell in Mazie's company without stirring up shit.

"Yeah, Jason said something about it, how you'd inherited this really cool old house from your grandma. It must be great to have a house. I live off Monroe in these really crappy apartments. It's all I can afford." The aggrieved tone reemerged.

Layla propped her arm on the window and drummed her fingers on the roof of the car. She wanted a cigarette but Mazie's odd way of twisting everything, of acting like Layla had this wonderfully cushy life, made her hesitant to ask if she could smoke in the car.

"So," Mazie continued, "You've been on your own forever, then? No one telling you what to do or anything? How cool." Layla checked Mazie in her peripheral vision, she looked somewhere midtwenties, long beyond the age when most of her friends considered parental influence an impediment to their own choices. "My mom and dad do nothing but freak. Finish college, change jobs, and on and on. I wish they'd die."

Layla sucked in her breath. She waited for the obligatory apology. It didn't come. "Slow down," she said, "the drive is right behind that hedge."

"Oh, wow. It's like a mansion or something." Mazie jabbed the brakes and the two women rocked back and forth. "Oh, wow. And, it's all yours? Some people have all the luck."

"It's a bitch to maintain," Layla said. "Pull around to the back."

Mazie crept down the gravel driveway and pulled up behind the back door. Layla wished she could think of a graceful way to avoid asking her inside. But Mazie hopped out of the car like a kid at the zoo. "Your back yard is as big as a park. Damn, this is like some place in a movie or something. You probably have great parties here."

Layla's boots crunched gravel. Mazie tottered along behind her, the rocks difficult for her high heels. She wobbled as she climbed the back steps, then fell into Layla's back. Layla fiddled with the back door lock. "It's an old lock, I have to kind of sweet talk it."

"But damn, girl. A whole freaking house." Mazie pushed through the door.

Layla really couldn't believe that Mazie was trotting on into her house behind her. She just wanted to get out of her filthy clothes, wash her spaghetti encrusted hair and forget the entire crappy week. "Soda and beer in the frig," she said as they walked into the kitchen.

"Thanks," said Mazie. "This house is so cool. I guess you have a trust fund or something. You in the market for another roommate? I guess not. Jason says that you and Matt have been friends forever and there's that other girl, what's her name?"

"Holly, Holly lives here too. Look, I appreciate the ride but I just have to get cleaned up. I can't stand it." Would the idiot take a hint? Was Mazie one of those curiosity seekers like the vultures that had hung around right after Mom died? Wasn't it a little late for that?

"No problem, I'll wait while you get cleaned up and give you a ride back to Jasons." Mazie settled into one of the kitchen chairs. She swiveled her head, taking in every aspect of the room.

"I don't think I want to go back out tonight. I'm kind of tired." Would she get it?

"I don't want to leave you stranded. I'll wait while you shower and see if you feel different then." Mazie wasn't going to budge.

"Well, okay," Layla said, feeling trapped. She scurried to her bathroom and peeled off her grimy clothes, leaving them in a pile on the floor. She soaped and rinsed her hair three times until it smelled like flowers instead of oregano and garlic. Damn Jason, that stunt with the hot pepper was ridiculous. Using a loofah, she scoured her flesh.

She couldn't see her reflection in the steam-shrouded mirror. Layla wished that Mazie had tired of waiting and shoved off. *All I want is to veg out in front of the TV; I don't have the energy to figure out her game.* Heading for her bedroom, she hoped that Mazie had taken the hint and drifted off.

Layla froze in the doorway.

Mazie stood by her dressing table, holding Mom's picture.

"What are you doing?" Layla's voice was sharp, accusatory. She felt invaded.

"I was just looking. Is this your mom?" Mazie looked up from the silver framed portrait. "You know, you could look like her if you did something with your hair and dressed up."

"Put that down and get the fuck out of my house." Layla felt icy prickles along the back of her neck. Her fists were clenched. Every muscle in her body was tense. She shook all over. "Put it down now and leave."

Social workers. Teachers. Tell me about your mother.

Mazie stood, wide eyed and fish mouthed. "I was just..."

"Just get the fuck out. Now." Layla's voice shot up ten

decibels. "Go!"

Mazie beat a hasty retreat, not even bothering to shut the door, her foolish stiletto heels clicking across the floor.

Still shaking, Layla's legs folded beneath her weight. She sat on the edge of the bed. Angry tears filled her eyes. Then, she filled her lungs with air and crossed to the dressing table. The sight of Mazie's fingerprints on the picture frame hurt her. Using the edge of her bathrobe, Layla rubbed the prints off the frame and carefully set the picture back on top of the jewelry box. Tightening the belt on the bathrobe, she left her bedroom.

Don't think. Don't think about why it feels awful to think about Mom, don't think about the past.

Layla ambled into the sitting room, flicked on the television, and began channel surfing. Clicking the remote lulled her into a detached calm.

Beneath the sound blast of MTV, a soft Scottish burr said, "She'll no bother you again."

SEVEN

The blue lights cast eerie shadows on the wall, odd deathly shapes choreographed by fear. The wail of sirens, the insect buzz of police radio, and the sound of engines ceasing and maneuvering superceded the cocoon of televised peace. Layla put down the remote and walked to the windows overlooking Queen's Road. Three squad cars, their lights flashing, blocked the road. An ambulance, its doors open, spewed out EMTs running toward wreckage.

Layla clutched her throat automatically. She could feel a scream trapped in her larynx.

An old blue Ford was half on the median, its front end accordioned into a huge oak. Smoke drifted from the hood. The rear wheels were off the ground spinning idly and impotently. As though she were dreaming, Layla went down the stairs and out the front door in her bathrobe, crossing the grass in her bare feet.

Standing on the sidewalk, she could see a million bits of broken glass echoing the night stars. The glass was spread across the asphalt in a parody of the heavens. The driver's side door hung askew. A piece of the door was ruptured. Fluttering against the trunk of a tree was the plastic bag Layla had used to protect the car seats from her spaghetti soaked clothes.

The night was in sharp focus. The lines of the plastic bag, the texture of the tree bark, each blade of grass were as separate and distinct as a pen and ink drawing on heavy paper. The whoosh of far-away traffic, the motions of the police and EMTs were like separate notes, randomly plucked, tuneless, reverberating.

Mazie lay a few feet from the crumpled car.

Had she crawled out? Did the force of the impact fling her out? Her eyes were shut, mascaraed lashes lowered on pale, plump cheeks. Her belly and chest were ripped open, as if the coroner had already begun his autopsy.

Ragged bits of skin, severed unevenly, framed her guts, steaming in the evening air. Layla put her hand in her mouth and bit it. Mazie's insides looked like spaghetti.

Part of the car door was sticking out of Mazie's chest.

Layla felt her dinner rising in her throat.

"Strangest thing I ever saw," a young policeman said. "It's like someone slashed her open with an axe." He made notes on a pad.

"Car door could've done it," an older officer added.

"We'll just leave it to the coroner," the first one replied. "Yeah, you're right. Check out that car door. It's obviously what sliced her like that."

Layla couldn't move. Her vision blurred. The officer with the pad approached her. "Miss, did you see the accident?"

Layla shook her head. "She was just visiting me. Mazie just dropped me off." She weaved back and forth like a branch swaying in the wind. Her hands twisted the belt of her bathrobe. The policeman put his hand on her forearm. "Do you need some help?" He glanced over at the paramedics loading the dead girl on a stretcher. Layla's face was fish belly white.

"No," Layla answered. Still, she did not leave. Mazie's blood was smeared across the street, a broad swatch of burgundy slick in the lights of the squad cars. Layla clasped her hands over her mouth.

A few feet away, an officer redirected traffic. A car door slammed. Layla thought she heard Matt. A car started. Layla looked to the left long enough to see Matt's Saturn reverse and pull into the neighbor's drive. She watched him walking across the lawn; he seemed to move in slow motion. The scene tilted and whirled around her, the earth seemed to fall away.

Through the thick terry bathrobe, she felt the warmth of Matt's hand on her shoulder. "Come on, let's go inside." She felt her own teeth dig into her hand.

Layla let him lead her into the house. She collapsed onto the chaise lounge. The television was on; an episode of *Real World* filled the screen. Layla picked up the remote and began to click rapidly though channels. Tears streamed down her face yet she didn't cry audibly. Matt pried open her fingers and placed a heavy glass in her hand.

She squinted at the glass. Then, Layla tossed back the amber liquid. "Dewars?"

"Yes, I figured you needed something a bit stronger than Miller Light." Matt's back was to Layla. He looked out the window. His back blocked her view of the world beyond the sitting room.

"Ah, yes. Dewars, despite not being the most expensive whisky on the market, definitely, it's the one with the most authentic taste of the Highlands. A blend, not a single malt, but still sincere." Layla set the glass down emphatically. "I am the child of an aristocratic drunk. I know such things. I also know when to wear white shoes and how to accessorize."

Matt let her babble.

"You know, I have a *Carrie* feeling going on. I didn't like her. I really didn't like her, I told her to get the fuck out of here and minutes later she's dead." Layla's tears gushed down her face.

"It's more likely a jammed throttle cable or an ancient master cylinder than your evil thoughts, precious. She looked like a woman unacquainted with car maintenance." Matt picked up Layla's glass. "Let those old engines get full of gunk and anything can happen."

"Seriously, I yelled at her, she left and now she's dead. I feel responsible." Layla hung her head down and wrapped her arms around her skinny legs. "She wasn't that bad."

"From what I heard, she was loathsome." Matt turned around and brushed Layla's hair out of her face. "No point in liking her retroactively now that she's gone."

Layla brushed his hand away. "I just feel responsible."

Matt picked up the remote and settled into the wing chair near the chaise lounge. "You always feel responsible, dear one. You seldom are." He flicked through the channels while Layla snuffled and wiped her nose with her sleeve. "I'll go to the funeral with you, precious."

"Okay," she answered and forced herself to look at the television screen. Matt had settled on an old Kung Fu movie. "Master cylinders and martial arts. You have anything to confess? You're getting a bit butch."

Matt raised one eyebrow and turned back to the screen.

◇

Mazie's funeral fell on a humid Wednesday. Unaccustomed to the rites of death, the Down Under crowd bunched together in the parking lot of Mattherly's Funeral Home, desperate for someone to take charge and tell them what to do. Layla's baggy pantyhose adhered to her skin. Short Jason was puffy-eyed and pale. Matt coached them. "Just say something like 'I'm so sorry' or 'we'll all miss her' if the parents do that awful receiving line thing."

"Receiving line?" Layla paused. "Isn't that for weddings?"

"Welcome to the world of white trash, princess. Don't be surprised if they have a glamour shot of the dear departed on top of the coffin. And, expect an open casket." Matt straightened the cuffs of his expensive white shirt.

Jason seemed about to wander off. Layla linked her arm through his and they walked across the parking lot to the huge wooden door.

It was a funeral super store. Placards in the hallway announced the times of different services. Separate lines, partitioned by velvet ropes, led into various rooms. A somber man in a gray suit nodded at them as they ascended the stairs, "And, your dear departed is?"

Matt whispered to Layla, "Smoking, or non-smoking?"

Layla muttered, "Oh, we're here because of Mazie Sewell."

"That would be the Dogwood room, third door on your left, miss." The man in the gray suit had an unvarying solicitous expression. He turned to greet a trio of elderly ladies clinging to each other.

One of the elderly ladies said, "I hope they didn't put all that make-up on Maybelle. Did ya'll see how they did up Loyal Sue Plyer last month? Loyal Sue never in her life wore eye shadow, she would have just died if she could have seen herself in that coffin."

Layla twisted her black skirt into place and took a deep breath. Her mother's pearls were cool against her heated flesh, bumping her collarbone as she walked across the parquet floor.

"Dear God, I hope it's not an open casket," Matt whispered.

Jason preceded them; he slipped through the crowd and met up with Twyla, her rose tattoo covered by a prim white blouse. Layla and Matt hung back. Twyla wrapped her arms around Jason and shep.arded him into the room.

"I want to turn and run," Layla said. "I really don't do funerals well, I cringed during the funeral scene in *Heathers*, I could scarcely sit through *The Pallbearer*, and I don't think Hugh Grant is the least bit cute."

Matt squeezed her shoulder. "We'll slip in, sit in the back, and get out quickly."

As they approached the door, it seemed evident that Matt's plan wasn't going to work. They were sucked into a line that snaked around the room and curled around a pink pastel coffin. "Oh God, what did I tell you? Glamour shot," Matt said directly into Layla's ear. "See the photo?"

The room was a bizarre hybrid of whorehouse-style flocked wallpaper, gilt wall sconces, and somber velvet draperies. A discordant brew of gardenia, lily, and hairspray hung like a sickly stench in the air. Over the discreet cough and murmur of church ladies, the mingled miasma of the floral sweet scent typical of southern women floated through the sadness. The smell nauseated Layla.

At the foot of the pink casket stood a gilt easel festooned with cherubs. A studio portrait of Mazie in a sequined gown rested on the stand. A telephone fashioned out of carnations and sweetheart roses was in front of the coffin. "Jesus called," proclaimed a gold ribbon trailing off the floral phone. Huge displays of lilies, bridal bouquets and wreaths suitable for the neck of a Kentucky Derby winner, and ringed the coffin like a multi-colored pyre.

A woman just ahead of them said, "It's just what she would have wanted. Bless her heart."

No, it isn't Layla thought. She would have wanted to live. Why do they say that it's what someone would want at their damn funeral? Who the hell wants a funeral?

As the crowd inched forward, Layla concentrated on her breathing. It wasn't her mother in the coffin. Matt managed to pull her out of the line and they slid into a pew while the mourners proceeded in their macabre line dance.

Don't think.

Somehow, Layla thought, somehow. I just need to sit here and stare straight ahead and soon it will be over. When the organist played "Amazing Grace," Layla thought she heard bagpipes.

Layla saw short Jason collapsing into Luke's arms. All she could see of Luke was sandy hair brushing the collar of a navy blue blazer. He folded the smaller man in his arms and stood steady, like a lighthouse, like the oak tree that had defeated Mazie's Ford. Then Matt spotted Luke. Layla felt Matt stiffen, heard the sharp intake of his breath.

Get through it, Layla thought. One minute and then the next.

Layla scanned the crowd. Twyla and Dave were next to short Jason and Luke. Tall Jason and Fred sat near Luke. Had she ever seen Fred in a dress shirt before? She didn't think so. Tracey stood looking like an exotic crow next to a cluster of curled and suited middle-aged ladies. Tracey had sprayed her hair funeral black and sparkled it with silver glitter.

Watch the crowd. Don't think.

"I have to get out of here, Matt. I have to, I think my chest is going to explode."

Matt and Layla beat a cowardly retreat to the parking lot. Layla couldn't speak to Mazie's parents, sad, gray people. She imagined their flesh would feel cold as the grave. What could she say to them? Nothing anyone had said to her when her mother died had made any sense or healed any pain.

Don't think.

She fastened her seat belt. Had Mazie worn hers? "Home, James."

"Yes, m'lady," said Matt.

When they got home, Matt occupied the kitchen. Layla watched as he pulled out the cutting board and an array of vegetables. The bell peppers seemed unnaturally shiny. The red onions appeared airbrushed. Matt's tomatoes were Technicolor. She watched in numb fascination. His behavior made no sense to her; Matt's movements seemed like some bizarre tribal ritual, confusion covered her face.

"It soothes me," he said, as though answering a question. He studied his spice rack. "What are you thinking about?"

"Entropy," Layla answered. "I seem to think of nothing else." Leaving her purse on the table, she slunk down the hallway to her room. Layla peeled off her panty hose feeling her leg muscles tense and relax. Her fingers were slick with her own perspiration. She turned on the ceiling fan. The cool air dried the sweat on her legs.

She bent from the waist, wilted. Layla massaged her calf muscles with the heel of her hand. Standing erect again, she stretched, then reached behind her head, kneading the sore muscles beneath her neck.

Her body was tight, trapped in tension.

Even in her room, she couldn't escape the southern funeral scent of perfume and gardenia. The sweet smell of death permeated the curtains and swirled around with the churning fan. The fabric softener wafting from her sheets echoed the hideous floral fragrance of the funeral home.

Carefully, she unfastened the fishhook clasp that held Mom's pearls around her slender neck. Her fingertips lingered on the pulse in her neck. Layla placed the necklace reverently in its velvet case, a tiny coffin for the pearls. Averting her eyes from her mother's picture, she put the case in the jewelry box. She unbuttoned the black linen skirt and stepped out of it, leaving the garment to lie like a lifeless body on her bedroom floor.

Death made her body lonely. She ached for touch.

Layla ran her fingers through her hair and let it fall to her shoulders. Shrugging off her blouse, she let it flutter to the floor.

Don't think.

Crossing her arms behind her, she unhooked her bra, sighing in relief as it came off. Layla rubbed her ribs just beneath her breasts where the bra's elastic had left angry red welts on her flesh. Her hands moved up, she squeezed her breasts, cupping them in her hands, her thumbs stroking the nipples. Slowly, her hands slipped away, her nipples erect, her breasts tingling.

Layla turned back the covers and lay on her bed. The fan went round and round, its gold chain swinging, its blades clacking. The breeze cooled her hot skin. With tears creeping across her eyes, she watched the fan. Her right hand rose from the sheets and slithered past the elastic waist of her panties. Lightly, her left hand rubbed back and forth from one nipple to the other.

Mindlessly, without intent, without question, she stroked herself. First, she brushed the surface of her sex with her fingertips and then she used her index finger to tease herself with circular motions. She was wet. Wet and alive. Entropy, she thought, slipping her finger into her moist core. Entropy wins. She slipped her finger in and out and pressed her palm against her curls until she shuddered and sighed.

EIGHT

"The ghost isn't here when you don't work," said Brandy. Leaning over the desk, her light hair slipping across her shoulders, Brandy looked like a model in a teen fashion magazine except for the pregnant belly concealed by Layla's desk. "I figure it must be a ghost that has something to do with *you*, not the building. I feel the spirit when you're around. When you aren't here I don't feel a haunt." Brandy sucked on a lollipop and twisted a curl around her finger. Over her sweatshirt, she wore a pacifier on a strip of ribbon.

"Is that for the baby?" Layla nodded at the pacifier. Layla deflected topics easily. When she didn't want to deal with things, she changed topics.

"Nah, it's my paccy," Brandy removed the lollipop and stuck the pacifier in her mouth, crossing her eyes. She giggled and spit it out.

"Really? What's that about?" Layla couldn't keep track of the fads and foibles of the girls. A few months ago, a group of them wore sweatpants with cropped shirts showing their big bellies. Before that, black nail polish had been de rigueur. Today it seemed like a pacifier on a chord was a must-have.

"Oh, it's just a thing everyone does. Having a paccy." Brandy rocked sideways and fidgeted while she spoke. It was a quiet evening; most of the girls had gone to a movie. A few of the older residents had commandeered the TV room. Brandy propped her elbows on Layla's counter. The pacifier bounced on her breasts, a bit of saliva catching the light.

Creepy, that's what it is, Layla thought. Pregnant young women sucking pacifiers. "Yeah, well, I guess most people have a thing."

"Like your cowboy boots. No one else wears them anymore." Brandy smiled encouragingly. "I'm not talking bad about your boots. It's just, they're your thing." Brandy scanned the area for other people, and then leaned farther over the front desk. "I figured it out. The ghost is haunting you, not the building. That's why it's only around when you are. I felt something this afternoon as soon as you clocked in, like it goes where you go."

Layla had no clue what to say to Brandy. She rustled the papers on her desk and looked at the appointment book. Brandy didn't hang out with the other residents. She just did her schoolwork and talked to Layla.

"My momma is a secretary," Brandy said. "She says if you just let everything on your desk pile up long enough it becomes garbage and you don't have to do anything with it." Brandy jiggled around like she was dancing to music that Layla didn't hear. She stopped abruptly. "Momma doesn't come up here to visit me. She says she's too busy. I think she's ashamed."

"I guess sometimes people just avoid you when they don't know what to say. It doesn't mean they're ashamed, it just means they don't know what to do." She wished Brandy would talk about this stuff to her social worker. Layla didn't have any idea what to say to her.

"Nah, she's ashamed. I kind of am, too. You know, a few months ago, right before I got pregnant, I got saved. A couple months later, I was in church, right there in church, on Sunday. All I could think was, here I am in church pregnant, and I'd rather die than marry Wayne Lee. You ever go out with someone like that? I mean, real cute and they kiss well, but you know, you just know that if you married them it'd be holy hell. Wayne Lee has a temper and he never will hold a job. But, darn he was pretty. You know what I mean?"

Layla nodded. Wayne Lee sounded a bit like Luke. Brandy had a round sweet face, creamy skin, and a tiny upturned nose and she was too perceptive by half; it seemed like the kid read her mail. "No matter what, Brandy, I'm really glad that you have the sense to break off with a bad-tempered guy."

Brandy gave her an enigmatic smile. "It isn't easy." She sucked on her lollipop a second. "I've got to go work on algebra.

If I stay ignorant I might get stuck with some loser like Wayne Lee." She smiled impishly. "He sure could kiss though."

Brandy walked off in the sad waddle of last trimester pregnancy. Her high-pitched giggle contrasted sharply with her swollen ankles, puffy fingers, and the dark circles beneath her eyes.

After Brandy left, it seemed unnaturally quiet in the reception area. The phone seldom rang after eight in the evening. Few of the residents had weekend visitors, the buzzer near the gate slept. The day staff hit the door between five and six. Without the click of high heels and perpetual paging, the building seemed nearly empty. The skeletal staff that monitored the residents overnight had no time for gossip or plotting against each other. They left Layla to her own devices.

Layla pulled a book from her backpack. It was a biography of Mary, Queen of Scots. Mary's life story was familiar. Layla shifted through the florid descriptions of Mary's beauty rapidly. She skimmed the familiar recital of events, Mary's French marriage, her second marriage, the murder of her Italian secretary and the murder of Lord Darnley her second husband. Husband number two fit parts of the Wayne Lee and Luke mold. He'd been a bossy pretty boy with a mean streak. Layla could understand why Mary may have plotted to have him blown up.

Layla was shocked by the biographer's blunt description of Lord Bothwell, Queen Mary's third husband. She'd always imagined that particular marriage had been a love match. This account indicated that the third marriage, like the two previous ones, had been politically expedient. What was the point of being beautiful and a queen if you were married off like an auctioned cow?

She read further. Layla had seen a few movies about Mary Stuart and had always imagined a hideous female rivalry between Mary and her cousin, the English Queen, Elizabeth the first. It seemed that was more romantic garbage. It looked like Mary's problems were all political, that Elizabeth had ordered her execution because of Mary's legitimate claim to the English throne. So much for garden-variety female competition.

Layla used a torn scrap of paper to mark her place. Maybe I should go to school and major in history. I could teach. Looking up at the clock, she found that she'd read away the evening. Five more minutes and she could switch the phone to voice mail and clock out. She checked the mailboxes, making certain they were locked. She glanced at the security monitors, then left the booth to patrol the first floor. It took her three minutes to set all the alarms. After that, she switched over the phones, locked the booth, and punched out.

The night slapped her face with an invigorating cool. After being incarcerated in the stuffy building, Layla was energized. Wide-awake and restless, she didn't want to head home. If Matt were home, he'd be getting ready for bed soon anyway. As soon as she stuck the key in the ignition, she decided to head over to Down Under, have a beer, and see who was out on a weeknight. She sped past the hospital, intending to cut down to 7th street to head uptown.

Passing Mid-town Square, Layla thought about the weirdness of Charlotte. The Mall had gone through several incarnations during her short life. Once it had held flagship expensive stores with frothy merchandise that folks believed was "just like the New York stores." Now Mid-town Square housed dollar junk stores and dress outlets full of cheap synthetics. It boasted a parking lot full of crack dealers. Things change too fast here. Charlotte eats her history.

Layla thought she'd like to travel.

Maybe somewhere like Scotland, where it seemed people clung to the past like lichen on stone. Maybe if she understood her own past, she wouldn't be so confused. But then, she thought, maybe if I find a parking place near Down Under all of my angst will disappear.

She spotted a place just across the street and around the corner. Leaving her car, she sprang out into the night. The lower buildings along North Davidson left room for plenty of sky. Several miles distant, downtown loomed, where the huge skyscrapers blocked the stars. NoDa, the North Davidson area, had the ambiance of a southern mill village gone psychotically bohemian. Layla could see the stars in NoDa, the buildings were dwarves, the tallest of them only three stories high.

Tracy was on the corner near Down Under, dancing in the music-less night. *I keep running into them what hears that different drummer,* Layla thought ruefully. She crossed with the traffic light.

Short Jason was slumped on the overstuffed sofa near Down

Under's front door. "He's down for the count," tall Jason said. "Don't try to wake him. It's best if he just passes out. It's just how he has to be for awhile."

"I understand," said Layla straddling a bench next to a picnic table. "I was wanting to ask you something...that painting in your kitchen? Jason said you see other people's past lives."

"I talk a lot of shit when I'm stoned, don't I?" Tall Jason wandered over to the sofa. He stood watchdog style in front of it, insuring that his roommate's drunken slumber would not be disturbed.

Layla watched Tracy moving awkwardly in a characteristic hybrid of belly dancing and hip-hop. A Rastafarian stopped and talked with her for a second. He left, heading down North Davidson. After an interval, Tracy followed him, a zombie grin on her painted face.

Layla watched Tracy sway down the sidewalk, streetlights catching the glitter in her hair. She heard the bench creak and felt it shift.

"Hey, pretty lady. Can I get you a beer?"

The familiar sound of Luke's drawl made Layla turn her head.

"Hi. Yeah, I could do *one*. I'm not making a night of it." She lit a cigarette.

"Miller Light?"

She nodded. "Yeah, thanks."

Luke went inside to the bar. Down Under sank in the weeknight doldrums. No band played. A few regulars sat shipwrecked on the patio. Layla saw the inside of the bar as Luke exited, plenty of room in there, only a few guys bellied up to the bar. He put a can of beer in front of her. She ran her thumb up and down the condensation on the can before she took a drink. Layla spun the big aluminum ashtray around the table. Luke made her nervous. So many chances to say or do the wrong thing when he was around. She said nothing.

He smiled and leaned close to her, making eye contract and then looking away. "You still playing hard to get?"

"I'm not playing." Her voice sounded harsh, angry in her ears. Layla didn't feel apologetic.

"Oh, honey. I know you're not. And I deserve anything you want to say or do. Hell, I'm grateful you'll even talk to me. I was just trying to make a joke. Honest." He smiled again, a practiced smile, one that had worked in the past.

Layla looked at the ragged cuticles and chipped nail polish on her fingers. It wasn't his fault Mazie had died. Luke had nothing to do with her crappy job. "Sorry. I over reacted."

"No problem, it's okay." He leaned back on his elbows and stretched out his long legs, effectively boxing her into a corner. "I'm surprised to see you out this late."

"Well, they changed my schedule at work for a few days. I go in at three and get off at eleven the next couple of days."

"What about Saturday?" Luke said the words softly, his slow speech conveyed intimacy.

Layla bit her lip, her stomach fluttered. "I don't work Saturday." She looked at Luke with clinical detachment. She'd always thought him attractive, but tonight something seemed off-putting about his pretty boy features. His lips were overly full, soft, and effeminate. She heard a whine infesting his voice. The careless fall of his sandy hair across his forehead was childish, no longer endearing. She recalled his kisses, sloppy moist, his lips too soft, the flick of his tongue too tentative. He kissed like it was an unavoidable task to be endured before the main event. Layla shuddered. Slimy, that's what his kisses were, *slimy*. His tongue was wormlike.

"I'd like to take you out Saturday," Luke said.

Guilty over her critical assessment of Luke, Layla said, "Yeah, sure. I mean, okay." She smiled a tight little smile, like a kid masking gas pains. She noted that he hadn't indicated what he had in mind. "So, where do you want to go?"

His hand snaked around her neck. He leaned into her mouth. His tongue tentatively brushed her lips as he gave her a smeared kiss. *His lips were too soft.* "We'll think of something." Layla drew back. She didn't even try to hide her revulsion.

With his fingers tangled in her hair, his thumb stroking her neck, he held her eyes with his. "No, honey. I didn't mean like that. I'm sorry. I just couldn't help it."

Again, Layla felt the sting of guilt. "It's okay." She set her half finished beer on the table. "I really need to go, I'm tired."

Luke grabbed her hand and brushed the knuckles with his lips. Even his hand kissing was too wet. "Saturday, still? Please, I'll behave."

"Okay, yeah. Sure." Layla pulled her hand out of his grasp

and took quick steps to her car. *My fault, I know it's my fault. I have to stop doing this shit. I send out the wrong messages. It must be subconscious. Maybe it's bad blood.*

She leaned on her car for a second and watched a shooting star in the velvet sky. *I hope Matt's home,* she thought, then got in the car. The city streets were deserted. It was after midnight on a weeknight.

The tree that Mazie had hit loomed ahead of Layla's headlights.

A segment of bare wood gleamed bone white in the light. Every time she approached her driveway, she saw it standing like an alternate tombstone. An animal – a cat or a possum – darted across the road. Layla hit the brakes hard. The small Toyota fishtailed. Layla saw the carnivorous tree approaching the windshield.

Her hands convulsed. She had no control over her fingers. Layla shut her eyes. Her foot lifted off the brakes. Alone in the car, she felt a body lean across her chest. Opening her eyes, she saw the steering wheel spin to the right. The car straightened. Then it stopped moving.

A sheen of perspiration glazed her face. Her heartbeat roared in her ears. Layla hyperventilated until she felt light headed. She could hear the ragged sound of her own breathing. Willing herself to function, she lifted her hands, grasped the steering wheel and turned into the drive. Once the Toyota was off the road, she stopped. Layla couldn't force herself to go down the drive to the rear of the house. Leaving her car in front, she walked around to the back of the house.

She fixed her eyes on the path ahead. An owl hooted. Moths suicided into the porch light. As Layla came around the back corner of the house, she saw Holly's blue Jetta. Matt's Saturn was absent. *Great, Holly came home and they've gone out without me.*

The back door stuck after she turned the key in the lock. She shoved hard until it clattered open. A suitcase on wheels was parked near the kitchen table and a pair of medium heeled dress pumps lay in the center of the floor. A box of expensive chocolates plastered with duty free stickers and a bottle of Tresor sat in the middle of the kitchen table. A note was propped on the cologne bottle:

Even cowgirls need jerking out of the blues!
Brought you some goodies. Matt's out with his new eternal love
and I'm down for the count. I've logged a zillion miles in
the past couple of weeks. See you tomorrow.

Holly

Layla put the note in her pocket. Holly seemed to have a sixth sense about when she or Matt needed extra attention. Layla grabbed a soda and balanced it on top of the presents. She walked to her bedroom with extra caution, avoiding the squeaky floorboards. Holly must be exhausted; the energetic flight attendant was usually a night owl.

She put the Tresor on her dressing table, popped the top off the soda and ripped the wrapping from the chocolate. Layla debated the merits of a raspberry jelly coated in dark chocolate over a hazelnut truffle before opting for a nut cluster. She chewed the candy while she took off her boots, dropped her pants to the floor, and picked up the paperback on top of the pile teetering on the floor beside her bed.

Before she opened the book, she seized the raspberry confection and put it in her mouth. Leaning back on a pile of pillows, Layla shut her eyes as she mashed the candy against the roof of her mouth, letting the dark chocolate and tart fruit tastes merge. "Damn," she said, "that's better than sex."

She felt the presence before she opened her eyes.

"Is it now?"

Layla's eyes sprang open.

He was standing by the window, hands folded behind his back.

He chuckled. "If that sweetmeat is better than sex you've made some astoundingly poor choices."

She cringed into the pillows. Layla was overwhelmed, too much had happened, too much continued to happen. She could not name the emotions that warred within her chest. Odd things, inexplicable things kept happening.

Don't think.

"I'm famous for poor choices," she said. "It's why I don't finish school. I've got a PhD in bad judgment." She reached for the box of chocolates. "Would you care for one?" Her skin tingled, a chill wrapped around her body.

"No, thank you," Ian said. He nodded again, the same nod of acknowledgement he'd given her during their first meeting. Hands still clasped behind his back, he began pacing back and forth. After the third or fourth foray across the room, he passed through the far wall and reappeared in a matter of seconds.

"Well, damn," Layla said. "Damn."

"It's nothing you didna know. I just reckoned I'd force the issue," Ian said. He turned to her and smiled. A mesmerizing smile, a smile that prompted Layla to think of things she seldom dared put into words even within the privacy of her own thoughts. His smile heated her flesh.

"So, we've established that either I'm insane or you are a ghost." Layla sat up and drew the bedclothes over her legs.

"And what would I be if not a ghost? What I am doesna make you mad." Ian sighed. He tilted his head to the side and let his eyes drift up and down her body.

"Oh, so you're letting me know that you can watch me whenever you like?" Two pink spots flared on Layla's cheeks. She clutched the covers up over her ribs.

"Actually, I can't," he said. "When I am about, you know it. You've felt things before, things you couldna explain rationally." His voice was soft and tinged with sadness. "I canna explain it myself. But, I seem joined to you, handfasted beyond the grave. I've no control over when I'm about." Abruptly he averted his face.

"There's something you aren't saying." Layla's voice was firm.

"There is that." He looked out the window.

"Well, then." Layla pursued him. She wanted to know what had brought the stranger into her life. Light reflected off the gilt framed picture of her mother.

"You remind me of someone. You are very like someone I once knew. I'll say no more about it for now."

Layla was alone in the room.

Robotically, she emerged from the cocoon of bedclothes and went to the bathroom to brush her teeth.

NINE

"So, what if someone has always had trouble talking to guys, and what if she meets someone and it's easy to talk to him?" Layla dumped a huge serving of potato salad onto her plate next to the fried chicken breast. She pushed a scoop of squash casserole to the side to make room for it.

"I'd kill for your metabolism," Holly said, drizzling low fat dressing over her cucumbers as she eyed her skinless broiled chicken breast. "Or yours," she added as Matt scraped the rest of the potato salad onto his already crowded plate. "I'd say either it's a good match or you are finally getting over some stuff. What do you think, Matt?"

"Insufficient information, tell me more." A timer went off and Matt jumped up, "My biscuits. Hold the juicy details." He scampered to the oven, snatching an oven mitt from a hook hanging beside the stove and jerked out a pan full of perfectly browned biscuits. With a deft movement of his wrist, he deposited the biscuits into a basket. Stopping by the refrigerator for butter, he landed biscuits and butter in the center of an assortment of serving bowls.

"Oh, super," said Holly. "More carbs and fat grams, just what my waistline needs."

"Hush, gorgeous. It isn't officially Sunday dinner without my biscuits. I'm surprised the food police don't storm in and ticket you for refusing fried chicken." Matt spliced open a biscuit and smeared a generous portion of butter on it. He put it on Layla's plate then fixed another. Holly held up her hands to block the biscuit. Matt put it on his own plate. "All the more for me. But, really gorgeous, you only get home-cooking about two times a month, and cooking is what I do second best."

"We don't need to ask what you do best," Holly said.

"Doesn't worry me if you do. I have references." Matt refilled his tea glass. "Now precious, you mentioned something about my favorite topic? Men?"

Layla put down her fork and stared at her food.

"Is there a sacred oracle in the squash casserole that I misplaced?" Matt leaned over and looked at Layla's food.

"Okay," she said. "Last night I went out with Luke."

Holly's lips thinned, her nostrils flared.

"I thought we were going to talk about *men*," Matt said.

"No, come on guys, I'm serious, here. Anyway, last night I went out with Luke. It was okay. He behaved himself. We had Thai food and then went to Down Under for a while. No big deal." Layla shoved a forkful of potato salad into her mouth.

"Another four hundred calories," commented Holly, taking a biscuit and slicing it in half. "Just a half, no butter. Go on, Layla."

"Anyway, all night it was like work. It was so darn hard to talk to him, not because of what happened before. I've always had a hard time talking to him. I feel like one of those kids who needs to read magazine articles on 'how to talk to guys'. I never know what to say to Luke and I'm always anxious about saying the wrong thing." She picked up her biscuit and bit into it.

"So, what about the other guy?" Holly leaned forward.

"Oh, he's all in theory. I was just thinking about how I can talk to guys that I'm friends with, but not to guys like Luke. I mean, guys I date." Layla gulped her iced tea. "I really don't know what I mean."

Holly put down her fork and studied Layla. "You know, it sounds to me like you have a crush on someone. Have you met someone?" Holly poked at the cucumber on her plate, disregarded the vegetable, and snatched the second half of her biscuit; she spread a thick layer of butter over it. "Actually, you're acting like you've seen someone that you *want* to meet."

"No, I was just thinking." Layla hid her emotions by grabbing a bowl and spooning mixed vegetables onto her plate.

"Are you holding out on us, precious? Have you met a mystery man?" Matt took the bowl of vegetables from her and started picking out the cauliflower and depositing it on his plate. "Where is this mystery man?"

"Only in my dreams," answered Layla.

"Aren't they all?" said Holly. "What's for desert? Did you make pineapple upside down cake?"

"I thought you were dieting," Matt said.

"I was. Past tense. Since I already committed major sin by biscuit, there's no point in dieting today. I'll start over tomorrow with Atkins or something." Holly reached for the squash casserole with its thick cheesy crust. "Yeah, eat, drink, and be merry 'cause tomorrow you diet and do aerobics."

"Back to you, precious. Have you ever thought of getting your life moving? Maybe if you were doing things you wanted to do, you'd meet the man you want to meet." Matt reached for the platter of chicken.

Layla rolled her eyes. "See Holly, when you aren't here to distract him, he watches Oprah and starts believing that crap." Layla mopped up stray vegetables with a piece of biscuit. "I just wondered if there was some way I could talk to guys I'm attracted to as easily as I talk to friends, and he starts reorganizing my life. If he threatens to empower me, I'll scream."

"Let's drop the serious stuff and eat dessert," Holly said. She picked up several empty serving bowls and dropped them into the sink. "Cake. I sense cake in this kitchen." She started sniffing like a cartoon doggie. After a few seconds, she removed three plates from the cabinet and brought them to the table. "I did my part."

"You win," said Matt. He stood up, crossed over to the counter, and returned with an old-fashioned covered cake dish. "Now if this were a movie, when I lifted the top off there'd be a large rat. But instead you get cake." He pulled the cover off with a flourish, revealing a pineapple upside down cake.

Layla scraped the crumbs from her plate greedily. "I love your pineapple upside down cake, baby brother."

"That's because it's almost as perfect as I am," Matt said. Turning to Holly he asked, "So, gorgeous, are you in town for long?"

"No, I'm back out Tuesday. I have Charlotte to Gatwick for most of the month. I'll post my schedule and stuff so ya'll can reach me. Call collect if Layla brings home a man."

"Thanks for your support." Layla lit a cigarette and leaned back in her chair. "I'm about stuffed. I could darn near take a nap."

"Me, too," said Holly. "I still haven't caught up on my sleep."

"You know girls, sloth is an underrated sin. I'm all for sloth. Granted, it's not as good as sodomy or drunkenness but it does have its place. Why don't we leave the dishes, take naps, then rent a few chick flicks and make the world go away."

"Sounds good," said Layla, "if you are willing to classify *A League of Their Own* as a chick flick."

"Sure, I'm a liberal," said Matt. "I can tolerate sports."

Holly stretched and yawned.

"By the way, precious. Nap time is prime time for a nice thick layer of moisturizer. You may not be eternally articulate, but your skin can glow." Matt piled up dishes efficiently and took them to the sink.

"Yes sir," Layla said. She stood up and stretched. When the phone rang, she answered it mid ring. "Right. Well, Holly isn't home long. Wednesday would be good. See you then. Ciao."

Holly and Matt looked disgusted.

"Layla?" Holly began.

"Okay, it was Luke. I'm seeing him again." Layla started down the hall. "Don't worry, guys. It's no big deal." It isn't like I get a lot of offers, she thought. I mean, they don't get it. Matt has a new love puppy every few weeks and Holly can pick and choose.

A few steps out of the kitchen, Layla overheard Holly, "Matt, I'm worried. Really. She could do so much better than Luke. She won't even try. It's like she has to punish herself for something, I don't get it."

Layla didn't wait to hear Matt's response. She hurried to her room and shut the door emphatically, let them sort out her life; she was tired of fooling with it. Shucking off her shorts, she obediently rubbed moisturizer over her face and curled up in bed. Yesterday she'd received a big delivery from Amazon. Layla had a new book on the Stewart monarchy, a book on royal mistresses, and two novels waiting by her bed. "Let's see, dead kings or romantic suspense?" she said aloud.

The book on the Stewart succession was on top of the pile. Layla looked at the glossy cover with small oval portraits of Mary, Queen of Scots, her son James, Charles the first, Charles the second, and Bonnie Prince Charlie. Reverently, she opened the cover and let her fingers drift down the unsullied pages. Layla adored books. She greeted every new volume like a long-awaited lover. Curled on her side, knees bent, head propped up on her arm, she began reading.

By page thirty-six, she was hopelessly confused. The material on clans swirled in her mind like a wayward Highland wind. She tried to decipher the difference between a handfast marriage and a betrothal. She'd thought that handfasting was a pagan deal or a Wiccan ceremony. The book said it dated to the days when remote Highlanders hadn't easy access to a priest and made their own marriages. But the author confused her by saying that the arrangement lasted a year and a day unless a child came of it. Layla gnawed her lip. Was it a fertility test or an expedient way to get hitched without local clergy?

Then there was clan leadership, the idea of being a MacDonald and being *The* MacDonald. It seemed there were circumstances where a woman could inherit and those where she couldn't. Frustrated, Layla marked her place and closed the book. She was restless, tired, but not sleepy.

Still on her side, she wrapped her arms around her body. Ian would know all about the clans, she thought. Yeah, like I can call Ghosts 'R Us and make an appointment. Like he even freaking exists. If he existed, I'd be scared of him, wouldn't I? I'm not scared; therefore, he doesn't exist.

Layla had that creepy-middle-of-the-night feeling. Despite the sunlight waltzing through the curtains, she felt the odd isolation of the small hours. Each creak of the house startled her. The indiscriminate thumps, the irregular buzzes of bug against screen, and the rasp of the wooden floors all pierced her bones

With each noise, with every lull into afternoon silence and solitude, her unease increased. Even the shift of her own weight on the bed made her heart swell in her throat. Caught like a bug in sap, she was stuck in irrational fear of something unknown. Still, she thought of Ian.

And as she thought, unplanned, unbidden, her hand made circular movements across one breast. The palm polished the nipple, carelessly, as if by accident. Her hand circled idly, intermittently squeezing the soft small breast. With thumb and forefinger working in concert, she stroked one nipple until it was erect. Licking her finger, she wet the tip of the nipple then squeezed her thighs together. She licked her lips. An intense longing pumped through her veins.

Her hips bucked and twisted. She wanted. She wanted. She wanted. Layla's entire body was inflamed.

Pressing her legs tightly together, she moved her hand to the other breast. Deep in her belly she throbbed, she ached with emptiness and desire. Her wayward fingers toyed with her breast. The nipple was already erect, quivering, protesting its neglect. Layla rolled to her back. She used one hand to brush back and forth across her breasts. Her other hand crept up her leg, a tentative finger slipped beneath the elastic band of her panties. She caressed her soft hair, moved her fingertip back and forth.

She thought of Ian, of what his face framed in red-blond hair would look like as he rode her hard. She knew he'd hold his weight on his own arms when he came, driving deep inside her core.

Layla jerked and placed her hands on either side of her, palms pressed against the mattress. Damn, I am screwed up, she thought. I'm playing with myself and thinking about a freaking ghost. Fuck, I'm crazy.

Jumping out of bed, she searched through the pile of clothes and chose nearly clean jeans. She shimmied into them and stuck her bare feet into sneakers. Her t-shirt fell over the loose waistband of the jeans. I need to get out of here. Take a walk, do anything. Something is really wrong with me.

I have to get out of here.

Layla stuck her cigarettes and lighter in her back pocket. She picked up her keys from the hook in the hallway and sprinted out into the sunshine. I'm crazy. My fantasy fuck is either a ghost or a hallucination.

Walk. That's it, she thought, walk. Layla headed up Queens Road, certain that if she walked flat out, full steam ahead, she'd soon stop thinking. I can run from damn near anything, she thought.

Don't think.

By the time she passed the tennis courts, she broke a sweat. Turing in by the tennis courts, she humped it past the playground and motored toward the lake. Kids on swing sets blurred. Teens carting huge radios blended into the pine trees. As she passed the old locomotive put in the park for kids to climb on, she heard a familiar voice. Brandy. Nothing odd about that, girls from the Home hung out in Freedom Park all the time. No, it was unsettling. Frightening.

Brandy was screaming.

"Wayne Lee, let go of me. You can't tell me what to do, you don't own me." Brandy's voice dripped panic.

Breaking into a sprint, Layla moved swiftly around the old train and saw Brandy.

A man with short dark hair grasped her upper arms. He shook the pregnant girl back and forth. Brandy's head jerked. "Wayne Lee, you stop it!" She looked terribly small. His face was contorted, eyes bulging, lips drawn back to expose tobacco stained teeth.

"Bitch, I done said we're getting married and we're getting married. You ain't giving away my baby." He gave Brandy a furious shake and flung her against the engine.

Brandy turned her head as she slid backwards into the locomotive and caught her face on the metal side. Blood spurted from her lower lip. Her face went dead white as the burgundy droplets smeared across her chin. Instinctively, she crossed her arms over her belly and turned away from her assailant.

A few feet away a man and woman on a bench gathered their newspapers and coffee cups, slinking off, heads down. A mother pulled her children to the far side of the outdoor skating rink, distracting them, glancing over her shoulder at Brandy with a look of contempt.

Layla dashed up to Brandy and Wayne. "Leave her alone," she shouted, vibrating with rage.

Wayne Lee reeked of a week without showers. "Who the hell are you?" His face was slick with mad dog sweat. He whirled to face Layla, his fist drawn back. Brandy whimpered.

"I'm her friend," Layla said. "You can't go around forcing people to do what you want." Brandy didn't move, her hand was pressed to her mouth, blood oozed from between her fingers.

"The hell you say, bitch." Fist clenched, Wayne stepped closer to Layla, his face carnivorous. His expression telegraphed raw violence. He drew back to hit her.

Layla *knew* he was going to knock her into the middle of next week.

Suddenly, he was hurled backwards onto his ass.

He pushed the ground with his hands, but he was unable to

stand. Something had him pinned. Wayne recoiled as if he'd received a punch to his jaw. His head twisted to the left. Rolling onto his side, Wayne thrashed about like he was being kicked in the stomach.

Layla stared at the spectacle like a rubbernecker watching a five-car pile up. Brandy moved behind her, peering over Layla's shoulder.

Wayne Lee rolled in the dirt, cussing and snarling. He looked like a dying catfish, flopping and thumping. His hands shielded his face, but cuts and bruises erupted on his cheeks. His nose bled. One eye was already swollen shut.

"Well, if he ain't calling me everything but a child of God," Brandy whispered under her breath. She scrunched into Layla.

Wayne held up his hands, pleading, "Please, please." Blood covered his t-shirt. Two fingers of his right hand bent at a peculiar angle. He was having trouble breathing.

Then a polished steel dagger appeared, hovering in the air a foot above Wayne's chest.

"No, no," Layla screamed. "No!"

The knife vanished.

Breathing raggedly, Wayne stumbled to his feet and walked away from the two women. He didn't even look back. He got into a battered Chevy truck and drove out of the parking lot.

Layla put her arm around Brandy. "Let's go by the emergency room and get you checked out."

"I told you the ghost goes wherever you go," Brandy said. "I told you."

TEN

After a quick stop at the grocery store, Layla headed down East Boulevard on her way home from work. It hadn't been bad for a Monday. Brandy was fine despite the bizarre incident in the park. Wayne hadn't returned. Most of the managers were off-site all day, wallowing in policies and procedures in the throes of yet another massive reorganization. Yep, just doing that ol' empowering, visionary two-step, Layla snickered.

On the sidewalk, she spotted the bounce of Holly's ponytail against a green t-shirt. Holly was into some serious sweat. Layla honked her horn and waved at her jogging roommate. It's not a bad gig being ordinary looking, she thought, the maintenance is low. Layla passed Holly. In her rear view mirror, she saw Holly's face, a grim determination to stay a size six plastered across her features.

Matt was already in the kitchen chopping dill when Layla came in juggling two grocery bags and her backpack. She let the backpack slide to the floor.

"How did the strawberries look?" He reached for the grocery bags, set them on the table and began unloading the contents. "Oh, super," he said, holding a carton aloft. "Holly's back in diet mode, so I figure fresh fruit salad for dessert. And, I'm doing a poached salmon thing that's to die for. Did you get asparagus? Yes, what a good little shopper you are."

Layla got a canned soda from the refrigerator and dodged Matt's frenetic kitchen dance. She popped the top and took a large gulp. Lighting a cigarette, she leaned back and luxuriated in the end of her workday. "Suck day done."

"Is that an invitation for the career move lecture?" Matt

scrutinized his spice rack, then ran the asparagus under cold water.

"Not today," Layla said. "I'll take a rain check."

"Steamed or stir-fried, what do you think?" Matt held up the asparagus.

"Oh, whatever you think. Wait, the calorie countess will probably want steamed." Layla gulped the rest of her soda, then crushed the can.

"Oh, a real man," said Matt.

Holly burst through the door. "Water, water, must have water." Matt stepped back as she dashed to the sink and turned on the faucet. Not bothering to use a glass, she slurped the running water and then stuck her head beneath it, emerging dripping and grinning. Big splotches of water darkened her t-shirt.

"I hope that's a prelude to a shower. Ashley's coming over to meet my harem tonight." Matt examined snow pea pods with the attitude of a diamond cutter. "And it would be so gratifying if you both behaved like good little girls."

"Ashley?" Layla's brow furrowed, her voice squeaked up half an octave.

"His mother had this big *Gone With the Wind* thing. His baby sister is named Scarlett," Matt said.

"It could be worse," Holly said. She started doing her doggie sniffing food routine.

"Salmon, mixed snow pea pods with water chestnuts, asparagus, and potato soufflé," Matt recited.

"And what wine are we serving in first class?" Holly ran her hands through her wet hair and re-did her pony tail.

"Shit, I forgot wine," Matt said.

"Not to worry, we'll go get some and be back in time to shower," Holly took her car keys off the hook. "It's actually safer to stay out of the path of the master chef. Come on, ride shotgun, Layla."

Layla picked up her backpack. "What goes with salmon, Chablis? Chardonnay? You need anything else?"

Matt stared into space a minute, "If you see any stray raspberries, I'll give them a good home in the fruit salad." He nodded at Holly. "I'll leave the wine to your discretion, gorgeous. But Mr. Ashley does love his Riesling."

Layla tossed her backpack into the back seat of Holly's Jetta and snapped her seatbelt. "So, what's on your mind?"

"You, I guess." Holly backed down the driveway. "I really have a bad feeling about you and Luke."

"There isn't any 'me and Luke' anymore. I'm just seeing him occasionally." Layla picked her cuticle. Holly's car was a no smoking zone.

"Seriously, I have an overwhelming sense of dread about you seeing him at all. I just have this feeling that some kind of disaster is going to occur." Holly changed lanes. "Look, remember when you told me you had feelings like some force was around, a benign protective something, and you thought it was your mom? Well, I admit I was pretty much an asshole about that, you remember? I told you it was just normal wishful thinking. Well, I'm sorry. I didn't get it. Lately, I've been having feelings, weird shit. I can't quite explain it. But, I just think that if you keep seeing Luke, something awful will happen."

Layla didn't respond for a few minutes. Then she said, "Thanks, I know that was hard for you to say. I'll think about it."

Holly pulled into a space right in front of the grocery store.

Impulsively, Layla leaned across the car seat and gave Holly a quick hug. "It'll be okay."

"I hope so. Come on, let's spend too much money on vino." Holly's long legs exited the car first.

As soon as Holly uncoiled and stood, a slack-jawed, snake-hipped man in a Red Man Chewing Tobacco hat gave her a wolf whistle. "Hey Baby, if I said you had a beautiful body, would you hold it against me?"

Eyes forward, both women sped up and moved past him.

"You think you're too good to speak?" The man spat chewing tobacco on the sidewalk.

Winking at Layla, Holly looked over her shoulder and said, "As a matter of fact, I *am* too good to speak to you."

"Bitch," he snarled.

"You know, Holly, for pure charm, you just can't beat a real southern gentleman," Layla said. They both collapsed into giggles. As they wheeled their shopping cart through the store, they kept giggling.

When they exited the store with three bottles of wine and four cartons of raspberries, the man was waiting for them. He wore a feral, predatory look.

He took a step toward them. It was payback time for Holly's smart mouth comment, for Layla's giggles. Layla felt her stomach knot in fear. She saw a glint of something in his hand, a knife? A razor blade? She put her hand on Holly's arm. Should they run to car? Back into the store?

He took another shuffling step closer.

He opened his mouth to speak.

Then he staggered back against the bags of charcoal briquettes piled in front of the store.

Layla's heartbeat escalated. Her skin felt cold.

Holly didn't seem to notice anything odd. "I hope Matt's southern gentleman is closer to quality folks than ours."

Matt was fluttering around the kitchen when they came in with the wine. "Both of you hit, the showers. Now," he commanded. "I've got to chill the wine, finish the fruit salad, and set the table. We will be using the dining room," he said in a don't-dare-argue-tone.

Layla considered wearing her pearls with a pair of jeans and a Harley t-shirt but decided not to screw around with Matt. This was the first man he'd brought home for a social event in months; she discounted the unintended encounters with the occasional stranger over morning coffee. Ashley must matter to Matt. Showered, with her hair neatly braided, she stood in front of her closet. Not much to choose from. Layla grabbed a navy blue cotton knit dress that fell to midcalf and shoved her feet into clogs.

"Thank God, you look like a human instead of a refugee from a beer joint," Matt said, shredding romaine lettuce.

"As always, I appreciate your confidence," Layla lit a cigarette. "Is there anything I can do to help?"

"Everything is under control."

Holly came in wearing a taupe tunic over wide legged navy blue pants. She did a runway model twirl. "Will I pass?"

Matt put an arm around each roommate and gave them both a squeeze. "Ya'll look fabulous, darlings. You'll love Ashley, I just know it."

And as it turned out, Layla *did* like Ashley.

He was perfect for Matt. When she helped Matt clear away the salad course and tote out the vegetables and salmon, she whispered, "I always thought that a 'charming accountant' was one of those ridiculous things like 'military intelligence', but, darn he's a sweetie."

Her usually cool roommate blushed. "He is that, isn't he?"

When they returned, Holly and Ashley were hot on a comparison of their favorite museums. Without a pause, Ashley included Layla in the conversation. "Matt tells me that you read a lot of British history. Did you know the Mint Museum is gearing up for an exhibit of 18th century English furniture?"

"Well, actually, I'm more interested in Scottish history than English history," Layla said. Then, fearing she's been rude, she added, "but that sounds interesting. Thanks for mentioning it."

"Oh, yeah, MacDonald." Ashley commented, "You would be interested in Scottish history. Have been able to visit Scotland?"

"Not yet, but I guess I've always wanted to. Holly prefers Paris."

"This week," Holly said.

"Our girl Holly is not a model of consistency, but Layla has always had a freak interest in Scottish history. More wine?" Matt picked up the bottle.

"Take notes, Layla. See how Matt does it, first he gets his prey tipsy and then..."

"Stop it Holly or I'll tell people what you weigh." Matt laughed and squeezed Ashley's hand.

After coffee and fruit salad, Layla picked up two glasses, a corkscrew and an unopened bottle of Chardonnay, "Let's leave the gentlemen to their brandy and retire to the sun room, Miss Holly."

"Why I'd be delighted, Miss Layla," Holly answered.

They settled into wicker rockers, the bottle of wine on a wrought iron table between them. "I really should use this room more," Layla said. "It's the greatest room in the house. Huge windows and all the shrubs growing around. It's like being inside a tree, or being in fairy land or something. I feel safe out here." She flicked ash into a crystal tray.

"I know what you mean," Holly said. "It doesn't feel like the city at all."

"Ashley is really wonderful, isn't he?" Layla exhaled and watched the smoke rise.

"Yeah, he and Matt seem a good match. But, I worry. It'll be harder for you with Matt involved with someone. I was serious as a heart attack when I said what I did about Luke. I can almost fell evil hovering over him." Holly poured herself more wine. "I just have the weirdest feeling, not like anything I've had before. I can't explain it."

Layla didn't want to talk about it. She was mortified that Holly thought she needed Matt to tend to her. "I've been thinking I might start school again. Between school and work I won't have time to get into trouble."

"Hey, that sounds great," Holly said. They sat in comfortable silence listening to the leaves whisper against the screens. Holly drained her wine glass. "I'm heading up to bed. That run took it out of me."

"I think I'll just visit with the night awhile," Layla said. "Good night."

Holly went up to bed. Layla sat in the darkness, listening to the rustle of leaves and the sibilant hiss of the night bugs. Car headlights bathed the room in a brief, dim glow, then passed into obscurity. She heard chairs move across the floor, footsteps, and the sound of muffled voices. Then, she heard the stairs creak and the heavy finality of Matt's bedroom door shutting out the world.

Layla stretched out her legs and leaned back. She poured herself another glass of wine and sipped slowly, letting the wine drift down her throat, letting go of the day. It was late, how late she didn't know, but the neighbors' windows lights blinked off one by one. The city was going to sleep.

The chair beside her rocked.

She was not surprised to see Ian sitting beside her. He fit the soft evening, the secretive shroud of darkness, the molten scent of dying gardenias. The creaks and whinging of the old house suited him.

Layla thought about speaking, considered several clever or pleasant things she could or would say. She chose silence. She didn't need to talk, to fill the still air with noise to keep her anxiety at bay. Something in Ian eliminated the need for vague phrases or empty words.

"It's time we talked," he said.

Layla nodded.

"I know you want answers," he continued. "I've no answers for you. I don't know that there are any answers. But you do deserve to know why I'm here." He looked different. Tired, worn, his face lined, his eyes red rimmed. Speaking seemed to cost him, as if the words bled out of him.

"I'd like to know what's happening," Layla said. "I don't know that I deserve it. I don't know that anyone ever deserves anything."

"Well then, there's this," Ian said. "I think we've all the right to know where we stand with each other, that's only justice. Minimal justice at that. Which means you do not deserve to know everythin' about me or how I feel about it. You do deserve to know the place I've taken in your life. I'm here to protect you."

Layla set her wine glass down on the wrought iron table. The clink of the glass striking metal and the sound of her breath were the only noises evident in the night. She folded her hands in her lap. Time seemed to slow to a stop. This moment, this one moment, when she sat in the ebony night with a ghost and listened to his soft voice, the careful articulation of some consonants, the dropping of others, the gently rolled 'r's and the hypnotic quality running like water through a mountain stream, this moment seemed all that was, all that would be.

She waited.

The stillness, the sepulchral silence of the night wrapped around her.

"Culloden," Ian said. He repeated the word in ominous tones, "Culloden."

Layla did not say anything.

"April 16th, 1746. The last battle fought on British soil." Ian's voice was low, yet each word was distinct. Layla felt his voice vibrate her bones and mingle in the flow of her blood. "I was doomed from birth."

Layla jerked, his words could have come from her mouth. She straightened her shoulders and looked at him, his face obscured by the night, the muted tones of his plaid blending into the shadows.

"I was born the same year as Bonnie Prince Charlie. I was in my twenties during July of 1745, when the Prince landed on the white sand of Arisaig. We came from the Highlands, down from the glens, from hidden crannies in the rock. Some of us believed that we could throw off the yoke of English oppression. Some of us believed that fat German George had no right to rule Scotland, let the English have him if they wanted. Many

Highlanders were Catholic and longed for a Catholic on the throne. Some of us were hot-blooded young men who wanted war, imagined the glory and knew nothing of gore."

Ian stopped speaking. Layla poured wine into her glass and waited.

"I didna remember why I went. I only recall how he looked on his colossal white war-horse, wearing the white cockade, a plaid fluttering about him. He was the perfect image of a prince – bold, charming, charismatic."

Ian looked up but did not appear to see the room. A transitory splash of light from a passing car displayed his face. He seemed to be watching a world that Layla could not glimpse.

"That was the beginning, a glorious beginning. All lost causes have glorious beginnings. With his army of Highlanders, the prince marched south to Edinburgh. It was a soft Scottish summer, the air warm, the sea winds mild. We were healthy and young and met no opposition. From Edinburgh we fought our way south to Derby, 120 miles from London."

Ian stretched out his legs, for a second he leaned forward, covering his face with his hands. Then, he laid his arms on the armrests, kicked back in the rocker, and looked at Layla. "Highlanders didna fight like the English army. We didna march in formation to meet on a flat field. We learned to fight in the mountains, swooping down on our prey. We owed allegiance to our prince, but we took orders from the clan."

He continued, "When we were encamped at Derby, winter came to the midlands. We were far from supply sources. While there was no real opposition, there was no support either. Cumberland, bloody Butcher Cumberland, sent a spy into the camp. The spy convinced the prince and his advisors that a British army, thirty thousand in number, was marching toward us."

Ian shrugged. "We marched north. Despite our early success, it seemed to make sense to wait for spring. We'd been on the move for months, we were ragged, tired." His voice broke. "We'd left loved ones behind. Woman and children, unprotected."

He reached over to Layla and traced the line of her cheek and jaw with the tips of his fingers. A patina of melancholy coated his features. Ian cleared his throat. "It was a long march back to Scotland for the five thousand who followed the Bonnie Prince.

We beat the English at Falkirk. That battle left us without ammunition. After a few weeks at Stirling we made our way home to the Highlands."

He rubbed his hands together as if they were chilled. "A Scottish winter is a different cold, it cuts through to the bone. The wind whips through your flesh and even your heart freezes. We made camp in Inverness. Many of us drifted back into the Highlands. We went home. Home to wives, to mothers, to sweethearts. I didna go home."

Layla moved closer to Ian. His voice was barely audible. "I didna go home," he said again.

"And, then?" she prompted.

"Culloden," he answered. "We were in Inverness, freezing, starving, pelted by ice and battered by gale force winds screaming up from the Moray Firth. Cumberland's army a mere fifteen miles away in Nairn. Just over one thousand of us, myself among them, marched overnight to Nairn to attack the English. We failed. We failed miserably, the first of many failures that served to kill a free Scotland."

Layla's skin was cold; she could feel freezing rain pelting her skin, icicles forming in her hair.

"Dawn broke like a deadly flat line across the gray horizon. We'd marched all night. We stood, half-starved and exhausted, on Culloden Moor. With sunlight came the English marching across the flat surface, rolling their cannons, coming and coming again in row after row of well-fed mercenary flesh." Ian shook his head. "We didna ken wha' to do."

Layla heard the sounds of thousands of booted feet, the sounds of the horses' hooves.

"They slaughtered us on that misty moor. It took an hour, only an hour to kill the future of Scotland. Sixty minutes to butcher the proud young men of the Highlands, to leave the land bereft and bleeding, to widow and orphan the clans. English artillery ripped our bodies. English horses tramped us.

"To my left, Jamie MacGregor, my cousin, was turned into a mass of stinking offal, his guts spewed across the dry heather. He begged me to kill him, to do what I'd do for a horse. His innards mingled in the mud and horseshit, his entrails steaming in the freezing wind. I couldna do it. I had no bullets and I couldna bring myself to slit his throat.

"The battlefield was littered with limbs, arms and legs flung willy nilly like some mad bloody puppet factory. All around me the dead and dying, pleading for water, for prayer, for someone who'd take word to a woman waiting back home. The wind was a widow keening. Wet snow, wet sloppy snow turned pink with blood, brown with gore.

"I saw a threadbare bit of MacDonald plaid, rough woven, pressed against a gash in the chest of a headless man. His fingers gnarled and twisted, holding the piece of plaid to a hole where he'd had a heart. He didna have a head."

Layla's breath sounded unnaturally loud. She felt bile pushing up her throat. Tears welled in her eyes.

"It didna end there. Not in honorable battle. Butcher Cumberland sent back his men after the battle to trample and hack away at the wounded, to use their wealth of bullets to dispatch the disabled. Highlanders were hunted down. Women who sheltered wounded men were dragged from their houses, raped repeatedly, English sabers shoved up their cunts before their houses were torched, the wounded inside roasted alive."

Layla covered her mouth. She struggled to stop herself from vomiting.

"No honor. He had no honor. I should hae gone home." Ian's voice was flat.

"Then I did go home. I walked the frozen rocky ground, my bloody bruised feet wrapped in rags. I chewed bark and begged meals. The sky was glorious blue, blue as the Campbell tartan. But the earth was blood stained and hungry, the ground cried out for blood and more blood."

Despite the darkness, Layla could see every detail of Ian's face, the haunted eyes, the twitching muscle in center of his clenched jaw.

"Through Inverness, and up through the Highlands I passed the skeletal remains of burned, blackened buildings still sheltering the crumbling bodies of old men and young women. By the roadside, I saw young mothers, babes in their arms, rifle stocks shoved up them, throats slit, still breathing, bleeding to death in the snow. A mile from home I saw the corpse of a young woman tied to a spit and roasted, – *they'd roasted her alive* – drinking and making sport while she screamed."

Layla bit her hand, to stifle her stillborn scream, to spare herself the humiliation of spewing dinner across her lap.

"My home was gone. The land had swallowed my past, leaving only blackened rock and the wandering specters of those I couldna protect. Those I had failed."

Layla held her hands in front of her mouth. She felt as if the blood had been drained from her body. Shaking and sweating, she tried to speak. She nearly choked. She gave up on talking and surrendered to tears.

"That's more than enough for tonight," he said.

Layla sat alone until near dawn.

D. G. K. Goldberg

a good little girl."

Layla sat at the table drinking coffee and watching the two men work in concert. They shared the kitchen like long-term partners. Emptying her cup quickly, she stood up and moved back to the pot. "Oh shit," she yelled, "work."

"This is a woman who loves her job," Matt commented.

"No, I have to call in. I can't face it today." Layla retreated to the hall phone and called the agency voice mail. She left a message for her supervisor pleading a stomach virus.

Layla dashed back to the kitchen for more coffee. Leaving Matt and Ashley to their breakfast, she headed toward her bathroom to shower. In the shower she decided to spend the day in the library. She had a strong sense that there was something she needed to know, something vital Ian had not told her. Showered and dressed in jeans and a t-shirt, she collected her keys as she passed through the kitchen on her way to her car.

"I thought you weren't going to work today," Matt said.

"I'm not. I'm headed to the library. It was great meeting you Ashley." Layla shouldered her backpack and left.

Driving through work-bound traffic was onerous. Cars crept along the snarled streets. Drivers honked and gestured. Layla rolled up her windows and turned the air conditioning on full blast. The day was already muggy and mosquito ridden. She missed the turn she wanted and spent fifteen extra minutes circling through downtown to get into a parking lot.

Sticky heat hit her when she surfaced from her small car. She felt immediately dirty, grubby. Exhaust fumes and construction site dust swirled through the humid air.

Layla stopped in front of the entrance to the library for a quick smoke. Passers-by hurried down Tryon Street with its soaring skyscrapers housing innumerable offices. Women in skirts and blazers wore atheletic shoes and socks over stockings, their plain dress pumps carried in bags or left beneath a desk. Shorthaired suited men strode briskly up and down the sidewalk, their nondescript suits making it impossible to tell a CEO from a recent hire. A twitching woman, her possessions garbage bagged and jammed into a shopping cart, ambled past muttering, "They think they know what's right. They don't know." Down at the end of the block, a street preacher set up his PA system and harangued the crowd.

Stubbing out her cigarette, Layla turned and walked into the cool quiet of the Main Library. She started her search in the Carolina Room. Layla found realms of information about the early settlements but nothing grabbed her. She couldn't define what she was looking for, but it wasn't there.

Leaving the Carolina Room, she wandered through the stacks picking up novels by Sir Walter Scott, atlases of the American colonies and an armload of books about Scottish history. She walked awkwardly beneath the load of books; the top three balanced precariously, the weight of the pile braced on her hip.

Several hours passed before she found a clue to the baffling obsession that had sent her to the library. A book on Bonnie Prince Charlie fell open to a chapter titled, "The Aftermath of Culloden." Horrified Layla read of Scottish prisoners locked in jail, naked in the freezing weather, starved, and deprived of all necessities, even water had been denied them. She winced while reading about small children and pregnant women massacred by the English troops.

Then she came to a short paragraph. One thousand Scotsmen, survivors of Culloden, had been sold to Carolina plantation owners.

From her earlier research, she knew that the Carolina colonies had been harsh, primitive, wild lands. Devoid of the delicacy of Williamsburg, divorced from the international harbor of Charleston, the inland plantations were hellish places. Slaves worked the heavy red clay soil for nine months of the year in blistering heat, yet winter was cold enough to kill. She shut the book with an attitude of finality.

So, that's how Ian came to North Carolina.

Layla took the books to a cart and left them to be reshelved. With her fingertips brushing the railing, she glided down the stairway, much as her mother had drifted down the stairway at her debutante ball.

She paused in the library lobby. It was so nice and cool inside and she knew it was sweltering outside. Couldn't be helped. She left the library and moved slowly through the heat. On the square, at the corner of Trade and Tryon, she stopped and bought a chilidog with slaw. Perched on a wall, she ate her messy lunch and mopped her face with a napkin. After a cigarette, she popped a breath mint into her mouth.

People walked by, all of them with a goal, a destination. Layla had the day off, unanticipated, formless and vague. I've spent the morning researching the history of a ghost, she thought. Maybe I should have checked out some books on psychology, maybe I'm going nuts.

Layla really thought that she was regrettably sane, dismally, depressingly, cursed with sanity. She was quite sane and Ian was quite real. Sometimes he seemed far more real than her coworkers with their ceaseless talk of what's on television and which store is having a red dot sale.

Yeah, I'm normal. I just have a ghost that drops in occasionally; he says he's here to protect me. Yep, that's the deal.

Layla's jeans were faded, her t-shirt crumpled. She had a headache. The heat from the sidewalk seeped through the soles of her boots. Layla walked the few blocks to her car, thinking about how awful it must have been, the stifling heat of centuries ago when Mecklenburg County was nothing but swamp and forest. What was it like, what could it have been like to come from the cool Highlands to this miasma of damp decay?

Her car radio jolted her with its volume. Late afternoon. She'd spent far more time reading than she thought. Well, at least I don't have time to shop, she thought. If I'm going to lay out of work, I darn sure can't afford a mall crawl. Layla did a mental review of her wardrobe while motoring down Tryon. She really wanted something special to wear for her date with Luke tomorrow and really didn't want to want it. I can see how he gets confused, under my faded Levis he can count on finding Victoria's Secret's latest lace. Yeah, I'm confused.

No wonder Luke is confused, she thought, I don't know what I want from him. I want him to want me, but I want him to want me my way. I'm making myself crazy.

Deciding she needed to be with people, that the noise in her own head, the obsession with the ghost, were sending her down dark corridors, Layla drove down Tryon toward NoDa. It was close to five o'clock, someone should be home or hanging out at the Jasons. house.

Tall Jason sat on the front porch with Tracy. They watched Sarah dig a hole as Layla pulled up in front of the small frame house. Tracy held a paper pinwheel on a stick. Layla got out of her car and called to the large dog, "Hey, Sarah, come here girl," while she patted on her thigh. Usually the big dog greeted her by jumping on her, wriggling with excitement and slurping her face. Today, Sarah stopped digging, her ears flattened against her head. She lowered her belly close to the ground and bared her teeth. "Sarah, Sarah. Come on pretty girl."

Sarah crouched on the ground, a slight growl emanating from her.

Jason stood up and walked to Sarah. "I don't know what's wrong with you, Sarah. It's just Layla. Hell, maybe Sarah has PMS." The dog continued growling, her eyes fixed on Layla. Jason put his hand through Sarah's collar. "If you can't be polite, you can just go in the back yard." Sarah whimpered as Jason jerked her to her feet. She stood rigidly, staring at a point just to Layla's left. As Jason pulled her to the back yard, she barked and turned to snap at Layla.

"I don't know what her problem is," Jason said as he returned to the front of the house. Tracy had put her pinwheel aside and was painting her toenails a metallic green.

"Just my winning personality," Layla said.

"Oh Layla," Tracy said, "you aren't that bad once people get to know you. Do you think I ought to put silver stripes or gold dots over this green polish? You know what I think? I think maybe Sarah saw a spirit hanging out near you. Dogs can see things we can't."

The woman next door came out on her porch holding a broom. She wore a baggy flowered housedress and still had pink foam curlers in her hair. The neighbor craned her neck and looked pointedly at Layla's car parked in front of the house. "Don't you be having another party. I'll call the law." The door slammed emphatically.

"Does she ever take those curlers out?" Layla lit a cigarette.

"Not as far as I know," Jason answered. "I think they're her communication device for keeping in touch with the mother ship."

"Is having too many parties against the law?" Tracey studied her collection of nail polish. "I think I'll put silver on one foot and gold on the other." She shook a bottle of silver polish.

"No." Jason began.

"Why not? Don't you like gold and silver?" Tracy picked up

a bottle of purple polish.

"No, I meant having parties is not illegal. She's just some sort of a human cuckoo clock. She comes out on her porch every three hours or so and mouths off." Jason stood up. "I'm dying of thirst, ya'll want anything? Your choices are water, iced tea, or water."

"Tea would be great," Layla said. "Or water."

Jason returned with three glasses of tea. Short Jason staggered out behind him wearing a pair of sweat pants and a ragged tank top, his hair loose, his eyes puffy.

Layla tensed. She really didn't know what to say to Jason. Mazie had died leaving her house. She filled her mouth with iced tea.

Tracy gave the top of her nail polish bottles a few extra twists and dumped them into her shoulder bag. The tiny mirrors on her bag sparkled in the sunlight. She reached into the bag and pulled out a tub of glitter. "Want some?" Tracey held out the glitter. "You know what I think? I think maybe we need to ask Mazie's spirit to let go of Jason."

Short Jason gripped the porch railing. It seemed that the rotted rail was all that kept him vertical. Layla peeked at Tracy. Was she serious? Tall Jason turned toward Tracy, his teeth clenched.

"I think that's a good idea," short Jason said. "Let's do it."

Layla reached out to short Jason and patted his arm.

"Really, I think it's a good idea," he said. "Tracy, do you know how to go about it?" From the backyard came the sound of Sarah whimpering.

Tracy didn't bother to conceal her smile. "I'm pretty sure I can do it. I've always felt like I had some kind of power, and I've been feeling kind of weird, electric or something, all day."

"You been doing coke?" tall Jason laughed.

"Look, she may be able to do it," said short Jason. Tall Jason and Layla made immediate eye contact. Tall Jason shook his head; Layla took that to mean, 'let's just go along with it'.

Tracy jumped to her feet and brushed off her pants. "Let's go inside." They filed in after her. "Can ya'll pin the curtain things or something, to cut down on the light? Do you have candles?"

Short Jason overlapped the Indian print bedspreads that

covered the windows and secured them with safety pins. His roommate went to the kitchen and returned with a few white candles stuck into empty wine bottles. Layla went through her pockets and found her lighter.

"Great," said Tracy. "Now sit on the floor in kind of a circle." Her voice was tinged with excitement, her face looked as if she'd just been elected prom queen.

Things are pretty freaking desperate when we start taking Tracy seriously, Layla thought. She handed her lighter to Tracy. Yeah, the flake of the New Millennium is going to wake the dead. Layla focused her eyes on the opposite wall. She felt nauseous, and something else, something very similar to the way she felt when Ian appeared.

"I know there are spirits present." Tracy sounded like a televised advertisement for a ghost hotline. Layla would have laughed at her except for the pitiless chill that crept through her chest.

Layla saw an auburn haired woman in a portrait-collared dress with a cinched waist stand by the wall, the dress looked like something from the "I Love Lucy" era. The woman was translucent. That'll teach me, Layla thought, you let one ghost into your life, and there goes the neighborhood.

The woman smiled sadly and faded into the floorboards.

Layla scanned her friend's faces. Tall Jason looked resigned. Short Jason looked hopeful for the first time since Mazie's death. Tracy looked like a kid loose in Toys R Us; she hummed a little tune while she lit the candles. It was clear to Layla that none of them had seen the apparition.

Why did I see her? Why can't anyone else see her?

Don't think. Don't think, don't question.

When the candles were lit, Tracy said, "Okay we all have to hold hands and concentrate on being receptive."

Short Jason's hand felt clammy to Layla. Tracy gripped her other hand so tightly that Layla's fingers grew numb. Candlelight cast spooky shadows on the wall and softened the planes and angles of her friends faces. Layla watched the other three carefully.

The auburn haired woman appeared again. She had morphed from translucent to transparent. Layla could make out the outlines of a Doors poster through her form. She smiled at Layla and gave her the same nod of acknowledgement that Ian employed. Layla had a sense that the woman had lived in this house.

Then an elderly black man with a salt and pepper beard passed through the wall near the kitchen door. He wore a dark blue suit with wide lapels. Catching Layla's eye, he gave her the nod and kept walking. He exited the house through the rear wall. Somehow, Layla knew that he strolled through the neighborhood often.

Layla studied her friends in sequence: Jason, Tracy, Jason. She knew that they hadn't seen the spirits. She struggled against the awareness that Ian had somehow changed her, that she could no longer ignore the uncanny sensations, the glint of moonlight on the silver birch tree, the mist and haze of moon shadow in her peripheral vision. Layla saw ghosts where others saw car headlights. It was a fact like height or eye color. She couldn't escape it.

I won't think about it. In control. I am in control.

Layla's left leg was asleep. Her hand hurt where Tracy squeezed it.

"Nothing is happening," said short Jason, his voice laden with tears.

"We're almost there," Tracy said squeezing Layla's hand. Whether she was signifying that a ghost was coming or whether she wanted Layla to go along with the deception, Layla could not say.

The candle erupted in a sudden series of sparks and shooting flames.

The light radiated across the peeling paint. No noise drifted in from outside. The traffic and the neighbors might have been a thousand miles away, might have been as yet unborn. Orange, amber, hell flame tinged with blue flared and flickered in the near dark dusk.

"Shh," said Tracy, "Something is happening."

Darkness came swift and sudden. The room dripped gloom, dark save for the flicker of the candles.

The room was charcoal gray. Color died. Layla felt Tracy and Jason's hands drift off as if she left her body, as if she left her time. She knew Ian was here now, but she could not see him, could not feel him.

Tracy's eyes, rimmed with purple eyeliner, were wide. Her

expression expectant. She leaned toward the candle. "Come to me, come to me," she intoned.

Damn parlor game, Layla thought, doesn't she know this shit's serious? The candle sputtered and went out unexpectedly.

Outside, Sarah began howling. A siren shrieked. The neighbors slammed doors and screamed domestic bliss. "Okay," said tall Jason, "this has gone on long enough."

Layla heard his heavy footsteps, his puffed breath, as if he was completely exasperated with the entire séance trip. The lights came on. The room seemed too bright.

Tracy slumped on the floor, breathing. Purple marks encircled her neck, as if someone had tried to strangle her.

"It's no a game," is what Layla heard.

No one else seemed to hear a thing.

And Sarah howled like a wolf without her mate.

TWELVE

Layla shimmied out of her jeans and chucked them on the rising pile of rejected clothing. She pulled a black jersey dress over her head and checked it out in the mirror. No. The black jersey flew through the air and topped the discard pile. What a crappy day: a nasty comment from Saundra about yesterday's sick day, followed by another schedule change, and culminating in a classic case of fifteen minutes to get ready with nothing-to-wear.

Even though Matt would have a shit fit about her seeing Luke, Layla wished he were home to help her sort out her clothing conundrum. But Matt and Ashley were MIA. Holly was out of town. Layla looked at a cotton sundress and shook her head. *If I asked Matt, he probably would have told me to wear a suit of armor.*

Layla reached into the closet with her eyes shut – *okay, wherever my hand lands.* Her fingers brushed the hem of a denim skirt. *It'll have to do.* She pulled out a black shirt to go with it. She caught a glimpse of herself in the mirror. Leopard print panties with a matching demi-bra, not that she intended for Luke to see them, were bad karma for this date. Layla stepped out of the sexy underwear and pulled on a pair of plain white cotton undies and a worn white bra. Then, she put on the skirt and blouse. Her black cowboy boots completed the ensemble. Impulsively, she sprayed on the Tresor that Holly had given her. *It's not for seduction* she told herself, *it's for confidence.*

The doorbell rang just as Layla finished brushing her hair. She experienced a familiar panic. Her clothes were wrong. She'd sound stupid. Her foot slipped on the stairs and she seized the railing, breaking a fingernail in the process.

"Hi," she said as she opened the door, blocking the entranceway with her body. "Let me just get my bag."

"You look great," Luke said, inching into the house.

Layla stepped back.

"Surprise," Luke said showing her several bags, "I brought Chinese." He had enough food to feed six people. Two cartons of soup wobbled on top of the bags

"Oh well...come on in," Layla said, masking her disappointment.

It was happening again. Luke was controlling the situation. Discomfort curled in her belly like a poisonous snake. Slow down, girl, she thought, he's just trying to be nice. "Do you need help carrying that?" She took the soup containers off the top of the stack.

"I got won ton and egg drop," he said. "I couldn't decide which to get and I got two kinds of shrimp." Luke followed Layla to the kitchen. He started unpacking the bags while she reached into the cabinets for plates, tossed silverware onto the table, and then opened the refrigerator to assess the drink situation.

"Pepsi, Diet Pepsi, or Miller Light?" Layla fought her irritation. Fried rice and spring rolls didn't constitute a threat.

"Miller Light. Why don't you put on some music?" Luke arranged the cartons on the table. He took serving spoons from the silverware drawer and put them on top of the cartons.

Layla stopped moving for a second. That *one* action. Luke causally fetching the serving spoons – reminded her how familiar he was with her house, how much he acted like both she and her home were his territory. She rushed to get paper napkins before he rifled through the pantry in search of them. "Has that got everything?"

"I think so," he said, then popped a jazz CD, one of Matt's collection, into the player. Luke sat at the table and filled two plates with food, "You like Moo Shu beef," he said, piling it next to a spring roll, Hunan shrimp, and fried rice.

Layla *didn't* like Moo Shu beef. She took a swallow of beer. Luke was trying hard to please her and she was nit picking. He'd been right weeks ago, she never let up, never gave anyone a break. She smiled and picked up her fork. "Thanks, this is better than going out," she said. "You sure got a lot of food."

"Well, I thought maybe Matt or Holly might be home," Luke mixed the Human shrimp on his plate with the fried rice.

Layla hid her face. She'd been suspicious of Luke since he walked through the door, interpreting his take-out food as part of a plan to be alone with her, and he'd thought that her roommates might be home. The spicy shrimp was tasteless. Layla's throat narrowed, it was difficult for her to swallow the food.

Luke reached across the table and squeezed her hand. "Friends?" He shoved a mouthful of chicken, water chestnuts and rice into his mouth and chewed hastily. "I'm trying, babe. New start and all of that."

The ringing of the telephone interrupted the infant conversation.

"Better get that, babe," Luke said. "It could be your other boyfriend." His laugh was the self-assured sound that Layla dreaded, conveying his certainty that he was the only man putting in a bid on her time.

"More than likely a telemarketer selling light bulbs or cemetery plots," Layla answered.

"Or, maybe a combined deal on both. Worried that the light at the end of the tunnel is burned out? Prevent a bad death experience by taking your own five hundred hour bulb to the after life with you."

Layla giggled and heard Matt's voice leaving word that he'd be at Ashley's all night. Luke stood up and walked to the other side of the table. As he spooned some of the chicken dish onto Layla's plate, bending down he pressed a quick kiss to her neck. "You smell great. Is that the stuff Holly brings you?"

His quick question and rapid return to his seat deflected any comment Layla could have made about the kiss. It was just a friendly peck, anyway. Besides, she was the one who'd dabbed perfume on her neck. "Yeah, she buys it in duty-free." Layla pushed food around her plate like a four year old.

Luke refilled his plate. "I think I read something about duty-free being phased out somewhere. I never can remember what I read."

Okay Layla thought, we have a topic. Now, what can I say about duty-free? "Holly hasn't mentioned it." Uh-oh, that killed the topic. What do I do now? "This shrimp stuff is really good."

Luke kept on chewing. Layla's fork was slippery with her nervous sweat. She ate mechanically, hoping that Luke would say something. The refrigerator motor seemed unnaturally loud, the ticking of the kitchen clock and the sound of a neighbor cutting grass all served as reminders of her inability to talk to Luke. A bug slammed into the kitchen window. Layla watched it.

"How's work going?" She relaxed and took a bite of fried rice.

"Oh, you know, same old, same old." Luke smiled.

Layla continued eating. She wasn't hungry. The music stopped. She thought about putting another CD on, but it seemed too much effort.

Luke rummaged through the bags and containers. He unwrapped four appetizers, meat, and vegetables on small skewers. Popping the top off a small tub of sauce, he said, "You have to try these, they're killer." He leaned over and put a skewer up to Layla's lips.

She took a bite of meat and chewed. Layla nodded to signify that it was good and held out her hand to take the skewer. Moving quickly, Luke was beside her. He picked up her hand and kissed the palm, closing her fingers around the kiss. Bending over her, he licked a stray speck of sauce from her lower lip.

Kneeling beside her chair with one arm on the table, he moved closer. He held a bite of meat between his thumb and forefinger and dipped it into the sauce. "Open up," he said, his voice almost a whisper. Layla opened her mouth and he popped the bite inside. He followed it with a kiss as she swallowed.

He turned her chair slightly so that she faced him. With a hand on either side of her hips, he moved in and gave her a wet kiss, his tongue invading her mouth.

Layla shivered. She turned her head to the side but he followed her mouth, nibbling her lower lip, sucking her tongue. His weight pushed the chair backward until it leaned precariously on two legs for an instant, before it slid out from under her body.

Luke wrapped his arms around her and caught her, lowering her to the kitchen floor.

He crawled on top of her, pressing quick kisses across her face. He covered her cheeks and forehead with kisses. Layla wiggled around, trying to move from beneath him. He held her firmly, arm around her back, hand brushing the top of her hips. With his free hand, he stroked her hair. He rubbed the top of her hips with his fingertips.

This was happening too fast. It was too much like before. She didn't want Luke, not like this. Layla started to speak. Luke seized her open mouth and devoured it. Her words were muffled against his mouth. His tongue darting in and out, he began hunching against her. Layla felt him harden against her belly. She could hardly breathe. His weight crushed her chest. She couldn't free her mouth. Her right arm was caught beneath her own body. With her left hand, she pushed against his chest. Luke grabbed her wrist, his thumb caressed the palm.

Shifting his weight, he got his leg between hers. Layla's skirt bunched up between their bodies. Still kissing her, he moved back and forth, rubbing his leg against her. Layla bucked against him. Initially her movement was resistance. But Luke persisted, his hand rubbing her ass. She was getting wet.

Layla squirmed and twisted. Luke captured both her hands, holding her wrists easily in one hand. Ignoring her protests, he slithered down her belly. Layla pressed her legs tightly together, but Luke pried them apart, then licked her through her panties, She could feel his hot wet tongue moving over her, snaking beneath the elastic leg.

Damn, she didn't want to want him. Layla pushed into his mouth.

She moaned, arching toward him. He released her hands and she stroked his hair. Expertly he pushed her panties down. He sucked, nibbled, licked, and kissed until she screamed. He traced the lines of her sex with his tongue, and then blew lightly on the moist skin. His tongue circled and flitted inside her. His hands captured her breasts. He squeezed them and then made circling motions, teasing her nipples. So sensitive and inflamed that she was close to pain, Layla ground into Luke.

"You know you want it, baby." He altered position again. Propped on his elbows, he moved on top of her. "You've been playing games too long."

Her lust turned to hate.

Still quivering from her orgasm, drenched in self-loathing, Layla shook her head from side to side. She felt him pressing at her entrance and tried to scoot backwards. Fear and anger made her tight.

He pinned her to the floor. The linoleum was cold on her ass and legs. "Don't play that now, baby." His face was feral.

"No, no." She buried her face in his shoulder and bit him. She couldn't free her hands; they were caught beneath her again. "I don't want to." She bit him again.

"Bitch." He slapped her hard across the face. "Tease." He shoved into her so hard and fast that despite her earlier arousal, pain shot through her core.

Eyes wide open, she watched Luke thrust. His face was contorted. He finished pretending to make it good for her. "Bitch, bitch, bitch." His hand twisted in her hair, he jerked and pulled.

Finally, he came, collapsing on top of her.

"Don't start any shit, baby. You wanted it." Luke rolled off. "It was fine when I was eating you, you just don't like playing fair."

Layla pulled her skirt down. "Not like that." She stood up and backed away from him. "I want you to leave. Get the fuck out of my house."

Luke picked up her beer and took a swallow. "I'll leave like I do everything else, when I'm good and ready."

Chinese food cartons spewed their contents over the table. Moo shu beef dripped down onto the floor. The tub of sauce lay on the linoleum, the sauce spreading like blood oozing from a wound. Chicken and vegetables congealed in milky-white fluid.

Layla backed against the wall. "I said get the fuck out of my house."

"And I said that I'd leave when I was good and ready." He set down the beer can; it slipped in sweet and sour sauce, spilling beer onto the floor. He crossed the few feet between them. He covered Layla's breast with his hand and then gave her nipple a sharp twist. She whimpered in pain. "Maybe it's time for desert."

The temperature in the room dropped suddenly.

Layla shook with the unusual chill. Numb with fear, she watched Luke's face, a droplet of saliva clinging to his lower lip, moving closer to her. He tweaked her nipple again. When she tried to move out of his grasp he pulled it sharply.

The room filled with fog.

Ian emerged from the wall.

His stride long and his step emphatic, he grabbed Luke by the throat. Ian's face was hard, his features seemed carved from stone. He flung Luke across the room, knocking over the table, crashing into the refrigerator. Luke sank to the floor.

Ian shouted, an unearthly, indecipherable noise that pierced Layla's ears. He held a large battle-axe over his head. He stood above Luke. "Make your peace with God, man," he said, his voice conveying finality.

Luke's eyes widened. A dark splotch on his jeans told Layla he'd pissed his pants in fear. He was crying now. The only coherent words he managed were, "please, please, please, please."

He was saying 'please' when the axe fell, cleaving his chest in two.

Layla heard the crunch of steel splitting bone. An explosive sound, like a huge balloon popping, followed the thump of metal on cartilage. Bits of bone, white as clouds, rattled onto the floor. Blood seemed to bubble out of Luke's chest.

Still Ian hacked away at the corpse. The hand that had inflicted so much pain on Layla's breast skittered across the floor. A vein in Luke's thigh spurted blood. Intestines erupted across the floor.

The blood darkened, from bright red to rusty burgundy to near black as it splattered across the walls, and seeped from Luke's body. Slivers of flesh, fragments of bone, a hank of hair and a few teeth scattered about the room.

Layla saw a finger on the kitchen counter.

One hand shoved in her mouth, Layla swayed. Blood covered her clothing. She sank to the floor, then crawled on all fours, vomiting until the dry heaves took over. She retched and choked.

Finally, Layla looked up and saw Luke's penis, neatly severed and stuffed in the gaping wound that had been his mouth.

Layla screamed. She screamed until her throat burned and the noise faded to a rasp. Her throat was raw. Her stomach rolled and churned. She curled, wordless and anesthetized, into a fetal position and put her head on what was left of Luke's lap. Blood soaked her hair, relics of Luke, tattered flesh and bone dust, covered her body.

Ian was gone.

Layla laid mute, head on Luke's mangled corpse.

And still hadn't moved at all by the time Matt came home. Two days after the murder.

THIRTEEN

"Oh my God, oh my God," Matt screamed.

Layla saw Matt drop a bottle of wine. She watched it shatter on the floor. She heard him scream. She blinked. He was making a lot of noise. The overhead light glared. Blood and flesh covered the floor. The wine washed through blood, diluting it, a small pink trickle moved around broken glass. Odd, how pretty broken glass looked.

Layla curled up, knees to chest. She wanted Matt to be quiet. It was okay as long as it was quiet.

Matt ran to the fallen table, then back to where Layla cowered. "Oh God, oh God," he repeated. "Oh God, oh God, oh God." His footsteps were heavy. Dishes rattled with the force of his movements. "Layla, precious, what happened? Are you hurt? What happened? Oh God."

Matt bent down and stroked her hair. "It's okay, precious. It's okay. It's going to be okay. Oh God." She cringed at his touch and moved closer to Luke's remains.

Matt jerked upright and raced around the room. He moved to the hallway, and froze. "I won't leave you. We'll get help." He came back into the kitchen and grabbed the phone.

Layla hadn't moved.

She heard him punch three numbers. Who was he calling? She heard him recite their address. He sobbed and babbled, he kept saying oh God. How could the person on the other end understand him? He was hysterical.

He hung up the phone and squatted down next to her. Matt won't sit down, she thought, too messy for Matt. Luke made a dreadful mess. "I've called the police," Matt said.

Layla heard sirens.

Matt got up and ran to the front door. She heard him talking to someone. He still seemed to be saying 'oh God' over and over. More footsteps, she heard a thundering herd, heavy steps, and radio static.

Matt was framed in the doorway, a group of policemen behind him. She heard someone say something about an ambulance. She heard beeps, clicks, and static. Why wouldn't they all go away?

A tall officer put his hand on Matt's shoulder. Matt turned, his hand over his mouth and walked away with the policeman. Layla heard more footsteps. She heard the toilet flush and then heard Matt wailing, "I don't know. I don't know. Oh God."

She shut her eyes.

Layla felt fingers on her shoulder, a light touch. Touch was vile. Touch was evil. She moved slightly to escape the touch. A woman's voice said, "Layla, Layla?" The voice was tentative, as if she wasn't certain that Layla was the right name. Layla opened her eyes and saw a round female face fringed with brown bangs and wearing a cop cap. The woman had big brown eyes ringed in gray eyeliner. Her face was covered with freckles. Layla shut her eyes again. "Layla," the voice repeated.

Layla sighed. She scrunched her eyes tight.

"I think she's in shock," said the female voice. "We need to wait until the ambulance gets here to move her, she may have injuries. It's hard to tell with all the gore." More footsteps, voices in the hall, Layla heard a man say 'ambulance'.

"It's on the way," a male voice said. "Just from CMC so they ought to be here any minute. Jesus. I've never seen a crime scene like this, never."

Another voice, a deeper voice said, "I think the EMTs might need to sedate her roommate or whoever he is. I can't make any sense out of him."

"Just be certain you get prints on him," answered another officer. "Didn't he say something about a boyfriend and another roommate? It sounds like half of Charlotte used this kitchen."

"We've called his boyfriend to come over. The poor guy needs some support," said the female officer. "Can you imagine coming home and finding this?" She held a handkerchief over her nose.

Layla stared at all the shiny shoes. The officers wore lace up oxfords with dark socks. Only the female who'd approached her came into the kitchen. The rest of them hovered in the doorway.

The voices blended into an indiscriminate clamor. Layla concentrated on ferreting out Matt's voice. He seemed to have stopped sobbing. "Luke has always been dangerous. I mean, who knows who or what he was into, I told Layla to stay away from him. I think he sold coke. He was the type. You know, edgy, sociopathic."

Layla heard some more noise, then Matt's voice said, "Oh, no. She absolutely did *not* do coke. Other than Luke, I don't think she knows anyone that would have." The din increased, she heard vague snatches of conversation.

"I don't think they were really dating anymore. They quit dating a few weeks ago. Layla thought they could be friends," Matt said. "They'd had dinner once or twice since they broke up."

Layla heard the female officer's voice, "Just lift her onto the stretcher, and try not to touch anything else in the room." More footsteps.

Six hands were on her body. Layla's muscles tensed. She shut her eyes. Someone was making cooing sounds. Words swirled around her. She was on a stretcher. She straightened her legs and folded her arms across her chest. Layla thought about the EMTs who'd picked up Mazie after the wreck. They'd worn white uniforms; probably these guys were in whites. Stupid uniform color for medical people, all that blood and gore, white gets dirty easily. Layla wondered why they wore white as they carried her out of the house.

She didn't open her eyes in the ambulance. It would have been too much trouble.

The emergency room smelled of Lysol. It was cool. Layla shivered beneath the cotton blanket. She was cold, horribly cold. Not as cold as Luke, she thought. Someone inserted a needle in her arm. Someone tightened a blood pressure cuff around her other arm. The room had no door. She heard the sound of a curtain, suspended on rings, sliding back and forth on a rail. A female voice commanded her to open her mouth. She touched a thermometer with her tongue. A machine beeped.

Someone shut off the beeping, "I have to change your glucose," a voice said. "You're dehydrated."

Dehydrated, Layla thought, how is that? Bodies are full of water, blood, all kinds of fluid. The emergency room was noisy. She kept her eyes shut. They'd stopped asking her questions; that was good. Layla didn't want to talk.

She thought she heard Matt asking, "How is she? When can I see her?"

She didn't hear anyone answer him. Then, she thought she heard Ashley's voice but she couldn't tell what he said, wasn't even sure it was Ashley.

A woman's voice said, "Except for severe dehydration, it doesn't look like there is any physical damage. Of course, we're going to do a rape kit."

Someone told her to put her feet in stirrups. It was easy to obey, easy to do what they wanted as long as she didn't have to open her eyes or speak. Layla put her feet into the stirrups. She felt rough sheets swaddle her legs.

"Scoot your bottom to the end of the table," a female voice said.

Layla pushed her hips to the end of the table. She heard wheels grate against the hospital floor.

"I'm just moving your IV unit down here with you so you don't hurt yourself. Okay, try to relax for me. I'm going to put a swab inside you. It will only take a second and then I'll be done, promise."

Layla felt cold metal down below.

"Come on, sweetie," the female voice said. "Try to relax for me. Exhale."

Layla puffed out air. She felt something stiff and cold move inside her. She screamed. "Stop, stop," Layla shrieked, "get it out of me! Goddamn you get out of me. Get that fucking thing out of me." Her voice carried through out the emergency room.

"It's okay, I'm done now," the female voice said.

Layla continued screaming. Eyes shut, motionless, her feet still in the stirrups, she shrieked and screamed.

She was dimly aware of a cool dab on her upper arm. A pinprick. She screamed – and then she slept.

❖

She awoke disoriented. A silent television, its vacant screen staring sinisterly, hung from a bracket on a bare white wall. On the bedside table were a plastic pitcher and a thermometer in a plastic tumbler. A large sign at the foot of the bed told her the day and date. A needle in the back of her left hand linked her to a plastic bag of fluid.

She sat up and looked around. A small sink with a mirror was to her right; windows covered in Venetian blinds covered the left side of the room. In the armchair near the foot of the bed sat a stranger, a small woman close to Layla's age, wearing a navy blazer and long floral print skirt. Her light brown hair was tied back. She wore wire-rimmed glasses. Layla had no idea who the woman was.

"I'm Addie Johnson. I'm a clinical social worker and I need to ask you a few questions, Layla."

"I don't want to talk to anyone." Layla pulled the blanket over her face.

"Well then, " Addie replied, "we have a joint goal then. Our goal is to get me out of your face. I'm not leaving until we talk a bit. Sorry."

Layla lowered the blanket. She almost smiled.

"I'll start with the stupid questions," Addie said. She had a pen in her right hand and a clipboard on her lap. "Would you mind telling me what day it is?"

"That one's easy, sign on the wall," Layla answered.

"Well, then, would you mind telling me who you are?"

"Another gimme," Layla answered. "You called me Layla, I answered, ergo I'm obviously a woman named after a rock ballad." She shook her legs nervously beneath the bed covers.

"Okay, and for the third pitch, do you have any idea where you are?"

"Well, gosh, Toto, we're not in Kansas anymore. My best guess is that I am in a hospital."

The woman smiled and made notes. "Layla, do you have any idea how you came to be here? And, before you answer, I need to tell you, in the state of North Carolina, I really don't have confidentiality privileges. Do you know what that means?"

"Not really," said Layla.

The woman put down her pen and leaned on her clipboard. "It means that I can be compelled to testify about anything you tell me. If you've been involved in a crime, don't tell me anything you don't want the police to know. If there is any possibility that you could be in trouble, you need a lawyer much more than you need a social worker. Is that clear?"

"I didn't kill him," Layla said. "It's my fault he's dead, but I didn't do it."

"I didn't ask," Addie responded. "Let's go back to the last question, do you know how you got here?" She hadn't picked up her pen.

"An ambulance," Layla said. "Now, if I recall correctly, you go through the do-you-hear-voices-routine."

A flicker of surprise crossed Addie's face. "You know the drill. Have you ever been in a psych hospital?"

"No, but I've played a mental patient on TV." Layla sat up and crossed her legs. "Actually, I saw a busload of shrinks when I was a teenager. My mom was murdered when I was a kid, then a few years later the Department of Social Services took over my life. They sent me to mental health for a while. Outpatient."

"Was therapy useful to you then?" Addie's voice was neutral.

"As much as I'd love to say it wasn't, it probably helped a bit." Layla ran the bedspread through her fingers. "You wouldn't happen to have a cigarette would you?"

"You know, you aren't allowed to smoke in here," Addie said, holding out a crumpled pack of Winstons and a pack of matches. "Wait until I leave. And you didn't get them from me."

Layla hopped out of bed and dragged her IV unit with her to the small closet. "Damn, hasn't Matt brought me clothes yet? I thought I could just go outside and smoke."

"I don't think that's a good idea," said Addie. "You really need to avoid the press, and they're swarming all over the hospital grounds."

Deflated, Layla sank back down on the bed. "I didn't kill Luke. I can't explain what did, but I didn't. I'm responsible. It's my fault. But I didn't do it."

"Don't tell me if there are going to be criminal charges," Addie began.

Layla cried wordlessly. Addie stood up. Layla shuddered. If she hugs me I'll deck her, Layla thought, goddamn social workers always hug you. But Addie walked over to the window and looked out, her back to Layla. "You may as well smoke," Addie said.

Layla filled the plastic tumbler with water and lit a cigarette.

"Thanks."

Addie remained at the window. "It's been difficult for you."

"Difficult? You have a talent for understatement. Do they teach you that in grad school? Sorry. I can't seem to help it. I either don't talk or I say stupid, smart-ass things. I always said stupid things to Luke. Or, I felt stupid whenever he was around. I don't know." Layla sucked in smoke. It made her dizzy. "What are they going to do to me?"

"I don't know," Addie answered. "I honestly don't know."

Layla inhaled greedily. Tears wet her face. She coughed. "Did anyone tell you about Mazie?"

"No, I haven't talked to anyone other than Dr. Hoskins. She said that you were brought in, non-verbal but responsive and that when she did a pelvic exam on you, you lost it. She thinks you're a hysteric. They don't teach ER docs current psychiatric nomenclature."

"Do you think I'm faking something? Is that what hysteric means?"

"That's two questions," Addie said. "No, I don't think you're faking anything. I think you've had significant stress compounded with some real bad luck in your past. If you *weren't* a bit emotional, I'd be more concerned. And, hysteric means, to Dr. Hoskins, throwing a fit in her nice tidy emergency room." Addie paced back and forth, she didn't turn to look directly at Layla. "So tell me about this Mazie."

"She was a girl. She was kind of starting to date a friend of mine, she and I were at a party, and she accidentally threw spaghetti all over me. Anyway, she gave me a ride home and we had an argument, so I told her to get the fuck out of my house." Layla's voice broke. "She did and she ran her car head-on into a tree right outside my front door. Killed instantly." Layla drew her knees up to her chest, folded her arms on top of them, and put her face down. Addie didn't move while Layla cried. After a few minutes, Layla raised her head. She dropped the cigarette in the water glass. "People around me just die, they die horribly. My daddy had mama's blood all over him when he woke me up to tell me she was gone."

Addie jammed her hands inside the pockets of her blazer. Layla lit another cigarette.

"Mazie had this weird curiosity about my mom. I yelled at

her because she was going through the stuff on my dressing table. She picked up a picture of my mom. It sounds silly, but I don't like anyone messing in my stuff. Especially stuff that has to do with Mama."

"You felt invaded," Addie said.

Layla nodded. "Isn't this where you tell me that none of this is my fault? That I didn't kill my mother. I didn't cause Mazie's car wreck. I didn't kill Luke."

"Would it help if I said those things?"

Addie's ponytail was beginning to come loose. Layla wondered how long the social worker had sat in the room waiting for her to awaken. "No," she said, "it wouldn't help. It wouldn't change anything. I had an argument with mom the day she died. Matt's the only person I ever told about that. I wanted to go out on a single date. I was fourteen, I was allowed to group date. I wasn't allowed to single date, or go on a car date. The guy I liked was older. He had his driver's license. I begged mom to let me go. She said I couldn't. I was a real brat. I sort of knew what she was up to, I mean, *everyone* knew, but no one talked about it. I called her a whore. She slapped me. That was the last time I talked to mom."

Addie stood, hands still in pockets. "Tell me," she said softly.

"Luke slapped me, too. Right before...the thing...*happened* ...the thing that killed him." Layla's voice was flat. "I don't want to talk about it."

"You don't have to," Addie said.

"What then?" Layla fidgeted with her cigarette.

"Well, you can talk about whatever you like."

"Do you know if anything is physically wrong with me?"

"Not much," Addie answered, "You were badly dehydrated when they brought you in. You've got some nasty bruises and there's some internal injuries that Dr. Hoskins will discuss with you. Did this Luke rape you?" Addie's voice was matter of fact, as if she was asking Layla if it was raining.

"I don't know," Layla answered, shaking her head. "I'm not bullshitting you. I really don't know." Layla squirmed around. "I'll really have to think about that." Layla stared at the wall for a moment. "If not all that much is wrong with me, why I am in the hospital?"

"I suspect that they want to observe and make certain that

not that much is wrong." Addie's voice trailed off.

"And, they think I'm crazy."

Addie twisted her right foot in its neat navy leather pump. Her hands pushed on the blazer pockets.

"Come on, " Layla said. " You've been straight up so far."

"Well...yes, there is that," Addie answered. "I think they may want you to spend a few days over in the pscyh hospital."

Layla looked at the neat center part in Addie's shiny hair, watched her draw a circle on the floor with the toe of her shoe, watched Addie bite a hangnail. "And, you're going to recommend that they do that, aren't you?"

The social worker raised her head and made eye contact with Layla. "I think that's what I should do."

"It's okay." Layla forced a smile. " Just bring me Marlboros, all right?"

Addie nodded.

"And can you fix it so that I can talk to you? If I have to put up with some menopausal bag hugging me, I'll flip."

"I'll be your social worker," Addie said. She picked up her clipboard. "I'll see you tomorrow."

FOURTEEN

Layla plunged the plastic spoon into the congealed salad and smushed it around petulantly. She picked up her plastic knife and hacked away at the gravy covered mystery meat. The small cup of coffee was tepid. The surface of the milk carton felt warmer than the coffee. She wasn't hungry. Layla destroyed the meal like a four year old admonished to clean her plate before going outside to play.

The heavy door swung open, banging against the robber doorstop. Layla looked up from her food expecting an aide with a blood pressure cuff or someone coming to retrieve her lunch tray.

Two policemen in uniform marched into her room.

"Am I under arrest?" She'd almost expected this.

"No, ma'am," the younger of the two said. He looked like a kid in a costume; he appeared younger than Layla by at least five years. "We're here to take you over to Mecklenburg Mental Health Hospital for an evaluation."

"Well, okay," Layla said. "They didn't have to send you guys. I said I'd go." What had Addie gone and done? Had she been stupid to trust her?

"We have a petition for involuntary commitment, Ma'am," the kiddie cop said. "I'm real sorry, but I'm going to have to ask you to let me put these handcuffs on you."

Layla cringed back into the pillows for an instant. "What is that all about? I told Addie I'd go over there."

"Ma'am, I don't know who Addie is. The petitioner is a Mr. Matthew Ledford. Now, if you'll just let me have your hands please."

"Matt?" she shrieked. "Matt signed those papers?" Suddenly Layla felt cornered and betrayed. Intending to simply get up, she moved suddenly. The young officer put a restraining hand on her arm. "Don't touch me," she yelled, "Goddamn it, don't you touch me!" Layla flipped the lunch tray up in the air. Lime green congealed salad splattered the front of the young officer's uniform.

He jerked her out of bed and pulled her hands together, shackling her wrists.

The older officer looked bored. "I told you about crazies," he said. "They can go off on you without warning."

Shoeless and wearing only a hospital gown, Layla was mortified. "Please, can I put on some more clothes?"

"You should've thought of that before you went off." The young cop's tone was belligerent now.

"Calm down, missy," the older officer said. Approaching her gingerly, he wrapped another gown across her back and tied it beneath her chin. "That ought to keep you covered." He opened the closet door and took the jeans and t-shirts that Matt had brought and stuffed them into a plastic bag.

"I'm barefoot," Layla said.

The older officer got out her boots and put them in front of her. Layla shoved her left foot into a boot. She slipped and crashed into the bed.

The younger cop grabbed her arm, his tight grasp cutting off her circulation. "Act right," he said.

"Don't touch me," she screamed. "Keep your goddamn hands off me!"

The older man looked out the door to the hallway. With a quick glance at his partner, the younger man responded, "Act right." He gave Layla a hard shake, then dragged her from the room. She limped along on one boot with the dual hospital gowns fluttering. All the doors on the corridor were closed. The aides must have run up and down the hallway shutting them before the officers came into her room. They moved swiftly to a service elevator and went to the basement.

They dragged Layla through the hallways, past the basement pharmacy and the morgue. She blinked in the sunlight when the older officer opened a door. The squad car sat right outside. Hand on her arm, the officer prodded her into the backseat.

Layla stared straight ahead through the screen that divided the front seat from the back as the police car passed her house. The officer drove through streets that Layla habitually traveled. The car passed over Briar Creek and turned down Wendover. Layla thought about convicted felons riding to prison, did *they* gaze hungrily at the world, or was it to painful to say good-bye? Maybe I'll find out, she thought. I didn't kill anyone, but I *am* responsible.

Mecklenburg Mental Health Hospital was a gigantic, sprawling light brick edifice covering several acres of prime real estate. The building bridged two worlds. The squad car traveled down Randolph Road, site of old homes valued in the high hundred thousands, and turned down Billingsley Ave, passing the Kuralt Building which housed the Department of Social Services. Behind the hospital nestled the public housing developments, elderly frame houses, and crack dens of Griertown, one of Charlotte's worse neighborhoods. The nearby Taco Bell had closed following repeated robberies, and children roamed the potholed streets near midnight.

The squad car crawled over the speed bumps in the parking lot. They drove up to the Emergency entrance. Kiddie cop hopped out, swaggering slightly as he yanked Layla from the car. "She's ready to go live, watch it," he said to the county security officer who met them.

"Pull on over to police parking and bring her inside," the county officer replied. He smelled of beer, his uniform was wrinkled.

Layla limped along on one boot and one bare foot between the two city officers. The older officer and Layla waited in uncomfortable plastic chairs while the younger cop strutted up to the desk. Next to Layla sat a chubby boy, about eight years old, picking boogers from his nose and smearing them beneath his seat. The woman with the child read a dog-eared copy of *Glamour* magazine.

Several seats over, an emaciated young man, bangs flopping in his face, shouted, "Yeah, and that's what the liberal, running-dog, fascist lackey media *want* you to think. They want you to think that whoever you elect is whoever you elect, but once elected they become *the* elect. You know what that means."

A middle-aged woman who sat next to him rummaged

through her cracked vinyl handbag. "You want to go out for a cigarette?"

"Don't try diversionary tactics with me," he shouted. "Don't you think I know who pays you?"

A slim woman with multiple scars criss-crossing her wrists walked up to the desk and rapped on it with her skeletal fist. "I've been waiting for hours," she said. "I haven't slept in years. You people don't seem to care." She had a streak of emerald green sprayed into her mousy brown hair.

The kiddie cop wore a look of disgust. "I'm really sorry, officer," said a woman with an auburn page boy haircut. "You'll have to wait with everyone else."

The young policeman stomped across the waiting room. Standing in front of Layla, he spoke to the older officer, "Like all we have to do is pick up crazies."

"We're on the clock," the older officer said. "Just sit and don't sweat it." He picked up an old copy of *Sports Illustrated* and paged through it.

"Well, I'm going to go check the radio and see what's happening," the kiddie cop said, leaving the older officer with Layla while he went outside.

It was over an hour before a tall woman with a bad perm and bright pink lipstick called the older officer up to the desk, "We'll see the patient now, but you can't leave until the doctor makes a decision. You understand? She's your responsibility."

The younger cop had still not returned from his foray into the parking lot to 'check the radio'.

Layla followed her to a small, windowless room. The woman held a sheaf of papers. Layla sat in another plastic chair. She noticed that the lamp on the particleboard desk was bolted to it.

"You've been having a rough time," the woman began.

"I want to talk to Addie," Layla said. "She's my social worker."

"You can see her once you're on the unit. I have to ask you a few questions and then Dr. Caldwell will see you." The woman didn't look up from her papers. Layla spotted several wiry gray hairs sticking up on top of her head.

"Okay, I know who I am, where I am, and what day it is. The only voice I hear is yours. Any more questions?" Layla wanted a cigarette.

"Look, we're trying to help you. Your boyfriend is concerned that you might try to hurt yourself." The woman's voice sounded bored.

"He's not my boyfriend," Layla said.

"Well, anyway. Your friend seems concerned that you might hurt yourself. Can you tell me about that?"

"Ask him," Layla said. "Look, if you'll just get these handcuffs off me, I'll sign myself in. This is absurd. Who the hell can act sane when you have them dragged out of bed by Barney Fife and brought over here without even letting them get dressed?"

"The officer reports that you became combative and threw things at him."

"Yeah, well, that's *his* story," Layla said. Talking to the woman seemed pointless.

"Would you like to tell me your side of it?" The woman still had not looked up from her papers. She wrote the entire time she spoke.

Layla turned her face to the wall. It was easy to stop speaking.

"Isn't there anything you'd like to tell me?" The woman's papers rattled.

Layla didn't answer. In a minute or so, the woman got up and left the room. Layla sat in the chair; through the open doorway, she could see people rushing past.

Finally, a short young man with dark circles beneath his eyes rushed in; the ubiquitous stack of papers in his left hand. "Good afternoon," he said. "I'm Dr. Caldwell." He held out his right hand for a handshake.

Layla glanced at his hand and then looked pointedly at her shackled wrists.

"Oh...I see." The doctor cleared his throat. "I'm sorry."

Layla shrugged.

"Now, Layla, could you tell me a little bit about how you come to be here today? Miss Tragotti seems to feel that some difficulties you are experiencing might make you dangerous to yourself. Would you like to tell me about that?" He sat down and leaned forward. He made eye contact with her and smiled.

Layla thought that all his movements seemed rehearsed. She imagined him in shrink school learning things like 'Trustworthy

Expression Number 653' and 'Caring, Compassionate Voice Tone Number 138'. She decided not to speak.

"Well then, we'll see if we can't get you feeling more like talking in a few days," he said. He scrawled something on the papers. The tall woman reappeared and took the papers, then scurried off with them. "We really can help," he said.

Yeah, right, Layla thought. I've been abducted by the reality police and transported to Hotel Silly, and my best friend is the bastard that did this to me. Not so incidentally, I have a resident ghost with a homicidal streak protecting me right into prison. Yeah, you're gonna fix *this* with Prozac.

The doctor left the room without a backward glance. Two men in scrub jackets and jeans replaced him. One of them said, "We're here to take you up to the unit, as soon as we can find the officer with the key to those cuffs. If you'll just be patient with us, we'll try to have you out of them as soon as possible."

Layla didn't feel like talking. She looked up at the men, smiled, and nodded. One of them disappeared and returned with the older cop. "I think my partner already left, how much longer will it be before you decide what you're going to do with her?"

"If you'll just unlock the cuffs on this young lady, sir, you'll be free to go."

The officer swung the cuffs with a flourish before hooking them back on his belt.

Layla stood and followed the two men. They passed down a corridor toward a key operated elevator. One of the men consulted the inevitable clipboard of papers. "I don't think those idiots down at Emergency Admitting even bothered to tell Addie that a patient of hers was brought in."

The other man nodded, "Yeah they do about as little as they have to."

A garbled message blared over the loudspeaker, something about the parking lot and the word "Stat."

One of the men gently pulled Layla back against the wall of the hallway as three men in white ran past.

She heard a siren, or *thought* she did.

A woman in street clothes rolled a cart of file folders down the hall, "Weirdest thing, an officer in the parking was sitting in his patrol car and..."

"Shhh!" One of the men tilted his head toward Layla. "Don't talk about it in the hallway."

The woman glanced at Layla and moved on.

"Some people," said the man. He guided Layla through the hall. She heard the voices of white clad, name tagged people. Their words swirled and flowed around her: dead... freak accident... maybe a knife...why didn't his partner?

Don't think.

The voices dimmed when they got on the elevator. When the elevator doors opened, Layla saw an elderly woman, so scrawny that the miniscule amount of meat on her bones seemed to flutter inside a baggy dress wrong-side-out. She stood in front of the elevator urinating. Over by the nurses' desk, a plump young woman stared impassively at the floor while kneading her own breast. Layla heard screams, wild laughter, and cursing.

She didn't want to get off the elevator. Layla followed the men to the charge nurse's desk where they handed over her papers and left. The nurse efficiently took her vital signs, weighed her and left her in a small windowless room. Layla quickly put on her clothes and sat down on the single bed. She poked her head out into the hallway where a toothless woman wearing a plaid skirt, a striped shirt, and backless bedroom slippers was picking at lint and threads.

Layla backed into her room.

She listened to the drone of hall noise. Layla thought she heard Addie's voice, she ran to the doorway, nearly colliding with the small woman.

"Whoa," said Addie, stepping back. "I hear you're not talking today."

"Well, not to some people. Can you explain this shit?" Layla sat cross-legged on the bed. "And where in the hell do you go to have a cigarette here?"

"Come on, let's go to my office, you can smoke there." Addie turned, her ankle length skirt billowing out, and walked quickly out of the room. Layla trotted beside her.

Once they negotiated the elevators and hallways to Addie's office and Layla was settled in a wicker chair, Addie handed her an empty soda can. "Ashtray," she said.

"I take it this is a smoke-free facility."

"There's a smoking area in the hospital unit. The rest of the building is no smoking." She spun around in her desk chair and punched buttons on her phone. "So we won't be interrupted," she explained. "Okay, here's the deal. I heard from Matt and your Dad this afternoon."

"My Dad?" Layla's mouth dropped open. "And who the hell dialed the phone for him?"

"Let me finish. The District Attorney is hot to charge you with murder. Apparently, your Dad took his hat in his hand and paid a call on Wendell Thompson. Mr. Thompson has agreed to represent you. He'll be by to visit you this evening. As your lawyer, he felt it was best to have you here. He thinks it will be easier to keep you out of jail. Since Matt had recent contact with you and your Dad hasn't, Matt had to sign the petition for involuntary commitment."

"Why couldn't they just let me sign myself in? I told you I was willing." Layla inhaled and flicked ashes into the soda can.

"Because Mr. Thompson says that if you are here on an involuntary that it's less likely they'll move to arrest you quickly. If you signed yourself in, you could sign yourself out whenever you liked."

Layla pushed at the floor setting the rocker in motion. Addie's office overlooked a small garden outside the outpatient section of the clinic. The summer sun had scorched the hostas, impatiens wilted in the heat. She examined the office. No personal photos, just some anonymous pictures of landscapes. A clean stoneware coffee cup on the edge of the desk was the closest thing to a personal touch. "Hey, your desk lamp isn't bolted down," Layla said.

"Excuse me?" Addie looked puzzled.

"In the emergency area they bolt the lamps to the desks," Layla said. "Don't you get dangerous lunatics in this end of the building?"

Addie appeared to consider Layla's comment seriously. "Actually, it's the alleged normal people who are more likely to be dangerous."

"What about me? Didn't you just say I might be charged with murder? Aren't I dangerous?" Layla's cigarette sputtered out in the dregs of the soda.

"I don't think you're dangerous," Addie tore at her cuticle and bit her lip. "Mr. Thompson said some other things. He said that he's looked through the crime scene investigation, the autopsy report, and a preliminary forensic report. You couldn't have killed Luke. It isn't physically possible."

Layla twisted and stared out the window. She pushed off the floor, setting the chair to speedy rocking. "Can I smoke another cigarette before I go back to the snake pit?"

"Sure," Addie said. "You know what I think? I think someone else was there, and that someone else killed Luke and that you're scared. I think that's why you choose to stop talking sometimes. I also think something else could be true. I think maybe whatever happened there was so horrible that you don't know *who* was there or really recall what happened. That could be true. Help me out here, Layla, which is it?"

"Sorry, wrong number." Layla lit her second cigarette.

"It really isn't important for you to tell me what went on," Addie said. "But, it's really important that you tell your lawyer what you do remember."

"You know why he's helping me, don't you?" Layla blew a smoke ring. "Damn," she said. "Did you see that? I hardly ever get them right."

"I presumed that he and your Dad were old friends or something."

"Not that simple. Start drooling, Addie, this one is a Freudian feast. Mr. Thompson's wife killed my mother." Layla leaned back and rocked. The social worker looked stunned. "May Thompson got off. She walked. And, by the way, don't let your supervisor see that expression. You just flunked the 'Maintains Neutral Expression' bit."

Addie straightened her glasses. "Are you comfortable with Mr. Thompson as your attorney?"

"He's doing it for free, isn't he?" Layla rocked back and forth.

"I believe so," Addie said.

"Well, the price is right."

FIFTEEN

"Salmon with mango chutney, green beans almondine and mashed potatoes," Matt announced unwrapping the plate and placing a cloth napkin to the left of it. "They won't let you have real silverware, so the plastic will have to do. It's common knowledge that one serves white wine with fish, but I'm afraid that it will have to be Pepsi." Matt arranged the food and withdrew a small plastic container, which he filled with water from a drinking fountain. He stuck a small bouquet of daisies in it, then sat across the Formica topped table and looked intently at Layla.

"Mashed potatoes?" She prodded them with a plastic fork.

"Plebian, I know, but you need the starch. You're wasting away. You look like you weigh around ninety eight pounds." Matt drummed on the table; he was fidgeting more than usual, his eyes darting around the room. "Forgive me, precious?"

"Of course I do. My God, you were trying to keep me out of jail." Layla took a bite of potato and chewed. Matt relaxed as soon as she spoke. She glanced at her hand, pale and sickly under the hideous fluorescent lighting that gave everyone corpse-like skin tones. "Did you bring my make-up?"

"Be still, my fluttering heart." Matt put his hand on his chest and fluttered his eyelashes in an exaggerated imitation of a southern belle. "Did you bring my make-up? Words I've longed to hear." He popped the top on his own soda and took a swallow. "Yes – make-up, navy blue knit dress and appropriate foot wear. But the watchdogs of your psyche would not let me bring moisturizer or jewelry. I don't get it. I'd go barking mad without proper skin care. What's with the blessed but sudden interest in appearance?"

"I'm meeting with my lawyer." Layla took a bite of salmon. "Hey, this is great."

"I keep telling you I can cook. Ashley should marry me." Matt leaned across the table monitoring each bite that went into Layla's mouth. They were alone in the visitor's room. The TV in the corner was silent. The rest of the patients were in group therapy or Arts & Crafts. Layla's legal situation excused her from most group activities. Addie had explained that it wasn't fair or realistic to expect the other patients to keep Layla's information confidential. "So, this lawyer knew your mom, didn't he? Is that why you want to look good?"

"I *have* a therapist, Matt. I don't need you to be one." Layla shoved her green beans around. She was losing her appetite. It seemed to happen after a few bites.

"You're not eating. I'm not a therapist, I'm a Jewish mother trapped in the body of a gorgeous young gay man. Eat, eat, models in New York are starving."

With Matt's eyes on her, Layla ate the salmon. She cut off bites with her fork and dipped the fish into the mango chutney. "It'd be easier to eat if the disinfectant and piss smell didn't override every other available sensory experience here."

"Is it that horrible?" Matt looked worried.

"Not as bad as jail. Will you bring me the books by my bed tomorrow? Just the whole pile. I really will go nuts here if I don't have something to read. There's only so many times I can re-read two year old copies of *People* magazine." Layla finished off most of the salmon and potatoes.

"You did well," Matt said as he packed up the plates. "I'll bring you your books."

In the corner of the visitor's room, Layla saw the outline of Ian's form. By the window, just a shadow, a dark wavering shade. She gasped and stared, transfixed and fearing what was to come. The outline of the Scotsman appeared for milliseconds, then he stood there, translucent. Ian glimmered briefly and was gone.

Matt packed up the plates. Layla stood and leaned into his hug, holding him tight. "Ashley is a fool if he doesn't love you," she said, speaking into his shoulder. Matt held onto to her and rocked her back and forth.

"Tomorrow?" He picked up the satchel with the plate

and napkin.

"Yeah, I reckon I'll be here."

He ruffled her hair and left. Layla sat at the table and looked at the far corner. Ian wasn't there. Gathering the bags with her clothing and make up, she retreated to her room to prepare for the visit from the attorney.

Returning to her room, Layla shook the knit dress and then hung it in the small closet. Standing in front of the sink, she scrutinized her face. She saw no real resemblance to her mother, a resemblance Mazie claimed to have seen. Same eye color, same hair color, but her mother had a different attitude; a dark sensual magic had infused her features. Shaking a bottle of foundation, Layla poured a blob into her palm. Carefully she dabbed it around her face, then sponged it evenly over her skin. She patted powder on top of the liquid make up.

Using a brush, she smeared blush across her cheekbones. Shit, I look like a clown. She rubbed off the blush with a scrap of tissue. That'll have to do, she thought. After applying a minuscule amount of mascara, Layla rubbed a clear gloss on her lips.

Mama had sat down in front of the dressing table to 'do' *her* face. Mama had gone through a half hour production culminating in a spritz of perfume and a kiss thrown to her own mirrored reflection. Layla wondered what had happened to Mama's silver hairbrush and mirror. So many of Mama's personal things had disappeared after she died.

Maybe Daddy Useless pawned them.

It was eight o'clock when an aide escorted Layla to a small, anonymous office to meet with her attorney. Suddenly shy, she paused in the doorway gazing at Wendell Thompson. He was still an attractive man, his thick hair graying at the temples; his lined face full of what effusive magazine writers would call 'character.' His eyes were bright blue in his tanned face. His firm belly and trim waistline spoke of hours spent in a gym.

Layla thought of her father, of his blood shot eyes, the broken capillaries that rubbished his skin, the slump of his shoulders. Daddy had been a good-looking man once. Her shyness faded, replaced by anger. "So, how's your wife?"

Thompson looked up from the papers he studied. "She's well, thank you." His tone and face betrayed nothing.

Layla knew she'd been put in her place. She slunk into the

room and wilted into a chair. Thompson closed his leather briefcase with an ostentatious snap of the hardware.

"Thank you for being willing to help me," she said in a soft voice. She laced her hands together to conceal their trembling. Thompson nodded in response to her statement. He smelled of clean scented soap and the freshly laundered aroma of detergent. His fingernails were neatly trimmed and buffed to a gloss.

"I am assuming that you didn't kill Luke," Thompson said. His look seemed calculating to Layla, she felt as if every iota of her skin, each strand of her hair was being evaluated.

"Well, I didn't actually kill him." She pressed her hands together. Layla felt sweat in her armpits, in the crease of her knees, and beneath her hair at the nape of her neck.

"Good," the lawyer said. His smile seemed artificial to Layla, it seemed like a used smile, one he pulled out as the occasion demanded. "Now, tell me about your relationship with Luke."

Layla turned her head to the side. She expected to see Ian, but he didn't manifest. "I don't know where to begin."

"How long had you and this young man been acquainted?"

"Well, I guess I've really known Luke about three years. No, not 'known'. But I met him three years ago when he worked with a friend of mine. He started hanging out with the same group of people I hang with, but not always. Just from time to time. I'd see him at parties and stuff." Layla tried to sort out the details of the relationship in her own mind.

"And the two of you became a couple how long ago?"

"I suppose we started dating about a year and half ago. Luke was still seeing other people for about three months, then we more or less became a couple until about two months ago."

Thompson leaned forward. "What happened then, two months ago?"

"I felt like we were going nowhere. Luke just assumed I'd be willing to see him whenever, but I wanted a more...a more conventional boyfriend-girlfriend thing." Layla's eyes teared up. "I was tired of waiting all night to see if he'd pay attention to me and he drank a lot. He was mean when he drank."

"Did he get violent with you?"

"Not really. Not while we were dating." Layla wished she knew what he wanted to hear.

"What does 'not really' mean?"

"He only hit me once." Layla's tone was defensive. "After we broke up, and I pushed him into it."

Thompson looked like a man who discovered a scratch on a brand new Mercedes. "You were angry at him?"

"No," Layla said, her voice louder than she'd intended. "No, not at all. That was about six or seven weeks ago, we didn't see each other again for about three weeks, we'd just started going out again when Luke died."

He offered her a Kleenex from the box on the desk. "So, at the time of his death, you were his girlfriend?"

"Not really, we were just seeing each other as friends."

He paused for a minute. "So, you really don't know much about his other friends, anyone else he might have dated during the last few months?"

Layla shook her head no.

"I hate to go into this, but I'm afraid I have to I need you to tell me everything about the night Luke died." He leaned back in his chair.

A few tears eroded what was left of Layla's make-up. "We had plans to get together. Luke came by about six thirty, he brought Chinese food. We had dinner. We talked about things." Layla folded her arms across her chest and stared at her lap. "We fooled around a little bit."

After several seconds elapsed, Thompson asked, "Did you have intercourse?"

"Kind of. Well, yes. I think so," Layla felt panic erupting in her chest. Her heartbeat accelerated. She pursed her mouth shut.

Taking his cue from her facial expression Thompson said, "Was it consensual?"

Layla exhaled a gigantic gust of air. "I don't know."

"You don't *know?*"

"Well, I started out wanting to. . . I mean, I wanted to fool around, I guess. But, things happened so fast that I'm not sure I really wanted to have sex." Layla's breathing was ragged. "I don't think I did. I got angry. I told him to leave."

"Then?"

"Then...Luke was killed." Layla wished she was invisible. She wished she could make herself shrink into the chair and disappear. How could she tell him a ghost killed Luke?

Had a ghost killed Luke or had she invented Ian?
Don't think.
"Who else was there?"
"What do you mean?"

Thompson wore a no-nonsense expression; compassion was erased from his stern face. "Layla, *you* could *not* have killed Luke. He was viciously hacked to death by someone with enormous strength. His bones were splintered, his internal organs beaten to a pulp. He wasn't even recognizable as human when they were finished with him. I understand fear. You were obviously frightened. So frightened that you stayed by his corpse for over forty-eight hours. Now, who was it? What did you see?"

Layla shook her head. She was cold, so very cold.

Thompson shifted gears. Layla was fascinated by the way the lawyer's masks and identities morphed. He spoke softly, "Of course, you're traumatized. You've been unable to speak for much of the time since this horrible incident occurred. You've stared in the face of your own death, known fear the nature of which most people never face."

She didn't speak.

"Is it possible that you really don't remember?"

Layla seized his question gratefully. "I really don't. I don't know what happened." It was more believable than the truth.

"Amnesia is a bad defense," Thompson mused. "Juries tend to think it's too convenient. See if you can remember anything. Maybe therapy will help you recall something. Right now, all that stands between you and an arrest for murder is the fact that you couldn't have exerted that much physical force."

Layla cringed. He was going to help her, but he wasn't on her side. She could feel his contempt like a physical presence in the room. Had he been disdainful of her mother? Had he made love to Mama while he condemned her for being a slut? Had he been like Luke, screaming, "Bitch" while he fucked her?

"Let me make it easier for you to understand," he said, standing up and straightening his jacket. "I hope that you won't even be charged. If you are, I need to construct a story sympathetic to my case. A terrified woman who remains mute out of fear is a sympathetic story. An angry, vengeful girlfriend who won't identify the murderer is suspect – maybe she set the victim up, maybe she orchestrated his death." Thompson picked up his briefcase and walked briskly out of the room, leaving the door open. "Think about it. See what you recall. Good evening."

Layla sat in the chair until an aide finally noticed her alone in the office. The aide was a short plump little woman with shoulder length hair that fell in movie star waves. "Layla. Layla," the aide said, "don't you know how to get back to your hall from here?" Her voice was kinder than most of the voices in Hotel Silly. "Come on, I'll take you back, your lawyer sure was here a long time. I bet you're exhausted. Lawyers can wear you out. I had one when I was in a car wreck and he made me tired."

Layla let the woman's words wash over her as she walked.

"Yeah," the aide continued, "even when they're on your side they can worry you half to death. 'Are you sure that happened? What about this?' They go on until Christmas if you let them."

Layla thought about Thompson's insistence that someone else had been in her house the night Luke died. She saw herself becoming the white woman's OJ, hanging out on talk shows babbling about 'the real killer' ad infinitum. Layla couldn't suppress a giggle. Shit, she thought, I can't walk around giggling over nothing; people will think I'm crazy. Wait a minute; I'm in the nuthouse. If I can't act crazy here, where can I act crazy?

"Here we are," said the aide when they reached Layla's room. It wasn't the woman's fault, she was doing a miserable second shift job, and she'd tried to be kind. Layla didn't want to speak, but she smiled.

She took off the knit dress and pulled on a worn t-shirt. Layla stepped out of her shoes and panties. After scrubbing off the remnants of her make-up, she brushed her teeth. The aide's cheery voice informed her that, "Lights go out in fifteen minutes, hon." Layla nodded as the aide trundled off down the hallway.

She shut off the light and sat on the foot of the bed. The institutional sheets were abrasive against her bare thighs. They reeked of strong bleach. Longing for a cigarette, Layla listened to the rhythm of the air conditioning. The lights in the hallway dimmed. The crepe soled shuffle of staff shoes faded. She overheard voices; they were discussing a carton of black cherry yogurt left in the staff refrigerator.

Damn it, Ian. You owe me an explanation, she thought. Then, quickly tensed. How *could* she, how *dare* she demand an explanation? He was amoral, wasn't he? Or at least, the rules she knew, the things she believed, didn't apply to him. Or, maybe Ian was evil; maybe this was all some form of amusement for him. After all, the centuries must pass slowly when you're dead.

Maybe Ian didn't even exist?

Don't think.

Layla's eyes adjusted to the half-light of third shift. She lit a cigarette, how much trouble could she be in? She smoked slowly, not even bothering to wave the trail of smoke away from the ceiling mounted smoke detector. Nothing happened. She flicked her ashes on the floor. When she was done, she scooped up ashes and butt, depositing them in the drawer of the bedside table. She heard someone walking down the hall, footsteps accentuated by the rattle of keys. Whoever it was walked by without glancing into her room. So, much for surveillance.

Damn it, Ian. Explain this. All right, she thought, Culloden, fucking Culloden, a bloody fucking wasteland, the death of Scotland. But, me, what about me? What about *my* life here, in *this* century?

Layla tried to synchronize her breathing to the air conditioning. She wanted to calm down. She didn't want to lie awake, ranting against a ghost.

It didn't work. She panted and wheezed and continued to rail against him in her mind.

Damn it Ian, why?

He stepped from the shadows in the achromatic half-light, the colors of his plaid muted, his hair unearthly bright. Layla felt the now-familiar chill, followed by a piercing of lust both hot and bittersweet. "Damn you, Ian," she whispered. "Damn you."

"Damned I am indeed," he said. Then he laughed, a rich, pure sound unlike Layla's bitter laughter, unlike the mad laughter of the lunatics down the hall. Ian laughed like a very young man who knows that life and love lay before him.

It was the saddest sound Layla had ever heard.

She watched him laugh and cursed him for his relentless beauty. It wasn't fair for a man, a ghost, to be so compelling, so perfect in his entirety that she lost the capacity to think. Layla knew that if she described him she could never explain exactly what about him made her wet with longing and crazy with desire. His features were flawed, he was too thin, and there was something sad about him, but it was the total, not the separate parts that drew her.

Ian abruptly stopped laughing and stared at her, "It wasn't Culloden. It was the bloody aftermath." The room grew colder; a dreadful roar seemed to fill the air. "My Maggie," he said. "They raped her. Then left her to die."

Layla felt her heart creep up her chest and clog her throat. She could scarcely breathe. "Is that why?"

She couldn't speak any more but it didn't matter whether or not she could speak. She was all alone in the room.

SIXTEEN

"I need to tell you a little bit about how I work," Addie said. "I say things like 'it seems to me' or 'it looks like' and I have to trust you to tell me when I'm wrong. If I say that it seems that something makes you sad, or angry or that I think you are avoiding something, I need you to tell me if that's right or wrong. If you don't do that, I can't help you. Therapy isn't an exact science. I can't read your mind."

"Does it seem to you that I want a cigarette?" Layla pulled a crumpled pack of Marlboros out of the waistband of her jeans.

"It seems to me like you always want a cigarette," Addie answered. "It also seems that whenever we get close to discussing any emotion you've ever had, you bring up cigarettes or make a joke." Addie handed Layla an empty soda can. She rocked back and forth in her desk chair, her paisley skirt twirling around her booted ankles.

Layla lit the cigarette and watched the smoke drift upwards. She waited for Addie to say something else. Silence made Layla anxious, she wanted to fill it with a joke, but after what Addie had just said she would have felt stupid about doing that.

But Addie didn't speak.

"Okay," Layla said, "I can't really talk about how I feel a lot of the time because I don't *know* how I feel. I don't think most people do, I think they just *say* that they feel whatever it's socially acceptable to feel at a particular moment. Like those screaming idiots on television talk shows, there is a cultural agreement that if your boyfriend screws around, you feel angry, or if someone insults you, you're angry. It's like all those people saying they care, what does that mean?"

"We aren't talking about most people," Addie said. "We're talking about you."

"All right. I don't know how I felt about Luke because it kept changing. I'd be angry one minute, hurt the next and then I'd feel guilty because of how I acted. I don't know how I feel about my job. I hate it one minute and other times I think it's pretty okay."

"Feelings aren't static," Addie said.

"So, how is talking about them going to help me remember what happened the night Luke died?"

"I think that if you need to remember what happened, you will," Addie said. "I don't know any card tricks that will make you remember."

"I thought that was what ya'll did, made people remember stuff they repressed." Layla fidgeted in the chair. It wasn't a question of recall. She'd be damned if she'd tell anyone what happened the night Luke died.

"No," Addie said shaking her head, " all I want to do is help you function, help you move forward to lead the best life you can in the future."

"It's not going to be much of a life if I have to spend it in prison."

"You're scared," Addie said.

"You're goddamn right, I'm scared. I'm scared of going to prison. I'm scared of what might happen next. I'm scared of being in the hospital. I'm scared of going home. Everything I can think of frightens the hell out of me. I wake up scared. I sleep scared. I'm fucking haunted." Layla dropped the cigarette into the soda can between her knees. She grabbed the arms of the chair and white knuckled them.

Oh shit, I shouldn't have said that.

She looked down at the carpet. "I'm scared that I really am crazy. I'm scared of whatever, whoever killed Luke. I'm scared I killed Luke," she said.

Stop it! Don't think.

"You couldn't have killed him," Addie said. "Physically, you couldn't have done it." The social worker's calm face, her placid expression and the certainty in her voice, underlined her belief that Layla had not murdered Luke.

Layla looked around the room again, but Addie's office held

no clues that she could use. Layla wondered if Addie had a boyfriend. What was Addie's belief system? If she told Addie that a ghost had killed Luke, would Addie think she needed anti-psychotic medication or would Addie patiently explain that people-who-have-undergone-severe-trauma-often-think-they-see-ghosts? Maybe Addie had a guardian ghost as well? Maybe hers had told her to apply to graduate school instead of murdering people.

"But, I still might go to prison," Layla said.

"Which is it? Are you scared of going to prison for something you didn't do, or scared you did it?"

"I'm scared I'll go to prison. I know I didn't kill him," Layla said. "I'm always scared, it seems like I've always been scared. Not always. But ever since Mama died. I was alone after Mama died."

"What about your father?"

"Daddy Useless? He was right there when Mama died and he didn't do anything to save her. He was covered in her blood and he didn't do a damn thing to stop it."

"Like you when Luke died?" Addie leaned forward.

"Exactly," Layla shouted. "It was his fault."

"He didn't pull the trigger. And you didn't hack Luke to death."

"He could have done something," Layla sniveled. "He was just there." She drew her legs up into the chair and wrapped her arms around them, curled up like a small, forlorn child.

"People can't always save other people or fix things," Addie said.

Layla rested her chin on her knees. "I know that. But it feels like he should have done something. Like maybe if he'd done something, she wouldn't have died. She *was* screwing around. Maybe he wanted her dead."

"Luke raped you. The medical report makes it clear that he raped you. Maybe you were angry. Maybe for an instant you wanted him dead. That doesn't mean you are responsible." Addie's voice was flat. She stated facts.

Layla blew out her breath in frustration. Balling her hands into fists, she hammered her thighs. "Do you ever feel like what you think or feel puts out a kind of energy that causes things to happen? I already told you about Mazie. She left my house and died in a wreck. I feel like I put out bad energy. Like I'm haunted." Layla shook her head while pulling out another cigarette. "I know it's not true. But, I feel like I have this horrible effect on things." She lit the cigarette. "I argued with Mama the day she died." She exhaled. "I feel like I'm just toxic."

Addie nodded encouragingly while Layla talked. "I suspect that most people have that feeling from time to time," Addie began. "You see, the world pretty much operates on chaos, and that's scarier than any system or reason we can come up with for why things happen. Humans have to find reasons for things. We use religion, or social theories, or superstition to explain things." Addie chuckled. "Some of us even use various schools of psychology to explain why people behave particular ways. But, in reality, it's all chaos."

"So, it's really about entropy?"

"I think so," Addie answered. "But, what I think isn't important. We need to look at what you think."

"I don't really know what I think. Well, I do sometimes. I sometimes think that I just happen to have rotten luck. Still, it feels like my emotions cause things to happen. Like there is some demon in me. I get angry at someone – they die." Layla paused; she was dangerously close to describing the relationship she thought she had with Ian. "My thoughts and feelings just seem dissonant, incongruent."

"Layla, from where I sit it seems like your thoughts and feelings haven't even met each other."

Layla sneered. "So, you're going to help me get in touch with my feelings?"

"Not necessarily," Addie said. "Unless you want to do that. What I am going to do is support you through the next few days while we wait to see the outcome of Mr. Thompson's meeting with the district attorney. Then after that, you and I will decide if there *is* anything else I can do for you."

"The next few days," Layla said. "The next few days kind of determine my entire life." She hung her head. "I hate this. I hate waiting. I hate it that there isn't anything I can do."

"You can decide what you are going to do when you leave the hospital. If Mr. Thompson succeeds in keeping you from being charged, what are you going to do?"

"I hadn't thought of that," Layla admitted.

"Maybe you should. How about between now and when we meet tomorrow, you think about what you are going to do with the next part of your life."

"Oh, goody, homework. I may as well go back to school."

"It's something to consider. Okay then, same time, same station tomorrow."

Layla stood up. "Thanks." Addie remained seated in her chair.

Addie nodded in acknowledgement but only said, "Tomorrow."

Shoving her hands in her pockets, her face hidden behind her hair, Layla walked quickly out of the office. She took long steps down the hall, hurrying to the tiny area near the day room where patients were allowed to smoke. The disinfectant smell, the constant paging, the rushing staff and somnambulant patients – all of it aggravated Layla. She hated being hospitalized but didn't want to go home.

She recalled something Addie had said a few days ago: *"You're grieving. You're mourning, you may not admit it even to yourself. You focus on any stimuli you can find to distract yourself, but inside there's a deep reservoir of pain."* She was pissed at Addie crawling inside her head. Damn, a ghost outside and a therapist inside. No wonder I'm in the nuthouse.

In the small smoking area a young woman with platinum blonde hair and black polished fingernails sat on an upside down trash can. Layla turned her back to the other patients and removed one cigarette from the pack concealed in her pants. During her first few hours she'd learned that pulling out an entire pack brought the patient population down on her like vultures on carrion.

Layla walked up to the scruffy looking tech that lit cigarettes. Patients weren't allowed to keep lighters or matches. Layla kept her lighter in her underwear; she wouldn't put it past them to search her room while she was out of it. She thought about curtsying and calling him 'keeper of the flame' but decided against it. "Thanks," she said when he lit her cigarette.

"Do you think I should get a boob job? I think I need a boob job," the platinum blonde said. "It would improve my self esteem and I wouldn't keep ending up here." The woman rocked back and forth. She held out her arms, displaying multiple horizontal slashes from wrist to elbow. "Definitively need a boob job."

Layla turned to the wall. In movies about mental hospitals, the patients were always brilliant or interesting. But boring, sad, repetitive people surrounded Layla. They cycled through the hospital the way other people went to the dentist or filed their taxes. She heard a page summoning her to the visitor's lounge. She put out her cigarette and raced through the halls, eager to see someone who *wasn't* doing the Thorazine shuffle.

Matt spread books of wallpaper samples, paint chips, and swatches of fabric all over the Formica topped table in the visitors lounge. "This hideous lighting makes everything look weird," he said. "You'll have to take the things you like over to the window to see them in natural light before we make any decisions."

"Decisions about what? The décor for my cell on death row? What on earth are you doing with all that crap?"

He shoved a huge binder full of samples with several bookmarks hanging out of it. "They've finished treating the kitchen like a crime scene and we're free to get it fixed up. I'd thought about surprising you, but it *is* your house, even if you have rotten taste and need to rely on my superior sense of style and color. Seriously, I expect that you'll be out of here in a few days and I think it will be better if I have the kitchen redone before you get home." Matt lined up two paint chips and a scrap of wallpaper in front of her.

Layla thought about making a series of sarcastic comments. She considered accusing him of running her life. Let's see, how do I really feel about this? Grateful. I feel grateful. I don't want to go home to bloodstained walls and slashed linoleum. "Thanks, Matt. I'm grateful," she said.

"Oh," said Matt. "We're making 'I' statements and sharing our feelings. Therapeutic progress." He added two fabric samples to the collection.

Layla's hurt was etched on her face.

Matt stopped his busy work. "I'm sorry precious. I'm walking-wounded too. I don't accept compliments or thanks very well." He squeezed her hand. "Take a look at my number one choices. I figure we have most of the walls done in the light cream matte finish with the moldings and trim in the russet. Then, this wallpaper has light cream back ground and picks up russet and blue for accent colors."

"What's the fabric for?"

"I am so over the mini-blind thing. I thought we'd go with the russet and blue plaid for the valances and tie backs with the solid blue for the body of the window treatments." Matt's voice telegraphed his excitement.

"Are you still seeing Ashley?"

Matt looked up from the samples. "Yes, of course, why do you ask?"

"You sound like a man who's dating a decorator."

"I'll have you know, precious, I put these pieces together all by my little inspired self. And, here's the best part: I figured we could stain the cabinets to a white pine and then have a laminated white pine floor." Matt gauged her reaction. "Unless you want to look at some other options."

"It sounds perfect. I really like the wallpaper. I would have just hired someone to slop yellow paint on everything." Layla squeezed Matt's hand.

"Yellow kitchens are so pedestrian, so mundane, so –" Matt began.

"So, heterosexual? Seriously, Matt I really appreciate it. It will turn the kitchen into a whole new room." What she left unsaid was the thought that she urgently *needed* the kitchen to be transformed. Otherwise, she simply could not live in her house. Somehow, Matt had known that. "Have I mentioned lately that I love you?"

"No," Matt said, "but I figured it out." He packed up the samples. "I brought your books, and a course catalogue for UNC-Charlotte. I figured that you could fit filling out a college application into your busy schedule. And, on the off chance that you might consider eating them, I happen to have a few walnut fudge brownies."

"Hand over the chocolate and you won't get hurt," Layla said. "Just put it on the table and back away slowly." She unwrapped a thick brownie and bit into it quickly. "Heaven. In heaven the saints eat brownies like this." Layla finished the brownie and moved the others over to her side of the table. "I'm not taking any chances that you'll want to take these back."

"I would never come between you and brownies, precious."

"Matt, remember when we were little?"

"You're still little. In fact, I've been meaning to mention that to you. Based on my research, I believe that women are supposed to have curves, not angles. Have you considered eating daily, whether you're hungry or not?"

Layla ignored him. "No, seriously Matt, remember when we first met? How easy it was for us to be friends because we'd both lost so much? Well, I figured out that one of the things that made it so easy is that we accepted each other's weirdness without questioning. Well, partner, I'm putting you on notice. I have some more weirdness for you to accept, but I am not going to tell you about it until I'm released from here."

Matt nodded. "Whatever you need, precious."

Layla's eyes felt gritty. Her head felt like a tight band was wrapped around her temples. She wanted to come clean, she wanted to tell Matt about Ian, about Luke's death, about the incredible series of eerie events, but the words wouldn't form. "It's not time for me to talk, but it will be soon," she said.

Matt folded his arms behind his neck and stretched. He rubbed his neck and grimaced. "I have a confession, precious. I don't know how you'll take this one."

Layla propped her face in her hands. Was he going to tell her he was moving out? Would she gain her freedom from the hospital only to find Matt moved in with Ashley? "Go on," she said.

"Luke was no loss. I know it's supposed to be terrible to think ill of the dead. But listen, precious, Luke was no loss. He raped you. He hurt you. God knows how many other people he hurt. I'm sorry you're in a tight corner, but I'm not sorry he's dead. Luke needed killing." Matt lowered his hands to the table. "There, I've said it. Be mad at me if you need to, but I can't stand to see you eaten up with guilt over that worthless piece of scum."

"Matt, don't let anyone hear you say that. Not ever. Mr. Thompson more or less said he was confident I wouldn't be charged because I couldn't have killed Luke, I don't have the size or the strength. Baby, that leaves you. So shut your goddamn mouth."

Matt shrugged. "I just don't want you feeling guilty. I want you home and okay. Don't worry about me. I was forty-six other places. You just be okay."

"I will be, you just watch what you say. People can get weird ideas. I'll be home. I'll be okay. You know, it's strange but a few weeks ago, I thought my life sucked. Now, all I want is to get that life back. That dreary little life with a boring job, frequently delivered pizza and evenings listening to below average music played by friends. I want it back. You know what I've figured out? I figured out that when you go from work to a bar, from the bar to a restaurant where you drink strong coffee and then home to bed – if you keep moving, if you spend a lot of time going from point A to point B, then you never have to think. I like not thinking. I like it a lot."

Matt looked at Layla like he didn't quite recognize her. "You think more than anyone. All that reading you do – history, philosophy, theories about this, reasons that could happen."

"That's not thought," Layla said. "It's just a higher quality of noise."

.

SEVENTEEN

The charge nurse spooned cottage cheese into her mouth while leaning over *The Charlotte Observer*. Half of the local section hung down from the front of the desk. The nurse peered through her reading glasses at the bottom portion of the newspaper.

Layla approached the desk with feline caution. She believed that staff was shielding her from coverage of the investigation into Luke's murder. She knew they avoided mention of whatever it was that happened to the young cop. Mr. Thompson hadn't called or come by in days. When she'd last spoken to him, he'd told her not to worry, that everything would work out. Fine for him, she thought. Layla wished she wasn't wearing her boots, her footsteps sounded thunderous as she inched toward the desk.

The nurse looked tired. A pile of charts teetered precariously on the front of the nurse's station. Post-it notes covered the charts. The notes were full of emphatically underlined phrases and multiple exclamation points. From her job at Windale, Layla understood the nurse's exhaustion, she knew that all those notes represented deficiencies in the charts that the nurse would need to correct before she could leave for the day.

Dread clenched Layla's belly. Her mouth was dry. She suppressed a cough. A simple thing, reading the newspaper, became a glittering privilege after a little more than a week in a mental hospital. The sound of the newspaper rattling was deafening. The nurse sighed and massaged the small of her back with her right hand. Layla stopped moving and noted the time, the twenty-four hour clock over the desk read 06:35, less than half an hour until shift change. Would the nurse fold up the paper and stick in her satchel? Would she leave it on the desk for her day shift counterpart? Or would she casually discard it in the trashcan behind the desk?

Layla's boot heel thumped on the floor. The nurse looked up. Layla inhaled. The noise of bodies getting out of bed punctuated the silence. "I couldn't sleep, so I decided to get up," she said, hoping her smile was innocuous, ingratiating. "Do you know if there's a tech in the smoking area this early?"

"I'll page one for you," the nurse said. As she turned to pick up the phone, Layla moved beside the desk. Quickly, heart pounding, she scanned the paper.

A massive amount of cocaine had been found in Luke's blood. The police were investigating the possibility that his death had been drug related.

The nurse paged for a tech and hung up the phone.

Layla moved back slightly. She'd wanted to read a bit more. As the nurse turned around, her elbow caught onto the paper. The paper, the cottage cheese, spoon, and several medical charts tumbled to the floor.

"Oh dear," the nurse said bending over to gather charts.

Layla snatched the paper while the nurse blotted up cottage cheese with paper towels. "Thanks for helping me," she said. Layla stuffed part of the paper into her back pocket while the nurse threw the paper towels in the trashcan. "I appreciate your help. The tech should be in the smoking area now."

"Thank you so much for paging someone for me," Layla said. "I'm sorry about the mess." She sidled toward the hall, concealing the paper in her back pocket.

"It wasn't your fault. I'm always clumsy when I work third shift," the nurse said, picking up the remaining charts.

In the smoking area, Layla got a light and moved to the vinyl couch in the far corner. The tech seemed abstracted. She stared at the clock. Feeling like she was in middle school, Layla unfolded the paper and slipped an old *People* magazine in front of it.

A local sob sister had revived the story of Layla's mother's murder. She'd written a nauseating column suggesting that Layla may have a unique capacity for being in the wrong place at the wrong time, or that she could be a homicidal maniac inspired to wreak revenge on the world for the death of her mother. The writer's purple prose concluded with a paean to the concept of innocent until proven guilty, with an aside noting that even if Layla *was* guilty now, she'd been an unsullied child when her mother died. Whew, that covered all bases.

Disgusted by the column, Layla moved on to the news item about Luke. She recoiled at the evidence of her own naiveté. How could she have missed a major drug habit? Cocaine explained the erratic behavior, the sudden temper and the rapid changes in Luke's personality. Layla stuffed the newspaper down between the sofa cushions.

A twinge, a pinprick of grief, burrowed worm-like through her brain. If Luke *had* been an addict, it wasn't his fault. She knew what Addie would say about that. Addie would tell her that Luke made his own choices about cocaine. Layla sealed her grief away; she felt the familiar freeze, the numbing of emotion that had been part of her survival gear for half a lifetime.

Don't think.

She had time for one more cigarette before making an obligatory appearance at breakfast. "May I please have another light?"

"Sure," said the tech, pulling out a lighter. "Sorry, I was about to doze off."

"Thanks," said Layla. The nicotine helped her function. Layla didn't feel as if she'd slept. Night after night in the hospital she obediently laid in bed at lights out, she drifted, she nodded off briefly, but she didn't really sleep.

The tech cracked open a thick math textbook and studied it, a frown of absorption covered her face. Layla watched the smoke from her cigarette curl toward the ceiling. The ceiling tiles displayed brown stains, the legacy of years of schizophrenics' chain smoking. Layla felt uneasy, not from sleep deprivation, not from worry about her legal situation.

Her discomfort stemmed from a specific sense that Ian lurked nearby. Layla sensed someone watching her.

She left the smoking area and headed to the cafeteria. She straightened her shoulders and sucked in her non-existent tummy. Damn, I *am* crazy, trying to look good for a ghost.

The picture on the Jasons' kitchen wall suddenly flashed into her mind.

It was Ian in the picture. How had Ian done it? How had he compelled Jason to paint that scene?   Layla knew without understanding how it was that she knew that the young woman in the picture had been Maggie. 'My Maggie', Ian had called her. She felt a flash of jealousy.   Maggie – long dead, brutally raped and murdered, but still Ian had called her 'my Maggie.'

Standing in line behind the platinum blonde who wanted a boob job, Layla took inventory of her own body. Her jeans, once tight, hung off her protruding hipbones. She'd always had small breasts but now her bra hung loosely on her jutting ribs.   In Jason's painting, Maggie was small but sweetly curved. *Jealousy is cruel as the grave*, she thought.   Damn, I'm thinking Bible verses. I read too much.

Yeah, Matt would say that I should put down my books and pick up my fork.   Resolving to eat whatever slop was for breakfast, Layla picked up her tray. Breakfast was discouraging: instant scrambled eggs congealing on the paper plate, cold hard toast, and a clump of grits with a skin surrounding them. Sitting at the long table, Layla picked up her plastic fork and prodded the grits; the entire mass squirmed to the side.

A gray haired woman wearing a Charlotte Hornet's t-shirt over purple leggings said, "They're trying to poison us, you know."

Layla didn't answer.

The woman banged on the table and screamed, "They are!" No one looked her way. Just another day in the nuthouse, Layla thought.

The coffee was the color and temperature of dishwater. Layla longed for a cup of decent coffee. Tearing her toast into bits, she started cataloguing all the things she missed about freedom. Hot coffee, hot baths, going to bed when she wanted, walking outside. She dropped the toast, struck by a surge of yearning. She missed Ian. He could manifest in the hospital. He simply didn't visit often and didn't stay very long.

Layla held the thought of Ian in her mind like a captured firefly. I probably do belong here, she reflected. I miss a ghost, a violent ghost who's killed people. Not just miss, I lust after him, I get crazy at the sight of him. Layla decided that Addie would interpret her feelings as some peculiar mishmash of sexual avoidance and escapism.

She was so intent on imagining a conversation with Addie

about her hunger for a ghost that she jumped when Addie spoke. "Layla, as soon as you're through eating, I need to see you in my office," Addie said. "Sorry, I didn't mean to startle you."

Layla lowered her eyes to the decimated food littering her tray. "I'm through." She picked up her tray and walked to the counter. As she walked, she felt a fog swaddle her, a thick, invisible, impenetrable entity wrapping around her. She was divorced from sensation, from feeling. Pains, hunger, grief, exhaustion – all of those feelings were distant. Emotion was somewhere *over there*, no longer real. Life seemed like a movie that she watched without interest.

Entering Addie's office, Layla stood uncertainly. She couldn't even decide which chair she wanted. Addie watched her closely, then finally broke the silence, "Sit there," she said.

Layla's knees bent, the chair was beneath her, she sat. In front of her she saw Luke as he had been two days after death. The stench of his corpse, the blackened blood coagulating on his colorless skin. She didn't cry. Layla had moved beyond tears.

"Have you thought about what you're going to do when you leave the hospital?"

The bloody image of Luke vanished. She blinked; she was in Addie's nice, neutral office, sitting in the streaming sunlight. "No, not really," she said. Addie usually was infuriatingly accurate in her assessment of what went on in Layla's mind. Thankfully, this time, she'd been unaware of the circuitous pathways taken by her tortured thoughts.

The sun came through the window, picking up haphazard strands of gold in Addie's light brown ponytail. The social worker wore a full skirt, pink peonies on a blue background with a blue blouse. Her nail polish and lipstick matched the flowers on her skirt. Layla envied Addie, all her disparate pieces fit together neatly, harmonized. Addie smiled. "Well, Layla, you'd best think about it. You're going home."

"Home?" Layla wondered what 'home' meant. *Her house?*

Would Luke's ghost join Ian? Would they battle it out nightly until she ran shrieking into the rush hour traffic on Queen's Road West? "Home," she repeated, without the inflection that implied a question. Unbidden images of stark rock against a chill blue sky, green meadows nestled in the cleavage of the earth and empty space full of promise, ran into her mind.

Layla looked down and thought, *My heart's in the highlands. My heart is not here.* Damn, I'm crazy. I have read too much. If I'm not quoting the Bible, I'm reciting Robert Burns in my mind.

Layla said, "What do you mean?"

"That's my line," said Addie.

"Huh?" was Layla's response.

"Oh, sorry," Addie said. "'What do you mean' is a question therapists ask all the time, I was trying to be funny."

"Seriously, what are you saying? Am I getting out of here? When?" She shook her left leg; her boot heel tapped the floor like Morse code gone manic.

"Well, we need to fill out some papers. It's called discharge planning. You'll need to call someone to pick you up. Then, you're out of here." Addie rocked back and forth in her chair, the pleasure on her face ill concealed.

"You mean that's all there is? No court hearing, judges, or anything?" Layla was amazed. For days, she'd lived in absolute terror of being stuck in an institution or charged with murder. Now, according to what Addie said, it was all about to be over. All the worries, all the papers, thrown in the trash like so many advertising circulars.

"Hey, this is real life," Addie said. "Sometimes it's anticlimactic." Addie scrawled notes on some form or another. "Seriously though, I worry about you." Addie softened her words with a smile. "I'd like to see you on an outpatient basis for a while after you leave. Your legal problems seem to be under control, but you're in a lot of pain, a lot has happened. We both know that. I think that therapy could be useful to you. What do you think?"

With Addie's dark brown eyes focused on her, Layla squirmed. She wanted – no she *longed* – she was desperate to spill out the entire convoluted story: Ian, her mother, all of it. But she knew that it made no sense. Layla looked at Addie, the therapist's calm countenance was like a lifeline. "I think that I'd like to come in and talk," Layla said. "I really haven't any idea about what I'm going to do from here on out. I feel haunted. I can't explain it beyond that. Just haunted, like everything is beyond my control and has to do with the past."

"I can see where you would. Go on," answered Addie.

"Do you ever...do people ever...shit. I don't know how to say this. Is it normal...do people ever, have..." Layla wrapped her arms around herself, holding her body. "I mean, I feel like it's all beyond my control. Everything. Like things that happened long ago dictate my life. It's beyond entropy. I feel fated, pre-determined. Like everything that happens to me is because of choices other people made long ago."

"I could see where you would feel that, go on." Addie was motionless.

Gulping air, Layla continued, "I feel like some kind of weird force has taken over my life. Now just suppose that it has. Some weird cosmic force is fucking with me or something, well, how would I know that was the deal instead of the deal being that I'm bat shit crazy. I wouldn't, would I? Look, I'm sorry you probably have an appointment. Other patients. I guess I should make an appointment. I *really* don't want to talk now. Really."

"How's next Tuesday at 3?" Addie's pen was posed over an appointment card.

"Okay, I reckon," Layla said. She shoved the appointment card into her pocket. Guilt pierced her in the chest. Would she keep the appointment? *Could* she keep the appointment? What if she told Addie about Ian? And, what was there to tell? That she wanted him? That a dead man killed Luke?

Damn.

"You can use my phone to call your room mate." Addie inched away from her desk.

"Thanks," Layla said and quickly dialed Matt's cell phone. Escape arranged, Layla stood. "Thanks for everything," she said. Then she left Addie's office and retreated to her room to gather her things together.

Layla crumpled clothing into a black duffel bag and piled her books beside it. After days of regimentation she was accustomed to waiting for someone to shepard her, tell her when and where to go and what to do. She sat on the edge of the bed and waited. An aide poked her head in the door, "Your boyfriend's here."

Layla looked up, her expression blank.

"Matt's here," the aide repeated.

"Oh, thanks," Layla said, not bothering to explain that Matt wasn't her boyfriend. She looked at the piled possessions. "Is it okay if he comes on back here? I don't think I can carry all this myself."

"I'll help you," said the aide, hoisting the duffel bag.

Layla grabbed the pile of books and followed. The heavy metal doors swung open and she was standing in the lobby. People milled around, most of them wore clothes that more or less matched. A few of them read magazines. No was conducting a conversation with an invisible companion. "Thank you," she said as the aide handed her bag to Matt. He grabbed the bag and wrapped his other arm around Layla, squeezing her tightly.

"So, how many roommates do I have?" Layla squinted in the bright sunlight as they walked through the parking lot. She hid behind the pile of books.

"What do you mean? Oh, Ashley. We're definitely an item, but I'm not rushing things." Matt sprang ahead of Layla, unlocked the car doors and threw her duffel in the back seat. "I'm not into instant commitment. But, I really do like him."

"Well, you're the one who mentioned that he should marry you for your cooking." Layla slid into the passenger side seat, fastened her seat belt, and sighed in contentment. "I can't believe that I'm actually out of there."

"Precious, was it really that awful?" Matt pulled out of the parking lot.

"Yep," Layla answered, "it was that awful."

"We've got another bit of awful to wade through, dear one," Matt said. "We need to go see your lawyer." He clutched the steering wheel with both hands as he merged with the traffic clogging Randolph Road.

"Matt, am I going to be arrested?" Layla went cold with fear. She looked out the window at the rows of medical buildings as they gave way to expensive condominiums. She could not look at Matt.

"I don't think so," Matt said. "I really don't think so. I think he just wanted to settle things." He parked near an anonymous looking office building near the Mecklenburg County Courthouse.

"Well, what did he say to you?" She got out of the car reluctantly.

"All he said was that he needed to give you information and resolve things." Matt locked the car and followed Layla up the sidewalk.

"I'm nervous. " Layla said.

"Well, of course you are, precious. But I think if it was a bad thing, Thompson would have sounded like it was bad. He sounded like it was no big deal."

Layla stopped to check the building directory and punched the elevator button. White shirted men and women in neat skirts carrying designer coffee entered the elevator with Layla and Matt. In her jeans and t-shirt, she felt conspicuous, as if she was obviously a criminal. She stared down at the scuffed toes of her boots; she fiddled pointlessly with her hair. It was limp and flat. She hadn't had a hair dryer with her in the hospital.

The petite receptionist's face split into a predatory smile when Matt and Layla entered the lawyer's waiting room. Layla giggled despite her feeling of approaching catastrophe. She often turned invisible once women spotted Matt.

"How can I help you?" The receptionist's eyes were fixed on Matt's face.

"Excuse, me. I'm Layla MacDonald. I think Mr. Thompson is expecting me." Layla's voice trailed off uncertainly.

"Certainly, have a seat," the receptionist answered. "Can I get you anything? Coffee, mineral water?"

Matt and Layla sat down on the small sofa. "No thank you," Layla said as she picked up a magazine. "Damn," she whispered to Matt, "another geriatric issue of *People*. Is it the universal waiting area magazine?"

"I guess," he answered.

Layla rolled up the magazine and tapped Matt playfully on the leg. "Such a waste," she said with a mock simper. "Maybe you just haven't met the right woman."

"Precious..."

"Mr. Thompson will see you now." The receptionist stood in the doorway.

Layla followed her down a wood paneled hallway lined with English hunting prints in heavy gilt frames. Thompson's huge office reeked of lemon oil and money.

"Please, sit down." With an outstretched hand, Thompson indicated a chair near his desk

Layla crept across the Oriental rug, trying to read the lawyer's expression. She sat in the chair, knees pressed tightly together, hunched over her own lap protectively.

"Well, Layla, it looks like things can start getting back to normal for you," Thompson began. He smiled like an indulgent uncle who just gave a favorite niece a new doll.

'Normal,' Layla thought. How does he define *normal?*

"It is very unlikely that you'll be charged," Thompson continued. "While nothing is certain, the District Attorney assures me that the existing evidence indicates the involvement of other parties. They may have to pull you in for questioning again at some point in the future. But I'll be right there with you if that should happen. It seems that your boy friend had some rather unsavory associates."

"So, I am more or less free?" Layla was trying to process everything. Her head hurt. How had things changed?

"I'd be more pleased if they'd made an arrest," Thompson said. "But we have to be philosophical about that. Many of these drug related deaths don't result in an arrest. They often remain unsolved."

What hung in the air between them was the knowledge of how quickly Layla *could* have been arrested without Thompson's expert assistance. Layla read the papers often enough to know that unsolved crimes did not sit well with Charlotte's citizenry. "Thank you so much, Mr. Thompson. I don't know what I would have done without your help."

"It's quite all right, young lady. Now," his voice lightened, "get on with your life." Handing her a business card, he added, "Call me if anything comes up. Anything at all. If they want to question you further, if the media annoys you. Anything. I'd be delighted to help."

"Thank you again," she said pocketing the card. Layla stood quickly and shook hands with the lawyer. She turned to leave the office.

"Layla, you look a great deal like your mother," Thompson said in a soft voice.

Layla didn't turn to look at the attorney. "So, I've heard," she said and hurried out of the room.

EIGHTEEN

"Just click your heels together three times, close your eyes, and say there's no place like home," Matt said as he turned into the driveway.

Layla gave him a gentle punch on the shoulder. "Sometimes, you carry this 'friend of Dorothy' stuff too far." She leapt out of the car while Matt was still undoing his seatbelt. "But, damn, It *is* good to be home." Neglecting her books and bag, she ran across the yard like an unleashed puppy, dashing up the back stairs two at a time.

Layla entered her house almost reverently. Her fingertips brushed the familiar molding in the hallway. She smiled at the usually unnoticed row of family portraits that lined the walls. Stopping in front of an antique mirror, she made a face at her reflection and then blew a kiss at it.

Suddenly, Luke – bloody and hacked to pieces – flashed through Layla's mind. I *can't* go in there. I *can't* go in the kitchen.

Matt was speaking. His voice sounded distant, as if he spoke from the bottom of a well. "You'll notice that the walls, windows, and floors are intact. Now, if you'll step this way to the kitchen, you'll see magic."

No!

Don't think.

Timidly, Layla entered the kitchen. The room was completely redone. The new color scheme, flooring, cabinets, and curtains had turned the room into a showpiece, something out of the pages of a glossy home décor magazine.

"Wow," Layla said. "Are you sure I live here?"

Matt stood behind her, one hand on her shoulder. Layla

reached up and patted his hand. "It's great," she said. "I can deal with this." *Yeah, as long as I don't think.* If I just look, then this is a different room, it never happened.

"No ghosts?" Matt's voice betrayed his concern.

"Well, I wouldn't say that," Layla replied, and then thinking better of it, patted his hand again. "You done good, boy. You chased away the haunts." Layla didn't think it was time to explain about Ian. Not yet, not when Matt still thought she might come unhinged at any moment.

Not when the quivering in her belly and the eerie electricity in the atmosphere told her that the Scotsman would come calling soon.

Layla fetched an ashtray from the cabinet over the stove. She got a Miller Light from the refrigerator and sat down on in one of the new kitchen chairs. "Damn, it's good to be able to have a beer and a cigarette."

"Keep it up precious and you'll fill three or four pages in your gratitude log," Matt said.

"I am so freaking glad to be home, that I'll forgive you for that comment." Layla took a swallow of beer.

"It's good you're in a benign mood. I have some bad news for you."

Layla white knuckled the edge of the table. "What now?"

"Precious, you're unemployed. Your bitch-goddess supervisor left a message about public image of the agency and a pile of other bullshit." Matt was watching her closely.

"Oh, is that all?" Layla slumped in relief. "I hated that job anyway. I can register with a temp service first thing in the morning, or call the Jasons and see if either of them know which restaurants are hiring. I'll file for unemployment. I really think I need something kind of trivial while I figure out what I want to be when I grow up."

"My goodness, precious, I fear your recent sojourn at therapy camp has caused a sudden outbreak of mental health." Matt got up and poured a glass of wine. "This calls for a celebration."

"Don't get too excited. I may decide that I want to be a slacker for the rest of my life." Layla swiveled around in the chair. "It's so great to be home. I can't wait to take a four-hour bath. Matt, sweetie, don't take this wrong. But, if you want to see Ashley tonight, please don't feel like you have to baby-sit me.

I really have been looking forward to being able to be alone."

"You're not just saying that? I'd love to see him later, but I really want to make sure you're okay. I've missed you," Matt said. "Besides, I've got dinner planned. Not to mention the facial that you desperately need. Oh, and tomorrow, first thing, when you crawl out of bed. Call Holly in London, she's at the Forte Crest Heathrow, the number's by the hall phone."

"I thought she flew into Gatwick," Layla said.

"She's doing some weird route. Charlotte to Philadelphia to London to Frankfurt. She has a few days off in London. If she doesn't hear from you soon she'll probably cause a nasty international incident."

"Okay, so I have an agenda for tomorrow. Call Holly, call a temp agency, take a shower and then plan life. Gosh, I wonder if I can manage to devise a national health care plan and bring world peace before early afternoon." Layla lit another cigarette.

"You know, it's none of my business, except I love you more than anyone else does, precious,..." Matt fumbled with his empty wine glass. "I hope you are going to keep seeing Addie. She seemed okay."

Layla looked at the ashtray as if it fascinated her. She chose her words carefully, "I'm going to try seeing Addie for awhile."

"Precious, I understand not talking about things. I didn't talk about my mom and dad for a long time. But, this thing with Luke... I think you need to talk about it. If you ever want to talk to me, I'm here for you, you know that. Or, talk to Addie if it helps. But it's too much to keep inside."

"I'll be fine." Layla hoped her voice sounded smooth. "And I know you're there for me, you always have been." She reached across the table and held his hand for an instant. "You're the best brother in the world. I'm glad I picked you."

Matt leaned over and kissed Layla's cheek. "Thanks, precious. But I picked you. And if you dare say 'whatever,' I'll smack you." Matt got up and moved to the counter where the CD player squatted. Nearby stood a new CD tower covered in the same wallpaper as the breakfast nook. Matt popped in Patsy Cline's *Sweet Dreams*. "See, I'm willing to compromise."

"Why, the boy did miss me," Layla said and chugged the remainder of her beer. "Do you mind if I turn that up? I want to go take the world's longest bath." Layla stood and stretched.

"Have at it," Matt said. "Dinner in about two hours."

Luxuriating in the tub, Layla suffered massive doses of guilt. Ian had killed Luke. Killed him because he attacked her. And *she* had caused the attack.

Hadn't she?

Mazie. Luke. The young cop. She'd caused their deaths. Hadn't she?

Don't think.

Routine. Layla grasped at the familiar female bath-rituals. She raised her leg and massaged cream into it before shaving it smooth. She was aware that she was anticipating the appearance of the ghost like a sex-starved lover. She couldn't stop her thoughts, her feelings. Layla rubbed soap around her breasts, not daring to acknowledge the heat rising in her belly. Damn.

"You look a great deal like your mother." Fuck Thompson. He didn't *have* to say that.

Layla splashed cold water on her face but it didn't cool her off. All she could think of was Ian. Not Ian the avenger, not the axe-wielding monster that turned Luke into gore. No, all she could think about was how agonizing, how excruciating, how sweet it was to want him.

Toweling off and padding to her bedroom, she heard Merle Haggard's voice coming from the kitchen. Matt was trying so hard to make her homecoming special, to make everything right. Layla pulled on a loose knit dress. She felt an urge to look good. Rubbing moisturizer into her face and putting on lipstick, she flushed in shame. It wasn't for Matt's benefit that she'd told him to see Ashley this evening, not really. She knew who the lipstick was for.

Layla complimented Matt profusely, but she barely tasted the meal. When he set a custard tart festooned with raspberries in front of her, she made appropriate noises of rapture. Yet, all through dinner she was thinking, 'please, let's hurry'. She poured another glass of white wine. "Is this Chablis or chardonnay?"

"You are such a peasant, precious. It's chardonnay." Matt started clearing the table. "What on earth am I going to do with you?"

"Oh, for tonight, I suggest you simply let me get drunk and go to bed." Layla topped off her glass. She was acting more intoxicated than she was feeling. She wanted Matt to think she was near sleep.

"I suppose a hangover is the best beginning for a new life," said Matt.

"Absolutely."

Matt ruffled her hair. "Don't make any commitments to telemarketers while I'm out."

"I'll play it safe. I won't even answer the phone." Layla poured more wine into her glass, emptying the bottle. "I'll finish this off and then go to dreamland."

"You're sure you'll be okay? Ashley's number is by the phone. Call me if you need me. I won't mind, really." Matt picked up his keys and looked at Layla.

"I'll be fine, sweetie. Probably asleep before you are out of the driveway." Layla smiled.

"G'night then," Matt pecked her on the cheek and left.

Layla lit a cigarette. Surely, Ian would come, any moment now. Minutes passed and she was caught in electric anticipation. She began jiggling her foot. She got up and paced the hallway.

Layla stopped suddenly every few seconds. House creaks, the noise, maybe a roach skittering across a counter, maybe a drip from a faucet – each noise etched on her flesh. Damn, I really am certifiable. Where was Ian?

Had there even been an Ian?

Had *she* killed Luke?

Had she seen someone else kill Luke? Had it been something so horrible she dared not remember? And, Mazie – what about Mazie? Had she deserved to die? The young cop – he was only doing his job. Was Ian evil?

Did Ian exist?

Her pacing brought her to the sitting room. Through the window, she saw the glimmering of a distant light though the trees. She cut off the overhead light and switched on a dim lamp. Putting out her cigarette, she curled up on the chaise lounge, shoes off, feet tucked under her bottom. The house noises, the scrapes, the rasps, the skipping sounds of water bugs that infest old Southern homes – all the sounds grew louder.

Unable to sit, Layla jumped up and ran to the phone. Addie. Her appointment card had an after hours number on it. She'd call Addie and...and what? She turned from the phone and sat down.

Layla listened to night noise, imagining that her heartbeat

roared as loud as a marching band.

She sat motionless and waiting.

Ian walked through the wall and stood in front of the chaise lounge, his expression indecipherable. Was it anger? Scorn? Lust?

Layla pressed her spine against the back of the chaise lounge. Holding her breath, still as stone, she willed him to speak, to explain, to set her mind at rest.

Ian shook his head slowly, sadly. Grief was as heavy as humidity in the tranquil air. Mourning morphed into a presence, an enigmatic entity that coated the walls like tomb-dust. "I've no more control than you do, Layla MacDonald," he said. "No control at all." He stepped closer. His image shimmered.

And then vanished.

Evil or amoral? What did he mean 'I've no more control than you'?

Layla jumped off the chaise and stomped out of the sitting room. Pinballing from room to room, her fist balled, hammering her hand against her leg, "Goddamn it! Goddamn it!" She rattled the windows with her footsteps. Reaching the kitchen, she pounded the freshly papered walls with her hand until her knuckles were red and aching. "That's it? That's all? You have no fucking control? What the fuck is that supposed to fucking mean?" Jamming her keys into her pocket, she rushed out into the night.

Layla stomped down the sidewalk, fleeing her own demons. Without looking, she stepped into the street. A horn blared, lights flashed, tires screeched. A lumbering Lincoln skidded to a stop, its bumper inches from Layla. She didn't look up. She just marched across the street.

This is crazy. I should go home. I can call Addie.

She entered the park and broke into a run. The asphalt sliced her bare feet. Layla skirted the road and ran on the damp grass, slipping and sliding, grimacing when her foot fell on a bottle top. Her knit dress dampened with the grass, slapped heavily against her legs. Layla lifted her head and fixed her eyes on the speckled stars winking in the night sky.

She huffed and panted but continued to run. Her chest burned and her lungs ached. She whizzed by the train where she and Brandy had confronted Wayne Lee. Layla picked up speed.

Was she running from Ian? *Could* she run from him?

She stubbed her toe crossing a small bridge near the train. Hopping up and down, Layla grabbed her injured foot and felt the stickiness of warm blood coat her hand. She wiped the blood on her dress. Limping, she climbed the small hill behind the roller skating rink. In the shelter at the top of the hill, she bent over a wheezing water fountain and gulped and gulped, holding the button down until her thumb was sore.

Water dripping down her chin, hair windblown and sweat damp, dress splattered with her own blood, Layla collapsed onto the wet grass. She sat cross-legged, her thighs getting itchy in the grass. As her eyes adjusted to the dark, she looked down the far side of the hill, opposite the direction of her house, at the small lake. The few stars scattered in the sky were reflected in the onyx surface of the stagnant water.

Across the lake, she saw headlights traveling down Princeton. She could not hear car sounds. The night was cotton in her ears, pierced only by the chorus of crickets. Layla felt the hair on the back of her neck stand up. She trembled slightly, the embarrassed shudder of an eighth grader walking to the chalkboard, exposing her body to her cruel classmates' scrutiny.

She wasn't alone.

Soundless, Ian was just behind her shoulder.

He wrapped his arms around her and pulled her back against his chest. She rubbed against him. A whimper, the tiny protest of a trapped creature, emerged from her mouth. Her heart drummed loud and anxious. Layla bit her lower lip. She wanted him to kiss her, to put his mouth over hers and have her helpless beneath him on the crushed grass. And she was terrified of him too; something amoral infused the air around Ian. She imagined his hands all over her, cupping her breasts, teasing her nipples, making circular motions on the inside of her thighs, moving under her dress, between her legs...then she imagined those same hands moving to her neck, gripping her throat, snapping her neck as easily as pulling the head off a dandelion.

Would he love her?

Would he kill her?

She exhaled, a titanic gust of air.

"It underlines the difference between us quite tellingly," the ghost commented.

"Huh, What?"

"Your breathing. It reminds me of the chasm between us," Ian said. "It reminds me that I'm dead."

Layla relaxed, leaning into him. His voice was tender, bittersweet. "Ian, you killed him."

"Aye, tha' I did," he said, his accent thicker than before.

Layla waited. Although he held her close, even while she longed for his hand to fondle her breast, he wasn't...*there*. She moved against him trying to feel him, her body hungering for warmth, for the firmness of his flesh and muscle.

Ian was there...and he was not there.

"I had no choice," Ian said. "You're mine to protect."

Layla drew her legs up to her chest, her damp skirt sliding up her thighs. She felt Ian's fingers brush against her leg and hastily withdraw. Layla wanted to turn to him, to slither around in his arms, to kiss him, drawing his tongue into her mouth and sucking it until he moaned into her mouth. She wanted him to tear dress off and straddle her right there on the wet grass.

She knew what it would feel like, the slight resistance as he pressed at her entrance, giving way to a stretching, then the sensation of fullness followed by glorious thrusting.

She shoved her clenched fist into her mouth and bit down hard.

Ian pulled her hand from her mouth. Layla turned. Their faces were close. She wanted to lean forward and kiss him. She looked again at the planes and angles of his face, the harsh lines. Layla drew back, "Enough," she said. "Explain it to me, 'protecting me'."

"My Maggie was raped. She was butchered and left to bleed to death on the frozen ground. They'll no have you." Ian's face was hard, his eyes opaque. "You're mine to protect."

Layla moved away from him and brushed grass off her skirt, then paced back and forth.

Ian watched her. "There's naught you can do," he said. "Naught I can do. It's simply the way of it. I've no control over what happens when I have to protect you."

"So, Mazie? The cop? The guy on the street? Luke? All of them...that was you?" She shoved her hands in her pockets so hard that the seams strained. "Do you have to kill? What's this about? Do you think I'm Maggie come back?" She braked her tongue before she asked the question that burned in her throat. She did not ask if he'd had anything to do with Mama's death. He couldn't have.

Could he?

She stumbled a few steps downhill. Ian grabbed her arm and steadied her. "I do what I must do to protect you," he said. "I've no choice in the matter anymore than you."

Layla jerked her arm free. "Do you think I'm Maggie?"

"No. You've the look of her somewhat. But no, you're not my Maggie." Ian sighed. "But you are mine to protect."

"Why? Why me."

"Why you?" He paused. "I don't know. It's an interesting question. I'd have to say – *because*. Just because it's the way of it, and neither of us got a vote regarding destiny."

"So, it's 'just because'. That's it?" Layla stepped back.

"Tha's th' way of it," Ian answered. He opened his arms and she fell back into them. She hugged him tight, her face pressed to his chest. Now he seemed solid, warm. She imagined she heard a heartbeat.

Then, she was alone on the hill looking down at the lake, the distant car head lights moving across the ebony surface like spook lights.

Peering into the smooth black surface of the lake, Layla became aware of a strange power. She had nothing to fear, not any more. Anyone that threatened her, anything that hurt her, would be destroyed no matter what she thought she wanted.

She walked home through the park slowly. The rustle of leaves, the infinite number of night noises did nothing to alarm her. She feared nothing. Layla knew it was unsafe to walk through the park at night. None of that mattered anymore. She could walk through the worst neighborhoods, knock on the doors of crack houses and ask for directions if she liked.

Layla strolled lackadaisically through the park. She had nothing to fear other than her own emotions. Pausing by the tennis courts, she watched the road. What would happen if she dashed in front of a speeding car?

What happened to people who threatened her?

She walked home, counting her steps to silence the questions in her mind.

NINETEEN

Layla rolled over in bed and shoved her head beneath the pillow, muting the morning sounds.

She curled up, snuggling into the mattress. Opening her eyes, she felt the moment of confusion that attends waking up in an unfamiliar environment. She flashed back to a hotel in Myrtle Beach. Luke and she had gone to the beach for two disastrous days last summer. He'd abandoned her early in the evening and returned about ten o'clock in the morning after she'd progressed from rage to worry. Oh yeah, she remembered it clearly. His "Damn, I must have been drunk," followed by a fast grope and quick sex.

Layla fumbled on the bedside table for her cigarettes, the rapid movement cleared the remnants of sleep from her head. She was at home. Not the hospital, not a hotel. Home. And Luke was dead. Her chest convulsed in a coughing fit. Layla stubbed out the cigarette, disgusted with her smoking.

She checked the time. Seven o'clock. Well, damn, she thought, I really do need to get on with this life thing. Layla grabbed a pair of shorts off the floor and stepped into them. Holly, I need to call her.

Addie, I should call her. I *need* to talk about...

No.

In the hallway, she could smell cinnamon rolls and coffee perfuming the air. Laughter and snatches of conversation mixed with the sultry sound of Roberta Flack's voice. She thought she heard tall Jason's laughter. After dialing the international code, she waited while the phone rang. Two rings, then a desk clerk. Holly had checked out.

"I couldn't get Holly," Layla announced as she entered the kitchen. Tall Jason sat opposite Ashley at the table, drinking coffee. Matt leaned over to pull a pan of cinnamon rolls out of the oven.

"Gorgeous," said Ashley, glancing appreciatively toward Matt.

"Do you mean my ass or the cinnamon rolls?" Matt parodied a pirouette and placed the pan on a trivet in the middle of the table.

"Both," answered Ashley, reaching for a roll. "Oh, hot!" He jerked his hand back.

"Now, I know you mean me," Matt said and winked. He fetched a spatula and four plates to the table.

"Young love, ain't it grand?" Jason picked up the spatula and scooped two cinnamon rolls onto a dish. "I'm a growing boy," he said, his tone slightly defensive as he shielded the rolls with his forearm.

"Oh, Holly left a message last night," Matt said. "You must have been sleeping heavily. Her schedule changed and she left London this morning. The bad news is that we won't hear from her for a few days. The good news is that she'll be home early next week."

Layla poured a cup of coffee. She hoped she looked rested or at least normal; Matt would go ballistic if he knew she'd been stalking around the park late last night. "So, what's the deal?"

"Holly didn't really say." Matt put a roll on a plate and handed it to Layla. "I got the impression that her schedule was reshuffled kind of quickly."

"Speaking of schedules, have I got a deal for you, Baby I'm going make you a star." Jason said, imitating a B movie producer.

"So, I should have my people call your people and we'll do lunch." Layla took a bite of the warm buttery roll. No one did childhood comfort food like Matt.

"Baby, we're doing a power breakfast right now," Jason said. "Here's the deal, I've started doing a night bartending shift at the Crossroads. We need someone to work the door. Seventy-five a night, three nights a week, in cash, off the books. It will keep you going until you decide what you're going to do. And – ta-dah! – since it's off the books you can collect unemployment from your job at the home."

"I should have known there'd be a scam somewhere," Matt said.

"Well, of course, *mon ami*, who you talking to?" Jason reached for a third roll. "The way I see it, Matt, you are one of those overly responsible hard-working types that's going to go postal one day. We slackers aren't any threat to society, right Layla?"

"Right," she said, screening her face with her hair. Layla concentrated on keeping her expression bland. She was a horrible threat to society. *Don't think*, she admonished herself, just don't think about it. Layla drank coffee, her internal tape playing over and over: *Don't think, don't think*, like the clatter of a train running a circular path through her thoughts. It occurred to her that she'd need to break her appointment with Addie. Addie made her think. Thinking was dangerous, thinking risked the tenuous stability that could keep her drinking coffee, doing laundry, getting through the days.

Layla could just see herself going into Addie's office and saying, "See, there's this ghost, and I keep imagining him doing me. I think about it constantly. Yeah, Luke raped me and that pissed me off but I imagine this ghost ripping my dress off and it's a real turn-on." Yeah, right.

Ashley's voice interrupted Layla's thought-trip. "I've got something for you." He held out a neatly gift-wrapped book.

Layla blushed in surprise, then regained her equilibrium, "Sucking up to the in-laws are you?"

"Just a homecoming present."

Unwrapping the package eagerly, Layla discovered a coffee-table sized book. "Scotland?"

"Matt told me you read a lot about Mary Queen of Scots and Scottish history these days. I thought you might enjoy seeing what Scotland looks like."

Impulsively, Layla hugged Ashley. "Thank you so much." She wiped her hands on her shorts and opened the book. "It's beautiful," she said, gazing at a photograph of the Highlands. "I better put it in my room so that I don't spill coffee on it or anything." She took the book to her bedroom and returned. Looking at her friends she felt a nagging unease. "Where's short Jason? I thought he didn't go into work until noon."

Terror sat like a lump of ice in her chest.

Ian hadn't...he couldn't have? Short Jason was no threat...

"Oh, the way of all flesh. Things change. The thing with Mazie," Jason said. "Her dying in that freak accident just when they were getting to know each other. He didn't want to stay in Charlotte. He went back home to Hickory to live with his mom for awhile, maybe patch things up with some girl he knew in high school."

Layla exhaled. Matt caught her eye. They exchanged the silent communication they'd employed for years. Layla's eyes asked him if tall Jason had said anything more regarding the accident that had killed Mazie.   With a slight change of expression, he signaled her to wait until tall Jason left. "Well," she said, "I can understand."

"Yeah, I can too," tall Jason said. "But it leaves me in the market for either a roommate or a new place." He looked at his watch. "I have to buzz. Layla, I'll see you at the Crossroads this Friday around six to set up."

"Thanks," Layla said as Jason left.

"I have to run as well," Ashley said. "Some of us don't have compassionate bosses who let us swan in when we feel in the mood." His voice was teasing. He kissed Matt quickly and ruffled Layla's unruly hair.

"Why do people do that?" Layla sighed.

"Cause you're cute," Ashley answered on his way out the door.

"So what are the first few things on your mind?" Matt sat down opposite Layla as the door closed.

"Entropy and dissonance," Layla answered.

Matt rolled his eyes. "And she's even sober. Seriously, what are you thinking about? I took today off, precious. I'm yours. I figured you'd need me today. Yesterday you really did need to be alone. But today, I thought we'd spend together."

Usually they moved from the kitchen to another part of the rambling old house to talk. Layla thought of the sunroom with its veil of greenery. But she didn't want to sit in the sunroom; traces of Ian's memories of Culloden seemed to cling to the walls.

"Layla?" Matt reached out and touched her face. "Layla, talk to me."

"I was thinking about entropy and dissonance. How, everything falls apart. How nothing fits together or harmonizes.

I guess I thought, even with all the awful, stuff that everyone would sort of go on being...well, *everyone*. You know." She looked at the room. Luke's body had sprawled right over there. Ian had walked through that wall, some weird battle-axe or something raised above his head.

"I keep seeing things," Layla continued. She looked into Matt's eyes and it was clear to her that he thought she meant Luke. "Mazie," she said, her voice flat. "That was a strange accident. A freak thing. How did she get like that?" Layla squirmed, she'd never lied to Matt before. She knew perfectly well how Mazie had died.

"Jason talked to her parents after she died," Matt said. "They're suing a guy who did Mazie's body work, something about a piece of the door cutting her like that. I understand that you feel badly about her, but it could have happened anywhere. Jason just needed to get out of town, precious. People handle things in their own way."

"Did you know we tried a séance? The Jasons, Tracey, and I. We were trying to deal with Mazie." Layla lit a cigarette.

"I heard," Matt said. "Tracy was up to her usual drama queen routine, bruised her own neck to add to the spooky factor. Tall Jason told me. I was surprised that ya'll did that."

"Matt, you're our generation's answer to Mr. Spock. You're the one with a rational answer for everything. We under-educated slackers just kind of grab at whatever floats out of the ether." Layla forced a laugh.

"I get really pissed when you talk like that," Matt said. "You're always putting yourself down."

"It saves other people the trouble of pointing out my considerable flaws and failures."

"Seriously, it makes me mad." Matt raised his voice.

Fear shot through every nerve ending in Layla's body, her eyes scanned the room in terror, awaiting Ian's inevitable arrival, awaiting more death, more bloodshed, more horror. *No, Ian*, she thought, as if she could telepathically reach the ghost, *he's not really mad at me. No, he's never mad at me.* Masking her fear as best she could, Layla gasped, "No, Matt, you aren't mad at me. You're never mad at me."

"Precious, you're right. Of course, I'm not really mad at you." He hugged her. "I'm sorry."

"It's okay," Layla said. "I'm just kind of...oh, I don't know, fragile now." Matt ruffled her hair and poured them both more coffee. She warmed her hands over the cup. "Let's try this conversation again, okay?"

"Sure, precious."

"Matt, do you ever feel like there are forces beyond your control? Things that we can't explain?"

"Yes." He paused. "And no." He took a drink of coffee.

Layla could read the thoughts flitting across his face. He didn't want conflict. He was willing to go with a little wooey-wooey if it comforted her.

"You remember that guy I dated before Ashley? Seriously, you remember Robert? He was into this entire Jungian thing, racial memory, archetypes, all that stuff. Well, I hate to admit it, but some of it makes sense. Like maybe we are compelled by a consciousness that we can't get in touch with. I don't know." Matt shook his head. "I'll give you this much. I think we don't understand everything."

That's a beginning, Layla thought. I don't want to push it. She sat silently, wanting to change the topic and not knowing how to go about it gracefully. She wasn't used to being on guard around Matt.

"I think that once you get a routine established, start doing normal things again, that stuff will make more sense to you," Matt added.

Layla was grateful for the opening. "You're right. I need to start off with a list of what I need to do. Really, I know it sounds cheesy. I can't just work the door at Crossroads a few nights and watch daytime television until I'm forty."

"In the meantime, if you want to believe in something, I won't take it personally," Matt said. "Religion, astrology, health food – whatever it takes to get you through the next little while – is fine with me. But I won't promise that I won't make fun of you."

"I wouldn't want you to," Layla said. "There's enough dissonance without you undergoing a personality transplant."

Matt stood up and took the remaining cinnamon buns over to the counter where he wrapped them in clear plastic wrap. "It's hard being a domestic goddess."

"I wouldn't know." Layla lit a cigarette, her free hand stayed protectively on the ashtray to defend it against Matt's cleaning frenzy.

"While you're sorting your life out, I'm going to clean the kitchen." He rinsed the breakfast dishes, then scoured the countertops.

"That was an unnecessary announcement," Layla said.

Matt arched one eyebrow. "I don't see any life sorting activity going on."

"Well, I'd like to learn to do that trick you do with your eyebrow. I'd love to be able to raise one eyebrow back at you."

Matt lifted the garbage out of the container and fastened the plastic bag with a twist tie. "I think it's genetic." He put a clean liner in the can. Heading for the back door, he said, "Get some paper if you're going to make a list."

By the time he'd taken out the kitchen garbage and returned, Layla was hunched over a yellow legal pad, the end of a pen replacing the usual cigarette in her mouth. Matt tried to peek, but Layla covered her notes with her hand. "I've decided not to decide for a few weeks," she said.

"Explain."

"Well, dear one, I think I'm in shock or a reasonable facsimile thereof," Layla said. "I feel an incredible internal pressure to do...*something*. You know, do SOMETHING in capital letters. I'm pushing myself to do something large and dramatic with my life. I think maybe I'm doing that to avoid feeling anything. It was like that after Mom died. I cut school, I ran around all night, back then it was doing something. Being a bad ass. I didn't deal with her death until years later. I feel the same way now. I'm sitting here, in the room where Luke died and I keep thinking I need the right course of study, the right job, the right boy friend and that will fix everything. But it won't. Not really."

"True. Now what are you going to do with your life?"

Layla flicked her lighter. It sparked but no flame appeared. With a cigarette stuck in her mouth, she walked to the stove. Holding her hair in one hand, she turned on the gas flame and bent to the burner to light her cigarette. Exhaling, she leaned against the counter. "I'm going to apply for unemployment, work those shifts at Crossroads, and see Addie for a few sessions. When I left the hospital yesterday, I sort of planned to blow

Addie off. Therapy is hard work. But, last night and this morning, I've been thinking about it and I really need to figure some things out. I think I may call her and see if she can work me in this afternoon. I don't really want to wait until my appointment. I might change my mind and blow the whole thing off..." Layla ran her hand through her hair then took a deep drag off the cigarette.

"Matt, sweetie. Do you ever feel haunted? I do. Not the house, but me. I feel haunted. Do you know what I mean?" She watched him, she measured each tiny motion of his facial muscles, assessed the shifts in his breathing, counted the times he blinked. Unable to endure the small silence, the wordless void, she spoke. "I feel haunted."

"Precious, I suppose we all have to feel something." His voice was so sad and empty that Layla felt a bit of her heart crumble in her chest. "I wish we didn't. I think it would be best to feel nothing at all."

"So do I," Layla said, walking across the room to her chosen brother. She wrapped her arms around him and they held each other, wordlessly, without tears. "Matt, I know you'd do anything in the world for me. But I think I'm going to call Addie. It doesn't hurt her when I'm in pain."

"I'm sorry, precious," Matt said. "But..."

"Don't ever be sorry for loving someone. Even if it's me." Layla moved back. "Damn, I nearly burned you with my cigarette."

◈

"I don't really know why I'm here." Layla bounced her foot up and down. She found the tap-tap-tap of her boot heel on the floor embarrassing, but she kept doing it. "I kind of panicked, I guess. It seemed that if I didn't call you and come in today that I wouldn't ever come back." She wanted Addie to say something, to tell her why she was here. She didn't want to talk. She just wanted to sit passively while Addie made sense of her life.

The therapist didn't speak.

"Why don't you ask me questions?" Layla's voice was impatient. Her foot jiggled nonstop, the tapping of her heel the only sound in the office. "I mean...I thought you people asked questions?"

"What would you like me to ask?" Addie sat very still. The pad and pen remained on her desk.

"Don't you usually ask people a bunch of stuff about their past?" Layla sounded belligerent.

"What would you like to say about the past?" Addie wore a dark skirt with a white cotton blouse. She looked unwrinkled, freshly ironed, even though it was past five o'clock.

"My mother. You don't ask about...I don't want to talk about...Aren't *you* supposed to be obsessed with my mother? Don't you people focus on how everyone's mother fucked them up? I mean, my mother had this sexual thing and she *died* because of it. She fucked around and she died. Isn't that important?" Layla was shouting.

"Is it?" Addie sounded mildly curious.

"What the fuck do you mean 'is it'? What do I have to do to get you to fix me?"

"I can't fix you," Addie said. "You can perhaps understand yourself."

"I don't understand, I don't understand one goddamn bit of it." Layla was shaking. "Look, my mother had this sexual thing, and it killed her. Maybe I have the same thing."

"Go on," Addie said.

"Goddamn it, I can't talk to you. Listen to me, goddamn it." Layla gripped the arms of her chair. Gulping air like she'd just run a race, she began, "I *am* trying to understand...I'm afraid."

"Anyone who has been through what you've been through would be afraid. I'd be more worried if you *weren't* scared."

Layla didn't speak, she held onto the chair tightly.

Addie continued. "It's been one horror show after another. Of course you feel crazy."

"Maybe I *am* crazy," Layla interjected.

"Maybe a lot of crazy things have happened to you and you're struggling to make sense of them. We do that, you know, we humans, we try to make sense of the chaos. It sounds like you have some feelings about your sexuality and some feelings about the tragedies that have happened and those feelings are all twisted together."

Layla nodded, a quick, almost imperceptible shake of her head.

"Why don't we start there?" The therapist leaned forward. "Tell me about how sex and death are connected?"

Layla looked up at the ceiling then down at her boots. She took a deep breath. "Is it normal for women to fantasize about something like rape?"

Addie moved back, a look of confusion crossed her face quickly covered by the therapeutic bland expression Layla was familiar with. "A lot of women have rape fantasies. What do *you* mean by rape?"

"I'm haunted by...I sometimes...I think about having sex with someone who just takes over. That way I'm not responsible and it's...I don't know. I have these thoughts where I just want a man to take over but when Luke *did* it was horrible, it was the worst thing...other than his death, what happened before was the worst thing since Mama died."

"Of course," Addie said. "No one likes to have anything forced on them. In fantasy, you are really in control. That sort of thing is very normal, most women have sexual thoughts that I suppose could be called 'rape fantasies' but those thoughts are radically different from the reality of rape. Daydreaming about a powerful lover isn't the same as wanting to be raped."

Layla let Addie's words sink in. She could see the truth of what the therapist said, *but* Addie didn't really understand. "You're right."

"But?"

"I'm haunted. I feel like I can't escape the past, like forces completely beyond my control have taken over my life. There isn't anything I can do. It's all about the past."

Addie nodded. "With everything that has happened to you I can see that you'd feel that way."

"I feel haunted."

"I think we can work together to understand those feelings." Addie scribbled on an appointment card. "I want to see you again soon and we'll work on this."

Layla took the card and shoved it into her pocket. "Yeah, we'll work on it."

TWENTY

Layla spread the roots of the mums in the potting soil. She picked up a watering can and sprinkled Miracle Grow over the plants. Every September she tossed out the geraniums and planted Chrysanthemums in the planters standing beside the front door. This year she'd chosen rose toned and mauve mums, sad melancholy colors matching her mood of mourning and loss.

Layla liked gardening years ago. When she'd moved into Grammy's house, she'd spent half the winter bent over catalogues, checking off perennials and considering seeds. But gardening got old. Pulling weeds, fertilizing flowers, careful cultivation of the soil – none of it fit the frenetic pace of Layla's life.

Grammy left gardening to the hired help. She hadn't known the names of the roses that bordered her back yard. Still, Layla had a memory of her Grammy: face soft in the morning dew, features shadowed beneath a broad brimmed hat, clipping gardenias to fill the crystal vases that peeped out of every corner of the house.

Sometimes Layla couldn't tell *what* she really remembered. Stories from her childhood, things her grandma had repeated, blended with images to form pictures. Even her mother's face – did she recall it? Or was her image of Mama patchworked from other people's perceptions?

Layla sat back on her legs. The trowel on her lap smeared dirt across her jeans. Staring at the silver birch, gray and mundane in the afternoon sun, she tried to summon her mother. Since Ian's appearance, she'd been seeing ghosts, so why wouldn't her mother come? Concentrating on her longing to see her mother, focused on what she wanted to say, Layla felt every fiber of her body straining toward the tree.

Layla felt a sob rising from her guts. The tears lodged in her chest. She wondered if her mother knew how badly she felt about the argument they'd had that last day. A stupid argument, the sort that all teenagers have with parents, meaningless really. If her mother had not died that day, she doubted that either of them would remember the argument now. If she could will her mother to appear, summon her back from the other side, then maybe she could begin to straighten out her life.

The amber afternoon light illuminated the mums, shooting through the leaves, contrasting with Layla's morose mood. She watched a jogger in hot pink shorts bouncing by her house. It's not exactly the right atmosphere to conjure up spirits, she thought. But still, she added wistfully, Mama liked good weather; drizzle and clouds seemed to leach away her sparkle.

She heard Ian's voice, a distant whisper. "It's no as simple as that."

He didn't appear. Layla wondered if she'd really heard him. She was getting to know him well enough to second guess what he'd say. He'd be right. It isn't that easy, she thought, I can't call Rent-a-Wraith and ask for Mama. Despite her sadness, she giggled.

We deal with the ghosts we're given.

Brushing the loose dirt off her jeans, she carried the remainder of the potting soil and her trowel back to the garden shed. Addie would say something about insight and guilt, Layla thought. I wonder if Addie is into that Jungian shit? Maybe she would have an explanation for Ian as a manifestation of my subconscious something or the other. She... I *tried* to tell her... she just didn't get it.

Going through the back door, she caught a glimpse of herself reflected in the windowpane. Her hair stuck together in sweaty clumps and dirt streaked her cheekbones. She didn't see a shred of the resemblance to her mother. She recalled the painting tall Jason had done of Ian and Maggie, but there was no resemblance to Maggie either. Layla pulled a soda from the refrigerator and rubbed the cool can over her face before popping the top. She made a mental note to ask Jason more about the painting.

Jason!

Damn, she was supposed to be at Crossroads to work the

door in about an hour.

Running down the hall, she slopped a trail of soda. Without bothering to shut the bathroom door, she pulled off her clothes, leaped into the shower and blasted herself with ice-cold water. Shrieking, Layla jumped away from the spray. Adjusting the temperature, she stepped back under the water.

"So now, we're recreating the shower scene from Psycho?" Matt raised his voice so that she could hear him over the running water.

"I damn near froze myself," Layla hollered just before she heard the sound of Matt shutting the door. Hastily shampooing her hair, Layla was through with her shower in minutes. Wrapped in her bathrobe, she slapped moisturizer on her face and pulled her towel-dried hair into a ponytail.

She raced to her bedroom and pulled on panties, a clean pair of jeans, and a black t-shirt. With a quick glance at her mother's photograph, she stopped for an instant before pawing through her jewelry box. Layla picked up a pair of opal earrings accented with diamonds. Her parents had given them to her on her fourteenth birthday, her first 'real jewelry,' according to Mama. No, not with jeans and a t-shirt to spend the evening checking IDs at a beer bar. Layla put the earrings down and inserted plain silver hoops in her ears.

Hair still damp, she pulled on mismatched socks and shoved her feet into black boots. A spray of perfume was her one concession to Friday night. Knowing that the air conditioner at Crossroads had a mind of its own, Layla picked up a denim jacket and looped the arms around her slender waist.

Matt was in the kitchen poring over a cookbook when Layla sped through the door. "You want me to drive you?" He didn't look up from the glossy photo of an elaborate chocolate torte. "You might want to drink tonight."

Layla snatched her keys from the hook by the door. "Nope, I'm feeling a regrettable need to stay sober." Leaning over Matt's shoulder, she examined the picture of the torte. "That looks better than sex," she said.

Matt rolled his eyes. "Your judgment is off."

"So, I've heard. So, when does that cake make its appearance."

"After I go shopping," Matt answered, "I don't have the pans

I need."

"Why don't you shop tonight?" Layla ruffled his hair. "Got ya," she said, moving away as he reached out to swat her butt.

She cut through a maze of residential streets and pulled into Crossroads' parking lot from the rear while rush hour traffic sat immobile in front of the bar. The long, low building didn't have the quirky charm of Down Under, but it had great acoustics and ample room. Sitting on Independence Boulevard, the bar had been through several incarnations – a dance club, a country and western bar, and a Goth club. The current owner was hoping to attract a blues crowd. Layla hadn't been in the building after the country and western era.

Her eyes adjusting to the dim light, Layla stepped inside. The new guy had obviously put some money into the enterprise, a second bar had been added reducing the size of the dance floor and creating a small table seating area. The smell of hot grease and onions announced that food was on offer. Jason was polishing the main bar with a striped towel. "Layla, over here," he yelled. Fred sat at the bar talking to Jason.

"Howdy, Jason. Fred." Layla leaned on the bar. Jason put a Miller Light in front of her. "Not tonight." She shook her head. "Could I just have a Coke?"

"Sure." Jason put the beer back in the cooler and slid a frosty mug of soda down the bar.

"You're getting pretty good at that slide thing."

Jason shrugged. "I'm a man of many talents." He pulled out a cutting board and started slicing lemons, methodically depositing them in a container like he was running on automatic. "Good knife skills, I slide mugs well, is there no end to my magnificence?"

Fred emitted a sound halfway between a laugh and a snort. "There is an end," he said. "And the end is near."

"In addition to being an asshole, did you know that Fred has the best collection of bad horror movies on video tape in the state of North Carolina?"

Layla lit a cigarette and coughed. "No interest in horror movies here," she said. "My life is one."

"Well maybe if you stopped chain smoking and started eating twice a week, things *might* improve." Fred leaned back, obviously gearing up for a lecture.

"Please...one male Jewish mother is enough. Matt's on my ass constantly."

"Pax," answered, Fred sliding his empty glass back toward Jason.

"Another one?" Jason dropped the glass into the sink.

"No, I'm on my way to work." Fred headed out the door.

Layla occupied the barstool he vacated. "Okay, tell me what I have to do tonight."

"Starting at six, you sit by the door and check everyone who comes in. The alcohol Nazis are really intense on the underage drinking thing. Anyone here before eight gets in free. From eight o'clock on there's a five dollar cover. We still use the nasty little hand stamp method so that in the morning people can tell where they met the stranger in their bed." Jason reached beneath the bar and handed over a cash box, ink pad and stamp.

Layla checked the clock behind the bar and remained seated. She had a good half hour before she went on-duty. "Are you painting a lot these days?"

"Yeah," Jason answered. Proceeding with his prep work, he stabbed orange wedges and cherries with toothpicks. His expression didn't shift, he continued with his work.

"So are you still telling folks that you see other people's past lives when you're stoned?" Layla drew circles in the moisture on the bar.

"Yeah, that's my story and I'm sticking to it," Jason said. "I just get images in my head when I'm high and I have to paint them." He wiped the bar down again. "Why?"

"Just curious," Layla answered. "Well, I better get in my place."

Layla arranged the cash box, inkpad, and an ashtray on the small table beside the door. Jason's answer left her uneasy. What if he *was* telling the truth, what if some kind of door opened in his mind and he really did see the past? She was still thinking about his painting when a cough startled her. She looked up and saw a freckled woman in jeans and a plaid blouse. "Sorry," Layla said. "I just stepped out of my body for a second."

"Is there a cover?" The woman's voice dripped impatience.

"Not yet. May I see some identification?"

The woman sighed elaborately and hoisted a huge handbag onto the desk. She pawed through it, scattering chewing gum wrappers, receipts, and ink pens all over the desk. Finally, she extracted a battered wallet, and flicked it open to show her license. Barely twenty-one. Layla stamped her hand.

A few more people straggled in after the young woman. Mostly an older crowd, Layla didn't see any familiar faces. A guy in his forties with long red blonde hair leaned on her desk for an instant. "Did they take out the pool tables when they remodeled?"

"Yeah, sorry," Layla answered. He turned and walked away.

Despite the slow start, by eight o'clock Layla had a line at the door. The band played an unrecognizable cover of something that might have been recorded by Muddy Waters once upon a time. Layla kept busy until ten.

By closing time, she was tired. Jason handed her seventy-five in cash. "You want to go get something to eat?"

"Not tonight, Jason," Layla answered. "Stamping hands is hard work. I think I'm just headed home. See you tomorrow." She folded the bills and stuck them into her front pocket.

A slight chill in the air prompted her to put on her jacket in the parking lot. Despite the hour, it was noisy on Independence – traffic sounds, random laughter, a wave of Latin music followed by the jarring sounds of hip-hop. Somewhere in the mix, Layla thought she heard a scurrying sound. It rattled her. Walking across the parking lot, she was certain she heard something moving. Not human footsteps, but *something*.

An eighteen-wheeler roared down the road, but Layla still heard a small clicking, a scratching sound. Whatever it was came closer. Her legs were paralyzed. Layla stood in the parking lot wishing Jason would come out, wanting anyone she could see, anyone other than Ian to show up.

The noise was only a few feet behind her now. Layla spun around. The parking lot *looked* empty. The nearby strip mall seemed deserted. She was alone. Alone with that persistent sound, like metal tapping on the asphalt.

She felt something brush her leg then looked down and saw an enormous rat. The creature fixed its beady eyes on her legs. The animal was the size of a cat, wicked teeth protruding, a long slimy tail, long curving claws scraping the asphalt.

Screaming, she ran to her car.

She jumped in and locked the doors. Calm down, she told herself. You can't drive until you calm down. Layla willed herself to gain control. Control, she thought, yeah right. Like anyone has control.

"It was only a wee beastie."

This time she was not imagining him: Ian sat folded into the passenger side of her Toyota, his long legs slanted to accommodate his height.

Layla cracked the window and lit a cigarette. "It was a rat. A fucking rat," she screamed at him.

Ian laughed at her discomfort and fear. "If you'd been in any danger..."

"You'd have made mincemeat of the rat," Layla interrupted. "Yeah, I'm getting the picture. Anything at all that you perceive of as a threat to me is immediately reduced to a hunk of hamburger." She started the car and jerked on the gearshift. The Toyota jolted backwards, tires squealing. "How in the hell can I have any sort of life with you popping in to wreak havoc whenever your cosmic pager goes off? Isn't there an easier ride in this rodeo?" She pulled into traffic, cutting off a Honda. The driver of the other car hit the horn. Layla reached out, her hand landed on Ian's arm as though she was restraining him. "They just honked, that's all. Control yourself."

"I've no control," he said, his voice soft and sad. Ian's face looked young in the faint light, he suddenly seemed no more than a boy. "I've no control," he repeated, and his face hardened back into that of a man who had seen too much.

Then he lifted her hand and kissed it.

A wave of desire washed over her. She longed to pull over to the side of the road. She wanted to fling back his kilt and bury her face in his lap, licking and sucking until she felt him tremble. She pulled her hand away from him and gripped the steering wheel until her fingers hurt.

"I've no control either," she said. She turned onto a side street, away from the leftover traffic on main roads. Layla slowed the car, listened to the sound of her own breathing, short, and shallow. She tried to staunch the flood of obsessive lust, but instead she imagined Ian arching into her mouth, moaning his need. She'd straddle his lap, taking the hot length of him into her, moving up and down while her tongue probed his mouth.

An animal darted in front of her headlights. Hitting the brakes hard, she bumped into the steering wheel. "Seems to be the night for destructive wee beasties," she said, hoping that her ragged breathing would be attributed to the near miss. A calico cat strolled idly across the road. "I don't suppose you can go out for coffee?" Layla giggled.

Ian looked perplexed.

"I was trying for some humor. I obviously failed." Layla drove on through the night. "Never mind," she said. She kept her eyes on the road. When she pulled into her driveway, the house was dark, the flat opaque eyes of the windows overlooked the shady yard. Matt's car was gone. She parked the Toyota and walked to the back steps.

Ian moved through the car and stood near the house, his head lifted to the night sky, his hair falling midway down his back. Layla sat on the steps, embarrassed that she looked at him with such alarming hunger. She devoured him with her eyes, tracing the lines of his muscles over and over again.

"You can hardly see the stars from here," Ian murmured. "North of Aberdeen, the stars glow like fire in the sky. Up in the Highlands the air is clear and the night sky seems full of fairy lights."

Layla wanted him to come closer, but he stood on the gravel, his face to the sky. She was drawn to him, but did not move. "Ian, what do you suppose it is that keeps you earthbound?"

"I've wondered that." He didn't continue.

She lit a cigarette. "Do you think that whatever it is that keeps you earthbound and that makes you haunt me is in control?" Layla shifted the cigarette around in her hand, and burned herself. "I'm not making sense, I know."

"Weel, nae," he said, his voice drifting into broad Scots. "I've had centuries to think aboot it. I used to think it was me own rage, keepin' me here. Now, I dinna ken wha' keeps me here." He paused. "I think I canna rest til I go home."

"What do you mean?"

"I'm not sure," he said. "I think I need to go back to Scotland."

"Do you think that the force, the thing in control, is some kind of evil?"

Ian turned and looked at her. His eyes were troubled, but a slight, bitter smile took over his mouth. "Ah, no, lass. If you want to look at the face of evil, try your mirror. Or, look at my face, or your fey friend Matt, or any stranger on the street. No force in the world contains as much evil as man."

She tried to frame an argument, but she couldn't. She let the cigarette slip from fingers and fall onto the gravel.

He added, "Yet, you'll see good in each face as well. Tha's the way of it. In each of us there's evil and good. The rest of it – the heavens, the cosmos – is only chaos." He smiled a smile that was seductive and amused.

Layla ground her cigarette with her heel and gazed at Ian as though he was a statue in a museum, painfully perfect in his rough male beauty. The lust subsided for a moment, replaced by an unbearable sadness. "Chaos."

"Chaos?"

"Chaos," Layla answered. "No good, no evil. The universe is amoral."

"Do you think so?" He smiled again, a smile that told Layla he thought she had only part of the answer.

"What then? You've had time to think it over." She pulled up her legs and wrapped her arms about them, curling up on the steps.

"Well, there's history. We're caught in a cycle, something that must be resolved or will go on and on." He resumed staring at the stars above.

It was deep dark in the back yard, shrouded by shrubbery and shaded by ancient trees. Occasional flickers of distant headlights bounced off black windows, then danced and feinted across the void. Layla attempted to make sense of Ian's words but was lost in the endless darkness. She sensed a meaning just beyond the edge of her understanding. "What is it? What must be resolved to stop your rage, to stop this spinning out of control?" Biting her lip, she swallowed the question she would not ask: if they resolved the mysterious force that resulted in death, would Ian fade from her life forever?

He said nothing.

"Ian, what must we resolve?"

"Ah lass," his voice shook, " I dinna know."

Layla put her head on her knees, only for an instant. When she raised her eyes to look at Ian, he was gone.

Layla was alone in the back yard.

Even the stars seemed cold and distant.

TWENTY-ONE

"Okay," Layla said, "so tell me about this Jungian racial memory thing."

"Take a course," Addie said dryly.

"Seriously, I want to know about it."

Addie leaned forward; and locked eyes with Layla. "I think I'd like you to tell me why you're interested in racial memory. What does that concept suggest to you?"

Layla watched a prism that hung from a thin wire in front of the window. The colors ricocheted around the room. "I don't know," she said.

Addie sighed. She put her coffee down on the desk with a resounding thump. "Let's try again. What are you really concerned about?"

Layla looked around the office, spotting Addie's diplomas. "You got your master's degree from Chapel Hill?"

Addie didn't answer, not even her standard therapeutic we're-here-to-talk-about-you-not-me. Neatly manicured hands folded in her mauve skirted lap. Addie watched Layla, cat-like in her silent scrutiny.

"Okay," Layla conceded, "We aren't going to talk about you and if I want to learn about Jungian theory I can go to school. Fine." She chucked her soda into the trash. "I'm sorry, I'm being a bitch. It's easy to fall into lately. Being a bitch. I seem to be doing a lot of it. I'm haunted, scared, or bitchy. Today it's bitchy."

She waited for Addie to reassure her, to tell her she *wasn't* being a bitch, and encourage her to go on talking. But Addie didn't speak. The therapist maintained eye contact but continued, sitting motionless, hands folded, a silent study in mauve and cream.

"Your office doesn't tell me anything." Layla railed. "I mean, it's so anonymous. I don't even know if that picture of the desert is really yours or if it came with the building or something. How can you expect me to trust you when I don't know anything about you? Yeah, I know, we're here to talk about me. But I still don't know how I can talk about me without knowing more about you. It's unnatural. I mean, with friends you sort of trade information, you get to know people and you know what you can say to them. I don't know what I can say to you. I don't know what you really believe." Layla rocked back and forth in her chair.

"All right then," she continued. "Do you suppose that maybe we're all controlled by things that happened long ago? That a chain of events once set in motion sweeps us down a path? Damn, I know I'm mixing metaphors all over the place. It would be easier if I knew what you believed in. I am scared I'm going to make a fool of myself, sound crazy or something. You're just going to tell me that your beliefs aren't important, that we're here to talk about me. Right?"

Addie nodded.

"And you probably think that I am so intent on knowing your beliefs because I'm not certain *what* I believe?"

Addie nodded again.

"Okay," Layla said. "Do you think it's crazy to believe that events from long ago cause things to happen in the present? Maybe we can't move forward until we understand those things." Panic seeped into her voice. "It's like I'm haunted."

Instead of the usual therapeutic 'what do you think', Addie replied, "I think that's it. Exactly. We have to know where we came from to know where we are going."

Layla shook her head. "I don't think we're talking about the same thing." She was certain Addie thought she was referring to her mother's death, or Luke's murder.

Layla glanced at the picture of the desert again. Maybe Addie hadn't bought it on a whim from a gift shop or found it hanging on her office wall. Maybe the photograph was one she'd taken on a vacation. Maybe the picture was of an important place to Addie, part of the tapestry of the therapist's life. Maybe Addie would understand, not all of it – not Layla's relationship with a ghost – but Layla's need to understand what had happened *before,* what summoned Ian to her, what forced her to guard her feelings so he wouldn't kill again.

"I don't think that where I come from begins with me," Layla said. "I think that everything in my life started...I don't know...I just don't think it begins with me."

"It seldom does," Addie answered.

"I think I need to figure out where I come from," Layla said. "Does that sound crazy?"

Addie laughed.

Layla flinched. Addie seldom laughed.

"Crazy is a word that has absolutely no meaning," the therapist said. "None whatsoever."

"I thought that crazy was your stock in trade. I mean, isn't crazy your business?"

"Crazy means different things to different people. You seem to use it whenever you are uncomfortable with something you think or feel, like that erases the feeling."

Layla shook her head. "No...that's not it."

"Tell me then."

"I sometimes feel 'crazy' or feel like I must *be* crazy to think what I think or feel what I feel." Layla stopped talking and shook her head.

"Go on..."

"I don't know that I can explain it any better than that. It's like, when you're up late at night, alone in the house, and you hear noises, imagine *things* and after a few minutes your heart starts beating double time and you're scared half out of your skin. Well, when you do that you know you did it to yourself, but the fear is real. I just think I make myself crazy."

"Go on..."

Layla shook her head. "I really *can't.* That's all I can say."

Addie waited a few minutes for Layla to continue but Layla just shook her head.

"Same time next week?" asked Addie.

"Yeah," Layla said stumbling to her feet and wondering if she could ever trust Addie enough to tell her the whole story. "I don't mean to be difficult."

Addie smiled and said, "Next week. Same time, same station."

Layla had already had a busy day. She'd spent most of the morning in the State Employment Office filling out reams of forms, then gone by Central Piedmont College to get copies of her transcripts from semesters scattered over the years. Before her appointment with Addie, she'd even stopped by a temp service to take a timed data entry test. Not having a job was hard work.

Leaving Addie's office, Layla stopped in a bookstore on Monroe Road. Bookstores and libraries soothed her. She derived a feeling of peace, of feeling 'at home' as soon as she entered one. She glanced in her checkbook before exiting her car, and decided she could splurge a little without putting her finances into crisis mode.

Like most of the businesses in this part of town, the bookstore was in a renovated old house. Layla dodged a white cat on her way up the stairs.

The cat humped its back and spat at her.

Startled, Layla dodged the animal. The cat stared at her and attempted to block the door. Layla stepped quickly around the cat.

Bells on the door heralded her entrance. Embarrassed by the cat's behavior, she slunk past a display of vegetarian cookbooks, and found herself in the New Age section. She picked up the nearest book. It was on tarot readings. Layla read parts of it while she thought about the aborted séance at the Jasons.

The white cat that guarded the doorway monitored Layla's movements. The green eyes seemed malevolent, hateful. She put the tarot book on the back on the shelf next to a volume on past life regression. Her fingers glided over the spines of books on spirit guides, karma, and graphology. But none of them seemed likely to offer any answers.

She moved on.

The cat followed. A few feet away from her, the cat padded silently, still watching.

Edging past a large woman picking up several books on astrology, Layla negotiated a path through the bookshelves to the history section. She reached for a copy of a history of Scotland called *The Lion in the North*.

In the travel section, she spotted a copy of *The Rough Guide to Great Britain*, and slid it under her arm.

The cat was perched on the top of a bookcase. Neck

stretched, eyes seeming to glow, watching.

She drifted into fiction. The paperback covers were a riot of garish paintings and sensual photos, bare chested Heathcliffe clones and orgasmic virgins on the romance novels, sultry dames twirling revolvers on the mysteries, silver suited spacewomen on the science fiction books. Layla's eyes lingered on the bodice rippers – dashing Cavaliers and roguish highwaymen clutching bosomy damsels.

Staring at a particularly graphic cover, she thought about how she wanted Ian to caress her breasts, how she'd like to stroke him.

She could almost feel it ...almost.

Leaning down, only a few inches from her face, the cat yowled, a hideous banshee sound.

Layla jerked back, her daydream banished.

She bumped right into Fred.

"We can't go on meeting like this," Fred said. "I'm beginning to get suspicious. What are you doing in a place that doesn't sell booze or cigarettes?"

"I'm looking for stuff to read."

"A bookstore is a good place for it," he answered. He was wearing a different Hawaiian shirt, this one featuring large red hibiscus on a dark green background. "What kind of thing do you like to read?"

"Oh, everything," Layla said, unable to describe her omnivorous tastes in books.

"Well, they don't have much of an 'everything section' here, but they're well stocked in horror. Oh, I forgot. You're the woman whose life is full of horror, so I take it you don't read much horror."

"Actually, I really read some of everything," Layla said. "If the horror section is good, I might want to check it out."

"In that case, back left corner. But you really ought to check out some of the stuff on how to stop smoking."

"Please, Fred," Layla began. But she and stifled a scream with her hand and then jumped back as a bookcase suddenly tumbled over towards on Fred.

Fred moved – but not quickly enough. Several hardbacks hit him, the edge of one book left a long scrape beneath his eye. As he tried to dodge the falling books, he reached for the heavy wooden shelf. A sickening sound, the crunch of his wrist splintering, rewarded his effort.

"No, no, he didn't mean anything!" Layla stood amid the wreckage and babbled. He was just talking about my smoking, he does it all the time, it's for my own good."

"Oh, my goodness." A gray haired woman rushed from behind the register, her long batiked skirt dragging the floor, rows of silver bracelets jangling. "Oh dear, I don't see how...Sir, sir are you alright?"

"I've had better days," Fred answered, getting up off the floor. Books were scattered everywhere.

The cat hissed.

"Let me call an ambulance." The woman brushed at Fred's shirt. "We'll pay for it of course. I don't see how that happened. I told Anita we needed to make certain those cases were stable. Do you think Miss Kitty could have knocked the case? Bad kitty, bad cat. I am so sorry, sir." The woman led Fred to a chair behind the register.

The cat followed Layla to the front of the store.

"Fred, are you okay? Stupid question, of course you aren't. Sorry. Can I get you anything?"

"Let's see, how about the actress that plays Gabrielle on Xena, three sausage pizzas, a winning lottery ticket and a hit man to take care of my boss?" Fred appeared to think for a second. "Give me time, I'm sure I can come up with a few more things."

"Seriously, I feel...really bad about this. Do you want me to call anyone or anything?"

"No one to call, I'll have a nice ambulance ride to the hospital and then make some other people feel guilty because I'm in pain," Fred said. "Don't worry, I'm sure you have a cigarette to smoke or something."

Layla felt helpless. She paid for her books, the cat spat at her as she edged out the door. "Sorry," she said to the cat.

The woman behind the register looked bewildered. "I don't know what's got into Miss Kitty today, she usually makes friends with everyone. You don't have a ghost around you do you? You know animals are sensitive to that sort of thing."

"Help, I am a prisoner in a New Age bookstore," said Fred.

Layla laughed nervously. "Well, if you're all right..."

"The ambulance will be along in a minute," the saleswoman

said. "I suspect they practice conventional medicine,"

"I'm going to be fine," Fred said. "They'll give me drugs and an excuse to miss work. Go, smoke and drink coffee. I'll give you a call later."

Blinking in the sunlight, Layla *did* light a cigarette as soon as she cleared the door. "Ian, Ian," she said, exasperation dripping from her voice. "He was only trying to help."

The Scotsman didn't appear.

Layla stumbled to her car. She did *not* want to go home. She drove toward Down Under.

In the lull between lunch and happy hour, only a few folks sat at the bar. Layla bought a hamburger that dripped with chili and slaw and carried it outside. Wrapping a double layer of napkins around the burger to protect the pages of her new books, she gobbled it down while skimming the travel guide. Drinking a soda, she flipped through the chapters on London and the Southeast, skipping over to the section on Scotland. A blob of chili landed on a description of Edinburgh's Royal Mile. Layla dabbed at it with a paper napkin.

She lit a cigarette and read further. After a description of St. Giles Cathedral, she leaned back and imagined the narrow stone buildings, the mammoth castle towering over the street, and the view from Edinburgh Castle. The pictures in the book Ashley had given her merged with her musings and with something else – something suspiciously like...*memory.*

In her mind's eye, she could see a dark winding street; see the upper windows of the houses on either side, close enough for conversation. She felt as though she recalled walking right up that street, slipping on its wet stones, and reaching the middle of the Royal Mile on a starlit night.

"Ian" she muttered under her breath.

Or, had her mental travel had anything to do with the ghost? Was it perhaps evidence of the racial memory thing? More likely a result of gobbling a hamburger with chili, she thought. Or, of months spent reading about Scotland.

Using a piece of napkin to mark her place, Layla shut the book. She'd been so preoccupied that she hadn't even noticed the after-work crowd drifting into Down Under. Dave wandered in, his arm around the red headed girl he'd been seeing. Tall Jason was close behind him. "Oh, you're going to be in serious trouble, girl," Jason said. "When Matt finds out you've been up here spoiling your dinner, he'll send you to your room for a week. I just saw him up at Reid's buying all kinds of stuff for a big deal meal."

Layla finished her soda. "I didn't know anything was up."

"Holly's back in town," Jason said.

"Well, damn," Layla shoved the book in her backpack. "You know more than I do. I've been out all day. If he'd tried to call, I wasn't home."

Jason made the sign of a cross and parodied warding off evil spirits. "You mean, you don't have a cell phone?" he said in mock horror. "I can't possibly go on speaking to you."

Layla laughed as she left. Jason was unable to keep phone service and often had to scramble to make his rent. Half her friends were on a fast track to something involving stock options and the rest of the group seemed to float from payday to payday, often as not spending their rent money on movie tickets or art supplies. Layla paused to look into the window of the Center Of The Earth Gallery, where a painting – misty mountains against a silver winter sky – seized her attention. If I had a job, I'd buy that, she thought. Standing in front of the gallery, she gazed at the stark scene and it filled her with an inexpressible sadness. The mountains seemed to pierce the soft underbelly of the snow-swollen sky.

A honking horn brought her back to the present. After-work traffic clogged North Davidson. She hurried on to her car, eager to get home and see Holly. Window down and radio blaring country, she cut through residential sections to try to beat the commuter onslaught.

Still in her flight attendant uniform, Holly unloaded her suitcase and garment bag as Layla pulled in the driveway. "Layla!" she squealed, dropping her bags on the gravel and running down the drive. As soon as Layla stepped out of her car, Holly enfolded her in a rib-crushing hug. "Oh damn," Holly shrieked. "Damn, I've been so worried about you."

"I'm okay," Layla said.

Holly pulled back and held Layla at arm's length. "Yeah, right," she said, a wry grin on her face. "And I'm the queen of England."

Layla curtsied then picked up her roommate's garment bag

and scuttled up the stairs. Matt flung open the door, "Well, it's about time someone showed up. I slave over a hot wok half the day and you'd think someone would appreciate it, you'd think someone would show up on time."

Holly grabbed Matt and hugged him. "I came all the way from Frankfurt for your cooking, so it had better be good." She kissed him on the cheek. "And, I got you some shirts in London that are to die for."

"Where's Ashley?" Layla dumped Holly's garment bag on the floor, "Isn't he coming over?"

Matt put a bowl of saffron rice on the table and piled lobster and snow pea pods onto a serving platter, "Just us tonight. Holly and I want to talk some things over with you."

"Give me a sec," Holly said, her navy blue airline jacket sliding to the floor. She left the room in an obvious hurry.

Layla watched Holly's retreat and wondered what Matt and she were planning. Were they frightened by her legal problems? That a grisly murder had occurred right here in the kitchen? Did they think she was going crazy? She wouldn't be surprised if 'the announcement' that was coming was, 'we're both out of here'.

"Quit pouting, I've killed a lobster in your honor, precious. A frigging lobster, I expect smiles and praise." Matt added a chicken dish to the laden table. Despite her suspicion, Layla couldn't help but smile. Matt was so pleased with himself.

Holly bounced into the kitchen wearing an orange pair of shorts and a London pub t-shirt. "I'm starving," she announced and heaped food onto her plate.

"I'm Matt," Matt said, "and we need to tell Layla what's up before she imagines some dark plot against her." Matt shoved a plate across the table to Layla. "Here's the deal, precious," he said. "Being unusually bright, we've noticed that it sucks to be you. Well, Holly can get you a free ticket to ride and I can give you some money. We think that you need to do the 'find yourself' ritual. You know, travel a bit. Then come back and do the school or job thing. We're both really worried about you and think you could use a break."

Holly reached over and grabbed Layla's hand. "You've never really explored the world. You just read about it. There are so many places you've only read about. We want to give you the chance to see them."

Layla's eyes glistened with tears. People just didn't do this for people. "I don't mean to seem ungrateful." But ya'll think I'm crazy, don't you? This is like some kind of intervention thing, right? You're scared I'm going to off myself or something?"

Matt sighed. "I'll ignore that." He handed Layla a pile of papers. "You'll need to fill this out for a passport. I know you want to say no, but just get a freaking passport first. That's all I ask. That way when you throw my money back in my face it will have much more of an impact."

Layla reached out for the forms. She couldn't quite accept what Matt was saying.

"Look," Holly said, "free ticket, anywhere in the world. You choose. It's as simple as that."

"Is it really?" Layla couldn't quite believe what was happening.

"Really," Matt said. "You don't have a real job right now. You aren't in school, why shouldn't you travel awhile? We can take care of things here."

"I don't know what to say."

"You start with 'thank you' and then tell me what a delicious meal I've cooked," Matt said.

"Thank you." Layla reached for the rice.

After dinner, Layla excused herself and went to her room to read. Following a whim, she leafed through one of her history books and guessed the route Ian would have followed out of the Highlands. Scottish prisoners of war had been marched to Edinburgh and then held in London before leaving from Plymouth. Putting the history aside, she turned to her guidebook.

Fred!

She marked her place with an empty cigarette pack and headed toward the kitchen to call him. Halfway down the hall, she heard Holly's voice.

"Matt, I really *am* worried. She's acting strange. I know that anyone *would*...but I'm scared of what might happen. We weren't even thinking about suicide and *she* brought it up. My God! It's worse than you said when you called. I should have come back home immediately. We have to do something."

"We have," Matt answered. "She'll take a vacation, it will put some time between her and everything."

Layla stood in the hallway. She remained motionless. *Eavesdroppers hear no good of themselves.*

"What if she won't go? Then what?"

Layla waited for Matt's reply.

"Then we move to 'plan B' or something," he said.

"What's that?"

"I guess we have to call her therapist. Maybe have her hospitalized again. I don't know. We'll have to talk to her therapist."

Layla felt betrayed. She'd call Fred some other time.

TWENTY-TWO

After a long night doing the door at Crossroads, Layla woke up early to dress for a day of temp work downtown. Filling in for a vacationing receptionist, she sat in the lobby of an accountant's office and answered the phone. During her lunch break, she made notes on a scrap of paper, figuring out how many days work she had to put in to save two thousand dollars. Even though Matt had offered to finance her entire trip, she really wanted to pay part of her own way. And working day and night got her out of the house. She wanted to avoid Matt and Holly after overhearing their conversation.

She dashed out of the office at five to make her six o'clock appointment with Addie. Layla was cruising down Randolph at ten miles over the speed limit when she spotted the blue light in her rearview mirror. "Shit." Layla knew how Holly would handle it; she'd do a lip lick and a hair toss and get off with a 'have-a-nice-day' and a warning.

Pulling over to the side of the road, Layla felt a flash of anger heat her face. Here she was busting her ass to get some quick cash together and another speeding ticket would send her insurance rates to the stratosphere. She rolled down the window and offered the cop her license and registration.

"Good afternoon. Do you know what I clocked you at?" The officer's gun belt was at her eyelevel. His tone reminded her of the young cop who'd dragged her to mental health. Cops, courts, and the threat of jail spun through her mind like an out-of-control roller coaster careening off a rickety track.

"No sir," she squeaked, her fear rising with each succeeding second. As he walked back to the car to call in her license number, Layla visualized shackles on her wrists. What if something had gone wrong, what if he'd been following her because they had decided to arrest her for Luke's murder?

With each step the officer took on his return to her car, Layla's fear increased. She was paralyzed with panic. He held out her license, and registration. "I'm going to have to write you a ticket."

Just beyond the cop, Layla saw Ian.

The ghost walked through a passing car, a grim look on his face. Hand in her mouth, Layla shook her head. Ian did not break his stride. He approached the cop, his face a study in vengeance.

Layla was desperate. She forced herself to mask her fear, "A ticket isn't the end of the world," she said, a forced smile straining her mouth. "A ticket doesn't scare me."

The officer looked at her like he thought she was crazy.

Ian stopped just short of the officer's shoulder.

The officer handed her the ticket. "Everything's fine, sir. You have a nice day," Layla babbled.

The officer appeared to deliberate. Layla wondered if he thought she was smarting off to him. She kept smiling like a kid running for class president. The cop straightened his hat and said, "Drive carefully," before he turned and walked away.

Ian faded into the asphalt and exhaust fumes.

Layla sat in her car shaking. She lit the filter end of a cigarette. Disgusted, she flung it out the car window and pulled out another. A coughing fit wracked her body. She struggled to catch her breath. As soon as she could breathe, she took another drag.

Don't think don't feel.

She repeated the words: *don't think don't feel,* clicked on the turn signal and cautiously pulled out into traffic.

She checked her watch as soon as she parked. Lighting a cigarette off the end of the first one, she walked to the door of the clinic. Standing to the side, she smoked rapidly before entering the building.

Layla thought her distress had to be plastered across her face.

She sat opposite Addie, assuming that the therapist would take note of her discomfort and make it easy for her to explain. But Addie maintained her usual relaxed style, immobile, waiting.

"What is it with therapists? You didn't even ask how I am."

Layla said. "I don't know what to say this week,"

"We've been working on you making a plan for what you'd like to do," Addie reminded her.

"Yes, well...Matt and Holly, my room mates, want to help me take a trip. They're worried about me. They think I am going to try to kill myself or something."

"And?" Addie looked into Layla's eyes.

"I don't like it...the two of them talking about me like I need...I don't know what." Layla stopped talking for a moment. She clenched her fists then stretched out her fingers. "They talk like I'm crazy. I don't like it. I know they care about me and I really appreciate *that*...but the rest of it, the whispered conversations like I am defective. I hate it."

"Go on," said Addie.

"I overheard a conversation. They were talking about how if I didn't take the trip they were going to talk to you about what they needed to do about me."

"I can't talk to them without your signed consent," Addie explained.

"I really *do* appreciate them wanting to give me a vacation..." Layla's voice trailed off. She leaned forward and propped her chin on her hands.

"You don't seem pleased about it," Addie said, her voice mild.

"I am. Really. I guess I'm kind of overwhelmed that they think they need to take care of me. It makes me feel like a huge fuck-up, like I'm not an adult. Right now their plan is that in a few weeks I'm off somewhere, and then settle into school or work when I get back."

"It must be confusing," Addie said. "You feel good that they care so much, but you want to fix your life yourself."

"Exactly." Layla looked down at Addie's burgundy shoes; they were the exact shade of her long burgundy shirt. Addie seemed so serene, her office so neat, her clothing always so perfectly coordinated.

"All of us need help from time to time. You've just been through some extraordinary events," Addie said.

"I'm scared of how I feel."

"About?" Addie let the one word question hang in the air.

Fear crept up Layla's throat, almost strangling her. She dug her fingernails into her palms. Her hands grew icy, as her terror increased; she had a sudden dread of Ian. She willed her breathing to slow down. She put her hands on the armrests of the chair and molded her body into a picture of relaxation. Acting as calm as she could, she said, "Whenever I feel angry or frightened, terrible things happen."

"Say more about that," Addie said. Even the tiny garnet studs in her ears echoed the color of her outfit.

"When I get scared or upset, it sets off a chain of events. Horrible things happen. I was angry with my mother, angry at Mazie, Luke frightened me. Look what happened." Layla looked beyond Addie. "Even the cop who picked me up when I went to Hotel Silly..."

Ian stood a few feet behind Addie's back.

Layla stared into his eyes. He seemed to be trying to figure out what was going on – whether Layla was threatened, glancing at the therapist, scanning the room.

And then, he disappeared.

"I can see why you'd think that," Addie said. " But *if* you made all these terrible things happen, *then* you could make them stop."

"I'm not making this up. Things *do* happen. You don't understand. There's more. Whenever I feel threatened, whenever I...there's always a risk...Anytime I feel angry or scared it seems like..."

"Bad things happen, but not because of your emotions." Addie rocked back in her chair.

"You just don't get it. I'm a catalyst or something. It's like I tap into some elemental force or something. But, *really*, when I feel things strongly...stuff happens. My emotions seem larger than I am, I can't keep them in my body. I mean, I know they're in me, but it *feels* like they are this external destructive force...That's the best I can do, I can't really explain it."

"It seems to you that experiencing your feelings sets off a chain of events out of your control?"

"Well...*something* like that happens," Layla said. Abruptly she added, "I'm not certain what my work schedule will be next week. I'll call for an appointment when I know."

"All right, then," Addie said, her face bland. "Good-bye."

Layla left the office.

She had no intention of returning.

Layla wanted to talk to Ian.

She wanted to work out some way that she could function without having to constantly monitor her emotions to prevent him from doing something terrible. She drove home in a daze, wondering if summoning Ian was a possibility.

I can't just call him. She began to giggle despite the appalling situation. *I have more in common with Ian than most of the men I know. Neither of us has a cell phone. Maybe we have compatible astrological signs.* She slammed on the brakes and narrowly missed running a red light. *Maybe if she visualized him and used her mind to call out to him, the specter of the Scotsman would appear.*

She was soon under the green tunnel of overlapping tree branches that created the soft sultry light of Queen's Road. Arriving home, she lingered in the back yard while the twilight faded subtly and night drifted over the pine trees. Matt and Holly weren't home.

Layla sat on the back steps and watched the blue smoke from her cigarette curl into the near navy blue sky. Reluctantly, she stood and went into the house. Hand on the door, Layla froze, questioning whether she wanted to turn the knob. For the barest moment, she was fearful that she'd open the door and find that something awful had happened to her roommates.

Entering the kitchen, she found a note from Matt. *"Figured you'd be exhausted, I'm at Ashley's if you need me. Hugs."*

A quick check of the answering machine revealed that Fred had recovered from the incident at the bookstore, Jason was going to be at Down Under, and Holly would be out overnight.

Alone for the night.

The full moon hung saucer sized in the sky. Layla looked out the kitchen window at the face of the man in the moon. When she was five or six, she'd seen it for the first time and puzzling it out had seemed like an accomplishment. She recalled her mother's manicured oval fingernail pointing at the moon, *"There are the eyes. Don't you see them?"*

Layla listened to the house creaks; night noises spooked her, the ubiquitous water bugs congregating beneath Matt's scoured sink made tiny restless taps. The old lady groans of the house mingled with the sighing of the wind and the restless scratching of tree branch against screen.

She opened the refrigerator and stared – food, wine, and soda suddenly a mystery, the cans of beer and jars of pickles indecipherable in the three-person clutter. Layla poured chardonnay into a jelly jar and carried it out to the sun porch. Sitting in a wicker rocker, wine beside her on a small table, she concentrated on Ian.

Initially, it was exhilarating.

Layla traced the lines of his body in her memory. She brought to mind his eyes, slightly slanted, over high cheekbones. Familiar warmth spread from her thighs, creeping upwards to her nipples. Her fingers strayed from the jelly jar to her neck then down to the sensitive spot near her collarbone. Blushing, she let her hand drift slowly across her smooth skin to her puckered nipples.

Then she allowed her fingers to trace her ribcage and slip beneath the waistband of her pants. She sighed as she brushed the soft curls and arched into her own hand, one finger flicking and stroking. While she sent herself into the heat and craziness, she thought about Ian, imagined his tongue teasing hers, thought about tracing a trail down his neck, flickering her tongue across his chest, making *him* crazy, so crazy that he pushed her onto her back and entered her with sweet, hot force.

She thought about him thrusting into her and shuddered with lust and shame.

She thought about licking the length of his leg, moving her tongue up the indentation of muscle in his thigh until...

She was burning with the shame of her lust for the dead man. She grabbed her wineglass and gulped half the jar down.

Exasperated, she trotted to the kitchen and returned with the half full bottle of chardonnay. The evening had a familiar tone of humiliation. Layla felt like she was sitting in a crowded bar alone waiting for an errant boyfriend, no different than so many nights when she'd waited for Luke for hours at Down Under, a smile stuck to her face while she watched the door, aware he had forgotten to come.

The wine and the silence bled all her energy, all thought. She waited, and it seemed to suck the life from her lungs, leaving her a husk. Tired – so tired – and mildly buzzed, she felt sorrow descend like a fog. She sensed Ian somewhere in the bleak night, but he didn't form. She could not see the ghost but she knew he was there.

Then, soft as a whisper and quick as death, he was beside her.

Shaken and shaking, she turned to him. "What am I going to do?" She gulped half the jar of wine then lit a cigarette. "I need answers. What the hell is going on?"

"Hell itself, I'd say." Ian laughed bitterly at his own words. "I think I've no control. It seems my rage outlives me." Ian's face, only a shadow itself, was lost in the shadows.

"Your rage," Layla began. "*Your* rage? I was going to ask you why you killed Luke when you did. Why not *before*. But I figured it out. You waited until the exact moment I wanted him to stop, until I wanted him dead. *My* anger killed him. I killed him as much as you did."

"No," Ian said. " I'll not hide from what I am. The rage that burns within me is stronger than death."

Layla twisted in the chair to look up at him. He was opaque now, solid. She chugged the rest of the wine in the jar, flinching as it hit her guts. Instantly woozy, she reached out and touched Ian's arm.

He felt like a mortal man.

Tentatively, and then with increasing pressure, her fingers explored his forearm and moved down to grasp his hand. It was warm to her touch. "The rest of it, Ian. There's more to it than rage."

"Is there now?" His tone was mocking, his expression one of mild amusement.

She leaped off the chair and the empty jar shattered. Layla wrapped her arms around his neck and plastered her body to his chest. She pulled his face to hers and kissed him aggressively, her tongue plunging into his mouth. He slipped one arm around her and caressed her rear with a circular motion, pressing against her. His other hand cupped her breast, thumb stroking the nipple.

She pulled back slightly, still on tiptoe, "That," Layla said insistently. "There's that."

"Oh lass," he said, each word dripping sorrow and regret. "Tha's naught at all. I were a man once. Tha's all there is to that."

Layla did not believe him. Her breathing was ragged. Her legs shook. She felt hot and hungry. "I think you feel something for me," she said.

"Tha' I do." His hair covered his face as he turned away. "Pity and lust. You're a pretty woman. And, you are mine to protect." He lifted her chin with his fingers. But his hand was icy now, insubstantial. "Giving your heart to a ghost is a wee bit mad." He lowered his voice. "My heart's in my Maggie's grave."

"Don't pity me."

She was alone. She didn't know if Ian had even heard her.

◈

"I'm sorry I called you over at Ashley's, that was incredibly selfish of me." Layla lit a cigarette.

"Don't apologize, precious. I'm glad you called. Lately it seems like you won't let anyone care about you." Matt poured himself a cup of coffee and sat at the kitchen table opposite Layla. "So you have a plan?"

"Sort of...well, yes. I do have a plan. It's just...well it could *sound* like I'm really crazy." Layla took a deep breath and exhaled slowly. "To start off with I *am* going to do some traveling like you and Holly suggested."

"Good." Matt looked puzzled.

Layla laughed ruefully. "Yeah, so why did I have to call you in the middle of the night, right? That's the complicated part...but I *finally* figured out what I need to do. And it's because I met someone."

"Someone?"

"Yeah. I met a man..."

"Not in the hospital?" Matt blurted the question out then coughed. "I'm sorry, I know how that sounds, but your judgment about men seems..."

"I know. I know," Layla interrupted. "But hear me out. I've met someone and he needs my help. I have to get to Scotland to help him. And there are some complications, the entire thing is really complicated."

"Scotland?" Matt looked bewildered.

"Yes, you see that is one of the complicated parts of the whole thing. I finally figured out that to help him I have to go to Scotland so that he can...he's kind of stuck with me...he goes where I go."

"I don't understand anything you're saying. This sounds crazy." Matt shouted at her. "Have you discussed this with that therapist you're seeing? Does she know about this?"

"I've tried to explain it to her, but she just doesn't get it. I figured that you were the only one who'd understand..."

"Precious, I'm trying to understand, but you aren't making any sense. What man? What complications?"

"Okay. Well...I don't know if you'd exactly call him a man. That's what's complicated." Layla crushed her cigarette out and reached across the table. She grabbed Matt's hand. "This is going to be really hard to explain. But you have to trust me. You *have* to believe me. I'm *not* crazy. But some crazy things have happened."

"I know," Matt said sympathetically. "What's the complication with this man?"

Layla took a deep breath. She listened to the ticking of the kitchen clock.

"Well what? Is he married? Running from the law? Gay? Does he belong to a weird religious group? What's the complication?"

"He's dead."

TWENTY-THREE

"I'm not bullshitting, Holly. She sat right there and told me she was involved with a dead man and that she had to go to Scotland because of him." Matt paced back and forth. He wore yesterday's shirt and his hair was a mess. "Damn."

"Have you called that therapist?" Holly spun her cup around nervously. Coffee slopped onto the table.

"Hell yes, I've called her therapist. It took me five tries to even get through to her and all she'd say is that she could not discuss any of her clients without their signed consent. If I had a concern about a friend or family member then I needed to get that person to sign a release of information."

"Jeez." Holly shook her head. "Did you tell her Layla was off her nut?"

"Yeah, she told me that if I wanted to have her committed to the hospital I had to show proof that she was mentally ill *and* dangerous to herself or others." Matt spun around frantically. "I got the distinct impression that she doesn't think Layla is mentally ill. Before, when I signed those papers to send her to the hospital, she'd sat in the kitchen with a corpse for two days – stopped speaking, screamed in the emergency – but now she *looks* okay..."

"What are we going to do? We can't just let her go halfway around the world while she's like this. Anything could happen to her." Holly gnawed her lower lip. "I know the trip was our idea, but I just don't see how...I don't think she's *really* mentally ill, but she's been under so much stress that she's unbalanced or something."

Layla froze in the hallway. They were talking about her

again.

"We can't let her go anywhere," Matt said.

Matt, I trusted you. Angry tears filled Layla's eyes. I trusted Matt and he didn't believe me. She held her breath. She heard Holly's voice.

"I've already given her the airline ticket. She has the ticket, her passport, I don't know how much in traveler's checks. We can't just tell her to give back the ticket. That might make her do something worse. Did you tell the therapist about her mentioning suicide?"

"She said that the danger had to be immediate," Matt answered. "She said some bullshit about that being too long ago." Layla heard Matt stomp around the kitchen, punctuating his path with random slamming of cabinet doors. "I bet she put the tickets and stuff in her jewelry box. We can just wait until she goes out and take it."

His words hit Layla like a sucker punch to the gut. They really were going to stop her. Matt would go into her room, plunder through her things.

Just like Mazie.

"Where is she now?"

"She's been holed up in her room all day," Matt said. "Reading, or talking to her dead man, I don't know what she's doing in there. She got really distant when I didn't accept...when I didn't believe her."

Layla stood rooted to the spot. Matt really didn't believe her. Her best friend.

"You don't suppose she's done...*something* to herself," Holly said.

"I've heard her in there and she came out and got a soda. But she hasn't spoken to me since that weird shit last night. We have to stop her."

The temperature in the hallway dropped. Layla felt the familiar chill that indicated Ian's presence. He materialized a half step ahead of her, emerging out of the wall. She reached out to touch him, but her hand passed through him. "Ian, Ian," she whispered.

Ian walked down the hall without turning around.

"Ian, please. *Please*," she begged, her voice louder.

"That's her," Holly said.

Layla rushed down the hallway and moved in front of Ian. "Damn it, no!" she screamed. "No!"

His face was stony, jaw clenched tight, eyes cold.

"I'm not in any danger, Ian. I'm not threatened. Please!" Layla grabbed his arms. Tears streamed from her eyes. "Please." She studied his face. Did he understand? *"Please."* Layla held onto Ian. Time stretched. Hours seemed to pass between each second. "Please." She dug her fingernails into his arms.

He was gone.

Frightened, exposed, betrayed.

Layla walked into the kitchen. Matt and Holly stopped moving, stopped talking. Both of them stared at her. Ignoring them, Layla flung open the refrigerator and pulled out a pack of cheese. She slapped cheese between two pieces of bread and smeared mustard on it. Neither Matt nor Holly spoke. "I'm making a fucking sandwich," she said. "You've seen sandwiches before."

Before either of her friends could respond, Layla took her sandwich and retreated to her room. She locked the door and pulled a large backpack from the closet. Propping her feet on the backpack, she ate her sandwich.

Only a few days ago Matt had said "I really wish you'd get a suitcase with wheels. This backpacking through Europe look is so retro." Now he was trying to keep her in Charlotte.

She had to leave.

Tonight proved that at any moment *something* could happen – to Matt, to Holly, to anyone. Leaving would protect them.

Passport, tickets, traveler's checks, the money Matt had given her – all there. Layla hastily folded a few pairs of jeans, a couple of shirts and tossed socks and underwear on top of them. Matt and Holly had to sleep sometime.

Hours later, she crept down the hallway. She couldn't say good-bye. They'd stop her. Sneaking out of the house, Layla controlled an urge to cry.

Don't think.

She sped through the night and pulled into a deserted parking lot on Eastway Drive. Huddled under her jacket, she napped restlessly. When sunlight and traffic sounds disturbed her, she headed to the airport.

Once she'd parked and taken the shuttle to the terminal

building, she wandered around looking for the right desk. It was surprisingly easy to change her ticket – in fifteen minutes, she was booked on a flight leaving in a few hours. She answered security questions, checked her backpack, and got her seat assignment. She reached the bar nearest her gate then chain-smoked one cigarette off the end of another.

"Nervous flyer?" The bartender placed her second beer before her

"I'm facing eight smoke-free hours," she answered. "I'm a madwoman, humor me." Finishing beer number two, she went into a shop and bought a box of envelopes, stamps, and a pen. Back in the bar, she put her car key, the parking receipt, and her registration into an envelope. *"This really is for the best,"* she wrote on bit of paper before addressing the envelope to Matt. She drank one last beer and sucked up three smokes before her flight was called. She missed Matt already.

Without any carry-on baggage, Layla settled in quickly between a businessman with a laptop and a woman in a leopard print jumpsuit. She pulled her London guidebook out of her pocket and studied it. She read about the Victoria and Albert Museum while the plane taxied down the tarmac and took off. After take-off, she read the airline magazine, drank white wine, and settled into her seat to sleep. Layla slept through the evening meal service and guiltily applied extra moisturizer when she awakened to a tiny cup of coffee. Unable to stretch in the cramped coach class seat, she kept her elbows close to her sides and filled out her landing card with the address of a bed and breakfast in London listed in the London guide.

As the plane bumped down at Gatwick, Layla's apprehension grew. She wished there had been a direct flight to Scotland out of Charlotte Douglas International Airport. She'd just have to figure out how to get there from London. She leaned forward and looked out the window. Airplanes from all over the world were parked or crawling slowly in the gray morning. El Al, Swissair, Air France, and the other airlines stood like huge sea mammals trapped on shore. Despite the announcement requesting that passengers remain seated, several men had already moved to the aisle and opened the overhead bins. Three seats up, a man in khaki pants struggled to keep duffel bags from hitting his head.

Layla's neck was stiff. Her eyes felt scratchy. But she was wide-awake, tingling, and anxious. When the plane stopped moving and people bumbled through the passageways, Layla's pulse raced, impatiently waiting while travelers arranged their luggage, put on coats, and blocked the aisle. She felt a pulling, a longing, almost as if she was close to home and desperate to arrive.

Move, come on, move. But the line moved at glacier speed. When she finally exited the plane into the hallway the chill in the air slapped Layla into maximum alertness. The worn carpet and the dingy paint in the hallway, were unexpected after the shiny floors and decorator touches of Charlotte's airport.

Layla staggered across the grimy carpeting. She hurried to passport control and joined a long line of sleepy travelers who had deplaned from several overnight flights.

Just ahead, a woman in a sari calmed a fretful baby. She heard another woman whine, "John, are you sure this is the right line? I'm not waiting all morning for nothing." Layla rocked back and forth, craning her neck to see how long the line was in front of her.

Reaching the end of the line, she was summoned by a young man whose thin lips, ivory skin, and starling blue eyes reflected a guidebook-perfect Englishman. She held out her passport and landing card.

"Are you on business or holiday?"

"Uhm...vacation."

"Oh, right, then, you're on holiday," he said. "On your own then?"

"Well...yes," she hesitated.

He gave her another glance and then handed her passport back over. "Thank you."

Layla followed the signs to baggage claim to retrieve her backpack. The overnight flight was hitting her hard, the room seemed to tilt and whirl ever so slightly, a funhouse mirror made real. The people she passed all seemed somewhat sinister. The lights in the baggage claim area seemed horrendously bright, screaming against her eyeballs.

Finally through customs, Layla caught the scent of smoke and coffee. On her right, she saw a Costa Coffee stand offering the standard international array of cappuccino, espresso, and dishwater American coffee. She bought a cappuccino and sat, lit her first cigarette with enormous satisfaction. Nearby, a woman with a Caribbean accent said, "I don't understand this bit about jet lag. They sleep on the plane don't they?" Layla glanced at her watch and calculated the time in Charlotte attempting to figure out how little sleep she'd had. It made her head hurt.

Weary and edgy at the same time, only caffeine and nicotine keeping her vertical, she wandered through the crowds to the train station inside the airport. Layla squinted at the train schedule. She couldn't figure out how to get from Gatwick to Edinburgh, and realized she'd best spend at least one night in London. She bought a ticket for central London. A creaky escalator transported her down to platform nine, where she waited for the Gatwick Express to Victoria Station. Two young girls with heavily mascaraed eyes stood smoking beside the tracks, their bare feet with candy colored toenails stuffed into platform sandals, their bare legs incongruous beneath heavy coats. Two cardiganed old ladies shared the bench, one complained, "Christmas used to wait a proper time, now soon as there's a snap in the air, it's jingle, jingle, jingle. I fear I'll be jingle belled to death."

A southbound train to Brighton whooshed past, the swirls of cool air taunting Layla with the promise of day. Three minutes later, the Victoria Express shuddered to a stop. Layla felt her achy leg muscles pulling as she stepped up onto the train. She balanced her backpack on the luggage rack and slipped into a window seat.

The arthritic train wheezed to a start and then shot down the track. Just outside the airport, Layla saw snatches of almost-countryside, the land so green that it nearly glowed emerald. The morning mist was still visible, rising wraithlike, ethereal, hanging over lawns and ball fields. Neat row houses bordered playing fields so eye-achingly green that they seemed Technicolor. Tiny gardens with effusive rose bushes trailing up walls, skeletal hollyhocks reminiscing about summer blurred beside roads snarled with trucks.

The landscape melted into the high rises and industrial clutter of London.

Between huge anonymous housing blocks, Layla saw random pubs that seemed relics of the seventeenth century. Between warehouses large as the pyramids and shiny Sainsbury's, she saw crooked streets dotted with tiny stores.

The train convulsed, then stopped at Victoria Station.

Layla jumped onto the platform, dragging her backpack. Nothing could have prepared her for the crowd in Victoria Station.

Hundred of Londoners in ubiquitous black rushed like wind up toys chattering on cell phones. Pinstriped men with dreadlocks sidestepped emaciated platinum haired beauties with elongated thighs. Young women with shiny, thick, rich-girl hair wore pearls and expensive boots and walked hand in hand with Mohawked men with bad teeth. People looked up to the train schedules, down at their shoes, dead ahead at their destination or at their cups of milky tea.

Layla couldn't figure out which way to go. Across the station, an escalator led up to shopping. Hordes of people swept by, trampled her when she stopped to read the directional signs. She hugged the wall and figured out the way to the tube – the subway.

But she had nowhere to go.

Scooting past a Boots and a Thomas Cook's, she wiggled through the crowd and reached a pay phone. Juggling her guidebook and fiddling with the unfamiliar coins, she placed a call to the first budget hotel listed. Luckily, they had a room available, *and* the directions seemed simple.

Just outside the station, she paused and leaned against the wall. A dark skinned man in a ratty overcoat stopped a few inches away from her muttering, "Princess Diana, she dead. So very sad." A younger man in a sweat suit touched him on the shoulder and they moved back into the flow of human traffic. Layla watched people pass down into the underground, like traffic on the interstate. She followed them down the steps.

Those steps were filthy. She kept to the right and moved without being able to really look where she was going. The station was full of people, rats in a maze zigging and zagging about. They all seemed to know where they were going except for the five folks bunched in front of the directional map.

Victoria line to Oxford Circus, change at Oxford Circus for Central line to Lancaster Gate. She headed down a hallway, teased by posters for plays, large showy pictures of exhibits at the Victoria and Albert Museum, special offers on cosmetics available at Selfridges and travel ads for unknown exotic sunny locations. The platform was a mass of humanity. When the train arrived, people unpacked themselves from a solid wall of flesh and spilled out onto the platform as even more people waded into the crush.

They reached Oxford Circus. Layla snaked out of the swarm and followed arrows directing her to the Central line.

Just ahead in the grainy light, she thought she saw a tall man in a kilt, a man with red blonde hair.

Jet lag.

She stumbled as she rounded the corner to the Central line platform.

People were mashed against the train windows. They crabbed sideways through the doors, brief cases held like shields, handbags clutched close. Layla plunged into the train, only a few stops to Lancaster Gate.

At Lancaster Gate station, she spewed out of the train. She rounded a corner and walked up an incline to get in an elevator. Layla read an advertisement for an Indian restaurant on Queensway Road and one for sung Eucharist at a church on Bayswater while the elevator shimmied.

Spit out of the elevator, she was swept through a narrow passage beside a dirty floor-to-ceiling window before exiting onto Bayswater Road. Across the traffic, Hyde Park glowed like living green silk, tiny jewels of flowers erupting, the trees portrait-sitting for an impressionist.

Two women in Regency dress passed by the edge of the park. A young girl in Edwardian garb, bright cheeked and pale curled, rolled an iron hoop on a non-existent path.

A misty lady in a medieval laced gown careful lifted her hem to avoid offal on the ground.

An elegant woman, in a suit that looked like Bette Davis should have worn in a film, passed Layla and walked right through the station wall.

Three Roman centurions marched down the center of Bayswater Road, right down the yellow line.

A Druid melted into the spray of a fountain in the park.

At the station front, Layla stood stupid and silent, looking across Bayswater to Hyde Park.

And then Ian passed through a black cab and crossed

through a bus to meet her on the street.

"You're seeing them all, aren't you?" he said.

Layla nodded.

"London is one of the most haunted cities on earth, layers of lost souls wandering," Ian said. "Somehow, I've opened a door for you. Perhaps one you'd have been better off leaving locked." She wanted him to touch her. He didn't. He stood, hands by his side, vigilant, looking across the street into the distance. They watched a bedraggled beggar, maybe medieval, with blackened stumps instead of hands, reaching out to empty space. The beggar faded into a newsagent's stand.

"Come along, you could probably use a coffee," Ian said. "Just down the road there's a pub. Claude haunts it. He's a bit of bore, he's been dead for about two, three hundred years. He had his last drink there before they hung him. It'll be all right, I won't let him bother you."

Layla nodded and followed.

"You don't know, do you?"

"What don't I know?" Layla's head was reeling.

"More than half the people you see walking the streets of London are dead." Ian smiled. "You've been among us all morning."

"I *need* a real drink," Layla answered. They crossed to a small island and then crossed again to a corner in front of a foreign exchange.

"Bit early in the day for that," Ian answered.

"I'm on holiday," Layla said grimly as a small boy walked through the wall of the foreign exchange.

"Here we are." They halted in front of The Swan, a pub with picnic table outdoor seating on Bayswater Road.

Layla looked around wondering out what to do; no table service. She pulled open the heavy door, entered, and went up to the bar. She bought a half pint of cider. Retreating to a corner table, she pulled off her backpack. Claude, the dead highwayman, was boisterous and drunk. "I wasn't an innocent man," he said. "Not me, not for a minute."

"I *hate* London," Layla said.

"As do I," Ian answered.

"So what the hell are we doing here?

"I think we're retracing my journey. London is the last bit of

Britain I remember. We were taken to London from Edinburgh before being moved to ships that sailed to the colonies. I caught the fever...I recall London and then the ship – nothing in between."

Layla drank the sweet cider. The alcohol hit her hard. She was tired, frightened, confused. "Edinburgh," she said, echoing Ian.

"I was happy there for a time – before Culloden. When Maggie was seventeen she stayed with her aunt in Edinburgh for the summer...that was when...when we *knew*."

"How old were you?"

"Twenty." Ian seemed more human, less ghostly than before, yet somehow *distant*...far, far from her.

Layla drank quickly. "How old were you when you died?" She spoke to herself.

TWENTY-FOUR

Layla paid for one night's stay. She dropped her pack on the floor of the tiny room. It was only four in the afternoon but she was exhausted. Without bothering to shower, she peeled off her clothes and climbed between stiff, scratchy sheets.

The alien noises of a large city announced morning. She sat up, stretched, and headed to the shower. The shower spit more than streamed and she danced around beneath it, teasing shampoo from her hair.

After breakfast, backpack cinched into place, she walked down the road to the tube station. Layla wanted out of London. Sunlight spilled through the clouds onto the white fronts of Georgian townhouses. Smells from kebab shops spiced the air. Different languages spun together in a tapestry of intonation and inflection. She descended into the dark underground and traveled to Kings Cross Station.

Layla jumped onto the platform through a wall of thick black smoke. Screams ricocheted off the walls. People stampeded, shrieking. The escalator erupted in a wall of flame. The blackened flesh of a woman flaked off her face leaving gleaming bone that crumbled into ash.

Layla gulped. She didn't smell smoke. It wasn't hot. She was seeing the images of the horrible Kings Cross Fire that killed thirty-one people in 1987. Bracing herself against the tile wall with her hand, she took deep breaths. When she looked up, the grisly images had faded to mere washes of color blending into the crowd of living commuters.

Straightening her spine and focusing on the top of the escalator, Layla stepped on board and rode to the top. The

British Rail station adjoining the underground was bright and modern. She fixed her eyes on the ticket counter and walked across the shiny floor. After checking the schedule to find the proper platform for the Flying Scotsman, the fast train to Edinburgh, she veered into a WH Smith's to look at magazines. Ian walked along beside her.

He flickered in and out. Layla wanted to ask him why she kept seeing other ghosts but knew she'd look like a loon walking through the station muttering to no one.

Her train shimmied to a stop; Layla hopped on the first car and rambled down the train to a smoking car.

A conductor positioned between the cars got her attention. "Excuse me, sir," she asked, "where's the smoking car?"

"Just two more down, miss," he answered.

Layla was well past him before the archaic quality of his uniform hit her. He seemed like someone out of a Second World War newsreel. She felt a scream stuck in her throat. But, what good would it do? Really? She could go barking mad on the fast train to Edinburgh, or she could carry on.

Carry on.

She shoved her backpack into the rack over two empty seats. She claimed the window seat. A tired looking young woman in a rumpled jumper proffering a box of Ribena with a sip-it straw in the general direction of her pasty faced kid took the seats opposite Layla. The child kicked at something unseen.

"We're only going as far as York," said the mother, her voice weary, her eyes red.

Layla smiled the watery vague smile of the childless caught in proximity to other people's offspring. She pulled out a notebook, intending to write a letter to Matt. Before the train leapt out of King's Cross, she began: *"Matt, I know that you'll think I am out of my mind. But, really, I am no crazier than usual. Ian is real. The other ghosts are real. Since I've got here it seems that the veil between the worlds is lifted, I can see..."* Layla sighed and started scribbling over what she had written. There was no way she could explain it, not at all.

The thump of the child's tiny sneakers was lost in the chugging of the train. The rhythmic rock of the train and the blur of the countryside behind the windows pacified Layla. She watched London fade. Outside of the capital, the train traveled through the postcard English countryside, squares of green framed by hedgerows with an occasional ancient spire marking the sky.

An hour out of London, Layla bought a cup of bitter coffee when the tea trolley clattered through the car. The steam rising from the cup warmed her hands. She lit a cigarette and watched the smoke and steam merge. The young woman and child nodded off to sleep. The noise of the train muffled the sounds of conversation.

Layla looked around the car. Several seats up, a young woman with industrially lacquered hair gestured wildly and spoke into a cell phone. Three boys, school ties askew, shared a skin magazine. She wondered how many people on the train were ghosts.

I can't live like this. I can't.

The train journeyed north. When it stopped in York, Layla immediately knew that the town was haunted by multitudes. Hordes of spirits drifted around the train. The restless dead drained her energy. Simply recognizing their presence was exhausting. Layla was a voyeur in a half-world of miserable dead. The mother and child bustled off the train. Layla barely noticed their departure.

The train lurched out of the station. Layla struggled to gain control, to reach within herself and find the capacity for not thinking, not feeling, not seeing.

Near Berwick, she saw the dismal coastline, the sea gray and misty, the rocks stark and treacherous. Staring out the window, watching the countryside slip away, she regained her equilibrium.

The first sight of Edinburgh hit Layla like a physical blow. Stark and macabre, rising on a pinnacle of black volcanic rock, the impenetrable city rose above the slumbering landscape. Twilight purpled the evening and a few cold stars blinked across the vast distance of space. Edinburgh Castle towered above the city. Tall houses, unlike any she'd seen in the rest of Britain, formed tight warrens and sinister alleyways amid the chill rock of Edinburgh's Old City.

She looked to her right and saw the lights of the New City, across Princes Street, quivering in the evening haze like remote fireflies. The drizzle distorted the store signs and pub lights, their bright colors swirling into the dying day.

Layla blinked in the modern bright space of Waverly Station. After windowed images of the Old City, the dazzling lights, hurried commuters and shiny floors shocked her into alertness. Backpack slung over one shoulder, she ambled over to the Tourist Information office to book a bed and breakfast.

Near the desk, a loud woman with an American accent wailed at the staff person, "Now, tell me again, what's 'en suite' and what's 'private'?" The woman's husband looked embarrassed.

Layla stood in line and shuffled from one foot to the other. She had a sense that she wouldn't be in Edinburgh long, that after a few days Ian would push her further north to the Highlands.

Layla gnawed her lip and wondered if it was okay to smoke while she stood in line. While she wondered, a tall skinny woman with spiky hair bleached white and tipped purple, elbowed her way to the desk, "Colin, my love," she said to the tourist officer, "I've got a two singles available and I'm on my way home, if you've got a weary tourist or two that could use a ride and a room."

"Elspeth, bless you. You're a Godsend. Look at this lot," answered the young man. "Hold on a minute."

Elspeth stepped to the side of the desk, her bracelets jangling and chain belt rattling. Layla counted eight earrings in her left ear, only three in the right. Elspeth wore a long black coat opened to reveal tight black pants tucked into knee-high boots. Her blouse was purple satin and a metal belt shook and shimmied around her impossibly narrow hips.

The young man in the neat blazer rapped on his desk. "Excuse me, are any of you waiting for a single? Anyone at all for a single, center city?" He peered over his desk at the crowd, his expression hopeful.

Uncertain what to do, Layla raised her hand.

"You miss?" The young man nodded at her. "Anyone else for a single then?"

"We were here first," the American woman objected.

"Yes, ma'am. I know ma'am. I'm terribly sorry, but I just had a property owner who's got two singles show up." The young man kept his voice even. "I'll be right with you. Miss, if you'll just step to the side, I believe Elspeth can help you." He motioned to Layla and then went back to the American couple in front of his desk.

Layla stepped out of the line and approached the tall woman.

Elspeth looked at Layla through a double row of false eyelashes, her eyes lined in sooty streaks of teal. "Hello," she offered her hand and pumped Layla's enthusiastically, "I'm Elspeth, I've a lovely Victorian home on Glengyle Terrace, only a stone's throw to the Royal Mile. Eighteen quid a night for a single en suite, breakfast included. All right, then?"

"Excuse me, but what does that mean?" Layla asked.

"Oh, sorry. Single room, toilet and shower, for eighteen pounds nightly," Elspeth explained.

"Sounds good," Layla said.

Elspeth turned back to the tourist desk, "Any one else for a single?"

The young man shook his head.

"Oh well then" she said to Layla. "We're off." Elspeth took great strides through the station parking lot to her small black Vauxhall, Layla half trotting to keep up with her. "It gets me from place to place," Elspeth said. "Hope you don't mind cats."

"No, of course not," Layla said. "Cats are fine."

Elspeth picked a plump calico cat off the front passenger seat. "Meet Mary, Mary likes to ride in the car." Elspeth cranked the car and took off like an Indy driver. "Your first time in Edinburgh, is it?

Layla nodded and carefully positioned her backpack in the backseat.

"Well, shag me, you've the sight. You do, don't you? I can always tell. You'll have an interesting stay, then. I reckon Edinburgh is about as haunted as it gets."

"I don't know what..."

"Oh, dinna fash yerself. That's broad Scots for 'don't get your knickers in a knot.' I can always tell when someone has the sight. I've a touch of it myself, nae as much as you. I can fair feel the spirits fluttering around you like midsummer butterflies."

The small car dodged narrow walls and groaned up steep inclines. Elspeth pulled out merrily cutting off taxis and buses. Her bracelets glinted in the dim light as she raised her scrawny arm in a cheery wave, shooting through a crowded intersection.

In the backseat, the cat yowled.

Elspeth veered around a group of pedestrians obviously befuddled by the Royal Mile. "I do a ghost walk for Mercat Tours every other night. You might like it. It's great fun. But, then again, it might set you off. Are you comfortable with them?"

"Comfortable with who?"

"The ghosties, of course. The spirits, the dead that walk among us. Does it bother you to see them or have you made your peace?" Elspeth's tone was conversational; she might have been asking Layla if she enjoyed Indian food or Celtic folk music. "Don't worry about how I know. I've told you, I've a bit of the sight myself."

Elspeth clipped an aluminum trashcan as she parked the small car. "My driving is great, my parking leaves a bit to be desired. Let me show you around Mary's Retreat." She bounced out of the Vauxhall, carrying Layla's backpack as if it were a small purse. A large gray cat scooted beneath the car. "That's another Mary." Elspeth escorted Layla into a Victorian parlor, doilies on every surface, chintz pillows and knick-knacks absorbing every bit of space. The carpet, curtains, and sofa all sported contrasting patterns of plaid.

Elspeth opened the top of a roll top desk and pulled down a ledger book. "The thing is, when your family lives in a place for generations, they all leave something. After a while you get a fine mess of tartan and tat." A small white cat rubbed against Layla's legs. "Her name is Mary as well. Are you beginning to see a pattern? Mary Queen of Scots had four ladies in waiting that were raised with her and stayed at her side until she died. They were all Mary's. And Mary, Queen of Scots never slept here. The house wasn't built until 1783. But, Mary's a nice name. Do you know how long you'll be wanting the room?"

"Not really, no. Is it alright if I smoke?"

"Please do." Elspeth pulled out a long black cigarette holder, a tin of tobacco, and a pack of rolling papers. She expertly rolled a cigarette and stuck it in the holder. "It makes me feel so much better about myself when other folk smoke. I didn't think any Americans still did. Don't they stone you in the streets for it?"

"Something like that," Layla said. She lit a cigarette and stifled a yawn.

"Oh, goodness. I've run on and on and you're fair done in."

Elspeth said. "You'll be wanting to get settled into your room. Let's say you'll stay at least three days. Not hardly enough to see Edinburgh, but enough to get the idea of the city." Elspeth scribbled in her ledger and took a ring with two keys out of the desk. "The large one is to the front door, the other opens your room. Breakfast is any time after eight and before nine thirty. Most mornings you won't see me, I sleep in. Gemma – she's my partner – does breakfast. I'm usually around from eleven onwards if you have questions. The Thistle and Castle down at the corner does the best pub grub in the immediate neighborhood." A black and white cat landed on the roll top desk. "No, Mary," Elspeth said. She picked up the cat and cuddled it. The cat leapt from her arms and marched along the top of the sofa before disappearing beneath a curtain.

Elspeth opened a cabinet and got out two thick tumblers and a bottle of scotch. She poured two generous measures into the heavy glasses. "I think you may need a wee drink tonight, until you get used to Edinburgh." She handed Layla the glass. "Follow me, I'll show to your room."

The promised single was a fairy princess boudoir with ruffled curtains, a single canopied bed and lavender flowerers everywhere. Even the air smelled of lavender. It reminded Layla of her grandma.

"I'm sure you'll be quite cozy here. Just watch out for Jamie." Elspeth said, drawing the curtains shut. "Jamie's my cousin. He's been dead for 'bout a hundred years but he still likes to pinch a bottom now and again. It could set off a terrible chain of events with that glowering ghostie who follows you about."

Elspeth said, "Cheers," and tossed down her own tumbler full of liquor before leaving Layla alone.

Layla fell into a cushioned chair and slowly sipped her whiskey.

TWENTY-FIVE

Layla sipped her mid-morning coffee in Elspeth's rear garden. Her three-day stay had already expanded to a week of late nights talking to Elspeth about Matt, about her life, about Ian...about everything.

Ian leaned against the garden wall, his arms braced against it. He gazed at Holyrood Palace. "He stayed there, you know. In 1745, briefly. It was all so brief. Just a drop in the ocean of history."

Ian stared into the distance. "I've not got it sorted, sometimes I recall how he looked on his horse and I think he *was* Scotland's salvation, that we died with his cause...other times I think he was a madman, driven by vanity. I don't know...I just don't know. It all blurs...I canna make sense of it."

Elspeth had told Layla that often spirits lingered beyond the grave because they had something to learn as well as something to *do*.

Ian crossed the close-cropped grass and sat beside Layla, "My memory is different here, in the land of my birth." He looked pathetically young, his opalescent skin and glossy hair underlining the cruelty of his death so far from home.

She thought a moment. Ian certainly seemed different now, less ethereal but still untamed, unpredictable. Layla exerted herself to find the right words. "You seem less otherworldly. More human." Her hands ached to touch him. She felt a hunger spread across her skin, an urgent desire to merge with him. Damn him.

"Well," he said, "I'm more confused, if that makes me more like a mortal." Ian shrugged. He drummed his fingers on the arm of the chair. It was an odd movement, almost adolescent.

Layla studied him. He was opaque now, as solid as the rock beneath Edinburgh castle. Ian looked exactly like a living man. "You *are* different," she said. "I can't see through you. You look just like a living person."

"I don't know that I've changed. I believe it's you. You see us all, all the uneasy dead."

A penetrating chill suddenly engulfed Layla. Wan sunlight careened off the stone wall, but did nothing to warm her. A damp cold seeped right into the marrow of her bones. "I'm haunted."

"So am I," Ian said.

"But you're..."

"I'm no less haunted..."

Wind chimes tinkled and the backdoor opened. Elspeth strolled into the garden with more coffee and an extra cup. She placed it all down on a small table and pulled up a chair. "Lovely day," she said. "Being a Scotswoman, I'm obligated to say that when there's anything less than gale force winds and a torrential deluge." She shoved the sleeves of her black sweater up her arms and crossed one black denim leg over another. "I'd offer you a cuppa Ian, but you've no use for tea or coffee, do you now? Stop glowering at me like you're an ogre, I didna ask ta see you anymore than you want to be seen."

Elspeth poured steaming coffee into Layla's empty cup before filling her own. She leaned down and fingered a dried plant in a concrete trough near her feet. "I'm always surprised when the lobelia dies, it's not a hardy plant at all. But still, it's such a pretty blue, I keep hoping it lasts." She rolled a cigarette with her quick skeletal fingers. Layla noticed how loose the watchband hung on her bony wrist.

Ian stomped off to the far corner of the garden. He straddled the low wall and looked downhill. The land was terraced; it was quite a drop to the next householder's back garden. At the edge of Elspeth's property, the wall seemed to keep out the sky.

"Ah Layla," Elspeth said as she exhaled, "your ghostie is having a bit of a sulk." Elspeth continued to pick at the bits of dried plant. "Were it a perennial, it'd come back in the spring. But, it's really gone."

Layla had the distinct feeling that Elspeth was telling her

something. "Have you always seen spirits?"

"Oh no. I've always been a bit sensitive. I grew up in this house, I've never lived anywhere else, and I never will." She looked into her coffee cup for a second. "When I was little I knew my gran was about, watching me, but I didn't exactly see her. After my mum and da passed over I felt them, but I didn't really see them."

Layla felt a familiar chill and wrapped both hands around her cup.

"Well, it's only since I've took sick, you know, that I've developed the sight fully." Elspeth said. "I think it's after easing my passage."

Layla studied Elspeth's elongated body, her short wispy hair, her hollow cheeks, and thought about her almost manic determination to cram as much into each day as possible. Instinctively, she reached out to touch the taller woman.

"Oh, don't go getting all American and touchy-feely on me. I'm not dead yet," Elspeth said. "In fact, I'm up for taking my rich American friend on a private tour of the Royal Mile today and letting her treat me to lunch at Jackson's."

"Your impoverished American friend who is spending her better-off friend's money would be delighted. I enjoyed watching you the other night when you did your regular dog and pony show for the tourists."

"That was just the standard Burke & Hair song-and-dance. You know, Burke & Hair aren't even proper ghosts, they were simply Edinburgh's most horrid murderers. I'm obliged to go through the tale for the tourist trade," Elspeth said. "They dispatched a number of their contemporaries in the 1700's and sold their bodies to the University medical school. Burke's skeleton is *still* displayed in the University library. Hair's skin was used for a wallet."

"Yuck," said Layla.

"I've seen worse," Ian commented.

"Stop it, ghostie. Layla, get your bag and jacket," Elspeth said. "Let's take a wee stroll down the Royal Mile."

Ian snorted. He swung a long leg over the wall and jumped down. Layla craned her neck but she couldn't see where he'd gone.

"He's not the only ghost in town," Elspeth said and grinned, her earrings jingling. "We girlies can be choosy. You don't like him what haunts you? Slip into the nearest pub and pick up another one."

"Back in a minute," Layla said. She rushed to her room for a jacket and her bag.

Elspeth waited by the front door as Layla tramped down the dark wooden stairs. "All ready," Layla said, her voice dripping artificial cheer.

"Your friend...Matt?" Elspeth said. "The one you told me about who is like a brother to you. Does he take precautions?"

"I think so."

Elspeth grabbed Layla's arm with her talon-like fingers. "You make damn sure he takes precautions, you do that for me." She let go and sighed. "We'll speak no more of this."

As they rounded the corner, Elspeth indicated a tall narrow house, typical of Edinburgh's Old City. "Jock MacDonald lived there, he's reluctant to leave. He's haunted the place since 1693. His descendant, Ewan died in 1859 and rumor has it he haunts just to get his own back from old Jock."

"Is every other Scot named MacDonald?"

"Well, yes," said Elspeth. "And did you know the truth of it, you're kin to half of history, Layla MacDonald." Elspeth panted as they trudged uphill.

"Do you need to stop?" Layla watched a bluish tinge wash beneath Elspeth's pale cheeks.

"Maybe for a bit." Elspeth rocked in the wind that blew off the coast. "You know, Layla MacDonald, it isn't the land that draws you back. That would be poetry. Instead, you're a soap opera, like most women. It's love of a man, not your tie to your MacDonald roots. Unfortunately for you, that man is dead. It's all for love of a ghost." Elspeth broke out in a rib-crunching coughing fit. "You're doomed, girl." She leaned against the side of the house. "Sorry, I over step sometimes."

"No, you don't. You speak the truth. I'm in Scotland because of Ian." Layla lit a cigarette, shuffling for balance on the steep incline. Looking downhill to Princes Street gave her a touch of vertigo. "I'm not sure whether it's ghosts or the damned hills in this city that make me woozy all the time."

"You can see why so many Scots are manic depressive. We go up. We go down. In the summer the sun's up until midnight, in the winter it gets dark around tea time. No wonder we're moody. We're bred for lunacy. You can see it all around you. It's why there are so many battle ghosts. We're a cursed, warlike people. If the English wouldn't oblige and fight us during a particular historical period, well then, we fought among ourselves." Elspeth giggled. "History according to Elspeth. Not always accurate, but always entertaining. And, I don't charge any extra for my theories."

Color returned to Elspeth's cheeks, "Come on then." She led the way down a narrow alley that ran parallel to the hillside. "This bit we're walking on, you Americans call it an alley...we call it a close. It's my mission to teach Americans to speak English."

Looking down to the New Town made Layla dizzy. She took a deep breath and kept her eyes on the purple streaks in Elspeth's hair. They turned up Lawyer's Close and started up the slippery stone stairs, until they could see the top of St. Giles Cathedral in the center of the Royal Mile.

Ghostly solicitors and the apparitions of advocates passed the two women. Bewigged and gowned, kilted and carrying briefcases, deceased attorneys floated through the close.

"Now would be a good time for a dead lawyer joke if only I could think of one," Layla commented. She dawdled a bit, rummaging through her pack, so Elspeth could pause, could extend the pretense that she was able to live normally.

Back straight, head held high, Elspeth strode across the Royal Mile to the Mercat Cross...her way of whistling in the dark.

The Mercat Cross was the epicenter of eerie Edinburgh, the place where heralds had once made announcements, miscreants were hanged and bloody brawls broke out. Housewives in bulky coats cut past it, running errands. Leather jacketed students strolled by. Tourists paused to photograph each other on the base of the cross.

The living were in the minority.

It was not yet noon, long before the Royal Mile swarmed with shoppers and sightseers. The broad flat stone around the Cross was damp, bits of windblown litter clung to the rock. Elspeth lifted her face to the bleak and cheerless sky; the wind ruffled her cropped hair. Layla stood a few steps behind, frozen, gaping.

Blood drenched soldiers in ragged plaids moved through the mist and rock. Wraithlike plague victims reached out, still beseeching, still imploring.

"We were a barbaric, pragmatic lot," Elspeth said. "We walled up the plague victims to contain the illness and we let them die. Mary King's Close is the worst example – hundreds just walled in. Even before I had the sight proper, I'd hear them moan when I walked past."

A fierce black horse dragged an apparition past. The ghost's long black hair was matted with blood, his tongue protruded, his claw like hands groped the air. Blood spilled from a slit in his belly, then vanished.

A blackened corpse-like figure ran from a house down the road. Scorched flesh revealed bone. Terrible screams sliced the morning. "He's awful, that one is," said Elspeth, her mouth set in a grim line. "He was tending a spit when he fell asleep, fell into the fire and was cooked with Sunday dinner."

A transparent cleric in medieval robes walked through the Mercat Cross. A young man in jeans and a black sweater wavered in the middle of the street and disappeared.

Elspeth put her bony arm around Layla. "That's just a glimpse. The sight is a curse." Elpseth sighed. "I brought you here because where you're going, you'll see much worse."

"Where am I going?"

"Wherever Ian leads," Elspeth answered, "And I fear for you."

Layla held Elspeth tightly and stared over her shoulder at a young girl in an Edwardian dress by a shop window. "Elspeth, there isn't anything I can do to stop that, is there?"

"I suppose not."

Layla gave the girl one last hug, feeling weakness, the disease, the nearness of death. She forced a smile. "Well then, since there is nothing I can do about the inevitable, let's go have lunch."

Elspeth laughed. "Yes, let's. Jackson's? They've lovely food and a fixed price lunch so you won't have to float a bank loan to feed me." Elspeth linked her arm through Layla's and pulled her away from the Mercat Cross.

They crossed the street diagonally and stood in front of Jackson's, an elegant restaurant set in a converted three hundred year old stable block. "It looks closed, " Layla said, disappointment tingeing her voice.

"No, they only open the downstairs for lunch," Elspeth explained. She turned off the High Street down Jackson's Close.

Layla skidded on the sharply inclined Old Town streets.

"You'd do a bit better if you'd packed hiking boots or trainers," Elpseth said. "Cowgirl boots aren't made for cobblestone."

"It's what I wear."

"I know how that goes." Elspeth ran her skinny hand through her short white and purple hair. "I used to have lovely, long red hair." She shook her head, her two skull shaped earrings bumped each other. "Death as a fashion statement. It's a concept."

Layla bit her lip and looked down at the cobblestones. "It's just not fair."

"Fair?" Elspeth laughed. "You do make me laugh. What an odd notion." She shoved open the heavy door and they filed into the wood paneled warmth.

As they walked to a table in the rear corner of the room, Layla noticed that everyone in the restaurant was alive. Elspeth seemed to know half the diners and all the wait staff. She nodded and spoke to people as they made their way across the room.

Seated, with the lunch menu shielding her face, Layla said, "They're all alive."

"Not only that, but the food is excellent. It is one of the reasons I like it here. It's the least haunted place in Edinburgh." Elspeth scrutinized the menu. "Both the salmon and the beef medallions are on offer today. Decisions, decisions. I'm spoiled for choice."

"You seem to think that your sight has to do with your health." She waited for Elspeth to notice her unasked question.

A waiter set a basket of warm bread on the table and took their order. Elspeth sat silently until he returned with a bottle of wine. After a sip, she ran her fingers across her hair. "My health? Rather my illness, or my death," she said. "The sicker I get, the more I slip into the space between the worlds. Some days the dead are more real to me than the living. I only hope it doesn't mean that I'm doomed to be tied to this world when I go. I've seen enough of poor wandering creatures to know that hell is being a ghost."

Elspeth stopped talking when the waiter appeared. She took a bite of her prawn cocktail.

Layla noticed that Elspeth's hand trembled as she brought

the fork to her mouth. Layla carefully spooned her soup. The room was warm, the polished wood and linen table clothes seemed a refuge from the grisly ghosts and loud tourists of the Royal Mile. She gulped soup and tears simultaneously. It was horrible to sit and talk while the wings of death beat the air around Elspeth. "I'm sorry I brought it up."

"Don't be, sometimes it helps to acknowledge it, to say I'm dying instead of 'lovely weather today.' But I sense that you want answers from me. All I can tell you is that I feel you're being pulled. Soon, you and Ian will move on, whether you want to go or not. When next you pass this way, I suspect that I'll have moved on. Though there is one other thing I can tell you." Elspeth's eyes were bright with unshed tears.

"Yes, what is it?" Layla leaned forward.

"Have the mocha torte for dessert," Elspeth whispered. "It's to die for."

TWENTY-SIX

Morning dew washed Edinburgh into pristine clarity. The entire city seemed poised on tiptoe like a ballerina, awaiting a photographer from *Travel and Leisure* to immortalize the beauty of the dark Old City, straining in contrast to the cobalt sky.

Layla's purple boots peeped beneath her Laura Ashley floral corduroy dress. The princess seams and leg of mutton sleeves were incongruously feminine for her personality, but the dress suited her fine-boned body. It was a lovely dress. She made a lovely appearance, standing on the sidewalk outside Mary's Retreat, her hair tumbling around her face, her backpack at her feet as she waited for a taxi to Waverly Station.

Ian was supposed to notice the dress.

He didn't.

Layla felt stupid. She'd spent more money that she could afford on a fairy princess dress, hoping that Ian would...

Elspeth slept through the morning. Layla thought how unfair, how horrible it was that she had met Elspeth, only to know she was dying.

Elspeth had not awakened to say good-bye.

The two women had said their whiskey-laced farewells the previous evening. Elspeth had hugged her tight and said, "Maybe, just maybe, I've helped you a bit. Maybe I'm through. I don't want to roam when I'm gone."

Elspeth asked Layla *not* to come back to Edinburgh for her funeral.

Layla curled up in her single bed all night, cursing Ian, but still longing for him. She wanted arms, even ghostly ones, around her through the night while she thought about the horrible timing of fate. But Ian did not come to her in the night.

He came at dawn.

They were leaving Edinburgh for Inverness.

He appeared beside her on the sidewalk, arms folded across his chest. "It's not like I have control over when I appear. I'm just as trapped as you." He sounded irritated with her.

Layla glanced at her watch, lit a cigarette and then paced back and forth on the sidewalk. "Look Ian, it's not that I *blame* you, but you have to admit that you've ruined my life."

The ghost looked confused.

"I'm in Scotland because of you. Everything in my life seems to have something to do with *your* life, with events that should have been resolved long before my birth. I don't understand what's happening. Now I'm going to Inverness and I don't even know why. I haven't known why anything happened for months. I'm just blown along."

"So am I," Ian said. "As hard as it may be for you to accept, I've no more control than you."

"Well, what was all of that bullshit about protecting me? About my being yours? You've fucked up my life completely." Layla shouted at the ghost. "Please don't protect me anymore."

"Protecting you? Yes, at the time I said it I thought that was the case." Ian paused. "Don't you see? We all try to make sense of what goes on around us. I assumed it was why I manifested when there seemed to be a threat to you. But as God is my witness, I don't know any more than you know." He moved away from her, his face bitter. "Maybe it's *you* that's drawn *me* back into being."

Layla looked downhill to Waverly Station but the taxi was still nowhere in sight. "We go in circles, don't we?" Ian looked at her quizzically. Again she was struck by how attractive he was, how much she longed for his touch. No matter, she thought. "We don't know and we won't know," she said. "We've no way of knowing whether something within me drew you more into the present or whether some crack in time cast you into my life. We'd best give up on assigning blame."

Ian nodded. A slight smile cracked his face. "It's a pity a man has to die to meet a rational woman."

Layla swung at him playfully, as if she could slap him. He caught her wrist in his fingers. "I was playing wit' you," he said.

"I know." Even the lightest touch of his fingers on her wrist jolted through her body. "Why do we need to go to Inverness?" Ian shook his head from side to side. "Because."

"Yeah, right. It's a ghost thang." Layla knew but she couldn't explain how she knew.

Ian had to go to Maggie's grave.

It was the only way he'd ever rest. And after that? Then what? Would he disappear? Would she spend the rest of her life seeing the troubled dead who could not quite leave?

The cab finally pulled up in front. The driver rolled down the window. "Waverly Station, miss?"

"Yes, thank you," Layla answered as the driver hopped out and stowed her backpack in the trunk. Ian and she got into the backseat of the taxi.

"You're heading back to London, are you?" The driver asked as he started the cab.

"No, I thought I'd go up to Inverness."

Ian was silent, looking out the window. Apparently, the cabbie didn't see him.

"Ah, going to see if you can catch sight of the Loch Ness monster, are you?"

"Something like that."

At the station, she handed over a five-pound note and told the driver to keep the change. Slipping on her backpack, she half-ran through the station, barely catching the 11:28 train to Inverness. Panting, Layla spilled into an aisle seat and stuffed her backpack beneath it just before the train whistle blew.

The carriage was half empty. No one seemed to react as Ian stumbled behind Layla, stepped over her legs, and settled in the window seat. The seats facing them were empty.

The stark majesty of the distant blue mountains was completely unlike the placid English countryside she'd passed through on her way to Edinburgh. The train plunged through deep ravines cut from rock, twisted across hostile fields and steamed along the rim of heathered moors. The land seemed silent, a secret-keeping land, the heather the color of blood.

The train continued northwards. With each passing mile, Ian grew more substantial, less ethereal. Layla saw his breath mist on the train window. She felt the heat of his flesh as she leaned across him. When the train lunged round a sharp ravine, she was caught off-balance and slid right into him.

She felt his heart thudding in his chest.

When she looked into his eyes, she saw fear. Ian's eyes were wild with terror, the fear of a condemned man waiting for a stay of execution, while he dreads eternity in prison.

Layla put one hand on either side of his face. She felt the muscles in his jaw twitch and jump.

Without thinking, she pulled his face to hers and kissed him.

Energy, primal and primitive, shot through her body. Then she felt herself chill; she was enervated, drained, as if the kiss sucked life from her. Ian's heart beat wildly. Against her chest, she felt his heart thunder. Layla pulled back, gasping for air. The closer they traveled to the Highlands the more mortal – the more alive – the ghost became.

The closer to death she drifted.

"What's happening?" Her voice was a whisper. Layla folded her hands in her lap, hiding the trembling in the folds of her full-skirted dress.

"I dinna know," Ian said. " But I fear we'll find out."

Outside the windows, the blood-tones of heather seemed to ache with the history of the land. The train rounded a corner and the onyx surface of Loch Ness came into view, smooth primordial water shrouded in mist, the stagnant depths disturbed by ominous dreams. Layla shivered. "I can almost believe there really is a monster there," she said.

"Oh, but there is," Ian said. "How can you doubt it?"

She looked at him, certain that he joked. But no, his expression was serious.

The train stopped abruptly.

Inverness, the capital of the Highlands. Layla expected a small, picturesque railway station, sleeping in the mountains. Instead, she stepped out on one of many platforms. Train departure signs blinked like Christmas tree lights. Travelers ran about like shoppers at a year-end sale. It seemed that anyone going anywhere in northern Scotland came through Inverness to get there.

She plopped down on a bench to consult her guidebook. Ian bounced on the balls of his feet, sniffing the Highland air, some magic at work on him. He seemed young, alive and in a hurry. "I've got to find a bed and breakfast," Layla explained. "And I need to call Matt and let him know I'm okay." She skimmed her guidebook. "Okay, I think I can find Tourist Information. I suspect I'll only get lost two or three times on my way."

Ian kept searching the faces in the crowd, looking for someone.

"She's dead, you know," she said.

"So am I."

"Well, you look well enough to carry my backpack." She tossed it to him.

No one even turned to look at the tall, kilted man with a backpack following the short woman in a posh Laura Ashley dress and cowboy boots. Inverness had seen weirder.

Following the directions in the guidebook, Layla turned left as she came out of the station and trudged on until she saw a Marks and Spencer. "Come along. Let's see, it said Tourist Information is up a small flight of stairs," Layla said. Looking around, she spotted the stairs. "Whew, Highlanders have an odd definition of small," she said. "I'm glad you're saddled with my backpack."

Layla secured a room in a bed and breakfast on Union Street just opposite the rail station. She hurried back outside. "We're going right back where we came from," she told Ian. "I've got a room right across from the station."

"I hope you've booked a double," he said. "It seems that people can see me."

"Well, if the landlord doesn't like it, you can just hack him up with an axe." She was tired, overwhelmed.

"I've no control, lass."

Within an hour, Layla was ensconced in a small room on the third story of an old house on Union Street. She curled up on the bed beneath the eaves, sipping milky tea and watching the pedestrian traffic on the street below. The clouds above Loch Ness were dark and full.

The proprietor had been polite, but not precisely friendly, indicating a folder near the front door full of area maps and directions to local restaurants. He hadn't seemed to see Ian. Layla felt alone, horribly alone. Matt was an ocean and several time zones away. Elspeth was dying. Edinburgh seemed like a dream to Layla. Ian seemed preoccupied. The morning drifted backwards in time until it seemed part of another era.

Something would happen to her in Inverness. Something unstoppable, out of her control.

Entropy.

"They're a rare mixture, the Highlands are," Ian began. "Not simply their beauty and their strength, but their endurance." He sat on the bed. "About eighty miles or so north of here are the Torridon Mountains, the oldest on earth I think. The quartz atop them sparkles like snow."

"I think I read about them," Layla said. "Something about them being so old that geologists can't find any fossils, that they were formed long before life of any sort began." She poured another cup of tea and lit a cigarette.

"Normal life can't be there, it simply cannot. Something old, something elemental owns that bit of earth. Something that has spread throughout the Highlands. It's drawn me back here."

"To those mountains?"

"No, to a different place. The force that drives life seeps through stone and pulls us each back to where we belong." Ian's voice was sad. Outside a mournful sound crept above the rumble of traffic and the grind of the railway. Layla heard a lone piper. His song was bittersweet and she did not recognize it, and the music filled her with a feeling she couldn't name.

Layla grabbed her jacket. "I'm going to find a pay phone and call Matt, then walk around a bit and have some dinner."

Ian shrugged. She stomped out of the room with the ghost following her. After locking the door, she pocketed the key and rushed down the narrow stairs. Ian followed. She heard his footsteps. Out on the street she saw a red phone booth. Checking her watch, she crossed her fingers, hoping Matt would be home. She dumped in a handful of coins and dialed her number.

Three rings. Matt's voice on the answering machine: "I'm not here. But Layla, precious, if that's you, please let me know where you are, *please let me know you're okay.* And if you need anything, any help getting home, let me know where to reach you, *please.*"

"I'm fine. I'll call again in a few days." She hung up.

Hands in pockets, head down, she walked into the nearest pub.

Layla stood in line behind a young couple with a toddler.

The child wore a t-shirt that said, "I'm a wee monster from Loch Ness." Layla bought Shepard's pie, cauliflower cheese, and salad. The bar maid looked right at Ian and asked what he'd have. "Nothing for me thank you," he said.

Layla poked her food with a fork then gave up. It tasted like ash, dry, sticking to her throat. Layla lit a cigarette.

"You'd do better to eat," Ian said.

"Oh, not you too. The last freaking thing I need is a lecture on smoking from a dead man."

"I was more thinking that you'd need your strength. Tomorrow is when it happens."

"When *what* happens?"

"When whatever will be, will be." Ian looked at the bar. "I wonder if I *could* drink a wee dram of whiskey."

"I don't think..." Damn. She was talking to herself. Layla jumped up and walked rapidly back to the bed and breakfast. Alone in her room she paced the floor.

Tomorrow.

What about tonight?

What about tonight and all the *other nights* for the rest of her life? She flung herself across the bed and pounded the pillow. Alone. Would she be alone forever? Was this it? A lifetime of talking to herself, walking with herself...of loving a man who disappeared in the middle of conversations, in the middle of...

"Ian, damn it, make *love to me.* Just once. Just once before whatever..."

Layla's voice was the only sound in the room. Outside a Highland wind rattled the windows. A lonesome train whistle, the rumble of traffic – then only the wind.

Layla rolled onto her back. The bedside lamp flickered, then died. Oblivion. No streetlight intruded. No sound save the wind. She felt a *presence,* a sweet welcome weight across her chest. Reaching into the night, her fingers traced a face, tangled in long hair.

A rough hot tongue traced a line down her neck to her collarbone. She turned onto her side and felt the pull and pressure of hands fumbling with her buttons, slipping her dress off her shoulders, down her body. Quickly she skinned off her panties. Moist kisses moved across her chest until a mouth sucked her nipple. A leg slipped between hers, she arched against it, moving against it and moaning. Her hands roamed across a body, stroking and clutching.

Feverish with need she pulled him to her. She shifted her hips so she was beneath him. He rose up on his arms and she reached for him, her hand grasping the length of him guiding him into her...

Then the lights came on...the wind stilled...

She was alone.

TWENTY-SEVEN

The wind knotted her hair, lashed her face and cut into her bones. A fine icy mist pelted her face. Layla flexed her fingers inside her pockets. The cold numbed her hands and swelled her joints. She could barely bend her fingers. But she trudged on through the darkness.

Ian had shaken her awake just past midnight. "It's now," he'd said. "Time to move on. We're here."

Without asking him anything, she'd dressed in the darkness. She'd known he was right. They'd traveled across a sea and through a country locked in an unholy alliance to reach a place where the mountains stood guardian to the past.

She'd followed the ghost out of Inverness, and hiked east, her lungs straining with the effort of matching his pace.

Five miles out of town, they reached Culloden Moor.

There the dead of Culloden, their wounds bleeding into the bitter earth, marched beside her. By the thousands they came, shimmering in the black night, dying again and again, marching back from eternity.

Screams echoed in the night. The ungodly death rattles of hundreds, the lingering moans of thousands...the desperate last prayers of the doomed.

She smelled a charnel house stench near the visitor center. Thirty Jacobites had been burned to death there, the horror replayed endlessly in the half-world. Blackened flash crackled and peeled off their bodies, fat sizzled, bone turned to ash.

A young boy in a kilt – he looked only eleven or twelve – clutched his stomach, guts oozing between his soft young fingers. It was dark. Stygian dark. But, somehow Layla saw the restless spirits fighting endlessly, their cause forgotten, their Prince long dead, their war endless.

She passed the clan graves, MacDonald, MacGregor, Sutherland, Stewart, and MacLachalan. The well of the dead, the nameless souls, the last great hope of Scotland roamed the barren moor where the wind skirled like the sound of a lone piper. She could not name the song that drifted cold as the grave and soft as solitude.

Still, she walked, the sound of armies clashing metal around her, the death throes of massive ghost horses, their thundering hooves pawing the air as the horses crashed to the earth, bellies pierced, eyes wild and uncomprehending.

Layla walked through the battlefield of ghosts, an impotent visitor from the distant future forced to witness for no good reason, seeing what she saw because of a bad hand of cards – entropy or random chance. Layla walked in lockstep with the ghost who'd brought her to this killing field.

For an instant, she thought she saw the Bonnie Prince, his enormous white stallion pawing the air, his black curls tumbling down his silk covered back. He appeared brighter, better fed, taller than the Highlanders. It seemed a grim betrayal. He'd lived, he alone seemed to glory in the slaughter, a smile upon his aristocratic lips while around him starved soldiers died in their threadbare plaids.

"That's the way of it," Ian said. "Those who lead us into war grow old and fat. They die beside a warm fire, speaking of glory." "You followed him. You believed," Layla said.

"I was young. I was pathetically young." Unlike the ghost armies, Ian was solid. "I've learned since then. I suspect that is the point of it, learning. We're all sliding toward inevitable decay. It's what we learn that gives it some meaning."

Layla sped up to keep pace with Ian. His path was deliberate. He walked across the moor, looking neither left nor right.

The mountains loomed ahead – ominous, threatening. The stars were bright in the Highlands – amoral, pagan. Those stars had seen the earth bathed in blood yet remained unapproachable, silent. Ian walked east as the sounds of death, the crashing weapons, and whinnying horses faded.

Then they were alone in a quiet so all encompassing that it

seemed the earth had perished.

Finally he stopped.

Layla felt hesitancy. The air itself seemed to warn her against approaching him.

Ian flung his head back and looked to the pitiless sky. Moonlight illuminated his face. He yelled, wailing an unearthly primitive sound beyond bereavement, the sound of the lone wolf who has found and lost his mate. The dreadful sound bounced against the granite and quartz of the mountains, flinging itself back a hundredfold so that the world seemed full of wailing, the cosmos drunk on grief.

Layla took a tiny shuffling half step toward Ian.

He didn't seem to see her.

She wanted to reach out to him but felt certain that if she touched him, he would hack her to bits and leave her to feed the omnivorous earth.

He wailed again, and now the sound of his voice was like the melody of a lone outlaw piper, piping the dead across the worlds to the other side.

The wind howled, a fearsome sound that washed away Ian's voice. The earth groaned and shook. A flash of something split the sky and fire rained down, sparks vanishing before they hit the earth.

"She's buried here," Ian said, his voice raspy and choking. "We stand on Maggie's grave."

Layla plummeted into his arms. He held her so tight she had to twist away to breathe. He bent down to her and slanted his mouth across hers, plunging his tongue deep inside. She pressed against him, his hard chest flattening her breasts.

His hand cupped her bottom. He squeezed and kneaded the sensitive flesh and she pushed herself against him. Layla felt him harden against her belly. Eagerly returning his kiss, she slipped her hand beneath his kilt. She wrapped fingers around the throbbing length of him. He was long and hard, the skin soft and the heat of his flesh compelling. She slid her hand up and down while her tongue twisted around his tongue.

His hand moved swiftly into the space between them and circled her breast. Holding it in her palm, he rubbed his thumb across her nipple. His other hand maintained a grip on her hips. He scattered small kisses across her face and then seized her mouth again.

Half breathless from the kiss, Layla moved her head back. She traced his collarbone with her tongue while he held both her breasts in his hands. Her hands grabbed his hips. She knelt before him and nuzzled his kilt with her face before moving beneath it to take him in her mouth. She sucked and licked, unable to control the tiny moans and whimpers of pleasure. She took him in her mouth, and relaxing her throat, tried to swallow the length of him, but he was too long. She swirled her tongue around the head of his manhood, her hands exploring him.

With a moan, he pulled her head away and dropped to his knees. He lifted her face between his hands and kissed her mouth until her lips were swollen. Layla tore blindly at his clothes, uncertain about how to deal with them. He shoved her sweater up above her breasts and suckled one while his long fingers toyed with the other.

Drawing apart, they removed their clothing.

Ian laid her down on the hard earth and moved between her legs. Layla had to draw up her knees. She felt stretched, and full. He lay on top of her for an instant. His eyes were damp. Then he moved, slowly at first, in and out. She bucked beneath him, her hands clawing his buttocks, urging him to move faster, harder.

He held her waist and turned them so that he had her on her side. He moved slowly, one leg over hers, his hands caressing her breasts. Then he rolled over on his back pulling her on top and licked her breasts while she straddled him.

He arched his hips and thrust up into her. She screamed. Ian held her on top of him and stopped moving. Eyes locked with hers, he turned again so she was beneath him.

He rode her hard and furious. Layla strained into him. As the sun rose red in the east, Ian rose up on his arms, his face contorted with passion. He looked down at Layla and cried, "Maggie."

He was gone.

The sun was a blood red smear on the horizon. Twigs and dirt clung to Layla's hair. She was scratched, scraped, and naked. Her body ached.

She was alone in a cold field five miles from Inverness. It was just after daybreak.

Dry eyed and numb, she pulled on her clothes and began the long walk back to town.

She was completely alone.

AFTERWORD

Matt turned the rented Mercedes down the tree-lined drive of the Heather Country House Manor.

It had been five years since he'd seen Layla and he was looking forward surprising her. Five years ago, he and Ashley had bought her house in Charlotte, sending her a cashier's check that allowed her to purchase a pub just outside of Inverness.

After Holly 'got serious' about some guy in Chicago, he and Ashley had endured a string of housemates. Now they were both doing so well that they had the house to themselves.

But Matt still wished Layla would come home.

Tossing the keys to a valet, he rushed up the stairs to the entrance hall and nearly ran to the registration desk. Next to the desk stood a suit of armor. Matt nearly giggled, "It's a bit ye olde, here." He couldn't wait to sit down with Layla and talk. No one, not even Ashley, could replace her.

E-mail and letters weren't good enough.

The perky young woman took an imprint of his Visa card and showered him with tourist brochures, flirting and fluttering. She didn't mention Layla's pub. "You'll want to take a boat trip on Loch Ness while you're here. We can book that for you."

Matt couldn't wait any longer. "How far is it to the Highland Ghost?"

"The pub the American woman bought?"

"Yes."

"Just down the road. But, you won't want to be going there. She's nice enough. But it's a wicked drive, particularly this time of year with all the fog. The Three Swans is closer and our restaurant here at Heathers is the best in the county."

"She's an old friend of mine. She's the reason I'm in the area."

"Poor girl, she's had a patch of bad luck. Every man that gets involved with her has a dreadful accident. It's the saddest thing. Her last boyfriend, a banker from London, he was up here on holiday when they met, he died in a car accident. The one before that, a local lad, had a horrible fall mountain climbing. Poor girl, she's cursed."

Matt picked up his room key. "Still if you could give me directions, I'd appreciate it."

"Fair enough." The young woman marked a route on a map. "We all drink in her pub, but tourists don't usually find their way there." She tapped a point on the map. "The trick is to make this turn here, before you're all the way into Inverness. If the pub isn't open, she'll be out walking the moor. She does that most days."

"Thanks so much." Matt hurried to the door and asked for his car to be brought round. He ran down the steps and sped off. Exiting the drive, he turned on his headlights. She wasn't kidding about fog. Matt crept along the narrow road, frustrated at the slow speed necessitated by thick fog and the clouds obscuring the sun. Trees bent in the fierce wind.

Glancing at the map, he slowed to a crawl. The turn should be just ahead. Got it! As he rounded a curve, he saw a stone building with tables outside emerge from the fog. The windows glowed amber in the dim day. Smoke rose from the chimney.

Eager to see Layla, Matt parked and leapt from the car in one unbroken motion. He ran into the building. It was dark in the pub despite table lamps and a blazing fire that warmed the room. No customers clustered around the bar or sat at the scattered tables. A gray cat hopped from the windowsill.

Matt's footsteps were loud on the hardwood floor.

A door behind the bar creaked open.

"Matt! Matt, Oh my God! I don't believe it. How...when... why didn't you tell me you were coming...Oh my God!" Layla hurled herself at Matt and hugged him. "I can't...Why didn't you...?"

"Precious, it's so good to finally see you again." Matt hugged Layla. She felt too thin, fragile. Her flesh seemed cold. "Let me look at you." He stepped back and held her at arm's length. "The longer hair is nice, your skin looks great. But what's with those clothes. I think I preferred cowgirl to Queen Victoria."

Layla wore a long black skirt, a white blouse, and held a shawl around her shoulders. She shrugged. "*You* haven't changed."

Matt looked at her closely. Five years was a long time, but there was something *very* different about Layla. Her skin seemed translucent, her face looked softer. She reminded him of the women on cameos and old paintings. She seemed to belong to an earlier era. "You've changed."

"Aye, that I have."

Matt quirked one eyebrow at Layla's assumed accent. Layla giggled at his reaction.

She took him by the hand and led him to a seat before the fire. Her hand was icy.

"I want to hear everything. How's Ashley? Is Holly going to marry that man in Chicago? What's everyone doing? Oh, I'm being awful, let me get you a drink. Some pub this is where you can't get a drink." Layla dashed across the room and returned with an amber liquid in a glass. "This will chase the chill from your bones. Now, everything... I want to know everything."

Matt held the glass between his hands. "First answer one question. You. Are *you* happy?" He looked at her pale face.

Layla smiled at Matt, a brief bittersweet smile. "Well now, I do as well as I can."

The best in all-new neo-noir, hard-boiled and retro-pulp mystery and crime fiction.

Autumn 2001 Release

FLESH AND BLOOD SO CHEAP

A Joe Hannibal Mystery
Wayne D. Dundee

The popular St. Martins hardcover and Dell paperback series is revived! Hard-boiled Rockford, Illinois P.I. Joe Hannibal is at it again, this time swept up in a murderous mystery in a Wisconsin summer resort town. Deception and death lurk behind the town's idyllic façade, when a grisly murder is discovered and Hannibal knows for a fact that the confessed killer couldn't have done the deed!

It'll take two fists and a lot of guts to navigate through the tacky tourist traps, gambling dens and gin mills to get to the truth, while dangerous dames seem determined to steer Hannibal clear of the town's darkest secrets. In the end, Hannibal himself, and everyone he cares for, may be in jeopardy as he learns that murder may be the smallest crime of all in this lakeside getaway!

1-891946-16-1   Trade pb, 272 pages

Winter 2001 Release

WAITING FOR THE 400

A Northwoods Noir
Kyle Marffin

They found the first girl in the Chicago train station, a dime-a-dance and a quarter-for-more chippy. Suicide. A train ticket still clutched in her hand: Watersmeet, Michigan, the end of line…

400 miles north, Watersmeet station master Jess Burton wastes away in his tiny northwoods depot with big dreams of big city life, watching the high-rollers and their glamour gals hop off the train for their lakeside mansions and highbrow resorts. Till the night Nina appeared on the depot platform.

Nina…Big city beautiful and clearly marked 'property of'. The kind of dame that can turn a man's head, turn him inside out and upside down till danger doesn't matter anymore, till desire can only lead to death. Because folks are dying now, and Jess is in over his head, waiting for the 400 and the red-headed beauty to step off the train with his ticket out of town.

1-891946-14-5   Trade pb, 288 pages

THE BIG SWITCH

A Brian Kane Mystery
Jack Bludis

Hollywood, 1951. Millionaires, moguls and movie stars dazzle in the land of dreams. Money talks, when desperate glamour girls are a dime a dozen. There's a seamy underbelly beneath the glossy veneer. Scandals lurk in every closet, sins too dark for the silver screen. It's all a sham, everything's a scam, everyone's on the make, no one's who they seem.

This is Kane's turf. Brian Kane, Hollywood P.I.

It's a standard case, as un-glamorous as they come: Hired by a mega-star's wife to catch her cheating husband with another casting-couch hopeful. Till one starlet winds up dead. Then another. When Kane's client turns out to be an imposter, and thugs are trying to scare him off, he's suddenly suspect #1 in his own case. And the body count keeps growing…

But it's personal now, and not even a vicious murderer can keep Kane from getting to the bottom of the big switch.

1-891946-10-2   Trade pb, 256 pages

Now try the finest in traditional supernatural horror!

Autumn 2001 Release

NIGHT PLAYERS

P.D.Cacek

Welcome to Las Vegas, home to glittering casinos, to high stakes, high-rollers, high priced call girls. 'Round the clock vice, where the nightlife never ends. It's the perfect place for a new-born vampire to make her home.

Meet Allison Garrett, the unluckiest gal who ever became a vampire, with an irreverently sharp tongue to go along with her sharp teeth. Meet her sidekick, Mica, a Bible-thumping street corner preacher. Both of them are on the run from the catty coven of L.A. strip-club vampire vixens they narrowly escaped from in P.D. Cacek's Stoker Award nominated debut novel Night Prayers. Hiding out in Las Vegas, Allison's now a night-shift showgirl, while Mica tries in vain to bring the good book to gamblers, crooks and hookers. And everything's as idyllic as it can be for a preacher and a vampire setting up house in sin city. Till the evil vampire that cruelly turned Allison shows up along with his bloodthirsty minions, and it'll take more than a gambler's luck to save Allison and Mica this time!

1-891946-11-0   Trade pb, 256 pages

Autumn 2001 Release

MARTYRS

Edo van Belkom

250 years ago, French Jesuits erected a mission deep in the uncharted Canadian wilderness, till they were brutally murdered by a band of Mohawks. Or so the legends say.

Today St. Clair College stands near the legendary massacre site, the mission's memory now more folklore than fact. Then St. Clair professor Father Karl Desbiens and his band of eager grad students set off to locate the mission ruins. The site's discovered, artifacts are found, the mystery of the Mohawk massacre may be solved…

…Till the archeological dig accidentally unearths an old world evil. There was no 'Mohawk massacre'. A malevolent demonic power was imprisoned in the remote Canadian wilderness by the original missionaries. But now it's been unleashed. Now the nightmare will commence. Father Desbiens has his own inner demons to struggle with, his own crisis of faith to overcome. He's an unlikely martyr to the faith he already questions, but the demonic presence has invaded St. Clair college, leaving a bloody trail of horror among his students.

1-891946-13-7   Trade pb, 272 pages

The Horror Writers Association

BELL, BOOK & BEYOND

An Anthology Of Witchy Tales
Edited by P.D. Cacek

Stoker Award winner P.D. Cacek brings you 21 bewitching stories about wiccans, warlocks and witches, all written by the newest voices in terror: the Affiliate Members of the Horror Writers Association. From fearsome and frightening to starkly sensual and darkly humorous, each tale will cast its own sorcerous spell, leaving you anxiously looking for more from these new talents!

1-891946-09-9   Trade pb, 320 pages

"If these authors are indeed the future of horror, the genre is in good hands…If you care about where horror is headed and who's going to take us there, this fine, spooky volume is a must read"
Garret Peck, Sinister Element

"Genre fans will obtain a taste of the destined in this witchcraft anthology"
Harriet Klausner

A FACE WITHOUT A HEART

A Modern-Day Version Of Oscar Wilde's The Picture Of Dorian Gray
Rick R. Reed

Nominated for the 2001 Spectrum Award for "Best Novel": A stunning retake on the timeless themes of guilt, forgiveness and despair in Oscar Wilde's fin de siecle classic, The Picture Of Dorian Gray. Amidst a gritty background of nihilistic urban decadence, a young man's soul is bargained away to embrace the nightmarish depths of depravity – and cold blooded murder – as his painfully beautiful holographic portrait reflects the ugly horror of each and every sin.

1-891946-08-0   Trade pb, 256 pages

"A rarity: a really well-done update that's as good as its source material."
Thomas Deja, Fangoria Magazine

"Depicting modern angst with unerring accuracy"
Reviewer's Bookwatch

GOTHIQUE

A Vampire Novel
Kyle Marffin

International Horror Guild Award nominee Kyle Marffin takes you on a tour of the dark side of the darkwave, when a city embraces the grand opening of a new 'nightclub extraordinaire', Gothique, mecca for the disaffected Goth kids and decadent scene-makers. But a darker secret lurks behind its blacked-out doors and the true horror of the undead reaches out to ensnare the soul of a city in a nightmare of bloodshed, and something much worse than death.

1-891946-06-4   Trade pb, 448 pages

"An awfully good writer...this is a novel with wit and edge, engaging characters and sleazy ones for balance, a keen sense of melodramatic movement and a few nasty chills."
Ed Bryant, Locus Magazine

"Bloody brilliant! A white-knuckle adventure filled with plenty of chills and thrills...this book just never lets up."
M. McCarty, The IF Bookworm

WHISPERED FROM THE GRAVE

An Anthology Of Ghostly Tales

Quietly echoing in a cold graveyard's breeze, the moaning wails of the dead, whispered from the grave to mortal ears with tales of desires unfulfilled, of dark vengeance, of sorrow and forgiveness and love beyond the grave. Includes tales by Edo van Belkom, Tippi Blevins, Sue Burke, P.D. Cacek, Dominick Cancilla, Margaret L. Carter, Don D'Ammassa, D.G.K. Goldberg, Barry Hoffman, Tina Jens, Nancy Kilpatrick, Kyle Marffin, Julie Anne Parks, Rick R. Reed and David Silva.

1-891946-07-2   Trade pb, 256 pages

"A chilling collection of ghost stories...each with a unique approach to ghosts, spirits, spectres and other worldly apparitions...Pleasant nightmares."
Michael McCarty, Indigenous Fiction

"A landmark collection...I loved this anthology"
A. Andrews, True Review

"This timely work refutes the current charge that ghost stories have lost their appeal... buy this book. Read it. Rediscover what is means to be a child cowering in the dark, listening for shuffling feet...and whispers"
William P. Simmons, Folk-Tales Review

STORYTELLERS

Julie Anne Parks

A writer who once ruled the bestseller list with novels of calculating horror flees to the backwoods of North Carolina. A woman desperately fights to salvage a loveless marriage. A storyteller emerges — the keeper of the legends — to ignite passions in a dormant heart. But an ancient evil lurks in the dark woods, a malevolent spirit from a storyteller's darkest tale, possessing one weaver of tales and threatening another in a sinister and bloody battle for a desperate woman's life and for everyone's soul.

1-891946-04-8   Trade pb, 256 pages

"A macabre novel of supernatural terror, a book to be read with the lights on and the radio playing!"
Bookwatch

"A page-turner, for sure, and a remarkable debut."
Triad Style

"Genuine horror and the beauty of the Carolina wilds. It's an intoxicating blend."
Lisa DuMond, SF Site

CARMILLA: THE RETURN

Kyle Marffin

Marffin's provocative debut — nominated for a 1998 International Horror Guild Award for First Novel — is a modern day retelling of J. S. LeFanu's classic novella, Carmilla. Gothic literature's most notorious female vampire, the seductive Countess Carmilla Karnstein, stalks an unsuspecting victim through the glittery streets of Chicago to the desolate northwoods and ultimately back to her haunted Styrian homeland, glimpsing her unwritten history while replaying the events of the original with a contemporary, frightening and erotic flair.

1-891946-02-1   Trade pb, 304 pages

"A superbly written novel that honors a timeless classic and will engage the reader's imagination long after it has been finished."
The Midwest Book Review

"If you think you've read enough vampire books to last a lifetime, think again. This one's got restrained and skillful writing, a complex and believable story, gorgeous scenery, sudden jolts of violence and a thought provoking final sequence that will keep you reading until the sun comes up."
Fiona Webster, Amazon

"Marffin's clearly a talented new writer with a solid grip on the romance of blood and doomed love."
Ed Bryant, Locus Magazine

THE DARKEST THIRST

A Vampire Anthology

Sixteen disturbing tales of the undead's darkest thirsts for power, redemption, lust...and blood. Includes stories by Michael Arruda, Sue Burke, Edo van Belkom, Margaret L. Carter, Stirling Davenport, Robert Devereaux, D.G.K. Goldberg, Scott Goudsward, Barb Hendee, Kyle Marffin, Deborah Markus, Paul McMahon, Julie Anne Parks, Rick R. Reed, Thomas J. Strauch, and William Trotter.

1-891946-00-5   Trade pb, 256 pages

"Fans of vampire stories will relish this collection."
Bookwatch

"If solid, straight ahead vampire fiction is what you like to read, then The Darkest Thirst is your prescription."
Ed Bryant, Locus Magazine

"Definitely seek out this book."
Mehitobel Wilson, Carpe Noctem Magazine

SHADOW OF THE BEAST

Margaret L. Carter

Carter has thrilled fans of classic horror for nearly thirty years with anthologies, scholarly non-fiction and her own long running small press magazine. Here's her exciting novel debut, in which a nightmare legacy arises from a young woman's past. A vicious werewolf rampages through the dark streets of Annapolis, and the only way she can combat the monster is to surrender to the dark, violent power surging within herself. Everyone she loves is in mortal danger, her own humanity is at stake, and much more than death may await her under the shadow of the beast.

1-891946-03-X   Trade pb, 256 pages

"Suspenseful, well crafted adventures in the supernatural."
Don D'Ammassa, Science Fiction Chronicle

"Tightly written...a lot of fun to read. Recommended."
Merrimack Books

"A short, tightly-woven novel... a lot of fun to read...recommended."
Wayne Edwards, Cemetery Dance Magazine

THE KISS OF DEATH

An Anthology Of Vampire Stories

Sixteen writers invite you to welcome their own dark embrace with these tales of the undead, both frightening and funny, provocative and disturbing, each it's own delightfully dangerous kiss of death. Includes stories by Sandra Black, Tippi Blevins, Dominick Cancilla, Margaret L. Carter, Sukie de la Croix, Don D'Ammassa, Mia Fields, D.G.K. Goldberg, Barb Hendee, C.W. Johnson, Lynda Licina, Kyle Marffin, Deborah Markus, Christine DeLong Miller, Rick R. Reed and Kiel Stuart.

1-891946-05-6   Trade pb, 304 pages

"Whether you're looking for horror, romance or just something that will stretch your notion of 'vampire' a little bit, you can probably find it here."
Cathy Krusberg, The Vampire's Crypt

"Readable and entertaining."
Hank Wagner, Hellnotes

"The best stories add something to the literature, whether actually pushing the envelope or at least doing what all good fiction does, touching the reader's soul."
Ed Bryant, Locus

NIGHT PRAYERS

P.D. Cacek

Nominated for the prestigious Horror Writers Association Stoker Award for First Novel. A wryly witty romp introduces perpetually unlucky thirtysomething Allison, who wakes up in a seedy motel room — as a vampire without a clue about how to survive! Now reluctantly teamed up with a Bible-thumping streetcorner preacher, Allison must combat a catty coven of strip club vampire vixens, in a rollicking tour of the seamy underbelly of Los Angeles.

1-891946-01-3   Trade pb, 224 pages

"Further proof that Cacek is certainly one of horror's most important up-and-comers."
Matt Schwartz

"A gorgeous confection, a blood pudding whipped to a tasty froth."
Ed Bryant, Locus Magazine

"A wild ride into the seamy world of the undead...a perfect mix of helter-skelter horror and humor."
Michael McCarty, Dark Regions/Horror Magazine